Tablecloth Scribbles

Tablecloth Scribbles

Christine Lemmon

Writers Club Press
San Jose New York Lincoln Shanghai

Tablecloth Scribbles

All Rights Reserved © 2000 by Christine Ellen Lemmon

No part of this book may be reproduced or transmitted in any form or by any means, graphic, electronic, or mechanical, including photocopying, recording, taping, or by any information storage or retrieval system, without the permission in writing from the publisher.

Published by Writers Club Press
an imprint of iUniverse.com, Inc.

For information address:
iUniverse.com, Inc.
620 North 48th Street
Suite 201
Lincoln, NE 68504-3467
www.iuniverse.com

Cover Design by Eye on Tomorrow,
Patricia Kindermann at (www.eyeontomorrow.com)

ISBN: 0-595-14067-X

Printed in the United States of America

This book is dedicated to

Laura Fleming

and

Betty Jann

"Show me, O Lord, my life's end and the number of my days; let me know how fleeting is my life. You have made my days a mere handbreadth; the span of my years is as nothing before you. Each man's life is but a breath. Man is a mere phantom as he goes to and from. He bustles about, but only in vain; he heaps up wealth, not knowing who will get it."

Psalm 39:4

Acknowledgments

This story has come to life because of three special people, and I would like to thank them for everything they have done.

To Georgia Hughes, for our walks and talks on writing, and for offering editorial guidance and encouragement on my original rough draft.

To my editor, Bonnie Toews, for inspiring me to remove this manuscript from my "nearly dead pile." Her positive feedback and editorial expertise walked me toward and through the finish line. (*www3.sympatico.ca/bonnie.toews/editorial.htm*)

To my husband, John Lemmon, for letting me rub his back in bed as I rambled on in all those late-night monologues about characters, problems and ideas concerning my novel.

I

Kristine Longheart sat staring at the row of red tulips framing College Avenue. She had sat there many evenings before but never noticed the tulips. Either she had taken them for granted or the stress of the semester had over-watered her mind.

That was a distressing picture, Kristine mused: a mushy mind. She shifted in her seat and turned her attention to the six tables, aglow in candlelight, that surrounded her. They decorated the sidewalk in front of *Till Midnight*, a café on College Avenue in Holland, Michigan. The quiet street, except for the soft chatter of college students and other outdoor diners, was a welcome relief from the dormitory. No television blared the night's game, no smell of fatty fried foods, and no rowdy voices. Instead, sun-dried tomato spread or lamb chops with red curried *couscous* craved savoring. The artistically garnished entrées invited mellow, more relaxing conversations, and guests who frequented the cramped gourmet café respected this.

Kristine became absorbed in the conversations at nearby tables. Some discussed ancient philosophy; others debated the difference between religion and spirituality, typical liberal arts conversations. The nature of their discussions drew her eyes back to the red tulips. How could she have not noticed them before? They were so incredibly gorgeous.

"Kristine? Hello! Are you okay?" Lauren Vanderhill asked as she sat down across from Kristine. In front of her waited a café mocha.

"You're studying that tulip like you're ready to pick it, and you know the fine for picking a tulip in Holland, Michigan."

"And hello to you too. You're late," said Kristine as she licked some whipped cream off her tall steaming mocha drink. "I was just thinking that now that exams are done, we have all sorts of planning to do."

"Planning? What are you talking about? We just survived a hectic semester. I say we need some rest and relaxation, beginning now."

Lauren pulled her navy sweater off over her head and hung it on the back of her chair. "I just want to breathe for a few minutes. Inhale, exhale, sip my coffee for starters."

"There's no time for that. I'm leaving for Florida in the morning."

"So what?" The expression on her friend's face dampened Lauren's impulse to tease her. "You're always so busy, so organized, so under control. Don't you ever want to break down, cry, go crazy… or something?"

Kristine rolled her eyes. "Who has time?"

Lauren took a long silver spoon and searched the bottom of her mocha for the sunken espresso bean. She was determined to find it before the melted chocolate slid off. "There is a time for everything, Kristine."

As the waiter set down a basket of assorted whole wheat, nine-grain, and sourdough rolls, the *chang, chang* of the city clock down the road whispered to outside guests a ten-thirty time check. It reminded Kristine that she still had until midnight to talk with Lauren one last time before summer vacation began.

"Okay, if you say so, if there truly is a time for everything, then right now it's time for planning the future," said Kristine as she dipped her silver knife into the melting butterball and painted her roll.

"The future? All I know is that you and I are going to Spain together come fall. Then we'll share an apartment on campus together, then graduate."

"Well, you're going to have to get much more specific than that. We need a plan."

Handing the menu to the waiter, Kristine used her white cloth napkin, still folded like a swan, to push bread crumbs off the table. Then she stacked their tiny plates on top of each other and neatly set everything in the empty bread basket. "Everything we're about to write is going to become sacred, set in stone. This is going to change the courses of our lives, Lauren."

"Goodness. What are you talking about?"

Kristine took a nibble of her cuticle while sneaking a quick peek at her friend. It was too late. Lauren reached over the table and slapped her hand.

Laughing like a child licking spilled milk off the counter, she raised her hands in surrender. "Okay, okay, you caught me. Why did God give us cuticles?"

She pulled out some honey lotion from her purse and rubbed her hands with the intensity of a massage therapist. "I want us to write something special on our tablecloth tonight and I want you to take this seriously," said Kristine.

"You mean something other than stick figures and flowers?" Lauren's silver necklace caught the light of the candle and danced in shadow form on the white paper tablecloth, like dragonflies in a headlight.

"No drawing pictures. Tonight we're listing. I want us to list things we plan to accomplish. You know…dreams, goals, ambitions." Kristine chose a purple crayon lying on the center of the table and let the white, yellow, and red crayons remain napping between the crystal salt and peppershakers. No, those colors weren't nearly noble enough for her purpose.

"Well, I do have a lot of dreams. I guess I've just never written them down before and never on a tablecloth," said Lauren. "We do have our entire lives ahead of us, so why don't we celebrate our youth and the fact that we have choices ahead of us yet?"

"Good. Now you're catching on to the significance of this activity. Everything that goes down in crayon tonight, must be accomplished. Okay?"

"Okay, Madam Type A. You start."

"All right, I will." Kristine grabbed the purple crayon and neatly wrote the words *Semester in Spain* on the white tablecloth. She clamped her mouth shut as an ambulance roared down College Avenue, reminding the outdoor candlelit diners that life speeds, slows, turns, and detours just as it likes without warning. "I know Spain is coming true. In fact, it's just four months away…you and I, American students in Spain. You may as well write it down too."

"Write it for me…over here. Good. Thank you," said Lauren.

"There. We've both got one goal down. I want you to write something now," Kristine insisted.

"Okay. While studying in Spain, I'm going to fall madly in love with a mysterious, intelligent, sophisticated Spaniard." Lauren wrote *Spanish hombre* and laughed. "Your turn, Kristine."

"Just five to ten pounds, nothing more. Lose it and maintain it for life." Kristine wrote *Lose weight*. "I know I'll be a slightly happier person once I lose just ten pounds."

"My turn, and hey, no mocking me for this one." Lauren scribbled *Noah*. "It's odd, but I just know I'll name my first son Noah. I've told you that a thousand times."

"You don't even have a boyfriend, let alone a husband, and you're already naming your first-born son."

All at once, as the waiter tried pouring water and ice through the mouth of the silver pitcher, the rectangular cubes took off like logs over a waterfall tumbling down onto Lauren's last goal. "There. I don't have to cross it out. Looks like Noah has been flooded out of my future."

Kristine laughed, displaying the tiny space between her two front teeth. "Okay. My turn." She moved her teacup over to make space for her growing list, then wrote *Nurture cuticles*. "If I don't stop biting them, I'm going to see a hypnotist or a shrink. It's really dysfunctional. I bite until they bleed. I've tried manicures, lotions, stress balls, prayer…I still bite. You go."

Family time, wrote Lauren. "This goal shouldn't be too hard to accomplish. I'm spending the entire summer in the same town, same house I've lived in all my life. I'll be surrounded by family."

Lucrative job, wrote Kristine. "Whatever I do after college, I've got to make a lot of money. And I've especially got to find a good paying job in Florida this summer…somehow."

"You really think having a lot of money is going to make you happier in life?"

"No, but I know that lack of money would make me miserable."

Walk through life with God as my friend, wrote Lauren.

"*Published Novelist*," wrote Kristine. "My grandma always said I'd become a novelist. We had this ongoing correspondence ritual in which I wrote her about every detail of my social life at college…whom I kissed on dates and whom I didn't dare…who I secretly obsessed over and who acted crazy in love with me. She claimed my lengthy, embellished letters kept her up at nights, more so than any of the books in her trashy paperback collection."

"Kristine, I just know that all your goals will come true. You're the kind of person who will make them come true." Lauren looked people directly in their eyes when she spoke. Sometimes it made Kristine's eyes water, so she'd pretend to fidget with something as an excuse to look away. She didn't like staring eye-to-eye in conversation, but Lauren said words only go so deep. *The rest of the message lies in the eyes. It's like reading between the lines.*

"Oh, Lauren, thank you. I know yours will too." Nearby faces gawked at the two pieces of French Silk pie passing by, and the waiter apologized for having to set the dessert plates right over the women's scribbled lists. "No problem," they assured him, and drew arrows to continue the lists along the round edges of the table.

Lauren pushed her empty café mocha to the edge of the table—a hint to the waiter that she wanted another. "This time, skinny on bottom, fat on top," she ordered politely. "Did I say that properly, Kristine?"

"Perfect. You'd like it with skim milk and whip cream, an oxymoron if you ask me."

"You know, if you spoke Spanish like you speak coffee, you'd survive just fine in Spain," said Lauren.

"Well, I get embarrassed. Speaking a foreign language feels like standing up on a stage performing lines in front of an audience. You know, the accent and all. I guess I'm shy."

Lauren laughed. "Oh shush, I've heard it all. You're not shy! But your Dutch accent gets stronger when you speak Spanish. I've never quite heard anything like it!"

"But I'm not Dutch." Secretly she felt thrilled, honored that after all these years she naturally sounded just like the rest of the town, the town she so grew to love, the town she called her home. She had heard the whispers and jokes in grade school that, if you're not Dutch, you're not much. She would sound Dutch, this she would do.

"Kristine, I'm one hundred percent Dutch, yet you've got a stronger accent than me. You grew up here. You say things like *goooood* and *youuuuu*, and you sound friendly when you're mad. But hey, consider it a compliment."

"Oh my goodness! How will I survive in Spain next semester?"

"I'll be by your side everywhere you go. Call me your personal walking, talking Spanish dictionary. Just don't try to blend in. You can't. Your blond hair, your pale complexion…you look American, like it or not."

"Thanks, now finish your list."

Lauren sipped her fresh coffee. *Become a Spanish professor.*

Eliminate caffeine from my diet. "Well, I might plummet into depression. My adrenal glands have long since withered away. Maybe this one isn't realistic."

"The earthquake that just hit Columbia and the shortage of beans?"

"Oh, right. Maybe we'll all have to forego."

Wake up early, wrote Lauren. *And do more with each day.*

Become a vegetarian. "It's that chick hatching out of the egg exhibit at the Chicago Museum of Science and Industry that did it to me. I'll never eat another egg again."

Lauren picked up the red crayon and scribbled one more thing. *Live the present.* She pressed so hard and passionately that the crayon broke in half.

"Well, you certainly set that one in stone," laughed Kristine.

Once they emptied their plates, the women split the check, said a few hellos to class acquaintances dining at the other small outdoor tables, and started walking the half-mile journey back to the dorm. They left their scribbles behind.

"Well, now that we've written down our futures, you might not like what I'm going to say," declared Lauren. "We've got to stop counting down for everything."

"Oh, stop with the wisdom," Kristine rolled her eyes. "We're only twenty-one years old. Why can't we count down?"

Lauren ran ahead a few steps and without warning performed a running cartwheel.

"You're crazy. You've got the energy of a kid," declared Kristine.

"Well, before we know it," said Lauren out of breath, "even Spain will be a memory. And someday our tight skin will be wrinkled. Our colorful hair will be white. We'll be rocking in our chairs looking through photo albums and soaking dainty white handkerchiefs. Soon our tears will stop, not because we stop reminiscing, but because at that age we won't have any tears left, because we've spent our life crying about every not-so-rosy incident that came our way and—"

"Okay, okay. Enough. But I won't have white hair. I'll probably have purple like my grandma's." Kristine pulled the blue flower scarf from her hair and let it fall in a mess on her shoulders.

"Oh, dear. I wished I remembered what color hair kit she used. I should have helped her with the timing part. Then again, she didn't need help. Her eyes worked just fine. I know this because she spent nights reading romance novel after romance novel. You would think she could read the instructions on the back of a hair coloring box. Oh, well. We all just accepted Grandma with purple hair."

"There was no warning before she died?"

"No. A heart attack in her sleep. Can you imagine?"

In truth, Kristine herself couldn't imagine her own grandmother dead. As the ducks flew south for the winter, so did Grandma, and as they returned to Lake Michigan in the spring, so did Grandma. She would nest in the tiny apartment behind the family businesses and every night the seventy-something-year-old and the young woman stayed up together burning sandalwood incense, dancing to Elvis Presley tapes, and reminiscing about Grandma's past. Now the world would never look as beautiful again. The seasons would still come and go, the ducks be here and gone, but their arrival would no longer mark the coming of Grandma.

"Not to change the subject, but do you have any more of those antacid tablets? This heartburn of mine feels like someone is dumping hot lava down my throat." Lauren pushed her chest muscles with her fingertips.

"I think so, but only two this time. You're overdosing yourself with these, Lauren. You're becoming a real antacid addict, and I'm worried." Kristine laughed, rummaging through her purse. "And no more cartwheels after coffee."

℘

Back in their dorm room, Kristine placed her silk herbal wrap over her eyes and her stuffed tiger next to her ears to shelter herself from a wicked breeze entering the window and tickling the nerves in her stomach. "It's May. How could it be so cold?"

"El Nino."

"No, he came last year. La Nina."

"Oh, whatever," said Lauren. "*Buenos Noche, Chica.* See ya in the morning."

"Not for long. I'm catching a bus to Chicago, then a flight to Florida."

"Well then, I guess this is good-bye." Lauren climbed down from the top loft, stepping as always on Kristine's mattress in the process.

"Hey, you're the reason my tiger has a flat head. Can't you use the ladder?"

Lauren walked over to the stereo, the only item not yet packed in the small dorm room. Gloria Gaynor's CD always occupied holder number four, and Lauren knew just how to click it in the dark to their favorite song, *I Will Survive.*

"Oh, come on, aren't you too tired tonight?" Kristine pulled the herbal wrap off her brown eyes.

"Excuse me, too tired? Too tired on our last night together? I don't think so. I purposely did not pack my stereo." She then reached inside her friend's bag and pulled out the sandalwood candle, knowing it had belonged to Kristine's grandmother. "I've got to light this. You're grandmother would be here joining us if she could."

Lauren's large furry white slippers made her look like a cartoon character as she sang and danced, utilizing all the space in the tiny dorm room. "I've spent oh so many nights feeling sorry for myself…"

Kristine, in her turtleneck nightgown, hopped out of bed, also driven by the music and candlelight. "I've got all my life to live! I've got all my love to give," she sang, holding up her long wool gown, gray, and resembling a gymnasium mat. Sexy didn't describe it. Warm did. As she sang into a hair spray bottle, she leaped over a box, tripping on her floor-length Michigan nightgown. This song had moved the women in pajamas so many times. It eased stress the night before exams. It cured insomnia. It made them laugh. It made them cry the night of the Valentine's Day dance when Lauren's date stood her up, and Kristine's blind date stood a good two feet shorter than her. Neither woman had danced at the disastrous event. Well, they danced to *I Will Survive* back in their dorm at midnight.

"Why do we love this song so much? It's so old and way before our times," shouted Lauren over the music.

"Don't ask me. I like it because you like it. You always play it."

"Listen to the words. It's not like we can relate. I mean, neither of us have ever really been dumped."

"It's got attitude. And who knows, maybe some day we will be dumped, and we'll know just what to say to the men who dump us." Kristine stared a moment into the tiny flame of the candle, which had vibrantly danced along, then blew it out.

"Well, I'm glad we did that. I can sleep now," said Lauren, nearly out of breath and climbing up to her bed. "Oh, I almost forgot."

"Forgot what?"

"Well, you're the one taking off to some faraway place this summer," said Lauren's voice from above. "So I've already said a prayer, asking God to delegate my guardian angels to you for the summer."

"What? Am I hearing this correctly? You're lending *me* your guardian angels?"

"Yes, just for the summer, God willing. Now it's not our jobs to employ the angels. They work for God. I've simply asked if they could hang with you for the summer."

"I've never in my life met someone as generous as you. Thank you," said Kristine.

"You're welcome. That's why I'm your best friend. Oh, hey, remember LaGuardia Airport in New York, September Ninth! We will depart for Spain together."

"Yes, meet me at the terminal and don't you dare board that plane without me!" Kristine said, turning out the lights. "14 weeks away. I can't wait."

"There you go again, counting down. Enjoy your summer in Florida first."

"Okay...I'll try. But hey, let's make our tablecloth scribbles come true. Let's do it."

"Sounds good to me. Now get some sleep."

Normally, Kristine felt cozy with tiger next to her and her best friend in the bunk above her. Tonight she felt a strange coldness enter through the window. She didn't try shutting it. Lauren liked it open. She liked to listen to the crickets and said they were performing like an orchestra for all the insomniacs. Kristine listened and could only hear their noise. She wondered if Lauren heard something different, something more beautiful than she did. Maybe Lauren's eyes and ears had some kind of audio screening devices that made everything sound crispier and happier and better. The crickets stopped momentarily, pausing to the honk of a car. Perhaps Lauren would hear it as part of the performance, the drums or something. It only made Kristine think of Lauren in the morning, heading for the comforts and safety of Zealand, just two miles away. Yes, tomorrow the naive and God-loving Lauren would be pulling into her driveway, and her mother would be running out with hugs and kisses to welcome her home. Her younger sisters would insist on bringing her luggage in, and her neighbors would come running over with greetings as well. It didn't matter that college stood just a song on the radio away. Like a puzzle of residents, Lauren's hometown missed a piece and her coming home filled the gap.

Then Kristine thought of her Grandmother's recent death with the same tempered frustration of a child searching for the missing puzzle piece under the sofa cushions, then the toy box, then finally giving up. It happened to be the centerpiece so the whole puzzle looked ruined without it. A corner piece might not be so bad, but the centerpiece, her grandmother, fit nicely as the core. The thought of her older sister, Jane, now married and living miles away in California didn't help. With her parents in Florida, too many pieces scattered. She forgot what her puzzle should look like. She felt frazzled and aware of the fact that she lived life from dot to dot on her list of things to do, and every so often she felt a need to do something, but if she didn't write it down, she would not do it. She wanted to tell Lauren how much she loved her as a friend and that she believed *her* dreams would come true as well, but who had time for such sentiments? She'd tell Lauren her feelings while sipping espresso in Spain in a few short months. She made a mental note to do so.

Good. She could hear Lauren breathing slowly and loudly in the bunk above her. Something about the sound of it, like waves coming in and out with the Lake Michigan tide, always told Kristine that she too could fall asleep, and tonight she felt ready, exhausted from the busy semester. She closed her eyes and tried to match her own breaths with Lauren's. This synchronized breathing took no practice. It happened naturally. Joining the chorus of a sleeping person's breathing might prove to be more relaxing than yoga. Neither taught nor contemplated, a sleeping person knew how to inhale and exhale perfectly. Kristine held her own breath to listen more closely, to listen to her friend's breath that suddenly sounded different…choppy. It sounded like a vessel struggling through very rough waters.

"Lauren. *Lauren.* Are you okay?"

She listened some more, then sat up in her loft, feeling her hair caught in the springs of the bed above her. "You're sleeping, aren't you?"

No answer. Then again, no one answers that question when they're sleeping. "You're my best friend. I hope I'm yours…Am I?" She asked, self-conscious her friend would wake, upset by her bedtime chatter.

She stopped talking. She listened. She no longer heard the crickets, nor cars, nor thoughts in her head. She only heard Lauren's breathing and felt the hair on her arms stand up to the cold wind. She felt dizzy, as if her mattress were in the middle of an ocean of rough waves and she couldn't see a thing. She didn't want to get out of bed, to step on the cold tile floor, but the sounds coming from her friend didn't sound familiar. She tossed tiger up above, then waited. Nothing happened. He stayed up there and now she wanted him back. Her friend began breathing desperately, and Kristine no longer thought. Nothing went through her mind. She had listened, waited, and thought enough. Now she could only act. Her body took over as she ran across the tile floor to the light, stubbing her baby toe in route. It took a couple seconds for her eyes to focus on her friend, struggling in bed, eyes closed, but fighting for breath.

She nearly tore the door off the hinges as she opened it and screamed down the hall, "Help, help, she can't breathe!"

She grabbed the phone and dialed 911. Others were entering their room now. One was climbing up on the bed and beginning CPR. Lauren had just learned CPR and had practiced it on Tiger a few months before. She had talked Kristine into taking it too, claiming it to be a responsibility people have for each other. Kristine agreed she would take it…sometime soon. Now she felt an arm around her, a life jacket that held her up. The cold breeze hit her in the face like a powerful wave and someone was shutting the window after Lauren's plant tipped over, crashing to the floor. Lauren loved that plant. *Aphrodisiac.* She named it that. It grew faster than the others. She declared it her favorite. Lauren talked to it all the time.

Blue and white lights were flickering outside the window. Men in blue were working on her friend, lifting her body from the top bunk and placing it on a stretcher. Lauren loved the top bunk, claiming she burnt at least a hundred calories more a day just climbing up and down. It always justified her daily handful of chocolate covered espresso beans.

"Can I go with her? She'd want me with her." Kristine asked a man in blue.

"I'm sorry. We did all we could."

Her legs shook as if she just swam a hundred laps in Lake Michigan. "Well, I'll go with her. I've got to be by her side. She'd want me to."

The man in blue held her arm tightly as the stretcher left the room. "Look me in the eyes, please."

He slowly waved his forefinger in the air catching her attention. "I'm so sorry to tell you this. Your friend did not make it."

"No, this isn't her time. She's got too much to do yet, so many untransformed scribbles."

※

After the storm came a Lake Michigan fog. People she didn't know. Faces she recognized from classes and the hallway, but never spoke to, now drifted into her room all hours of the night. She sat anchored on a box, Lauren's box of winter sweaters. She answered questions over and over to all kinds of people. Then came the woman who kept talking about her baby, of all things, at a time like this. She said she craved lemonade and peanut butter in the middle of every night and anxiously waited nine months for her first baby girl to be born, the woman who went through an uncontrollable nesting phase and painted the nursery yellow, then pink, perfect pink, in anticipation. This woman said she massaged her baby, then rocked her baby night after night, long after the baby slept, just to hold her, and dream about her life ahead, of preschool and art projects on the refrigerator and temper tantrums and college and walking down the aisle with her father. This woman now held her hands out in a cradle position, crying that her darling baby no longer safely slept in her arms.

Kristine couldn't look Lauren's mother in the eyes, fearful she might drown forever in tears. She only stared through the window, at Michigan's dark sky. She stared until it turned a hue of orange, then finally blue. The fog lifted some.

2

Kristine didn't care about making phone calls, nor pondering the night before, nor crying, nor further talking with people who may have been in the room when the waves came crashing in, nor people who may have needed more details. She made herself not care. She felt numb, a fly caught in a chip of ice. Nothing prepared her for this. For a moment, she wondered if she had misunderstood. She had never heard the men in blue, nor any of the voices from the night before, mention the word 'dead.' Maybe Lauren wasn't…dead? What were the words they used? 'Passed away,' 'gone', 'didn't make it', but no one actually said 'dead.' Kristine stood there a moment thinking about it, then closed her dorm room door, not bothering to lock it. No one would steal Lauren's boxes. No one would dare, not now. Her friend was…gone, permanently. She paused in the hallway, imagining the way their good-bye was supposed to have happened.

"Hey, I want you to do something," Lauren would have said. "I want you to give me that good-bye wave sort of thing you said your grandmother always did."

"Oh, I don't know. It was the last thing I saw her do before she died." Kristine didn't know whether she was speaking her reply out loud or thinking it.

"Please, *por favor*. Give me your grandmother's good-bye."

"Okay. Here goes."

Kristine turned her back to the door, kissed her forefingers, extended her arm backward and wiggled her fingers. Just like Grandma, she never looked back, since that would break the rules of the backward good-bye wave. She was glad Lauren couldn't see her tears dripping shamelessly like drips of melting ice cream, and wondered if Grandma too always shed tears when she waved without looking. She walked down the long hallway not looking back, as if doing so might turn her to stone.

As she walked the mile to the Greyhound bus station, she felt weightless without the heaviness of her suitcase. She didn't need it. She couldn't think about brushing her teeth, shampooing her hair, let alone carrying luggage at a time like this. Such things meant nothing to her now. And why bother to bring her wooden shoes to Florida where it would be too hot to wear eight pairs of socks and wood on her feet?

She sat down for a moment on a bench across the street from where she had sipped her last coffee with Lauren the night before. She sat staring at the same row of red tulips framing College Avenue. Now, with just a few minutes left in Holland, Michigan, the tulips reminded her of the green with white lace costume she had sold just two weeks before. Dutch-blooded or not, it had never mattered. Every spring she had danced down the streets in the tulip festival anyway.

The tourists never knew her secret. She didn't come from Holland at all. She came from Chicago. They photographed someone they assumed was Dutch, but she was Irish, English, and Czechoslovakian. The visitors had no idea she was Catholic, not Christian Reformed or Reformed. Often they left Holland by the hundreds on tour busses, taking photographs of the Dutch dancers with them.

As for the residents of Holland...well, they never left. Why would they leave a hometown like Holland? They were born there, grew up there, got married there, and...would one day die there. Kristine had skipped step one of this process. She was born in Chicago and didn't move to Holland until the age of nine. Back then, she had felt like a stranger. Even the tulips belonged to the ethnic background of her friends—her friends who couldn't ride their bikes on Sunday or say the name Jesus without first reciting a prayer. As a child, she lied about her Sunday family bike rides and refrained from saying things like 'holy cow!' at slumber parties. She only wanted to feel comfortable and that meant fitting in, making the strange new place her home. This she did through grammar school, through high school, and she liked Holland so much, she stayed through college.

She glanced down the same street she used to dance down with wooden shoes. She stepped and swept that street with pride, a trait she borrowed from Dutch ancestors who were not her own. Looking at the tulips, she marveled how they always bloomed just in time for the annual *Tulip Time* Festival, as if the little bulbs could hear the Dutch dancers clomping down the street in practice before they started. Yes, the festival would go on without Lauren this year, without even noticing she had died. That's what festivals did…carried on.

ಳು

Later, as the bus slowly passed the college campus, Kristine wanted to ask the driver to accelerate. The tulips outside her window streamed endlessly along, rows upon rows—red, purple, yellow, pink—and as the bus moved on, their colors blurred behind her. She could see black, too. That crayon, the one no one liked, made its way into her mind, shading the bus into a limousine. Like the pictures hanging on a mother's refrigerator, faces outside smiled and hands waved. The people of Holland, blonde with blue eyes, waved politely as they crossed the street in front of the bus.

Just twelve miles north of Holland, the bus stopped in the tiny tourist town of Saugatuck. Some called it the Martha's Vineyard of the Midwest. It stopped at the bus stop on the corner of Main Street. Kristine knew there would be crushing questions during its ten-minute wait, so she got out and ran past everyone who might stop her and ask what happened…past Stacey working behind the counter in the newsstand, and Vivian putting her apron on in the candy store, and Tweetie sitting on the bench in front of the drugstore, and Old Dave rounding the corner with a cane in one hand and the morning paper in the other, and Greg biking down Main Street with some books in his basket, always ready to talk to anyone who felt like listening. Yes, she knew this place, and she loved its people.

Kristine rounded the corner to the one-hundred-year-old pink building, once her family's ice cream shop, and went inside. She knew by heart where all the fifty flavors stood displayed in the glass freezers, and she made sure the new owners hadn't changed them around. *Mint Chip*, her older sister Jane's favorite, belonged next to *Chocolate Turtles*, her mother's favorite. Little Katie's *Blue Moon* had to be kept in the same cooler with all the crazy colored little kid stuff. Dad, a John Wayne sort of man, liked the rugged, nutty, chocolate ones down near the windows. Kristine's favorites were two from each cooler. She could never decide on one so she always insisted on scooping a cone with at least five flavors packed together.

Now, on the customer side of the counter, she knew just how to order so as not to aggravate the person scooping. After all, the shop got so busy at times that, if customers didn't specify plain, sugar or waffle cone…single or double…*French Silk Chocolate*…*Chocolate Turtles* or plain old chocolate, things would get held up.

She didn't feel hungry. The thought of food sickened her. Instead she craved comfort, and ice cream brought her to a familiar place, a cozy state of mind. She ordered in the tone of voice reserved for someone requesting a tissue to dry her eyes.

"I'll have a double dip sugar cone with Chocolate Rocky Road on the bottom and Chocolate Turtles on top, please."

She chose these two flavors because Grandma loved the first one and her mother loved the second, and she missed both right now. Now that her family had sold the business, she knew that for the rest of her life, licking ice cream could never simply be an innocent, mindless act. Each flavor sensitized a memory.

The teenage boy holding the scoop did not smile. He did not say a thing.

"No, wait a minute. Give me that scoop, please. I'll do it myself. My parents used to own this place. We just sold it a couple of months ago. You've got to let me dip my last cone."

"Sure. Whatever. I need a break anyway." He dunked the silver scoop in the water well, shook it off, and handed it to her.

She ran around to the other side of the counter. "Thank you." She dug hard and deep inside the box, making sure to rub her arm against the side. She had to get coated with ice cream just one more time. Closing her eyes, she smelled the freezer, the ice. That ice she had scraped down once a week every summer for eleven years. At the short age of nine she could barely reach inside, so her mother had her stand on a bucket. Now, at twenty-one years old, she recognized the work that had to be done: the box needed scraping and that boy shouldn't have been taking a break. She wanted the job. She longed to scrape with such intensity and passion that her father would reap more profits because she could gather more ice cream off the cardboard. Instead, she had a bus to catch. No, more than that, her family no longer owned the shop, the bed and breakfast upstairs, or the luncheon parlor next door. Someone else now wore the apron for the job she once had and loved.

She scooped the bottom dip bigger than the top so it wouldn't be top-heavy. Her dips never fell off. She knew how to dip ice cream the right way. She glanced at the old-fashioned pink radiator set against the window, and for a moment, she glimpsed her grandmother's frail little body dressed in purple, sitting there as she always did. Osteoporosis hadn't allowed Grandma to dip, but she always stuck around the family as they worked the business together.

She shut the freezer lid and plunged the silver scoop into the well, splashing herself. She laughed, then nearly cried thinking of all the times her father used to shake water at her as they worked side by side. She looked around. No one was watching. She pulled two thumbtacks off the board behind her and stuffed the label that read 'peppermint' under her shirt. Her mother had once painted each of the flavor labels by hand. She peeked under the wooden counter holding the cash register. Good, her family's scribbles still marked the wood. One night, they had written silly little notes on the counter, as if marking their territory. The scrawl in blue magic marker she immediately recognized was her own ten-year old had writing: *Scoop Ice Cream Forever!* She shook her head, realizing how much her goals at ten-years-old had changed from her goals at twenty-one. She couldn't dip anymore. The business was gone.

Pulling some napkins out of the silver holder, she felt sticky fingerprints all over it and started to cry. Kristine never let that thing get dirty. No, the napkin holders in her parent's shop never stayed sticky for long, not when she worked there. Just then, the bus slowly turning the corner caught her eye. It couldn't go without her. In a panic, she darted out the door, never leaving a dime behind for her cone. Somehow guilt evaded her. In her mind, she had earned it. She had worked there for years. Where would she work now? How could she ever possibly work anywhere else for the summer? Just about every summer of her life she spent scooping in that pink shop.

Gazing out the bus window, she watched her hometown grow smaller and smaller behind her. She didn't want to leave the Great Lake State, the eleventh largest in the country, she reminded herself. She loved Michigan. The Great Lakes formed most of its boundaries to the east, while Ohio and Indiana bordered the south and Wisconsin bound the west. She didn't want to leave her hometown. It was like a mitten on the map. The mitten felt cozy and comfortable to her right now. She didn't feel like taking it off.

As the bus continued past the area where she grew up, she pictured the house weeping. Yes, she decided, houses could weep. She imagined yellow and green paint running down the shutters as the new owners desperately painted over it with the ugly white they chose. The house hated the facelift. This she knew. Then she thought of the boxes, everything her family owned stored away temporarily in some warehouse. She wondered if others worried about the geographic scattering of the American family and the evaporation of their hometowns the way she did.

Eyeing some ducks flying north through her window, she became caught up in the irony. Who heads south in the spring? Her trip south seemed like a defiance of nature, of everything seasonal. She closed her eyes and let her thoughts drift. Her head slumped forward until it rested against the cold, misty-morning glass of the window. With each bump, her forehead banged against the pane. She liked the bumps. The repetitive thumping seemed to replace the painful thoughts of leaving memories of her grandmother and the family businesses, and now Lauren, behind.

She felt butterflies flapping about in the pit of her stomach, their wings—normally used for courtship, regulating body temperature and avoiding predators—now entangled and crumbling apart. They had danced about so many times through her life, she knew their choreography by heart. At times they made her nervous for no good reason at all. She often feared they might be bats, but how ridiculous!

Should she have stayed? Should she have talked longer with Lauren's mother? Would there be a funeral? Of course there would be, and she would miss it. She had a flight to catch in Chicago. She switched from thinking to picking her cuticles, and fearfully diagnosed herself with that psychiatric self-mutilation problem in which people physically injure themselves so as not to feel emotional pain. No, she still felt emotional pain, despite the sting of raw flesh framing her nail beds. But if she could hop in the ice cream freezer and numb herself for a few hours, she would have. She always diagnosed herself with something, and the family loved to tease this hypochondriac side of her nature that stemmed from childhood, when she would sit for hours flipping through the family medical encyclopedias. The gruesome pictures caught her attention first. Then, fearful that such bubbles or discoloration might some day appear on her own skin, she would study the symptoms and compulsively examine her body for such premature signs.

※

On the flight to Florida, she stared out the window and saw drips of rain dab one large continuing watercolor mural beneath the plane's wings. For a fleeting moment, she thought she saw Lauren in the clouds. She was diving for the espresso bean sunk to the bottom of her mocha coffee, and her look of utter disappointment when it turned up naked, stripped of its chocolate, made Kristine smile. She considered calling *Till Midnight* to see if someone had saved the tablecloth with their scribbles on it. How ridiculous, she chided herself. Especially with all the chocolate stains. No doubt the waiter had dumped it.

She opened her purse and pulled out the envelope addressed to her grandmother. She had kept it in her purse for months now and didn't know what to do with it. How could she have dropped a letter in the mail to Grandma without having put a stamp on it? A simple, careless mistake that sent the letter back to her. Why did it take so long to come back? She didn't know. Perhaps it got lost in the campus mail for a couple weeks. All she knew was that Grandma didn't get to read the letter and there was no point putting a stamp on it now and returning it. Grandma had died. She flipped the long letter over and started writing on the back.

Dear Grandma:
You once told me that the letters I wrote kept you going, added spice to your life. Well, I wished you had been more patient because my last letter simply got lost in the mail

without a stamp. You should have waited a couple more days and it would have arrived. I hope you don't mind my writing another. I promise to keep you going.

You won't believe this story! A twenty-one year old and a seventy-four year old, both full of life, both now dead from attacks in their sleep just a couple of months apart. My mind watches reruns over and over again...episodes of the younger one, and of the older one. In my imagination, I talk to them both as if they're still alive, and they talk to me.

I can hear the one named Lauren warning me that we spend half of life counting down to a long awaited event and the other half looking back, remembering. I hear the feisty grandmother reminding me not to worry about things I cannot control. I got so upset that time I visited you in Florida and it rained every day. Now I'd give anything for a rain-spent day inside with you, Grandma. No, we cannot control rain, or death.

I guess this all means there will be no more summer nights of eating Heavenly Hash ice cream with you, Grandma, and now, no sipping espresso in Spain with Lauren.

She folded the letter then opened it again. She had to write about the time Grandma walked the streets of Saugatuck in her pink fuzzy robe and slippers. She had to write it down because some day, when she would be rocking back and forth with a box of tissues, freckled arms and purple hair, she'd at least have her letters to Grandma to comfort her. They would describe the details her mind might forget, and they would keep Grandma alive forever.

℘

Dear Grandma:

Remember the time city cousin Michelle from Chicago spent the entire summer scooping ice cream in the shop. We were short some employees and needed the help, and besides, Michelle loved you and wanted to spend some time with you. The three of us night owls teased each other all night. Michelle and I used to call you "sexy woman," and you'd blush, saying, "Now, now girls." One night Michelle and I worked until midnight in the shop. The tourists just kept coming and I stayed open an hour later because it was the family business, and I felt we could rake in some extra cash. The bar at Coral Gables had closed, and lots of drunks were migrating from that bar to the Sand Bar. Luckily, our shop was situated right between the two. We were so nice when we scooped ice cream, and that night we got so many tips that, when we finally did close down, we decided to hang out for some late night pizza across the street at Morrows.

It was then that we heard loud pounding on the window near our booth. We looked out, as did everyone else in the restaurant, and to our shock, there you stood, Grams, with your pink robe and pink slippers. You were waving your forefinger at us, and pointing to your wristwatch. We should have told you we were going for pizza that night. You were up and waiting for us in your little apartment behind the shop. We should have told you. You probably would have liked a pizza and beer yourself. I know you only drink beer with pizza and would not eat pizza without a beer. I could go on and on.

Oh, Grandma, your refrigerator stored nothing but Kit-Kat bars, Swiss cheese, ham, butter, and thinly sliced rye bread. As for Lauren...I haven't meant to ignore her in this letter...well, she kept her dorm room meticulous. She alphabetized her books and fed her plants a weekly dose of Advils. They were gorgeous plants, growing out of control. Lauren spoke Spanish to them.

3

Kristine looked at her mother standing at the airport terminal gate and realized how young she looked with highlights running through her hair and a glowing tan. Then again, maybe she just felt older, making her mother look younger. She noticed her little sister Katie, a miniature of her mother, hopping about like a battery-operated toy. She wondered if that is what happens when people die. Their batteries run out.

As they walked through the airport, Kristine stopped to spread SPF 36 sunscreen on her forehead, nose, and shoulders—paranoid that a single dose of unprotected UVA/UVB rays might deter her determination to age gracefully. She never could forget the picture of melanoma cancer on the girl's arm in the medical encyclopedia. She rubbed the sunscreen obsessively in her hands. They felt cold although she now stood in Florida, not Michigan. Why? She wondered. That was easy. She had left behind the comfort and warmth of the great mitten on the map.

In the tiny backseat of her mother's white convertible, Kristine felt as if someone had squeezed a tube of humidity down her throat. Tightness gripped her chest. Maybe it was because her purse was still strapped over her shoulder. No, her purse sat on the floor. She took her sunglasses off because they constricted her eyes. She searched the car for an escape, any escape, just in case. Just in case why? She didn't know. Just in case she needed to break free. Having the convertible top up didn't help her planning.

"This sounds crazy, but I'm not feeling good. It's cramped and muggy back here, and I feel like I'm going to suffocate to death," she announced.

"I know honey. I wish the air conditioning worked in this car." Her mother accelerated through a yellow light at the intersection. "The convertible top isn't even working today."

"This is serious, Mom. I feel weird back here. It's so small, and I can't breathe!" She tugged at the neckline of her tank top.

"Okay, what should we do? Should I pull over?" Her mother glanced in the rear view mirror, and the car behind them honked a good three seconds for no reason at all.

"Mom, pull over quick! I'll switch to the front seat."

"No, no you won't! I want you to sit back here with me!" cried Katie.

"I want to sit by you too, but I can't breathe. I don't know why."

Little Katie sat closely, rubbing her arm kindly as if mothering her baby doll. "You will be okay. Mommy will pull over and let you out to breathe. Mommy, pull over now! Oh, wait, Mommy. Kristine isn't wearing her seat belt. Put your seat belt on! Daddy doesn't start the car if my seat belt isn't on!"

Kristine went through the seat belt procedure, setting a big sister example, then her mother pulled over. A bit embarrassed, she stood on the side of the unfriendly US-41, breathing in and out, in and out. A crazy thought raced through her head as she looked about: a postcard picture of Florida, US-41 would make an Indian on horseback cry.

With her mother and sister in the convertible laughing at her, knowing her to be the dramatic hypochondriac, and passing cars honking, she turned her deep breathing scene into a performance, clearing the air with her hands in a swimming gesture. A voice from a passing truck yelled, "Freak!" and she had to convince her own mind that getting back into the car wouldn't be so bad. I'll get back into the car, but I will never get into a coffin, she thought. No, I will never let them lower me into the ground.

Back at the furnished rental they lived in while looking for a place to buy, the family stood talking around the solar heated pool. They were a close family after eleven years of mopping floors, cleaning toilets, waiting tables and horseback riding together through the woods at their father's ranch, the last of his entrepreneurial endeavors. Since the sale of the businesses and the southward migration a couple months ago, they had only spoken on the phone and had so much to catch up on.

As she watched her little sister performing backward somersaults under water, Kristine felt glad to be talking, laughing, reunited with her family again, but guilty…as if she should be around people who knew Lauren and were mourning her death. She should be walking up to the open casket at a funeral, not splashing around in a solar heated pool! She didn't dare to smile too much because she should be wiping her eyes with a white handkerchief, not drying herself off with a beach towel. Instead of wearing a pastel colored bikini, she should be wearing something dark, solid, and solemn.

Her eyes caught the shadow of a pelican flying over the screen of the pool, and she felt horrible…as if she had stolen Lauren's guardian angels away. Maybe Lauren needed them. More guilt set in, the sort that comes after eating a double dip chocolate waffle cone, then dipping her fingers into the hot fudge and licking it off. No, her guilt felt all of this, plus ten-fold. Oh, why didn't she just skip her flight and attend the funeral? What had she been thinking? How could she have made such a rash decision? She blamed it on shock. It had to be shock, because it all happened so fast that she didn't know she had any options. Then again, she had to leave. Her hometown would always stay where it lies on the map, between Lake Michigan and Lake Huron, but everything comforting about it had changed.

It took her all day and into early evening to finally discuss with her family what had happened the night before. They were disappointed she hadn't called them immediately with the news. Why didn't she tell her mother when she got off the plane? Why hadn't she stayed in Michigan longer? How could she go this long without talking to someone about it? They hurt for her, holding her in their arms as they did when she was younger. She didn't want to cry because that would only rub in a fact she couldn't accept: her best friend had actually left this life without finishing anything she wanted to accomplish.

Katie begged and pleaded for her big sister to sleep in the same bed with her, and Kristine looked forward to the chatter, hoping it might keep her mind off Lauren. Instead, Katie fell into a deep sleep right after the second storybook, kicking her tiny legs into her sister, pulling the comforter over to her side of the bed, then entangling her arms around her big buddy.

Minutes, perhaps hours, passed when Kristine saw a white figure, enormous in size, standing, floating a few feet from the bed. Ten-foot wings, whiter than fresh fallen snow and carved with more detail than the design of a snowflake, reached steadily upward. Just as she took her eyes off the mammoth wings, the angel vanished. In her place appeared black curly hair tinseled in silver, royal blue eyes, an Etch-a-Sketch of Lauren slowly filling itself out in mid-air in the doorway to her room.

"*Hola*, Kristine. I've got a Heavenly secret to share with you. Death strikes in three, it really does. And, it's time for you to fall asleep now, too. Go ahead. Fall asleep. How can you die if you can't fall asleep? It's your turn now," echoed the voice.

"No, I don't want to die, and I can't believe you died! I will not fall asleep!"

"Kristine, you are my soul mate, and I miss you."

"But Lauren , you told me all my dreams would come true. I believed you. Why would you want me to die too?"

"Dreams not fulfilled on earth can still be fulfilled…"

Kristine sat up in bed rubbing her eyes, as the sketch of her friend slowly erased itself. She felt thrilled to have had the opportunity to see her friend moving and talking once more. She felt honored and wanted to memorize everything heard and seen. She wondered if she might get more visits and hoped she would. How could it be? Had she really visited her there in the room? Had she really crossed the life-death barrier just to deliver that message? No! Of course she hadn't. Kristine came to her senses moments later, and as much as she would have loved for her friend to visit, Lauren wouldn't be so selfish as to want her to die too. Lauren liked to share. She never stole.

She finally slept four of the eight hours she lay in bed. Lauren said it herself. *There is a time for everything*, or there should be, so Kristine declared night her time to mourn.

Her mourning began the next night. As she lay in bed at eleven forty-five, she envisioned her and Lauren finishing up their list of goals on the paper tablecloth at *Till Midnight*. Still awake at midnight, she analyzed age and how so many things had gone unfinished in Lauren's life. At one o'clock, she resented heart attacks for sneaking in and robbing her best friend and grandmother of life while they slept. Why did she feel so mad? It wasn't like a disgruntled gunman randomly opened fire.

No, death chose Lauren, and it chose Grandma. They must have been carefully selected for some Holy reason. What is it the very devout say? *It must have been their time*. And just as there is a time to be born and a time to die, Kristine decided there was a time to climb out of bed, to forget about falling asleep. She walked into the dark bathroom to run her toes under cold water. She had torn a couple of nails so low they now throbbed, and she hated herself for doing that, but knew it was a habit she couldn't break. The cold water numbed the pain, and she got back into bed. She hoped some day humans would evolve to the point that they didn't have toenails anymore and her children's would be the first generation so advanced.

At two o'clock, Kristine thought of the irony of life: half of life is spent looking forward, counting down to holidays, vacations, weekends, while the other half is spent pondering backward. But if she didn't let herself reminisce, things she once loved would die. At three o'clock, she promised herself that from this day forward, she would start living for the moment. At four o'clock, she cried for Lauren's family and their lost time together.

She tried counting sheep but instead turned to counting the number of *Tums* she had given Lauren. It must have amounted to a full bottle within a one-month span. She felt psychic as she watched each orange glowing second tick by. *I knew it would turn 4:46 at that exact second, I knew it! I knew it would turn 4:47 when it did!*

After getting a tension headache, she covered the clock with a shirt and diverted her observations to her sister's breathing in bed next to her. She envied her sister for sleeping so soundly. Why couldn't she too fall asleep? Why wouldn't she? She felt alone, lonesome in a world of sleeping people. Still, her sister's breaths became a comforting rhythm, while her own breathing changed. Perhaps, it changed because she thought about her every breath. She suddenly realized she skipped a breath or that her breaths were speeding up so she would try to slow them down again, and sometimes she felt in need of an extra breath but couldn't catch one. As the hours passed and the sun came shining through the blinds, Kristine realized she was becoming preoccupied with her own breathing and her own death.

Several times she dozed off and it felt good, natural. *No! Wake up!* an inner voice, a terrified voice, cried out. *Do not fall asleep! You might die!* The inner voice, her mind, tortured her exhausted body that was begging to sleep. This same attack of hair pulling insomnia returned night after dragging night.

4

Sinful. Kristine almost wished God never created night. But nights of sitting up alone in the living room recliner chair did pass, and during the days that followed, no one fully understood the extent of her problem. No one knew exactly what to make of it. Fed up, she declared her time of mourning over, done. She did her time and now she granted herself permission to enter REM sleep and whatever else happens after that. Naps on the raft in the sunlit pool hardly competed with a dream-spent night in bed.

She rejoiced with more gladness than ever when the days that God has created kept coming. But nights came too, part of the package. She couldn't have day without night, she knew that, but still, she felt like a first grader who screamed and cried and begged her parents to let her stay up. Bedtime—the bully, the bad guy, and the party poop—kept creeping up.

"When you have your shortness of breath tonight, just breathe into this here bag, girlie." Her father placed a brown paper lunch bag next to the recliner chair, her newfound bed. "Try relaxing your thoughts when it happens."

"But it's not my thoughts. It's kind of strange that my thoughts would do this to me. I mean, I know I'm not crazy, Dad!"

In truth she knew her thoughts of death made their way through her mind like objects on a factory conveyor belt. She couldn't bring herself to yank the bad thoughts off. She let them go by. She watched and listened to them as they made their way.

"It has nothing to do with being crazy," added her mother as she turned the television off. "Have you been drinking caffeine past three o'clock?"

"No. I'm down to half a cup a morning. No more." She pushed the lever on the chair and shot upward. She didn't want to recline. "I was thinking that it's asthma. Or who knows, my scoliosis might be constricting my lung cavity. We haven't had my scoliosis checked in years."

"Are you worried about anything?" Her father turned off the lights in the living room.

"Wait, keep that small light on Dad, please."

"How do you say please?"

"Oh, Dad!"

"No, come on. How do you say please?"

"Okay, okay…pretty please with real whipped cream, not the kind the competitors across the street used, but the kind we used, and nuts…not the peanuts but the chopped almonds and a cherry on top, but not a warm cherry, a cold cherry like we always served our customers. There."

"Very good. Mom and I taught you girls well. Now, are you worried about something?"

"No, I'm not worried about a thing. Just falling asleep, that's all. But you know I have gained some weight at college. Maybe the extra weight is squashing my organs." She sat in her pajamas in the recliner, ready to confront another night, cowardly, as if death might come like a thief in the night.

"Well if you'd like, I'll go with you to the doctor. We'll have you tested for asthma." Her mother kissed her and pushed her bangs out of her eyes.

"Okay, but it might be something else…like mitral valve prolapse or some irregularity with my heart, or angina." Secretly, she thought she had an undetected aneurysm ready to burst.

"Try to get some sleep tonight. If it doesn't go away, we'll get you checked."

As they left the room she longed for infancy, so she could throw a tantrum and gain a few more moments of attention. She would do anything to postpone going to bed. Her mind *ticked* along with the clock. So did her fingers, *tapping* the arm of the cold vinyl recliner. Watching the tube, she listened to the clock and the distant snoring of her father, convinced she was about to die. She dreaded midnight, the American flag, the national anthem, then static. Her parents hadn't hooked up the TV to cable in the rental home.

From the recliner chair, in an upright position, she tried to enjoy the flickering static show in the dark living room, like fireworks on a smaller scale. The *stststststtststststst* sound got to her and she knew she'd have to quietly exit the vinyl, walk over to the television and turn it off. Again, remote control would come in handy, but didn't exist with the television in the rental home.

Hours passed. She started to slip into sleep. *No, wake up and do not lose control. Do not fall asleep!* She manned the graveyard shift, while the rest of the world slept. The living room in the rental home looked ready for battle. A gaudy copper helmet posed on top of the TV, a medieval sword hung on the wall over it, and two black and gold shields were nailed next to it. Touched by sun, the decorations weren't so bad, but at night in the dark living room, they were creepy and eerie. She watched the walls, decorated by the elderly couple that traveled the world after retirement collecting cheap souvenirs. Nothing moved but a spider on a cross-country journey from the corner above the television to the corner above her recliner.

Day arrived, night followed. Over and over again. Who said it was all very good? She disagreed with the Creator on this one.

Sitting at the kitchen table in her pajamas, she stared at the cereal boxes erected like buildings that formed a city around her bowl of milk, perhaps a pond. She could feel her hair tangled from her night of tossing and turning, and she traced the skin on her face for pillow crevices. They remained, along with the head rush that should have disappeared a minute after first standing. She chose *Life, Quaker Oat Life*. She chose it because she liked its name and wondered if eating it might make her live forever. She read the nutrition facts on the side panel, then the ingredients below. She placed her health in the hands of whole oat flour (with oat bran), sugar, corn flour, whole wheat flour, rice flour, high starch oat flour, slat, calcium carbonate, sodium phosphate (a phosphorus source and dough conditioner), reduced iron, and many more ingredients. Yes, this combination created the cereal she now ate. The cereal called *Life*.

She could have easily stayed at the kitchen table all day if she didn't have to find a job. Something about the kitchen brought her comfort, and Mom's food and the aromas and sounds that went along with it. She admired Mom's creativity and discipline when it came to making hot breakfasts for her daughters every single school day of their lives. Mom never missed a chilly Michigan morning of waking with her girls, throwing on her robe, and making her way to the kitchen to prepare a breakfast that always featured some style of egg, a member of the fruit family, and a form of bread. In the month of December the girls ate the red and green swirl bread. On St. Patrick's Day they ate green bread. On Friday's, they ate toast topped with a thick spread of peanut butter, sliced bananas, and large marshmallows roasted in the broiler. Summer breakfasts differed greatly since Mom had to go to the business first thing in the mornings. Then, she allowed the girls to have ice cream for breakfast, as long as they made it into a banana split with peanuts for protein, and strawberries and pineapple instead of hot fudge.

In response to a lazy scream from her adrenal glands, she poured half a cup of skim milk into her coffee, then squeezed some chocolate syrup and stirred it all together.

"You know, Dad, I've never had the summer unemployment problem before. I always worked for you in the shop."

"I wish I had a job to offer you this summer, honey. I don't anymore."

"I try not to look back, Dad, but this time last year, I'd be ringing the silver bell, alerting the town that the ice cream arrived, that the season had started."

Her father set his paper down and stared out the window at a palm tree. "I'd be outside in front, painting a fresh coat of pink on those wooden benches."

"I'd be slicing strawberries for the guests' breakfast," added her mother, "and Jane would be sneaking testers here and there when I wasn't looking. Oh, Jane, I can't believe she's been in California several months, and we haven't seen her."

Katie's deep morning voice could be heard from around the corner where she was spying on the family. "I'd be rubbing blue ice cream all over my mouth this time." She giggled as she rubbed her mouth with her little hands. "Yummy. I like blue flavor."

The family laughed.

"And old Granny would be sitting in the window on the pink radiator," added her father.

"I feel horrible. I planned on making enough money this summer to at least reimburse you for my own airline ticket to Spain." Kristine sipped her chocolate coffee and burned the tip of her tongue, which ruined the experience of drinking the rest of her cup of coffee. "Is there a yellow highlighter anywhere? I've got to search the classifieds."

"I hate to say this, but it's been a couple weeks now, honey. If you don't find a job within two days, I'm going to *have* to buy you a plane ticket back to Michigan." Her father handed her the classified section, then sipped his black coffee. He drank his coffee dark but always had a glass of orange juice as if to chase it down after each sip. "You could at least live back in Holland with your friends and wait tables with them. That way you'd at least have some spending money for Spain. You can't go there with nothing."

"No, I can't go back to Michigan. I can't, not now." She poured herself more coffee and squeezed more chocolate. "Mom, Dad, I vow right now to find a job within two days. Maybe I just needed a deadline to work against, and now I've got one. *Two days.*"

She gulped the muddy drink as if injecting herself with some ancient formula. With each gulp she could feel her creativity awakening, her ambitions screaming out and her confidence building. "Someone will hire me, I know it. Just put me in front of an interviewer, and I will get the job."

"Whoa Nelly! You know this has nothing to do with you and your skills, but do you really think you're going to find a job here in the off-months?" Her father bit into a piece of toast, top heavy from too much grape jelly. He often spoke as he would speak to his horses back in Michigan. His favorite horse was named Kid. He loved them all.

"Dad, when I drink coffee, I can do anything!" She laughed and poured herself the last inch from the pot. "This liquid bean stuff turns me into a wonder woman of some sort. I get all kinds of ambition when I drink coffee. It makes me want to read the entire *USA TODAY*, or volunteer my time somewhere, or start writing. Not reading a novel, but *writing* a novel, yes, writing, editing and rewriting it to perfect publishable form. I do regret not drinking coffee before my SAT test! Why didn't I? Oh well. Coffee inspires me. Don't worry. I'll go out and interview today, and I promise I'll come home with a job!"

"Hey, hold the reins! Before you go, just remember you have a lot to offer those employers. Don't you forget that, kid. You hear? Mom and I say it all the time…anyone who hires you is going to be the luckiest employer alive."

"Oh, Dad, I wish I could still work for you." She knew her father loved her too much to send her back to Michigan. He wouldn't do that. He knew his daughter well. She needed a deadline, and now she had one. She worked well under deadlines. Now she wanted to impress him. She would find a job, and she would find one quickly!

"Get out of here, hit the pasture!" he said.

℘

In one coffee-induced hypo-manic day, she attended a four-hour seminar, almost became a purified water saleswoman, interviewed with Lee County to become a toll collector on the bridge linking Sanibel Island and the City of Palms, and phoned the Thomas A. Edison and Henry Ford Museums in Fort Myers, begging to get hired for anything, even as grounds keeper. When the man there asked her why she wanted a job at the museums, she had desperately replied, "Because I'm sick of fearing death." She knew it made no sense to a complete stranger, but the man once his surprise had passed, told her that, when Thomas Edison was in a coma and close to death, he awoke for a moment and looked up and said, "It is very beautiful over there." The man didn't offer her the job, but at least he gave her a glimpse of hope.

By noon, the coffee high wore off, but she kept going. Later, she filled out an application to be a manager of forty Spanish-speaking maids at a four-star resort. But after she and the person doing the hiring had a conversation together in Spanish, Kristine knew she'd never be called back. An old grandmother interviewed her for a cash register position at a shop on Sanibel Island called *She Sells Seashells by the Seashore*, but the woman kept calling her "sweetie" and "little girl," and Kristine didn't think that would work out. She left and attempted to apply for the Fort Myers Beach trolley driver position. They told her she needed a special license to drive a trolley. In sum, no one offered her a job. She felt defeated, over-qualified and under-qualified, and completely non-marketable.

On the second day, she did more of the same and returned home feeling rejected.

Under the dock behind the rental home, a manatee, about ten feet long, with a small wrinkled head and straight whiskered snout, snuffed its nose slowly above the surface of the warm water before disappearing into the shallow canal with a pump of its tail. Glancing up from the classifieds, already highlighted from her morning perusal, Kristine watched the rippling current of the canal. *Where are the currents going? Where are they coming from?* Four hundred miles of canals running behind the homes made Cape Coral the only city in the world with more canals than cities in Italy.

About three minutes later, the gray-black creature surfaced again, and this time brought with him one, two, three more manatees, each with cleft upper lips and bristly hairs. She couldn't tell if they were grazing for food on the canal's surface or simply spying on her. She waved to be friendly. She blew some kisses. She felt the urge to grab onto the corpulent body of one of the slow moving manatees and swim away with it and its family into the Caloosahachee River, maybe the Gulf of Mexico. She knew the canals led *somewhere* exciting and the manatees were surely living a more adventurous life than hers. She wondered if they had fears too of boats speeding down the canal and killing them, of crushing or drowning in flood gates, of eating a fish hook by accident, of getting entangled in crab trap lines, of pollution and animal haters with rocks in their hands, or red tide and cold water. She felt depressed. Of course they did. They and all the other great creatures of the canal, and of the world all feared something. And if they didn't, well, they should.

She felt desperate. "Oh, dear Lord," she prayed aloud, "please guide me to a job. Charter me wherever you like, oh, please." She then tossed the paper onto the dock, glancing one last time at the ads that left her no optimism. But there it was, hit by the first drop of Florida's daily summer downpour. She read it once to herself, then out loud: *Waitress with a sense of humor needed for island restaurant. Interviews start daily at 8:00 a.m., Island Marina. Call first.*

※

Early the next morning, she borrowed her mother's white Chrysler convertible and set off in due course to Island Marina.

She drove to Cape Coral's far north end and turned onto Pine Island Road. After a few miles, it converted into a narrow two-lane road with smelly swamp water on both sides. She laughed, recalling the man on the phone's vivid directions, "Once you enter a town called Matlacha, you'll see marsh water all around you. It's beautiful."

After a wooden bridge, she could smell morning coffee as she drove through the quaint fishing town with waterside fish houses and casual looking seafood restaurants—more designated landmarks. Between buildings, she caught glimpses of the picturesque Gulf of Mexico turning a shimmering orange from the dawn's emerging sun. She felt renewed, restored in some way, as if *she* were rising with the sun. She felt competitive, ahead of the day, and all the late morning sleepers of the world. They were still in bed, missing out on the sun's skyward ascent. She never noticed morning and all its traits before. Now that morning no longer meant rushing off to class, she couldn't help but notice things. Lauren had told her about this. Lauren told her to take time to notice things.

Despite a few old hotels and boat rental shops on the side of the road, Matlacha didn't *look* like a tourist town. It looked like more a lifestyle that had remained as so for centuries. Perhaps the local fishermen intended to keep their site a secret. Or maybe fishermen preserved it as a no-fuss, non-glamorous escape. She could smell raw fish, sushi. No, it was not sushi, just plain old raw fish, stripped of its scales, nothing glamorous, and certainly nothing edible in her mind.

North of Matlacha, she drove over a bridged creek and entered Salt Water Key, an island of its own. Continuing on her treasure hunt, she laughed when she spotted rows of banana trees—they meant *turn right*. She did so and lost site of the Gulf of Mexico.

Wow, she thought, turning a confident left at the orchard of mango trees. *Michigan has things like blueberries and apples, but nothing from the passion and citrus fruit families. Those would be tasty on ice cream.*

She unrolled her window, smelling a sharp citrus fragrance magnified by the crisp morning breeze. It satisfied her more than a glass of grapefruit juice. She daydreamed…

Me? Commissioned the job for naming a new lipstick shade? I'm honored to accept such a glamorous position. You can pay me my million bucks later. First, I just need a little brainstorming session. Moon-lit Mango, Sun-lit Papaya, Papaya Wine. No, no such thing…Mermaid Gloss, oh, stupid…Banana Peel, get off the rhyme, Kristine… Salt Water Drench, Whipped Banana…Ashes…Ashes to Ash…Dust to…Death Black… Heartbeat Red…Coffin brown…

The dead end diverted her thoughts as she made a sharp right and headed about two miles down a curvy road with old wooden stilt homes on one side and nothing but the wide open gulf on the other. Breathtaking, she thought, and turned at the sign that read, "Island Marina."

She took a seat under the bamboo hut and watched a nearly extinct Great White pelican balance itself on a narrow wooden dock post as she waited for the boat to arrive. When she called for directions, the man on the phone had told her it arrived every morning at around eight o'clock. She knew nothing about the restaurant, and didn't ask. She just knew that a boat would take her out to the island for an interview. On the island stood a restaurant that needed a waitress. She planned to be that waitress. She felt foolish and irresponsible for not asking more questions, but she impatiently wanted a job, and a boat trip sounded nice regardless. After all, her deadline to find a job expired today. So take it and stay in Florida or leave it and head back to Michigan, a place no longer comfortable.

What if there is no restaurant? No Tarpon Key Island? What if it's a big hoax? What if it's the type of place where the waitresses dance naked? Or worse? Why do they have to take me out to the island for the interview? Why can't they just interview me here at the marina? Perhaps it is just a joke, and I'm waiting for nothing, no boat. Oh well, I'll find out soon enough.

She opened her purse and turned her mace that hung on her key chain to ready position. She couldn't breath, but her chest pains were only slight *pokes*, not stabs. The blade of the knife moved under *her* control. She wouldn't let it stab, *not* right now. She closed her eyes, focused on each breath—pushing her abdomen in and out, not up, and down. She imagined mental gargoyles perching upon her thoughts and fighting off negative worries. This helped somewhat, then a few minutes later she picked up a cracked coconut, closed her eyes again and felt its rough, splintery skin. She concentrated hard on the coconut in her hands, anything to prevent her imaginative mind from wandering to the 'what if' thoughts.

5

A sure thing! Thank God, she thought, as she heard the motor of a small powerboat and opened her eyes. As it pulled up to the dock, she forced herself to yawn, stealing some extra air.

"You here for the interview?" asked a man with leathery skin tying the rope. He wore all white but for dockside shoes with no socks, and the lines on his face belonged. Like the crevices on a seashell, they had deepened with each current.

"Yes, I am. I probably should have asked a bit more about the job and the island."

Kristine reached onto the boat to shake his hand. "So tell me, what type of island is it?"

"Tarpon Key? Ah, how does one describe Tarpon Key? Well, dear, let me tell you. It's a *magnificent* place to eat. Simply *magnificent!*" He spoke with the passion of an auditioning actor. "You just need to *visit* Tarpon Key to understand it, and I'll take you there if you're ready." He extended his hand and Kristine accepted, stepping onto the boat.

"My name is Lawrence. I'm the Tarpon Key dock master. I just need to load up a few things and we'll be on our way, dear." He walked over to some boxes that were piled on crates under a Sabal Palmetto palm tree and started loading them one by one onto the boat. Suspiciously, Kristine peaked inside the boxes each time he'd leave for more. Bulk amounts of ketchup bottles, cleaning detergents, and cleaning rags—typical restaurant items.

Within ten minutes, Lawrence started the boat and they slowly pulled away from the dock. The smell of boat gasoline tickled her nerves as she watched the marina slip further and further away. She felt carefree and irresponsible at the same time, a dandelion blowing so far from home but having fun along the way. The gasoline smell reminded her of Saugatuck and the yuppie boaters who would sail from Chicago just to buy ice cream in their shop. But now as the wind hit her in the face, she wondered if leaving that comfort zone behind might not be so bad after all. Looking at the Gulf of Mexico ahead of her reminded her that this present situation—no friends, no job, no money, and no idea where the boat would take her—forced her to pay attention.

"Tarpon Key is a privately owned intra-coastal island where time is virtually *frozen*," Lawrence stood behind the wheel still smiling, and in doing so, deepened the engravings on his skin. "There's not much on the island, just the restaurant and bar, twelve adjoining guest rooms, six cottages, and a couple of private homes. But the place is simply *magnificent*, dear. *Magnificent*, I tell you!"

"Dear me!" Kristine smiled too, aware of the crow's feet forming around her eyes. She liked the charming way he attached the word *magnificent* to all his sentences.

"Dear, you'll want to take a seat now and hold on. It's just a little bumpy ahead."

She could feel the force of the boat's increasing speed sliding her and the cushion she sat on back toward the end of the boat. She tucked her hair into the collar of her shirt so she could still see and grabbed onto the side of the boat. Her lungs filled with the heavy sea air, as if someone had sprinkled a saltshaker over the boat.

A mile or two passed…a few distant islands and boats anchored everywhere, fishermen mostly. The eight o'clock morning sun provided a fresh perspective, vivifying everything…color, temperature, and sounds. The water looked like luminous turquoise stained glass. *Any chapel would pay big money for such windows*, she noted. The air raised goose bumps up and down her arms. The birds of the air chirped clearly, loudly, as if through a microphone echoing across the currents. *Any chapel would pay big money for such a choir.* She closed her eyes and prayed under her breath, "Our Father who art in Heaven, hallowed be your name."

Even if she *didn't* get a job, Kristine decided the boat trip alone made the early morning effort well worth it. Just feeling awake, alive, and on a boat before the official daytime actually began, rejuvenated her in a way that made her think of how an early morning poacher, who never got caught, might feel. Being alive under the incandescent, dawning sun made her realize that her late morning dreams didn't compare to what real life offered. She scolded herself for sleeping so late into the morning. *There's things to see in this world, things that look different early in the morning.*

She no longer had to hold onto the side of the boat as it approached a large island capped with about one hundred extravagant old Florida-style, pastel-colored homes, clapboard-sided and tin-roofed.

She suddenly bent down to scratch her ankle...well, to secretly catch her breath. She kept her sentences short, as always, when she sensed a breathing frenzy approaching. *Ouch, my heart. Darn, I'm a hooked fish,* she thought. "Is that Tarpon Key?"

"Oh no, dear. That's *Silver* Island. *Some* consider it *Fantasy Island*."

"Is Tarpon Key *that* gorgeous?"

"*Absolutely*, but Tarpon Key is more of a *Gilligan's* Island.

"Who lives there on Silver Island? I mean, how do they get there? There's no bridge, no road, and it's so far from the mainland!"

"You have to be a member of the Silver Island Club before you can own a house there. Anyone who can afford to be a member there can *certainly* afford to get there by boat."

"The homes look so new."

"Not as new as you think. This island was a refuge for President Theodore Roosevelt and his tarpon loving friends at the turn of the century. He sold it to New York advertising giant, Baron G. Collier, who bought the island in 1906 and built a *lovely* wooden mansion overlooking Pine Island South. His home became the Collier Inn."

The island looked luxuriant, and Kristine felt she'd be safe docking there. Maybe it was the pastel-colored homes that reminded her of her family's ice cream shop, she decided. But, as the boat passed the ritzy residences, panic suddenly gripped her. She felt a knife stab her chest and knew what a fish felt like being filleted alive. *Maybe it's a hoax. Maybe there's no Tarpon Key, no restaurant. What's the worst thing that could happen*, she asked herself. *I might die in some wretched way.* She didn't like her answer.

"*There's* Tarpon Key!" Lawrence fervently pointed as they passed a channel marker topped with an osprey nest.

"Oh, my goodness, it *is Gilligan's Island!*" She had never seen anything like it, except on television. A mound of shredded greenery appeared…one small, round island of about one hundred acres of lush green palms, lavish vegetation and tropical flowering plants. Unlike Ginger and Marianne's deserted island, some sailboats and several small boats bobbed in their births.

"Wow, what do they use on their lawns? Monosodium glutamate? I've never seen anything so green and beautiful," Kristine laughed, taking off her sunglasses to get a flawless view.

"No, no preservatives needed. It's *all* natural." He shook his head and chuckled. "Monosodium glutamate…that's the first I've heard that one, dear, and I've taken a lot of people out here, from all over. Some have walked the Asian tea gardens at Golden Gate Park in San Francisco. Others have ice-skated across the top of the mountains of Squaw Valley, or hiked the trails of Lake Tahoe, or set up camp in Yosemite. Still others have driven the Pacific Coast Highway from Sacramento to San Diego and picked a grape from a vineyard in Napa Valley. And these are just the West coast stories. People from everywhere tell me this place competes. I've never seen any of the places they talk about, dear. I have no desire to go either. This *magnificent* place satisfies me just fine."

"I've never been to any of those places either. I will tell you, though, this place competes with the rows and rows of apple orchids and the yellow sand dunes, and winter wonderland snowfalls and crispy orange leaves of Michigan. I can offer you that comparison."

As the boat drew closer, a white rustic building with a huge screened porch and green awnings loomed larger and larger.

"That's the restaurant and inn. It stands atop an ancient Native American shell mound, about thirty-eight feet above sea level. Once we tie up, just follow the sandy pathway up to the front doors and go on in, young lady."

Lawrence easily maneuvered the boat into a slip. "Long before it was ever an inn, it was the home of playwright and mystery novelist Emelia Willow. She and her husband bought Tarpon Key for a couple grand and later spent over a hundred thousand on the amenities. She had it built in the thirties on the highest point of the island. You can buy several of her books in the gift shop over there."

Kristine felt relieved to hear words like *gift shop* and *mystery writer*. As she walked up the coconut palm tree-dotted path, overtaken with ducks, she declared the tropical jungle her utopia. If she had had a flag, she would have stuck it in the dirt. No pavement, no light posts, no tourist signs, and no preservatives. It stood completely void of commercialization. The color green showed up everywhere, but not just green. If the landscape were a crayon-colored drawing, one palm would be emerald green; another, sea green. Yellow green and pitch green, and cat-eye green in some patches, shaded the grass. There were more greens than her brown eyes had ever seen before. Birds chirped, and the waves rippled slowly on shore. Some slapped against the wooden docks. The sounds harmonized better than any New Age audiocassette, better than anything she had ever heard. No honking horns like the city. Just tropical birds chirping and male ducks quacking, fighting over the females.

By the time she walked up the hill to the front doors of the white clapboard restaurant, she felt like she'd been on a ride at Disney World. *No, that's man-made, this isn't,* she reminded herself. She felt like she had gone through a facial, a back massage, and an aromatherapy treatment…completely revived.

Inside the shady building stood wooden tables painted white, with straight-back chairs that showed their age and displayed a 'don't-give-a-hoot' charm. Everything looked old, rustic, but clean. Shaded from the thick shadowing palm trees that looked like monsters with long slender bodies and wild, crazy green hair, it seemed dark and cold, and there were ashes in the fireplace. In one of the restaurant rooms farthest from the front door, Kristine noticed the wallpaper peeling off the walls.

"Go ahead, give yourself a look around," said a woman. "I'll be right with you. Those things you see falling off are dollar bills. Go, look up close." She disappeared.

Kristine walked around the dining rooms that encircled the bar. She recognized an old familiar voice, music she and her friends played as they huddled into the fraternity houses on winter weekends, drinking and dancing to keep warm. The words, blended with alcohol, carried them out of the gloom, the cold, and made them believe they really were in Margheritaville. At times it felt hypocritical to be shouting the tropical words of Jimmy Buffet while wearing boots and dripping from melted snow. Now, she felt so much a part of the world in his songs that she gave herself permission to sing the words "pencil thin mustache" out loud as she hurried around the corner and into the bar. Well, it sounded like Buffet's voice, yes. In person, no. It all came from the speakers. *Oh well.* It surely looked like the sort of place where he'd hang out.

She looked around. Autographed dollar bills posted with masking tape covered the walls like crisp autumn leaves ready to drop from their trees. Overhead fans, made of wood, whipped just enough of a breeze to loosen some bills, and they fell to the floor. Looking out the large screened windows, she saw a jungle of Indian banyan trees with ovate, heart-shaped leaves and remarkable aerial roots that grew down from the branches to form secondary trunks. Overshadowed by banyon and fanlike leaves of the palms, the rustic bar seemed more like a tree house to Kristine, a place where time stood still.

"Good, you looked around. I'm Ruth, the head waitress-slash-manager. Welcome to Tarpon Key. Years ago, an old fisherman put his dollar bill on the wall in hopes that, when he returned, a cold beer would be waiting for him. It started the paper-bill tradition, and our guests still do it today. It's worth more than twenty two thousand dollars, but the ones that fall go to charity."

Ruth spoke quickly, but her words sounded relaxed. "I run the restaurant all summer while the owners are away."

"I've *never* seen anything like this place! It must be Florida's best kept secret!"

Kristine looked out the front windows and saw water. She turned and looked out the back windows and saw jungle. "Does a restaurant like this get busy?" People used to ask her the same thing about the ice-cream shop, and within a minute, the crowds would be lined up outside the door and around the corner.

"You'll find out soon enough. The next boat doesn't go back to the marina until three-thirty today."

"So I'm stuck here. What does one do on this island all day?"

"For starters, we work." She sprinkled lemon oil on the wooden surface of the bar and rubbed vigorously with a clean white cloth. "Why don't you take a seat and look through our scrapbooks? How about something to drink?"

"Sure. Water, please." Actually, she craved a good old-fashioned strawberry soda, the kind her sister knew how to make properly. Fresh strawberry syrup stirred into soda water, then two large curls of vanilla ice cream dropped in...

"You might want to choose something else. Our water is for stomachs used to island water, if you know what I mean."

"Anything else is fine, thank you."

She flipped through pages of newspaper articles and clippings from national travel publications. Writers from all over the world had spent time on the island, reviewing it as a one-of-a-kind place. Several articles ranked it high among the world's best paradise get-a-ways. She could picture Ernest Hemingway, the novelist who journeyed from Illinois to Italy to France to Florida and Spain, making a stop here along the way. Had he ever drunk here in this bar with his friends? Perhaps he had come by boat one night. Key West wouldn't take long by boat. She wondered if Jimmy Buffet knew about it too. She could picture him taking a huge bite of a cheeseburger, licking his lips and singing, "Cheeseburger in Paradise."

"So why would you be good waiting tables?" Ruth handed her a Diet Coke and took a seat next to her at the long white wooden table.

"Well, I've grown up in service-oriented family businesses, so I've served customers just about my entire life. I'm serious about making money. I plan to take a year off college and save up before returning," she lied, saying nothing about going to Spain in the Fall. To justify the lie, she reminded herself that she wouldn't be going abroad at all. She always justified a lie because as her high school principal used to say, his students have a responsibility in life. They wear "Christian" on their backs and represent to others what Christians should be like. Even though his reminders went out to those wearing the school jacket, he said after graduation they would go about life with the invisible word "Christian" on their backs. She justified her lie and moved on.

"How did your parents start their businesses?"

She remembered how, at first, it was like a child's dream...easy. Later it became hard work. "When my dad left his medical sales job in

Chicago, we sold our boat and bought a well-established ice-cream shop in a busy resorting town. It had a bed & breakfast upstairs, and we lived in the house attached below. Eventually, we moved out of the house and converted it into a restaurant. About the same time, my dad started a horse ranch from scratch," she stated with pride.

"Do you consider yourself a hard worker? We keep busy here and the hours are long."

"Oh yes. I've grown up in a Dutch town that honored a strong work ethic. You know, do absolutely everything to the best of your ability, whether waiting tables or leading a country." She couldn't help but picture herself carrying three boxes of ice cream out from the backyard freezer into the shop. Her father somehow always carried four but could barely see where he was going.

"Well then, why don't you start bussing tables right now? We'll see how it goes from there. Like I said, you've got until three-thirty. That's when the boat goes back."

"Thank you." After years of adding exactly one tablespoon of malt powder to make the world's best vanilla malts, it seemed strange having to prove her workmanship to someone else.

"If you take the job, you'll have to live here on the island for about twelve days in a row at first, then the boat will take you back for two days off every week. Two days in a row that is."

"Live here? On the island? Where?" She still wanted to live with her parents and her little sister, to spend time with her family over the summer.

"We have two houses for the cooks and waiting staff. We also provide staff meals here in the restaurant before lunch and dinner serving hours."

"Does the waiting staff make good money?"

"They average about five hundred dollars a week in tips during the summer months. Since there's no place to spend money on the island, it's a great way to save."

Kristine laughed. "Well, I'm interested, and I do need a job!"

She wondered if the owners had any family members working there, like a grandmother, one who wore purples and reds and added much color even to an ice-cream shop.

"Then give it some thought while you're working today. If it goes well, you can start tomorrow or whenever you like. I'll show you where the rags are kept and how to set tables. We're going to be getting pretty busy soon, so we better get started."

℘

"Okay, so the fork goes on this rim of the place mat here?" Kristine asked Ruth in a conscientious tone.

"Over this way a little more, and make sure the napkin doesn't cover up any wording on the place mat."

Ruth had started out as head waitress and quickly advanced to manager, she told Kristine. She spoke matter-of-factly, displaying an overabundance of natural common sense about everything. A friendly person, the sort that might own a Saturn back on land, the petite fifty-something-year-old woman had lived on the island for years and swiftly waited the tables without showing any signs of tiring.

"Are you okay? You seem a bit out of breath," she asked Kristine.

"I'm fine. This is a better workout than kick boxing," Kristine lied, dropping a rag as an excuse to bend down and gasp for breath. She didn't know why she couldn't breathe. No danger lurked, and with the sun directly overhead, night stood hours away yet.

As Ruth explained the bussing procedures, both women recognized immediately that they shared common work ethics. They both set up tables with intensity, carefully aligning the silverware with pride. As Kristine folded a napkin neatly, she could almost hear her teachers from Christian high school telling her do everything with pride and to the best of her ability. She wondered where Ruth acquired her work ethic.

Learned? Taught? Innate? Regardless, their work ethic was bonding them, and the women respected one another from the time they first cleaned a table together.

While bussing her second dirty table, Kristine glanced out at the water. She was amazed to see boats of varying caliber, big boats, small boats, sail boats, fishing boats and yachts pulling up to the dock. Within half an hour, voices of every accent, language and pitch imaginable rang through the three-room restaurant. They sounded like a charismatic congregation speaking in tongues. Sun-tanned people in flip-flops started lining up outside the door and down the walkway. They spoke American, French, or German. A few minutes earlier, Kristine could never have imagined people from all over the world arriving on boats for lunch.

She sprinted from table to table as fast as she could, wishing she had more time to talk to Ruth about island life and the job. What would she decide come three-thirty when she'd have to catch the boat back? As dirty tables piled up, she had no time to talk to anyone, only to bus. Her family used to run around together like this every summer. She felt lonely without them working by her side, and it felt uncomfortably professional to call a boss by first name instead of *Mom* or *Dad*.

"Okay, you can stop now. The boat's waiting for you down at the dock."

Ruth walked up to the dirty table she was cleaning.

"It's three-thirty already? It can't be. I thought it was about one o'clock." For the first time all afternoon, she lost her breath again.

"Well, you were busy. And you did a fine job. If you're interested, you can be back on the boat any morning with your suitcases."

"You're offering me the job?"

"That's right. We need help right away. Try to come back on the boat tomorrow morning. Remember, you must stay out here and work twelve days in a row."

"I need to think about this, about living out here, on an island with no bridge, no recliner chair to sit up in, no…"

"What?" Ruth interrupted.

"Ah, when I took the boat out here, I didn't realize I had to actually live on the island. I mean, I've got so many things to do on the mainland."

"Don't we all?" Ruth picked up a ripe grapefruit left on a plate and began to peel it, dropping the peelings on Kristine's tray before pulling the juicy sections apart. "Want some?"

Christine took one piece. The juice burst inside her mouth, a sweet tart taste. She'd never eaten grapefruit like this in Michigan.

"Opportunity's like this ripe grapefruit," Ruth pointed out. "It's up to you if you're going to pick it before it falls from the tree."

*

Walking down the path to catch the boat, she could hear a drunken voice singing an old familiar song.

"…with Gilligan, the skipper too, the millionaire and his wife…the movie star, professor and Marianne…here on Gilligan's Isle."

Wearing cut-off jeans, the barefooted singer had a beer in one hand and a rope in the other. Next to his tiny, inexpensive, rusty old boat, a seventy-foot luxury yacht and a few cabin cruisers docked side-by-side, as unfitting as a grapefruit on an apple tree.

"Welcome aboard, dear! I'll take you back now," said the dock master, Lawrence, as he greeted her at the staff boat.

"Do you make two boat trips to the island every day, Lawrence?" Kristine stepped onto the boat, determined to fully understand all island transportation options, including escape routes.

"Yes. I pick up inventory or guests staying in the rooms…older couples on their honeymoons, writers looking for inspiration, all sorts who want to escape the busyness in their lives. There's also employees coming and going from their days off."

He stared at her for a moment and spoke again. "Dear, everyone comes out here for a reason. They don't always know the reason for several years…hindsight. The currents of life bring individuals to Tarpon Key. The canals we go down might not make sense as we're cruising along, but there's a reason why our motors run out of fuel, get caught up in a mangrove or run ground from time to time. You've got a decision to make, but if you turn it down, you might just be pushing yourself against the direction of the wind."

He turned the key in the boat's ignition, and they were off.

She put on her sunglasses, which were scratched and rose-tinted, and noticed a blue heron quietly stalking prey at the edge of the mangrove. She smiled, looking back at the island, then bent down to fidget with her shoelace and catch her breath.

6

She had a wonderful day interviewing on the island. Ten o'clock at night crept up way too quickly, and as the family watched television together, she tried catching her stubborn breath, while fighting nausea and a watering mouth. Rushing to the kitchen, she drank *7up* and devoured Saltines. Little ants were crawling inside her left arm as it fell asleep. She took hold of the heavy object connected to her shoulder and shook it frantically, but her fingers stayed numb. She ran to the comfort of the living room. Brief, repetitious, sharp pains struck where she guessed her heart was. Like *Pin the Tail on the Donkey*, the darts came close enough. She self-diagnosed a heart attack and silently waited for it to happen, wondering if Lauren suffered, if she tried calling out for help that night, but without a voice. She couldn't feel sorry for Lauren, now in the arms of God. She instead felt sorry for herself, not in the arms of God.

Everyone said goodnight and prepared for bed. In the bathroom, she examined her pupils in the mirror. Her eyes looked more brown than ever, and her black pupils, so tiny, were too tiny in proportion to the brown. Her knees shook.

"I'm having a weird pain in my heart area." Refusing to go to the recliner, she climbed into bed with Katie. "I don't understand what's happening to me. I swim during the day, but at night, I feel awful."

"Are your pains bad?" asked her father, as he stopped in to say good night.

"Like the blade of a windmill breaking off in a tornado and hitting me in the chest, Dad."

As he leaned over the bed, taking her pulse, Kristine noticed a dancing blue aura around him. She noticed things like this around everyone lately, even the dog. It meant nothing to her. She wasn't psychic, didn't read auras. Her brown eyes were teasing her. They were mad, grouchy, resentfully tired. She knew it. She promised she'd stop applying mascara. They were feeling weak and makeup only weighed them down. Rebellious, they entered the dream world without her. At first they'd fixate on something for so long that a blink felt like an eight-hour sleep. Soon, they'd spastically begin to blink, enjoying rapid eye movement though Kristine was awake.

Her father placed his two fingers on the pulse on her neck and she started feeling dramatic. She shook of laughter and couldn't stop—one of those laughs where there's absolutely nothing funny but it's uncontrollable, and tears came rolling down. Once her father turned the lights off and left the room, the laughing stopped, while tears silently continued. She took off her sheets and lay straight-backed, gazing at the ceiling.

Two minutes later, Katie fell fast asleep. Rather than relaxing her body parts, Kristine fought the drowsiness tugging at her eyelids. She didn't want milk, wine, Nyquil or any other insomniac remedy. Though her body and mind were exhausted, she resisted falling asleep. As she lay on her back under the entombing sheets, she felt like a body in a coffin.

Thinking back to the past few months of her life, she saw nothing but stress over little things. After studying ten hours for one exam, she still felt her blood pressure skyrocket as she sat in her desk, as if no amount of studying could ever be enough. After one hour of the boring stationary bike, she still felt that one hour and fifteen minutes would be better. After enjoying two cafe mochas, she then felt guilty, as if one should be plenty. After waking up at eight o'clock and running to class, she scolded herself for not having awaked at seven. As her car got stuck in five-feet of snow, she cried because she knew she'd miss class. Why didn't she laugh? Why didn't she lie down and do an angel in the snow? Why did it ruin her entire day—something so out of her control?

Because she let it, she realized. As she looked into fields of weeds, she only noticed the beer cans, the ugly stones, the dirt. She looked right past the wild yellow daisy on its tall slender green stem, growing alongside the trash. Now, pretending to be a body in a coffin looking back, she realized how insignificant most of life really was and how hard she had been on herself. *No wonder life is the four-letter word and death is five.*

Lying on her back, her heart pounded. She placed two fingers on her neck—*b'dum, b'dum, b'dum, b'dum.* Two fingers on her stomach—*b'dum, b'dum, b'dum, b'dum, b...b'dum.* It skipped a beat. *B'dm, b'dm, b'dm...* it sped up!

Is this what Lauren felt before dying in her sleep? Imaginary ants crawling from her left arm into her feet? *Where's my paper bag?* Turning over to her left side to reach for it on the floor, she suddenly felt a powerful wave of energy shoot up from her toes and spasm in her chest.

She bolted up from her prone position, clutching her chest, and heaved back a scream. Her throat felt dry, yet she couldn't stop heaving. Her sister awoke. As if escaping the dark, the bed, the room, Kristine sprinted into the dining room and turned on the overhead light.

On the car ride to the Cape Coral hospital, her mother and father sat in the front seat, while Kristine and Katie, making grouchy moans every so often, sat in the back.

"You just lie down back there." Her mother reached over the seat and rubbed Kristine's hand.

"Oh no, I can't lie down. That's when everything gets worse!" She sat upright in the middle of the back seat. "I feel so embarrassed for putting you guys through this worry. What's happening to me?"

"What do you think is happening?"

"A heart attack. I'm sure of it. I'm sure I just had a heart attack."

She drew comfort knowing that shortly she'd be in the company of medical professionals. She also liked having people awake with her at one o'clock in the morning.

Walking into the hospital's emergency room, Kristine accepted the nurse's offer and sat down in the wheel chair, while explaining her symptoms again.

"You look so young and healthy," said the skeptic nurse. "But the doctor will take a look at you in a minute." She walked away.

"Why is she so calm? Why so lackadaisical about this?" Kristine turned around to look at her father as he pushed the wheel chair. "I've just had a heart attack!"

As she lay on the table, the doctor hooked her up to the Electrocardiograph.

"This records the electrical activity of your heart. We're going to look for irregularities in the muscle, blood supply or neural control."

Kristine smiled up at her father and mother, then the doctor as he placed sticky things all over her chest. Inwardly she felt guilty because she liked the wheel chair better than the recliner chair tonight.

"Describe your symptoms to me, Kristine."

"A viselike squeezing sensation beneath my breastbone, pain radiating from the front of my chest."

She did feel that way, but in truth the vivid description came right from the pages of her parents' infamous medical encyclopedia she so carefully studied the night before. She figured she'd get further by communicating with the doctor in his own terms.

"Whoa. You are describing a heart attack. But no, rest assured. It is not a heart attack. Have you been under any kind of stress lately, Kristine?" The doctor looked back and forth between Kristine and her parents. "Because it might be that you're experiencing extreme anxiety, which is routinely mistaken for cardiac or respiratory disorders."

"Anxiety? No. I'm a pretty stable person. Pretty in control of my life, doc."

"Have you been under any kind of unusual stress lately, like a traumatic event or something?"

"My best friend just died of a heart attack in her sleep. I skipped her funeral."

"And her grandmother also died recently of a heart attack in her sleep," her father added.

"I'm sorry to hear that. But I want to assure you all that Kristine is not dying of a heart attack. She'll be fine, although her blood pressure has literally skyrocketed. She just went through some serious progressive stages of hyperventilation, and the next step, after the wave, would have been to pass out."

"So her heart itself is okay?" her mother asked.

"I'd say so, yes! Should it start to happen again Kristine, and it probably will, you need to talk yourself out of it," he explained. "Convince yourself that you're not going to die from this and just relax when you start feeling the shortness of breath. Hopefully you can stop it from getting to this point again, but it'll take some strong convincing on your part."

"Am I going crazy, doc?"

"Absolutely not! Anxiety disorders are the most common mental disorders in the United States, affecting two to four percent of the population."

"Mental disorder? It makes me sound crazy."

"I'm not saying you have a serious mental or anxiety disorder. Just that you let your thoughts affect your body. If you let it get out of control, you may need treatment. This might mean drugs, psychotherapy, behavior modification, relaxation training. Alone or in any combination."

"What triggers this sort of thing?"

"Well, some learning theorists say anxiety is learned when innate fears occur together with previously neutral objects or events. I don't know. You need to figure out what your fear is. Then face it in whatever way you choose."

Back in bed again that night, the spastic wave returned. It was not nearly as bad.

"Breathing is easy. See?"

Katie dramatically breathed in, then let out a long sigh and smiled. "I'm good at breathing. Mommy said I learned quick when I was a baby."

She eventually fell into a light sleep, but every so often she'd wake and check her big sister's breathing. "I want to see you breathe with the lunch bag. Please, breathe with the bag Daddy gave you. It's funny."

"Okay, thanks," said her muffled voice through the lunch bag. "I'm going to sit up all night, because every time I lie down, my toes get numb again. And some day, I'm going to invent quieter lunch bags!"

The twenty-one-year-old and the five-year-old giggled as if watching a Tom and Jerry cartoon.

Her shortness of breath lasted for hours, and she dreaded the darkness called night. Sitting up in bed, as the doctor had ordered, she told herself she wasn't going to die and that her shortness of breath originated from her own mind. Throughout the rest of the night, she'd drift hesitantly into a shallow sleep, then her inner voice would wake her. Her neck bone felt tender from resting against the wooden bed board, but she'd rather feel a stiff neck than all the other crazy things, she decided. Her eyes, shrinking into puffiness, watched through the blinds, and at four-thirty, the moon slowly disappeared behind a pattern of passing clouds. At five o'clock, the bedroom walls flickered with the headlights of passing cars. At five-thirty, birds began chirping—probably year-round Florida birds that didn't bother flying North for the summer, she thought. Or maybe they're mockingbirds, Florida's state bird. But if they were, she should hear them mimicking the sounds of other animals. But no, they were just normal *chirp chirps*, the happy stress-free kind.

Looking at the birds of the air, she felt disappointed with herself. If they weren't worried, why should she? As if worrying might actually add a single hour to life. She listened to the birds, as if hearing their chirps for the first time. She prayed to God, and then the sun rose and the show outside her window ended. Daylight, the sun, that was all very good, she thought. She felt like a hypocrite. How dare a Christian fear death? She had hardly discussed death, ever. During coffee, conversation and crayon time at the café, it had never crept up. Perhaps no one allowed it to. In college, she took classes on everything from world religions to ancient philosophy to chemistry to biology, but everything focused on life. Not death. So how dare a Christian fear death? Well, it was a great question because she did.

℘

"Mom, Dad, can either of you drive me to the marina this morning?"

She walked into the kitchen. The tangled hair and bags under her eyes reflecting back from the stainless steel coffeepot she lifted reminded her of the night before. "Would you hire me?" she asked the pot and shook her head with a stern grimace. Her feet suddenly felt heavy. Amused at herself, she looked down to see if she was wearing her wooden shoes by mistake, instead of her slippers. Then it struck her. "Oh, no! I didn't bring my wooden shoes to Florida," she cried.

"What?" her mother asked.

"Oh, nothing, nothing. Hey, I've got to catch the boat. It'll only take me a minute to pack my suitcases. Did you say you'd drive me?"

Her father gave his wife a look of consultation. "Honey, what are you talking about? It's almost noon. What boat?"

"The island. I forgot to tell you. I'm taking the job on the island, and I have to leave this morning. Oh, and I'll be living out there. You can pick me up every twelve days or so."

Her mother walked over, kissed her on the cheek and handed her a ceramic mug. "Here, drink this. It's strong Java."

Taking the mug that weighed about two pounds, Kristine felt like a spoon-fed starving, stubborn dog, a mutt walking the streets of Mexico.

She sipped the muddy coffee, then shut her eyes. Suddenly she heard voices in her head. She saw scribbles. Together the voices and the scribbles screamed to be heard. As if tossed into a windmill on a wildly windy day, they whirled around madly, yelling out the one or two-worded goals scribbled in crayon on the white paper tablecloth. She heard Lauren's dreams, like psychotic little voices in her head, crying out louder than her own scribbles. "Family time, family time, family time," the voices screamed.

She put the mug of coffee down and opened her eyes, noticing her parents watching her as if watching a performance of Phantom of the Opera. The voices in her head shouted, "Kristina, Kristina," then drowned in another sip of coffee.

"Okay, if I took the job on the island, I wouldn't be able to go to the concert tonight, and that wouldn't be good because I'm really craving some family time."

"After the night you had, I think you should get back into bed and we'll wake you in time for the concert." Her mother carefully removed the coffee mug like an owner steeling a bone from a dog.

§

"This will sure get his attention," her mother said as she drew *We Love you B.J.* in a thick red marker on poster board.

"You think he'll remember us, Mom?" She unfolded the blanket, spread it on the lawn and sat down.

"Of course he will. We haven't missed a concert since you were eight."

"True. I can't believe I blocked the door to his hotel room at one o'clock in the morning. And he picked me up and kissed me when he probably wanted to kick me." She picked a handful of the thick Florida grass and smelled its fresh green odor.

"He'll remember us," said her father, dipping into the cooler for some black licorice sticks. "I sure hope he sings his Christian songs."

B.J. Thomas music played when Mom cleaned. It played in the station wagon on family vacations. It played in the ice-cream shop over speakers. It played on Sundays when the family used to crowd onto the couch in front of the fireplace. Kristine knew the words of his songs before knowing children's songs. His music did something to her parents every time it played. Mom usually cried, and Dad looked as if he was in a mesmerized state of praise. Kristine knew that someday at her wedding, for the father/daughter song, she'd have to play a B.J. song. His words turned the gloomiest days into days of rejoicing. *Yes*, she thought, *music becomes just one board in the bridge that links the present with the past, the new with the old, and every so often, people love to run back and forth on that bridge. Music takes them to and from.*

To pass some time before the concert, Kristine walked Katie over to the bridge to look for fish in the Caloosahachee River below.

"Well kiddo, we're not going to see any fish down in that dark water, so stand over there and let me take your picture with the pretty sun setting behind you." Kristine was already peering through the lens of the camera, as she always set every picture up as if one day it might hang in a museum of world art.

"Tilt your chin, turn your head a bit to the left…no, that's your right, Katie. The other way is left. Okay, good."

"What do I say? How about Cheese?" asked Katie.

"You don't like cheese. No, I want you to say *hasta luego*, alligator."

"What's that mean?"

"It means, see ya later alligator, but in Spanish."

"*Hasta lego gato.*"

Kristine snapped the photo on the word *gato* before jumping at the sound of an interrupting voice from behind her.

"Really, I'm more than happy to take a photo of you two together." A man in his late twenties wearing sporty sunglasses got off his black bike with no kickstand and laid it down on the cement.

"Oh, okay. Sure. That would be great." She handed him the disposable camera she bought when Lauren wanted to take photos of frozen Lake Michigan. Now she felt eager to use up all the pictures and get them developed, hoping she would have at least one shot of her best friend somewhere in the background of any of the twenty-four exposures.

"Come on, Katie, let's put our arms around each other." Her eyes burned. It didn't help that she poured an ocean of eye drops in them before the concert. She hoped the signs of sleep deprivation wouldn't show up through the lens of the camera and that the man taking the photo wouldn't notice.

"You're too tall," whined Katie. "You have to bend down, Kristini."

Kristine wondered if her five foot eight inch body towered over the man holding the camera. It didn't. Good.

"All right girls. Say…"

"I won't say cheese," Katie called out in an angry voice. "I don't like cheese!"

"Okay. Okay," laughed the man. "How about…this world is great but the next is better," he said as he took a few steps back and turned the camera, making it a vertical picture.

"What?" Kristine asked. "That's odd. What do you mean by that?"

"Just say it. I bet it'll generate the prettiest smiles you've ever smiled before."

"No! I won't say it," snapped Katie as she fell out of her pose and onto Kristine's feet.

"Why not, Katie? Just say it so we can get back to the blanket because it sounds like the warm-up music is starting."

"No! Daddy says stranger danger."

On 'stranger danger' the stranger snapped the photo and handed the camera back to Kristine, laughing. "That's a good lesson, but if I meet your daddy I won't be a stranger any more." The sun setting behind him set his golden curls in a wreath-like glow, reminding her of a Roman prince. The only thing missing was his toga. Instead he wore a deep green T-shirt and black shorts. And he rode a black bike, not a flying white horse. *If he's a B.J. Thomas fan, dad will give us permission to elope.*

"I live downtown here and bike just about everywhere, well, except when I'm working." He handed the camera back to her. "My name is Steve O'Connor."

She noticed him staring her directly in the eyes as if reading a book. She didn't want to blink, for it might turn a page and his interest. She longed to be a novel, a wonderful mystery, adventure and romance all in one, something he couldn't put down, or maybe a political thriller. She hoped he didn't prefer science fiction because she didn't even believe in UFOs.

"Nice to meet you. I'm Kristine Longheart." She did a 365-degree turn, checking for her little sister. "Oh good. There she is. I've got to keep a quick eye on her."

"She's cute. So tell me, are you in school or do you work?"

"Well, I go to college in Michigan but I'm on summer break."

"Michigan? Never been there. Nice state?"

"Great. They grow lots of Christmas trees, and the whole state has about fifty-four thousand farms. I'm not sure how many trees they grow in Holland, the town I come from, the town in which everyone has blue eyes but me." She couldn't believe her answer, although she knew his looks caught her completely off guard and she didn't want to have an intelligent conversation. She wanted to stare. Maybe she could have *written* a great answer to his question, but then again it wasn't an essay contest, just a conversational question. Grandma would have loved this one in a letter.

"Pride in one's state. I like that," he said. "It would probably be a prettier place if there were more brown eyes around though."

She felt a smile from ear to ear and her face growing hot. He still stared.

"I think I've already got you figured out. I mean, I haven't known you for long, but you're a planner, aren't you?"

"What do you mean?"

"I read people like I read books. You like to have things all planned out. You expect life to happen as you plan it to happen."

"How can you tell that?"

"My secret. I'll tell you some day. Besides, I'm still in the first chapter. I'd like to read a bit further."

"We'll see about that," she smiled. "I'm only here for the summer, and I've got to find a job, quickly!"

"That could be a challenge. This is summer in Florida, the off season."

"Well, it is a priority. Finding a lucrative summer job is a written goal of mine. I need the money."

"Good luck."

"Thanks. Do you work around here?" Her sentences were becoming choppy. She couldn't breath. She hoped he didn't notice that and the dark circles under her tiny, red eyes that were brown just a moment ago.

"I'm a commercial architect here in Fort Myers. I moved down here from Mississippi after I finished school. I love it here. Oh, turn around, you've got to see the size of the sun now."

"It's almost blinding. Hard to believe such a color exists." She thought of Lauren, who told her to start finding new things to love. "Katie, we better go. The concert is starting. Nice meeting you."

"You too. Bye." He shook her hand lightly, then waved at Katie, who smiled like she was in love for the first time in her few years of life. Kristine sang along with the words as she squeezed Katie's hand and walked back over to the blanket, "Life has had its hard times when I felt the chill of winter...I can't forget the night when my sweet Jesus slipped away."

Their father kneeled in the grass, videotaping the stage as they approached the family blanket. Their mother sat with tears gracing her cheeks.

"Here honey, bring them up now, on this song. I love this song." Her mother handed her a bouquet of lilies.

As Kristine walked up to the stage, she could feel her heart dancing in rhythm with the music, and she feared that walking too close to the speakers might trigger the pain. She didn't want to die. Not now, not at a concert with her family in the park, and not with the handsome older man on his bike watching her from across the street. As she carefully walked around the blankets spread across the grass, so as not to step on any fingers, she glanced at the lilies in her hand. They wore natural purple, blue and white suits with ruffled blouses underneath. Somehow the lilies, once alive in the fields, reminded her not to worry about tomorrow, for tomorrow will worry about itself. She knew tulips belonged to the lily family. She knew all kinds of things about tulips because she had sold them at school. She liked the parrot tulip the best for its petals wrinkled at the edges. That is not to say she didn't love the Darwin tulip with its deep-colored blossoms.

"I know this family," B.J. Thomas said softly into the microphone that echoed throughout all of downtown Fort Myers. "They're dear to me. Security guards, let them back to see me later. I do love this family." He bent down, hugged her, and took the flowers.

The crowd screamed, Kristine's mother cried, her father kept videotaping, and Steve sat on his bike watching from the road. Later, Steve showed up at their blanket, introduced himself to Kristine's parents and handed her his phone number. "It's too loud to talk now, but I'd love to go out. Call me if you'd like." Then he looked at little Katie and said, "There. I'm no longer a stranger."

She giggled and nodded as she squeezed her daddy's hand tightly.

Kristine watched Steve take off on his bike and wondered if she could control the timing of achieving her goals. She didn't want to meet Mr. Right too soon in life. Admittedly, she viewed men as obstacles to all the things she wanted to do in life, before settling down. She wondered what he meant when he said this life is good but the next is better. What on earth was he talking about?

℘

They walked up and down Fort Myers Beach for hours, sometimes knee deep in the warm water and sometimes on the white, crunchy shoreline. It was the same beach day after day, but each time it looked completely different, just as a painting on the wall looks different with the lights turned off and the shades shut, compared to the lights on or the sun striking it from the window. Steve held her hand as they walked and always stopped for a moment to kiss her on her forehead, nose, then lips. They stopped to pool hop at resort pools and sometimes ordered tropical drinks under the bamboo huts designed for guests only. They ate gyros salads at an outdoor Greek cafe overlooking the Gulf of Mexico and watched a drunken man get a picture of an ugly trout, wearing a polka dotted tie, tattooed onto his arm. They sat until closing at a local jazz club, too loud for talking. Still, they sat. They walked through the outdoor mall, tossing all their extra change into the fountains. They sat on a blanket, listening to a band of retired jazz players, in the same downtown park where they had first met.

As she picked a handful of grass, she noticed it much longer than when she sat here with her parents at the concert. She felt a new urgency to find a job or take the offer she had on the island. Writing the goal on the tablecloth had made it all sound so simple. Achieving it was turning it into another story. And how dare Mr. Right sit next to her? She hadn't planned on him showing up for years yet, after she accomplished all her other goals. Somehow she'd discover a flaw in him, something to remove him immediately from the Mr. Right category.

"Steve, there are things I want to do in my life, lots of things. What if I don't do them? What if I lose control and never accomplish any of my dreams?" They lay on a blanket on their backs looking up at the darkened Florida sky.

"Oh, but you are in control, and every day we make choices. These choices either bring us a step closer or a step further from our goals."

"What if I die before getting there?"

"Kristine, you might die before reaching your goals. I might die before reaching mine. We all might. That's why the journey toward our goals, the daily steps, must mean something more. Make those steps count and make them fun. Hop, skip, jump, run backward, or walk passionately toward your goals. Those steps should add so much pleasure to your daily life, and if they don't, well, maybe you should reevaluate your goals to begin with."

She liked his answer. She liked him. So much so, that he suddenly looked like a roadblock, standing before her and all her dreams. She would disqualify him quickly. "Do you want to travel in your future?"

"Kristine, I've lived all over the country, the world for that matter."

"But have you seen all you want to see?"

"For now, yes. With a father in the military, I've done so much. I once paddled a canoe down a flooded street during a devastating storm in Japan. As a boy I watched a grizzly bear sniff the tires of our car in Alaska at a park where my family planned on picnicking. I drank my first cup of strong, black coffee while sitting under a full moon in an outside square in Madrid one night. It almost made me sick and I stayed up all night."

"In Madrid? You lived in Madrid?" Why hadn't she told him about her plans of going to Spain? She kicked herself at the thought of him not knowing, but maybe she wouldn't go without Lauren. She didn't want to cross the boundaries of being a horrible friend, taking off for the international adventure that her now deceased friend would have died for. "Are you sure you're done traveling, seeing the world?" Her Mr. Right would surely want to travel.

"Done. Here to stay. I need to belong somewhere, to establish friends that last longer than just a couple months. It's tough saying good-bye every time you really start caring for someone."

Suddenly she knew she had to take the job on the island. "So where was the most incredible place you've ever been to in all your life?"

"Kristine, there's no competition. I've been to a place beyond words, beyond anything describable."

"That sounds quite dramatic," she laughed. "You're not talking alien abduction now, are you?"

"Far beyond."

"Tell me about it. Do you have pictures or something you could show me?"

"No pictures. Although I've got this sketchbook, and for a whole year after I went there, I tried recreating what I saw in my sketchbook. I'll tell you about it sometime, but for now, it's still somewhat private. I don't want to talk about it."

"Private? How can a place be private? Where'd you go?"

"Later, okay? But hey, just know one thing. This life is good but the next is better."

"Yeah, you've said that before. Are you talking about reincarnation?"

"No, no. I'll tell you another time, okay?"

"Okay, whenever you're ready. I'm here."

She wondered where Steve had gone. Why did he have to keep so quiet about it? Maybe it involved his father and some confidential military assignment. Maybe something horrible happened to him in this place and he was still in the process of psychological counseling. Maybe he was on drugs and referred to that sort of trip. Perhaps it was alien abduction. Some day she would get inside his apartment and snoop around for his sketchbook. *No, it might be as sacred as my letters to Grandma and I'd die if he read those*, she told herself. Then again, she couldn't figure out why she herself hadn't told Steve about the breathing troubles, her panic attacks. Except for chronic cuticle biting, she always felt she had life under control. She couldn't understand how her mind could now be crazy enough to do this to her, and she feared she might be losing touch with her saneness. No, she couldn't let Steve think her crazy.

Dear Grandma:

It might not be the right decision, but I've made it. I'm leaving for an island in the morning. And that's all I'm going to say about that. Tonight I watched the players of a jazz band performing so confidently. Even as they approached the end of a sheet of music, they flipped that sheet, then continued playing with confidence. I know their secret. They rehearsed! They knew exactly which notes lay ahead. But life is not rehearsed. Not knowing what lies on the next page ahead makes it difficult to walk about so confidently. Life itself is the only performance we have. There's no rehearsal nor going back to do better the second time around. As for the notes we play, well, they might suddenly end and the page may go blank. How do we know if we can't rehearse?

The realization that I'm not going to live on this earth forever, that my life here is not permanent, shocked me. I've never considered death before. I never gave it any status in my future list of things to do. Now, I watch Bugs Bunny falling off a cliff and I have a panic attack.

Just one more thing, Grandma. I never wrote about the day Lauren cried in front of the mirror for an hour because her naturally tight spiral curls just wouldn't straighten. I stepped in with tissues, a fresh can of hair spray and a curling iron for flattening, but the stubborn white hair still rebelliously twisted. She was so upset because she had a date. Her plans were ruined due to her out-of-control hair. Lauren never could see the beauty in her naturally thick hair. She could see the beauty in everything else, including months of Michigan's dark, gloomy skies and dirty snow, but she could never see the beauty in herself. That's all.

7

"You just got home from college and you're off already." Her mother hugged her under the bamboo hut. "And you haven't told Steve yet."

"I know, Mom. I wished I didn't have to live out there, but it's great money and I'll be home soon for two days off. I'll tell Steve on those days off, or I'll write him a letter."

"No, you tell him in person!"

"I will as soon as he gets back from Mississippi. He's visiting his family for a couple weeks."

"Well, you know I love you, and I'll be here to pick you up on your days off."

"I know. I love you, too."

"Oh, do you have your paper lunch bag, just in case?" her mother whispered.

"She'll be fine, Ma'am. I promise," interrupted Lawrence as he loaded her suitcases onto the staff boat.

Taking the dockmaster's hand and stepping onto the boat at Island Marina felt like *deja vu* from a couple weeks ago, but this time, she had a couple suitcases with her.

As they pulled away from the dock, Kristine waved until she could no longer see her mother. She felt a panic attack and didn't know what to blame…the speed of the boat, the wind hitting her face, or the what-if scenario playing itself out in her mind? Deeply breathing, she could taste the salty air on her tongue. What if the boat tips over? What if it runs into another boat? What if it explodes suddenly in mid-air?

※

None of that happened. Instead, the boat pulled up to the remote island of Tarpon Key, where a man standing under a crooked, petite key lime tree walked up to the dock to greet them.

"Hello there, and welcome to Tarpon Key. My name is Denver, I'll get your stuff and take ya to the staff house." Without allowing Kristine to lift a finger, the skinny older man wearing a tight black Bad Company T-shirt loaded her suitcases from the boat onto a gulf cart. He wore his hair pulled back into a long, frizzy brown ponytail with split ends sticking out everywhere.

"Is that there all the stuff you got?" he asked. "You gotta see what all these waitresses bring out here with them. You got nothing compared to them."

Exactly, she thought. She planned to pack lightly for her first days on the island. That way she could quickly and efficiently escape the island if needed.

The golf cart took off at full speed down a winding sandy pathway through the subtropics jungle.

"The staff house ain't too far. It's just smack in the center of the island. You like music?" asked the man in control of the golf cart, and her life.

"I love it. Why?"

"I play the guitar. I sing too. Write my own lyrics. I'll sing for ya later." Driving up to a house built on stilts, Denver parked the golf cart and carried everything inside while giving a narrated tour.

"Meet Mr. Front Door. It doesn't have a key, so we just go right on in." He kicked the door open with his foot. "And this here, well, it's the facilities, as you can see. We all share it, but you ain't gonna share it with us because you're gonna have one in your bedroom."

Denver slammed the toilette seat shut with his foot.

"Sounds like you've given this tour before." Kristine coughed, allergic to cigarette smoke.

"Every few months, people, they're coming and going." With a tall, laid back slouch, Denver walked down the hallway, kicking beer cans out of the way as he went. "This is my room, and that over there is the bartender's room. Way on the end is Howard, the potato peeler's room."

"But I thought there were two staff houses. Why is this coed?"

Disturbed. Kristine never had a brother, nor serious boyfriend, and it just felt funny to live in a staff house with the same men she'd be working with, men she didn't know.

"Yeah, well, there's, um, I'd say, um, let me count and let me use my fingers to count. Three, four, okay, there's about six of us living in this staff house and the rest live in the other one. Mainly the cooks are over in the other one." He tossed his cigarette on the tile floor and stomped it good.

"Goodness gracious! I think it's dead," said Kristine.

"Gotta be sure with all this trash on the floor. Can't let a single spark go."

"So where's my bedroom?" She took a handful of her hair, smelled it, and made a disgusted face. It already smelled of smoke.

"Hark! Your room's down the hall way, just follow me." Denver slipped on a torn magazine page lying on the floor, but his reflexes were surprisingly agile and he barely missed a step.

"Oh, dear me. There are no sheets on the mattresses." Kristine pointed to a mattress on the floor. Then she looked down at her gold diamond sandals she bought at Payless and could barely see her plum-colored toe nail polish hidden under the sand. "And they don't supply us with towels? I should have asked more questions during the interview."

"You ain't got your own stuff? Don't worry. I've got an extra sheet and pillowcase you can use. I'll bring it to ya later. It ain't no problem at all!" Denver flipped the mattress over to hide the yellow and brown stain marks. "You don't want to sleep on that side, the springs are popping out."

"Oh, dear Lord." She knew that if she said such a thing, she owed the respect of saying a prayer. *Oh dear Lord, be with me out here. I trust in You and walk where You want me to walk. I know this is Your plan. If anything, I realize now I'm a bit spoiled.*

"Ya like your room?" asked Denver.

"Ahhh, well, it's pink. I've had a pink room just about my entire life so I guess it's a familiar pink...you know, comforting." She held her breath a moment because when she inhaled, her heart ripped. She only blamed herself for not asking more questions the day before.

"Ya like the staff house?"

"I like the stilts. I've never lived in a stilted house. We don't have stilted homes in Holland. Although a window would be nice, or a lock on my door."

"Trust me, now. You'll be safe. We're all courteous here. And don't mind the floors. Without pavement on the island, they can't stay clean. No one's to blame for it. Are you the clean type?"

"You could say that. At eleven years old I'd dust the head of every doll and vacuum my carpet once a week. So yes, I'm clean. In fact, I had this horrible habit for a while."

"Sure, I understand. Alcohol? Drugs?"

"No, no!" Dressed in a pastel-colored floral print sundress, she stared around the room as she spoke. "It's nothing like that. We're talking about cleaning, aren't we? I used to spray my light bulbs with Windex until they'd explode. That's before I learned to turn them off before cleaning."

"Then this might take some getting used to. But hey, I better get my bones back to the kitchen. You just make yourself at home here. Oh, been meaning to ask, are you from England or something? What's that sweet sound to your voice?"

"No, I'm from Holland. I guess I sound Dutch. Thanks for the ride and showing me around. You've been accommodating!" She inwardly scolded herself for always acting so overly courteous to strangers, like a Dutch dancer welcoming tourists to the Tulip Time Festival.

"Whoa. You've come a long, long ways," said Denver. "Welcome to America. I hope this untidy place doesn't scare ya too much."

"Well this is no time for me to be a utopian. I'll adapt." She forced herself to yawn, which always meant stolen incoming oxygen. She opened her suitcases, then decided to leave her clothes where they were. Ruth expected her in the restaurant for training.

Ruth lived on the island just like everyone else, but not in the staff house. Instead, the owners provided her with a tiny cottage overlooking the Gulf. She handled everything from scheduling the wait staff to conducting employee meetings. Above the Jimmy Buffet music, she matter-of-factly explained everything—from the potato salad or coleslaw choice, to telling customers, "yes, the shrimp deluxe is served hot and in the shells so you'll need to peel them."

Kristine periodically glanced out at the Gulf of Mexico, topped with bobbing boats, then returned to taking notes with the intensity of a reporter gathering something newsworthy.

"You're a type A like me. I can see it in you, but hey, you don't need to write all this down." Ruth looked her straight in the eyes.

"Short-hand, learned it in college," replied Kristine. "Ruth, if you don't mind my asking, what made you come out to this island? I'm just curious."

"Actually, I'm glad you asked. We all have our stories and we all like sharing them." Ruth tossed the rag aside as if sharing her story suddenly became more important than washing the dirty tables. "Coming here was the best decision of my life. Leaving New York City was the second best. I worked on Wall Street for ten years."

"A stockbroker?"

"No, administrative assistant to a group stockbrokers. I worked in a gorgeous skyscraper downtown. I answered phones and took messages with the same intensity you see in my scrubbing tables. But there, I looked up every day and saw a glass ceiling over my head. Out here, there's no ceiling. Well, there's God's ceiling of stars. Don't get me wrong. New York is one of the man-made wonders of the universe, but living there as long as I did, well, I got sucked up in the hustle and bustle and politics of corporate America. The piles on my desk formed a skyscraper of their own, and my paychecks were good, but what was I really saving for? Was it worth my saving if my daily life was misery? I was making great money but I was getting sick. Why spend our health making money? Then we have to spend our money getting our health back. I just got caught up in the errands of life."

"Yes, life can feel like a dot to dot, from one errand to the next. I've been feeling that way myself lately," Kristine put her note pad down and finally sat down next to Ruth. "I study like crazy. I get perfect grades at school, join every club imaginable, clean to perfection, work like crazy every summer and shop until I drop because I'm never satisfied with my wardrobe. I get frantic over a pimple on my cheek. Yes, Ruth, I'm such a perfectionist, yet what pleasure does all these efforts bring me? They don't make me happy."

"Then you've come here just in time. Every person needs to find an island they can escape to, some place, any place in the world that forces them to stop and think. This island will change the course of your future. You were meant to stop here, and you've come while you're still young. Me, I was caught up in the web of life so badly that it took me a long time to feel free again. I used to show up in my cubicle before the sun rose, and I'd leave after it set. What were the colors of a sunset? I couldn't tell you back then. My back ached from the inactivity of sitting at a desk all day. My eyes burned from staring into a computer screen for hours. I knew there had to be more to life than this. I knew that on my deathbed some day, I surely wouldn't look back on my life, wishing I had spent more time in the office. It's a common phrase and one I could relate to."

"Life can be exhausting," added Kristine. "But how can I relax? It doesn't matter what I'm doing…dipping ice-cream, mopping the floor, studying for finals, I do everything to the best of my ability and I wished I could just hang out and not care so much."

"You need to force yourself to sit in silence, force yourself to think. Often, we keep ourselves so busy that we never allow ourselves to sit and think. Sometimes I think our errands only bury the things we don't want to think about."

"But how can I stop being a perfectionist?"

"I'm not telling you to do less than your best. Let me tell you something Martin Luther King, Jr. might say. He might say something along the lines: *Scrub those tables with the same intensity as Michaelangelo painting and Beethoven composing music, scrub those tables so well that all the hosts of heaven sing out, now there lived a great table scrubber. That's correct. Never do any job in life without pride, without passion, no matter how small your job may be ranked according to this world. Whether a television anchor woman or a waitress scrubbing tables, work with pride and passion, knowing all the while that the voices of Heaven are singing out with you as you work.*"

Back at the staff house, her body ached as if it had just run the women's four hundred-meter low hurdles for the first time in a new track season. At around ten-thirty at night, she shut her door and slowly pulled Denver's torn bed sheet over the yellow-stained mattress. Then she pulled her orange and black stuffed tiger out of her suitcase and hid him under her sheet. She plopped down onto the mattress, kissed his furry black nose, and opened the never-ending letter to her grandmother.

℘

Dear Grandma:

Here I am, my first night on this island called Tarpon Key. I feel lonely and all I have are my own annoying thoughts to keep me company. Is there no escaping ourselves? With no lock on my door, I also feel threatened and somewhat paranoid, as if I can't protect that same self that annoys me. I hear a lot of voices down the hall, but I plan to stick to myself out here and just make money. I don't want, nor need, to get close to these people. I'll learn their names and that's all. I do believe woman can be an island of her own and I will prove so this summer.

As for my crazy panic symptoms, I thought that if I just kept busy and forgot about my fear, they'd go away. Well, life is one big trial and error, so I'm still looking for something that might work.

Now I hear someone playing the guitar. It must be Denver. He works in the kitchen, washing dishes and cleaning. His lyrics are kind of redundant. He's singing over and over that, "Life is so hard, life is so hard." I wonder why life is so hard for him? I also wonder if these people ever sleep? I guess I don't mind if they don't! Goodness, I should love people who don't sleep. In my own freaky manner, I'm one of them.

Today, a few of the cooks and the bartender made similar comments to me. One, who has a wild-looking black mustache, said I look so "clean cut." Another called me "proper." I've never thought of myself as clean cut and proper, then again, I've never been around so many men with pony tails and wild mustaches. Well, I'll just stay in my room with my door shut every night, and they'll think I'm sleeping.

Hey, I really am on a remote tropical island!

Kristine closed the letter then conscientiously did her "homework." She re-read all the watering notes she took from Ruth, then memorized the dinner menu, which featured fresh broiled fish and shrimp steamed in beer, entrees ranging from $16 to $20. There was no printed menu. Instead, the wait staff recited it by memory to the guests. She practiced out loud several times, unsure how to pronounce *Halibut*.

After turning out the lights, she imagined herself a vampire, given the right to stay awake all night. She thought about the tiny piece of land she now slept on way out in the Gulf of Mexico, and the gulf is a seven hundred thousand square mile arm of the Atlantic Ocean, bordered on the north by the United States and on the east by Cuba. She knew her geography well and now the facts haunted her. She wondered if a big wave might come and wash over the island and the small staff house, her new home.

8

Her second night waiting tables on Tarpon Key, Ruth informed Kristine of a top-ten reservation that would require extra special attention.

"Ethan Edwards is an elderly, well-established ship captain who will be bringing in a party of nine gentlemen tonight. Actually, they'll be docking any minute now." Ruth stood at the hostess desk and scribbled off the last name from the reservation book. "He is *extremely* well respected, one of our regulars for dinner, so we like to make everything just right for his table," she whispered professionally to Kristine. She was no drill sergeant, but spoke sternly and the employees seemed to respect her for this.

"Waiting tables is show biz, Kristine. No matter how you're feeling on the inside, you need to smile on the outside," prepped Ruth.

"No problem. I'll do my best." Kristine stared out the screen door. She couldn't tell where the water ended and the sky started, nor could she distinguish between the stars and the lights of approaching boats. She had watched every episode of *Love Boat* and wondered if this guy wore the white captain suit of a Miami-based cruise ship. She spotted lights approaching the island. They weren't bright, festive, cruising lights, but rather plain old spotlights used solely to light the way in the night. *A simple boat. Maybe the captain left his cruise ship home for the night.*

"That might be them now," said Kristine.

"Yes, and keep in mind there's no telling how late they'll stay. Remember to offer them Brazilian coffees with their key lime pies."

"Okay, and up-charge them from iced-tea to Long Island tea." Kristine laughed, then returned to her only other table of the night. During the day, the staff waited on up to ten tables at a time, but at dinner, two proved plenty. Evening customers loved to talk and dine for hours.

The dinner room glowed dimly, lit only by the red boat candles on each table. A man with long curly hair arrived on the island with a guitar earlier in the night, and now sat on a stool in the bar singing "Riders in the Storm" and other Doors music. In between songs, he reminisced to Kristine about the concert in New Haven, Connecticut many years ago, the night Jim Morrison got arrested and pulled off stage. He said he liked Morrison and all, could relate to his lyrics, making his blood dance in some weird way.

When the time came to service the nine-top, Kristine took a deep breath and approached the captain's table.

"Hello. Welcome to Tarpon Key. I'm Kristine." She struck a match and re-lit the wick inside the glass jar on their long wooden table. After several reciprocated greetings, one voice asked for a light.

"Okay. Do you mind lighting it yourself? Unless, is it the same as a cigarette? Because I've lit cigarettes before, well, not for myself, but, anyway, I've not lit a pipe." Nervous and ridiculous behavior, she knew it. But fearful she'd set his pipe on fire, she held the book of matches in the air, gesturing to the man on the end that he do it himself.

"You've not lit a pipe before? Hello dear, I'm Captain Ethan Edwards. So nice to meet you." He puffed his pipe before stuffing her matches in the pocket of his white captain jacket.

"Nice to meet all of you as well. So, you're a captain? Of what ship?" For the first time in her life she considered a career in stand-up comedy. She induced tears in one man, while another started coughing from laughter. The captain's face turned red. She didn't know if she should feel embarrassed or proud.

"Oh no, no cruise ship. I'm not that type of captain. I'm a fisherman. We're all fisherman." He offered no more information.

Kristine recovered, giving a salute with her hand, then returned to business, recommending the infamous Cabbage Creeper—a Piña Colada with kahlua. Seven of the men took her up on the offer, and Ruth, watching from the corner of the room, hand-gestured the okay signal, and disappeared to some paperwork in the back office. One man ordered a bottle of Joseph Droughin. Her mind immediately wondered at her continuing future as a waitress. She hated opening wine.

"Have you ever played poker?" asked one.

"No, why?"

"Don't. You'd lose. Your facial expressions are too honest. Would you prefer we all order that creeper drink instead of wine?" They laughed boisterously like pirates. "It was the way your nose scrunched up when I ordered the wine."

"Oh no, wine is fine. Oh, goodness, whatever you want. It's no problem. Really! I've got this modernized wine opener here. It came with the job. I'll be right back with your bottle of wine."

She fished through the liquor closet for the right wine label. Rodney Strong, Sonoma County Cabernet Sauvignon, Beaujolais Village. When she found the bottle of Joseph Droughin, she kissed *it*, her enemy, the wine, and returned to the table. Like a blond on *The Price Is Right*, she modeled the $85.00 bottle as everyone gawked. Then she pierced its cork with the modernized silver metal point.

"Well, she caught a fine one. Let's see if she can reel it in," said a fisherman sitting next to the captain.

She smiled and rotated the bottle. Holding the cork steady, she tried the opposite: holding the bottle steady. She couldn't remember which worked best during her last disastrous attempt. She unhooked it, then re-hooked it and started over. All eyes studied her struggle. A camera flashed. She had become someone's souvenir. She heard cheers, laughs. They were teasing her, as if she were catching her first fish. She both hated and respected the catch, the bottle, at the same time. She started reeling it in, but the fish, no, the cork, crumbled. Only half came out with the hook, no, the modernized silver wine opener. Someone handed her a knife, and she scraped the rest of the broken cork onto a bread plate, hoping Ruth wouldn't see. An inhumane catch, she had mutilated it and felt unethical for doing so. Ashamed, she poured the red wine with tiny cork crumbles into the clean, clear glass of the man who had ordered it.

He held the glass close to the table, lit only by the red candle. All became silent, but for the overhead wooden fans. "I must access its hue, clarity, depth and intensity, Kristine. This is important. Studying a wine's color helps me detect its age, as well as the way it was made," he spoke as if conducting a seminar.

"Well I hope it passes all such categories and I hope it's old enough. I'm not responsible if it's not." She wanted to take the glass in the kitchen for a minute, just to strain out all the tiny specs floating on the surface. Some had sunken to the bottom.

He held the base of the glass, rotating it gently. "Kristine, this swirling action exposes more of the wine to air and helps it release substances that form its bouquet, which will concentrate in the top of the glass." He lifted the glass to his nose and took sharp, shallow sniffs. "Ahhh, the more complex scent of this older wine is revealed!" He raised the glass to his lips and took a mouthful of wine, about a tablespoon. He tilted his head forward, pursed his lips, and drew some air through the wine in his mouth, holding his head rigid. He exhaled the air through his nose, keeping his lips closed. He moved his jaw in a chewing motion.

"Honestly, I'm curious. What's he doing? Does anyone know?" She smiled sincerely and it showed.

"Yes, he's letting the wine flow around his mouth and come in contact with his tongue and membrane lining the palate," answered the captain. "Now, comes the part we've all been waiting for. He'll either swallow or spit!"

He swallowed to everyone's surprise, then gave the verdict. "Earthy, muscular, mature…corky. Just how I like it." No one commented on the floating cork fragments after that, but Kristine noticed one man spitting casually in his white cloth napkin. The guy next to him picked some out of his teeth.

"I saw that. Thank you," she whispered in his ear as he laughed. "I'm interested. Where did you learn such a routine?" she asked the man who ordered the wine.

"I own a winery in Napa Valley."

"Oh."

By the time the party cleared the table and headed for the door, she felt tremendous relief. But, as she started to clear the dirty table, Captain Edwards returned. "Kristine, you're a real trooper. We had a wonderful dinner and a lot of fun. Don't run out the next time I show up. We're not always this rowdy."

"It was fun. I learned some things. I learned a lot!"

"Where are you from, dear?"

"Holland."

"The country?"

"No, Holland, Michigan. Believe me, it's more conservative than the country."

"And, Lake Michigan, some fine catches there. I fished the Great Lakes a long, long time ago."

"Did you catch anything?"

"Of course. I always catch something. How about you?"

"Okay, yes, well, not with a fishing pole, but with a stick in a river. I caught a disgusting, slimy vine of some sort."

"Oh, if only I were thirty years younger, I would have married you for your charm, young lady!" He laughed loudly for everyone to hear.

"Kristine, I take people from all over the world fishing. How would you like to go late-night tarpon fishing with me?"

"Tarpon fishing? Sure. I'd love to sometime."

"No, I mean tonight. I'm dropping my group off at the marina, then I'll swing back to Tarpon Key and pick you up."

"This late?"

"Absolutely! Eleven o'clock. Be on the front dock."

"Okay. Why thank you. I look forward to it!"

She ran into Ruth's office. "I think I did something wrong."

"What?"

"I told the captain I'd go fishing with him…tonight."

Ruth stared. "Why of course you should. That's not wrong! He's a respected man around here, and he's taken celebrities and famous people from all over the world out fishing. Carol Burnett went with him once. Do *not* miss an opportunity to go fishing with Ethan. You'd be a fool!"

§

God put those stars up there to separate day from night, she thought, as she looked overhead, mesmerized. Like staring into a fire, she could hardly drag herself to blink, and she hardly noticed where the boat headed. With not a cloud in the navy blue sky, the stars sparkled like a broken chain of scattered diamonds and her neck ached from looking up. She realized she had never noticed the sky before. She knew the basics, that the sky wore blue on sunny days and gray on cloudy days, but now she realized it wore much more, accessories and all.

She looked around her, studying the boat. No cruise ship, but in the realm of fishing boats, she considered it luxurious. The Captain kept his boat in tip top shape. Like the napkin holders in her parent's shop, the silver rims of his vessel sparkled in the moonlight, as if freshly wiped with Windex. *Pride of ownership.*

"We're entering Boca Grande Pass, the world's best spot for tarpon fishing." Captain Edwards had one hand on the wheel and another on a tropical drink garnished with a pineapple.

"Boca Grande means big mouth in Spanish, I think," said Kristine, dipping her hand over the edge of the boat to tap the dark, not too chilly water below.

"Yes, this is the mouth of the Charlotte Harbor and it's one of Florida's deepest natural inlets. The Calusa Indians loved its rich fishing grounds. Tarpon love it too. They usually hang out in warm, coastal waters."

"Do you think we'll catch anything tonight?"

"I *guarantee* you're going to catch a tarpon, and we won't leave until you do!" The saltwater guru sipped his drink. "We're not on a deadline here. We don't want to rush anything, but you *will* catch a tarpon. When? I don't know yet. Tonight? This morning? Absolutely!"

"But how do you know I'll catch a *tarpon*? Aren't there other fish out here too?"

"Oh yes, there are others…grouper, snapper, cobia, mackerel, sheepshead and pampano."

"Goodness! There's as many fish as there are bottles of wine!" The boat stopped and he unleashed the anchor.

"A bottle of wine to go with every fish."

"What sort of wine would you order with tarpon?"

"Oh no, we're not out here to bring a tarpon home with us. In all my forty-eight years of fishing, I've *never* killed a tarpon. They're the most prized of all saltwater fish, and there's a no-kill law. No, there's no reason to kill these gamefish. No one *wants* to eat a silver king, Kristine."

"So basically, we're here to hook one and let it go? That sounds simple."

"I wouldn't say that just yet. Keep in mind, we're aiming for tarpon, tournament-size tarpon. Nothing less, nothing more, and tarpon is what you'll catch. They can reach more than six feet in length and one hundred and fifty pounds in weight, and no fish is more unpredictable than the tarpon." He attached some small, live crabs to a fishing pole and cast it out, before handing the pole to Kristine.

It was men's moonlight madness as boats shopped the dark, deep water, searching frantically, though displaying the calmness of men who shop. Everyone had his own space, no shoving, fighting for the same sweater. Everyone owned part of the water. Just one more fish of the night, one more, then it's time to go home. As if the men pushed the mute button on the remote control, it proved a quiet sale, almost silent enough to hear a dolphin breathing or gulls calling. Kristine and Ethan didn't have to talk much. Though they were still strangers, they felt comfortable with the silence of the event. She liked his comfort zone.

"There. Listen. *Shhhhh*…a rolling tarpon, half mile down."

"A what?"

"Tarpon breathe air from the atmosphere like we do. They rise to the surface, exhale, inhale and roll under. If all is quiet enough, you can hear it."

"I do." In the silent darkness, they could hear the tarpon rolling and crashing about, porpoising in order to breathe air into its swim bladder. The fish rolled slowly in a horizontal direction with a soft, almost lazy sigh, sinking two feet below the surface. The captain attached some live, finger-size mullet to another pole and handed it to Kristine, taking the other pole she had been holding for about an hour. She cast it out and the mullet stayed on the surface. The boat kept drifting.

"I feel it! I think we've hooked a fish!" Kristine's bait was sucked under and her line went tight. She could feel the weight of something big, a tarpon tugging.

"Dip the rod to the surface to create controlled slack, Kristine." The captain stood there, calmly calling out commands. It all happened just below the surface, softness, not jerking, almost in slow motion. "Wait for your rod to bend sharply, Kristine. Tell me when you feel the full weight of the fish."

"Oh, dear God! I feel it. Help!" She still wore her long blue skirt and white blouse from dinner and didn't feel like embarking on the battle alone.

"Okay, now sharply sweep the rod sideways. A tarpon's mouth is as hard as concrete. You can do it. Steady, strong, pull on the rod. Keep constant pressure on the hook."

"Help! I'm going to need your help!"

Something silver exploded in the black water. The tarpon jumped, stung by the hook. A wild scene, it jumped out of the water, into the air. When it hit the water again, a flying wave of salty water slapped Kristine. "Please, grab onto my belt so I don't go overboard with this fish!"

"Okay, looks like you might get pulled. Need help now?"

"No! I can do it. I've got to do it!"

"Okay, ease the pressure and enjoy. You're now fully engaged in a battle with a silver king, Kristine."

By now the weight of the tarpon had pulled her feet to the edge of the boat. Her arms felt shaky, as if she had just lifted weights in the gym. Her dress dripped with water, and she anticipated going overboard in battle. A good twenty minutes passed, and she was still fully engaged in a stubborn battle with the powerful acrobatic silvery fish. The water below acted nervous, as the scale-encased muscle danced around. Her mind fought too. She couldn't give up now. She felt so ready to battle, so ready to face her fears head on, her fears that felt too big for life, her fears of death. She didn't know how to battle her panic attacks, nor her fears, but engaging in this physical battle with a fish felt good.

The captain took a Polaroid picture, then moved in to help. He took the pole over and lifted the fish to the gaffer. She noticed its bright silver belly against its dark blue body.

"Well, how do you feel? You've just caught an eighty-five pound tarpon.

"Like I've just experienced one of the wonders of the universe. Wow. I guess that sounds pretty dramatic, doesn't it?"

"People compare it to all kinds of things. Climbing to the top of a mountain, hang gliding, it means something different to everyone. It's personal."

"Captain, why do you do it? I mean, has it ever lost that first-time appeal?"

"How can I say this? Every baby born to a woman is given a life. But oxygen, and the capacity to breathe, the elements of scientific living, they don't bring a person to life. That person must decide if they want to live. Does this make sense?"

"I'm not sure."

"We can go through life living and breathing but this has nothing to do with truly living."

"Oh."

"Dear, we all have our domains: a rider on his horse; a dancer on the stage; a pianist at the piano; a fisherman on his boat. Our domains are one thing: the horse, stage, piano, and boat. What we do with our domains is another. We gallop, dance, play the piano, and fish. Only, we don't just go through the motions. We crave it, feel it, escape to it, savor it, and forget everything else in life. We get tired, we sleep, and we wake-up and long to return to our domains. Only we bring more and more to it and we get better and better, and learn more and more about our domains. In this age of information, we are only human, overwhelmed. We can't learn it all and never will. We can, however, learn all we want about our domains, the things that make us trot, sing, dance and catch fish. There are a lot of lost people out there, people without domains. Find a domain and bring passion to your life."

Kristine understood now his reputation for being the best charter boat captain around. She assumed he had told this story to others, to people who had come from all over the world for the tarpon-catching experience. Well, maybe he told it only to people who asked the simple question, *Why do you fish, Captain Edwards?* She wondered how many people caught a tarpon, then embarked on a journey in search of their domain.

※

At the pay phone out on the dock, she squeezed her dress and let the water drip freely onto the wooden planks. "Hello Steve, I miss you," she said into the rusty phone.

"Anything new and exciting in your life?" He asked from his parent's home in Mississippi.

She slapped at a batch of mosquitoes feasting off her arms and legs. "Yes, I just caught a two hundred pound silver king. We battled a good two hours before I won." She knew she embellished the story a bit, but hey, the fish story belonged to her, her first fish tale. "I've got a Polaroid picture of our struggle. It looks a lot smaller in the picture. It was huge in real life, and he did back flips about ten feet into the air."

"You went fishing? I just can't picture you fishing."

"Can you picture me working?" She looked at the ripples of water slapping against the wooden posts of the dock

"You found a job?"

"Yes, yes I have. And it's a unique one, quite unique."

"Congratulations. Where are you working?"

"Well, I've got a job waiting tables on a remote island in the Gulf of Mexico. You can come see me any time you want, but you'll need to charter a boat because it's just a few miles out and there's no bridge, no roads, no anything. In fact I'm talking to you on a pay phone outside on the dock."

"Oh." There was silence. "That's a lot to absorb. Um, it sounds like you're living on this island, this remote island with no bridge?"

"That's right, and it's paradise out here, really. There's no place like this, there can't be, it's literally paradise."

"No, don't say that. It can't be paradise. Don't say that until you actually see paradise. Now if I were there, I could tell you if it was paradise. I could make that comparison."

"That is not a fair thing to say, Steve. You actually think the places you've been are all better than where I'm standing right now? That's so arrogant of you."

"Kristine, I know that one particular place I've seen is better, and that's a fact, not an opinion."

"Yeah, but you won't tell me about that place. Maybe I'd like to go there, and if it's far away, maybe I can close my eyes and listen as you tell me about it. I can go there in my mind. If it is so important to you, I'd like to see this place, but you don't seem to ever want to talk about it."

He ignored her point. "Seems obvious to me that if you've taken a job that requires you to live on an island, you've basically decided we're over."

"No, not over. I can still see you on my days off."

"I guess that's better than not seeing you when you return to college in Michigan."

"Steve, I won't be going back there in the fall. I've been struggling with a decision. I'm going to Madrid for the fall semester, I think. I didn't want to say anything. I guess I've been confused lately, but I realize I want to travel."

"Well, that'll be an even bigger good-bye." He laughed and then there was silence.

"Yes, it will."

After a moment of silence, Steve cleared his throat. "Oh, why am I getting mad? You're so young. You deserve to do things in life. You deserve experiences."

"Steve…"

"I'll see you on your days off. Call me, okay? And just know I'm not mad. You're young and all this is good for you. How can I get mad?"

He hung up. There was no good-bye, and she forgot to tell him she cared for him, that he came so close to fitting her Mr. Right profile. She would tell him next time.

·

9

She sat on the mattress in her pale pink, sandy-floored room and let her mind wander dangerously. She had lived and worked on the island ten days and suddenly started feeling claustrophobic, like a plastic figurine in a glass dome with fake snow falling down about her. Did they ever want to break the glass and escape? Probably not, she decided. The dome housed their comfort zone. A nice world for plastic figurines, well, until some clumsy child dropped it, shattering the glass. No, she was no figurine, just a minute insignificant being on a small island in the large Gulf of Mexico. And, to make matters worse, she could think of no way to get off the island.

She felt sequestered, isolated, remote, stranded, a prisoner on Alcatraz, a shipwrecked sailor like Robinson Crusoe, a proper British schoolboy that might revert to savage brutality in a struggle for power and survival. No, this wasn't like what it was in *Lord of the Flies*. She couldn't call this an island of survival—just an island, like Great Britain, like Cuba, like Ireland, only smaller, *much* smaller. But what if she got a sudden chocolate craving and there were no grocery stores? Or worse, what if her heart pains returned and she had to get to a hospital? She declared that dilemma a thing of the past, unless of course, she'd let it return. Then it *did* return, making mind over matter a powerful thing.

Just the *thought* of heart pains gave her brain blaring signals that life-threatening danger lurked nearby. Her autonomic nervous system started pumping adrenaline and cortisol, the hormones that make her heart pound harder and her fingers itch. As her arms shook, she decided they were just recovering from the tarpon battle of a few nights ago. She felt pain in her heart, and a nerve reacting in her leg. No, it *couldn't* possibly be a nerve. Instead, it was something climbing over her leg! After springing up, she reached for the light. Two red cockroaches scrambled into the mattress hole down by her toes. They justified her decision not to fall asleep, nor to turn off the light.

She watched another red bug sprint across the sandy tile floor before grabbing an old coffeepot that served no purpose—it was just an accepted part of the room—and trapping the creature. Watching it jump around under the glass pot disgusted her so she threw a dirty towel over it. That still didn't satisfy her. She remembered her own feelings of claustrophobia and let the thing go. She felt pity for it, so ugly. How can people *not* hate cockroaches? If only it looked like a butterfly, she'd make the effort to free it outside. Instead, she wanted it dead, but hated the crunching sound that came from the last one she murdered. She wished it were a spider. They are so simple to kill…just a *smush*; not a crunch.

The music from down the hall grew louder, so she put her ear against the door and listened for some words. It grew louder again and sounded like Don Petti giving a concert in the staff house.

"She's a good girl, loves her mama, loves Jesus and America too," Kristine sang along quietly. "She's a good girl, crazy about Elvis, loves horses…" She stood with her ear to the door, relating to the words. She didn't move. But then, another song came on, one that stirred her like a cup of coffee, inducing a hypomanic phase of some sort. She wondered if Lauren ever danced behind closed doors. She knew Grandma did. Grandma probably couldn't contain herself when Elvis came on.

She looked at the cockroaches scrambling around the floor, having fun, and she started to dance, alone in her room. She closed her eyes as she moved and sang, carefree. "I've spent oh so many nights feeling sorry for myself..." It didn't matter that Gloria's voice came from speakers down the hall. She felt part of a party in her own room. With every twist and turn she felt the stress and burdening worries twirling away.

She spun, leapt and spun again, then hopped over the coffeepot. Dancing gave her positive energy. It released the negative. With no one to see her, she could let her emotions control her movements. If it had a name, it would be called the "emotional stress relief dance." After burning at least four thousand calories, she stopped. She couldn't help but miss Lauren who loved this song so much.

With no one to talk to and no way to sleep with cockroaches on the prowl, she took out her yellow powder-scented journal hidden under her underwear, which was still in a suitcase.

℘

Dear Grandma:

If I'm going to be an island, I better get used to solitude of thought. Instead, I'm feeling stranded and lonely. I also feel caught between two worlds—one that was comfortable and one that is new. When I close my eyes, I'm back in my old Michigan bedroom, looking out the window. I see Kid and Bay Pacer trotting through the yard below. When I open my eyes, I hope that once Mom and Dad find a home to buy, they will get the horses here to Florida. Again with my eyes closed, my mind tricks me into thinking I'm back in the twin bed next to your petite body. I open my eyes and regret that I never tape recorded your stories. I also understand that you hated writing letters. You just liked reading mine. I close my eyes again and smell Mom's homemade chicken noodle soup. I open them and realize I've hardly seen my mom this summer. So I close them again, and I'm suddenly on my old bike. I'm pedaling with Jane back from the beach in our bathing suits. We're in a hurry because I have to get to work at the ice-cream shop. We're hoping Dad doesn't notice the sand on our toes. I open my eyes and tell myself I will some day get out West to visit Jane. I thought I just heard little Katie calling me 'Kristini' and I hope she doesn't switch to Kristine any time soon. I close my eyes once more. "Now, now, now! Pull yourself together," I can hear you scolding me. "Okay, Grandma," I actually say out loud. "I am growing older, and at twenty-one years old, I now need to experience life. I need to live in the present; not the past.

℘

    She closed her eyes and could see the bridge that linked the present with the past. She stood on the side with tulips blossoming in a field and Lake Michigan glistening in the background. She longed to pick a bouquet of them, to touch their satin petals. Instead, she forced herself onto the wooden bridge and crossed back into the present. As she walked, she could hear a voice from history. "Every man is a piece of the Continent, a part of the Maine."

    She suddenly agreed with John Donne—no man is an island complete in itself—so she walked down the hall toward Denver's laid-back voice as it repeatedly and pathetically sang the same lyrics, "Life is so hard, life is so hard." She poked her head into the room and asked if she could join him.

    "There, enjoy a Cabbage Creeper drink," said Denver, turning up his stereo. He sank into the huge orange vinyl armchair that looked as if it belonged on the set of *Twilight Zone*. Positioned directly in front of the dark window and the palm trees that formed distorted shapes behind him, he looked as if horns were growing from his head as he sat in the chair.

"Come on now, don't be shy. I've got four more of those there piña coladas with khaulua mixed into them." Denver pointed to the cream-colored drinks with dark liquor sunken to the bottom.

"Well, thank you very much."

"Okay, girlie. Take a sip quickly. It's time to dance." He jumped up, tossed his cigarette onto the floor, stomped on it, examined it closely, and stomped on it again. Then he grabbed her hand.

"Me? Oh, no! Thanks anyway, but I'm just going to sip my Cabbage Creeper over here. Thanks for asking though." She had no desire to dance with a man who weighed half her weight and bordered being drunk.

"Child, I'm so laid back right now I'm about to slip into a coma. I *gotta* dance!"

She knew how to say 'no', how to scream, how to run out and how to just plain not do anything she didn't want to do. She knew all that, and she knew some karate to go with it all. She knew Denver belonged to another puzzle, and didn't match any of the pieces of her own puzzle, but something inside her suddenly craved some new design to her puzzle. She felt curious about why someone his age could just hang out on a little island, work in a kitchen and sit alone in his room, drinking and playing such pathetic songs on his guitar. Her curiosity drew her into some kind of ballroom-type dance with him as he invented new steps to Bad Company music on the stereo. Next, came *Tesla*, then *Damn Yankees*. Except for the spins and dips, during which Denver almost collapsed, Kristine didn't mind. They danced a long time. He sang to all the songs, and his angelic-sounding voice surprised her. She complimented him on it, but he didn't hear. Instead, he psychologically sank deeper and deeper within himself, dancing with his partner all the while.

In his own world, Denver seemed caught in some kind of trance. It gave Kristine time to reminisce about her grandmother and all the nights they had spent together in the little apartment behind the ice-cream shop. Grandma loved Elvis Presley, but she kept that her secret. After confessing it to Kristine and her city cousin visiting from Chicago one night, they bought some Elvis tapes and danced till morning. Grandma *loved* his yelps, hiccups and stuttering, though she kept it her naughty secret. She knew a lot about Elvis, more than just his songs. She once called his early rock-an-roll style "rockability."

"Ahh, let me think a minute. Okay, sure, sure. I think rockability, ahhh…ahh, yeah, it's a mix. You know, a mix of something like country and western with rhythm and blues, if I remember right," replied the stranger she now danced with.

Kristine came out of one of Denver's lethargic spins, not realizing she had said it out loud. "What? What did you just say?"

"Country and western…you like all that stuff?" he asked.

"I guess. I really like jazz, jazz with words. I also like your soft, mellow voice, but I'm wondering why you always sing such sad lyrics. Are they about your own life?"

"Hey, I gotta ask ya something." He spun her and changed the subject simultaneously.

"I think I was trying to ask you something, but sure. What do you want to know?"

"Have ya ever said a swear word before?"

"A swear word?"

"Yeah, a naughty, bad, awful word."

"I know what a swear word is, thank you." She laughed. No, of course she hadn't ever sworn before. "Silly question. Have I ever said a swear word before? Well, let's give it a try…Hell…there."

"What?"

"I said, Oh Hell."

"You said you were going to swear."

"Yes, yes I have. I just did and you were my witness. Oh Hell. Before this moment, have I ever sworn before? Well goodness, no I guess I haven't…Damn…hmm."

"So now what? Are you addicted? Have I destroyed you?" he asked.

"No. There's really nothing to it. I don't see why people have to put all their anger into one naughty word. I mean, why can't they just, you know, really discuss how they're feeling. I mean, do Hell and damn really sum it all up?"

"No, not really. I mean, there are plenty more descriptive words than Hell and damn. You really gotta use a combination to get your point across, and you know, you can mix them up in whatever combination you want…you know, what the Hell are you talking about? Damn that. I just don't agree," shouted Denver.

"That just doesn't sound like fun to me. I really think I could easily express my emotions without combining various swear words together in an effort to get my point across."

"Man. You gotta return to your own country, the Netherlands, or wherever you said you were from."

"Holland, Michigan."

"Oh, wait a minute. Oh…good song. I like this here song! After midnight, we gonna let it all hang down," sang Denver in perfect harmony with Eric Clapton. "I like this song, but I gotta turn it off now. Yeah, I gotta do it again, one more time today, tonight, this morning, whatever zone we're in." Denver led Kristine over to the orange armchair and nodded at her to sit down. Then he picked up a maroon-colored guitar, leaned his back against the panel wall, and stroked his chords as he slid down to his butt on the sandy floor.

"Life is so hard, life is so hard." As he shut his eyes, it was as if his spirit took over, singing its song through Denver's lips.

"I had it all, lost it all, it came, it went, it's gone. Oh, hell, oh damn, oh hellish damn, life is so hard, life is so hard, life is so bad, life is so bad. I had it all, then lost it all, it came, it went, and it's gone. Oh, life is so hard, life is so hard, life is so bad, yes, life is so bad."

Kristine listened to his song with the added swear word combinations until around three-thirty when she could no longer keep her eyes open.

"Well, party's over. I'll pound on your door in the morning. There'll be no oversleeping here." Denver took the final swig of Jim Beam from his plastic cup, then tossed it into the closet.

"Denver, where'd you get a voice like that? It's too good to be human." Kristine dusted the dirt off her jeans as she stood and stretched.

"I ain't got a clue. I just always sing. I love to sing."

"You're fortunate. I had a dream one night…"

"Oh? So did Martin Luther King and…"

"Now let me finish," she laughed. "I had a dream one night that I was on stage singing. At the end of my song, everyone was standing and clapping and crying and waving to me up on stage. Then I woke up and remembered I can't read a note. I lip synched my way through high school chorus. I'm awful! I envy you for your gift!"

"Gift? Never thought of it as a present. And heck, never dreamt of standing on a stage. I don't care where I'm standing, as long as I'm singing."

"Denver, why is life so hard for you?"

"You like your questions, don't ya?"

"I'm curious. Your song is so sad."

"Well, ya know, we're all just vessels. And gosh, there are so darn many sorts of vessels. You gotta figure out what sort of vessel you are in life, and I'm guessing you haven't the slightest idea yet what you are. Why me, I'm just a make-shift raft that keeps falling apart all the time. I'm in need of major repair."

"What makes you a make-shift raft?"

"The kind of vessel you are is a personal thing, ya know. I mean, it's who ya are in life. I don't try to be a yacht or anything. I mean I guess a make-shift raft could turn into a yacht with lots of effort and all, but ya know what? I'm a happy raft, I just need to keep myself together next time around."

"I have no idea what sort of vessel I am."

"Don't cruise any further until you know what sort of vessel you are. I can't give ya any better advice than that, girlie."

"Tell me, your song is so sad…"

"Why can't I be sad? What, don't worry-be happy? Listen, if something happens in life, and you feel sad, I'm not gonna tell ya to rent a funny movie. You know why? That movie's gonna end and your gonna feel sad again. No, let yourself feel down. It's okay to feel down. I'm sick of this world not letting people feel down. The theme of our world is be happy, but I think we all need to have days, weeks and sometimes even months of feeling sad. I think its part of life, that's what I think. We're gonna go through dark water and sometimes we just can't make it out in one day, it's just too big."

"Have you been in dark water long?"

"Hey, it's bedtime. That means lights out, music off, band getting grouchy." Denver made his way over to the lamp, first bumping into the wall, then turned out the light. In the dark, he knocked over a couple things and probably hurt himself in the process, but Kristine knew he'd pull himself together again in time for work in the morning.

10

Florida's sky modeled several fashions. Some nights it looked starched and smooth, except for delicate rhinestones sprinkled across the heavens. Other nights it looked so organized, with white clouds ironed into sheets of navy blue fabric. Then there were the sweet light blue nights dotted in puffs of low-hanging clouds, and angry black and blue nights where darts of lightening ripped through wrinkled folds. On angry nights, inky colors stained the sky. The sky dressed as it liked, not minding the event, or the occasions below. It dressed as its Maker told it to, not caring to please anyone.

Several nights were spent sitting on the top level of the island's wooden water tower, and the view from the top gave the same thrill one gets from taking the elevator to the top of the John Hancock Building in Chicago, or the Top of the Mark in San Francisco. Only instead of an overhead view of manmade skyscrapers, one gets to see God's skyscrapers. The towering palm trees formed a city of their own, but looking down at the top of their heads sure beat looking down at rooftops.

She liked the water tower, her nest, and didn't mind sharing it with Howard, a different breed of bird. The sky spread itself sweet tonight in baby blues, the colors of a nursery and she liked sitting under the friendly sky. She stared at the light blue canopy overhead just as someone shook a pillowcase and a star fell out. She wanted to ask Howard if he saw it too, but Howard didn't talk much. No one on the island seemed to know much about the forty-something man, just that he worked in the kitchen doing prep work and existing in his own happy go lucky world. Still, at night, he wore the same straw hat, and his scruffy shoulder-length hair and auburn beard grew like vines up his face. His conversations with the staff were limited because he spoke his own quirky language. Now, he sat on the top of the water tower, way past dark, yet he sat with a paintbrush in hand, making strokes on a canvas.

"I wonder if we'll see another shooting star," she finally said to break the silence, her voice like a coin dropping during a performance and rolling down the aisles. "But then again, you're busy painting, so you probably didn't see the last star." After another minute of silence, she added, "Yet you're painting on a dark night without a light so…I'm confused."

"Hey Dude, would be kind of cool, man, cool to see another." He tossed a twig over the side of the water tower and watched it drop. Then he quickly stroked his canvas.

She laughed. "Howard, where are you from?"

"Cowabunga, I'm from the creator. I'm from the same one who created that there ladybug sitting on your shirt. I noticed it in the dark. I can almost see its red shellback and how it's painted with little black dots—perfectly round. I couldn't draw such a perfect circle if I tried." He dabbed his finger in paint and dotted his canvas.

She picked the little creature off her shirt and tossed it over the side of the rail. "So you, I, and the bug come from the same creator, Howard."

"That, that, that, that's right!" he said in a *Tony the Tiger* voice.

"You're crazy," she said. "And don't you ever take that hat off? Are you hiding something? Who are you?"

Howard rubbed some paint on his lips, kissed the canvas in front of him, then wiped his lips on his tropical flowered button up shirt. "Who do you think I am?"

"I don't know. An artist gone mad?" she asked.

"No, but hey dude, let me tell you something about art," he said. "We're all artists. Yeah, that's right. Every living person has the ability. Listen to me now. We wake every morning with a clean, white canvas before us. As the day progresses, we paint that canvas with the words we use, the gestures we make and the thoughts we think. And cowabunga, by the end of the day, our canvas might look horribly disturbing or it might be a masterpiece. It's all up to us, you see," he continued. "We paint our own pictures. Now, who do you think I am?"

She didn't want to answer. She wanted to think about her canvas. What color has it been for the past several months? What color is it on a daily basis? She couldn't wait until morning to start with a fresh canvas, to paint something beautiful.

"Oh, come on now, don't get so serious. Who am I?" he asked again.

"Ah, well, Howard, my first guess...and, it's not a very good guess, would be Santa Claus, but you're too young and your beard is red; not..."

"Ho ho ho, no, no, no," he interrupted. "Try, try again."

"Okay, my second guess, ah, a criminal on *America's Most Wanted*, and my third guess, someone in the witness protection plan?"

"You are so far off. Denver, he likes to classify us all as vessels of some sort. In that case, I'm a caravel."

"A caravel? What's that?" she asked.

"It's a sailing ship, typical of Portugal and Spain. When I'm peeling potatoes, as I do almost three hours a day, I'm the Santa Maria. Sometimes when I paint, I'm the Niña, and right now, as I'm here talking with you, I'm the Piña. Just depends on my mood and what I'm doing. I mean, how can we go through life as just one vessel? We're constantly changing."

"Oh, so you're the three ships that Columbus took to America. Okay, and to think, the others on the island, they all told me you only talk jabberwocky. How dare them?" She laughed.

"It's not funny," he said. "I didn't come out here to get to know people or for them to get to know me."

"So why are you here and why are you talking to me?"

He paused for a moment, then said, "I'm here for therapy and you're attempting to have an intelligent conversation, and I respect that."

"Therapy?"

"Yes. I'm dying."

"Oh, my goodness! I had no idea. I am *so* sorry."

Howard laughed. He laughed uncontrollably. He laughed until he cried. Eventually he wiped his eyes and smeared his canvas. "Oh please! We're all dying, you see. Yes, your mother, your father, your siblings if you have any, your friends, every one of us on this island, on this planet, we're all dying. We were born to die, and every single day of life means one less day of our life."

"Oh."

"Come on, now you're the one who started talking to me," he said. "Don't just sit there in that fearful silence. I'll tell ya, parents need to do a better job of telling and reminding their children that some day, they're gonna die. Wouldn't this be a better world if children grew up aware of the fact that this life is quite short?"

"Well, it might frighten them."

"Ba…hum…bug! Why should death frighten anyone?"

"It scares me, Howard."

"Why! Tell me why!"

"It means separation from loved ones, it's unknown, it's…"

"The separation from loved ones is temporary, it's like going away on a trip, saying good-bye, but not forever. You're scared because the topic of death is taboo and you're not prepared to handle it. You're an educated woman, preparing for a career, for a house and family some day, for wealth and vacations, but I'll bet you're not taking any time out to prepare for death."

"Prepare for death?"

"Yes. It's silly and simple. All you have to do is live. You're book smart and that is a fine thing to be. However, now you need to live, become world smart, experience the world."

"Well, I was planning to go to Spain in the fall, but I'm not sure it's a good idea now."

"Why not?"

"Well, I was going with a friend of mine, but she backed out and now I don't want to go without her. I guess in a way, I'd feel guilty."

"Are you asking me for permission to set out for Spain?" He slid his eyeglasses back up onto his nose using his middle finger.

"No, of course not." She couldn't help but laugh.

"Well, then it sounds like you need permission from your friend before you set off. Let me help you with that. Get past the guilt phase. If she's a good friend, she'd want you to go, she'd want your dreams to come true."

"I'm also mad, I guess, at her."

"Forgive. You've got to push yourself out of your anger and your guilt. It might feel like walking a plank into dangerous water, but do it. Push yourself to move on."

Kristine tore a vein out of a fallen palm leaf. "I don't know that I'd feel comfortable going alone." She wrapped the leaf around her finger, looking only at her project as she spoke.

"I can give you a contact to look up when you get there."

"*You* know someone from Spain?"

"Quite well. I'll give you the contact information soon, not now, so don't rush me on it." He tore a jagged sliver of wood from the water tower and split it in two, as if fiercely competing in a turkey wishbone contest. "When the time comes, go and explore new worlds, new people. Sail away to Spain. It should only take about five and a half weeks with a crew of ninety. Sail away young woman, sail away!"

"Fine. Thank you."

"But remember, no matter where you go in life, and I know you'll go far, please don't ignore the small things, the details. Pay them attention, notice them."

"Like what?"

"Look at that lizard over there, behind you." He laughed as he picked the lizard up by it's tail, which subsequently fell off. "When cornered, did you know one type lizard sprays the intruder with blood from the corner of its eyes?"

"I had no idea."

"And…and another sort of lizard, ahh, the chuckwalla lizard, when he's being hunted down, he runs into a crevice of some sort and breathes extra air into his lungs so he gets bigger and can't be pulled out of his small hiding space. Oh, and the alligator lizard, he's got scales as mean as armor. The poor old lizards that don't have rough scales, they can dart quickly, to hide behind things and escape. The chameleon, well we all know they change colors."

"Goodness gracious! That's incredible! They're like art works, detailed art," said Kristine, smacking a mosquito that landed on her arm.

"I hope that answers your question, Kristine. I'm here on the island to notice things, smaller things in life. It is my own personal therapy right now. I'm here for one other significant reason, but it's personal."

His words echoed above the palm treetops, and this, she noticed. His words sounded refreshing, and she felt mad at all the thoughts she had allowed in her mind over the past several weeks, all the thoughts that smeared over her canvas in dark, dramatic, depressing colors.

"Howard, my canvas has been ugly lately. I'd like to paint a really fun picture tomorrow. Any tips on how to do this?"

"Yes, meet me at the dock tomorrow night after dark. Now get some sleep."

Her interest brewed strongly, like a pot of freshly ground Colombian coffee. Lawrence, Ruth, Captain Edwards, Denver, and now Howard…each life held so many themes, chapters for a novel. Not just on the island, but *anywhere*. People cruise along as vessels carrying secrets, stories. Island life forced her to take time out, to listen to strangers. She couldn't remember when she had last listened, *really* listened, to anyone, even those she loved.

৩

Dear Grandma:

I've finally made my decision. I'm going to Spain. If I stayed in Michigan, I never would have met all these interesting island personalities. I guess good and bad comes from leaving comfort zones. I just know there are more strangers in this great big world worth meeting, at least six billion of them, and some of them might be living in Spain. I know they're certainly not living on the pages of a textbook. No, they're a part of this present world, and it's a world worth discovering!

11

Working lunch, then dinner, with no time but a water break and wardrobe change in between, hadn't given her the opportunity to explore the island. She decided to do so before meeting Howard tonight on the dock after dark. Perhaps this way, she could come to him with a few adventurous colors already on her canvas.

"Knock, knock, knocking on Heaven's door. Can I come in?" Denver entered her room without knocking and collapsed onto the mattress. He always looked like he was physically falling apart, and this time, his ragged shoelace dragged on the floor and strands of his long frizzy hair poked down across his eyes.

"Make yourself at home." Kristine pulled her pajamas out from under him, stuffing them under her pillow instead. "I'm heading out to look around the island a bit," she said.

"Swift. You can go on two conditions. First, you spray this stuff all over you." He tossed her some *Skin So Soft*. "And second, you take me with you."

"Sure, you can come."

"Swift," he replied again. "You better bring a flashlight. There ain't no lights out there. And put some real shoes on. You can't run in those things. They've got diamonds on them," he stated, pointing to her feet.

"They're not *real* diamonds. And run? Who says we're going to run?"

"Well. if you see a snake, you'll run. I guarantee!"

They made their way along the rugged trail, leaving footprints in the sand as they went, as so many islanders had done before them. If the island could talk, the stories it would share. But wind, rain, and years gone by had wiped all such imprints from its surface, leaving not a trace of the Caloosahatchee Indians nor any other visitors from the past. Oh, if the trees could share the secrets they had heard through the centuries. Instead they stood tall and proud, reaching out with their branches to the breezes and strangers coming their way. Peacefully, silently, they reigned.

As they walked the sandy path that formed a circle, not a safe and perfect circle, but more of a twisted, rebellious, curvy circle, around the plush two-mile island, Denver carried a tree branch, using all his power to dig it into the ground with each step.

"I'll tell you, it's funny seeing you making your way on this trail," he told her. "You just don't seem like the type to be living out here." Denver pointed to a turtle, frozen in the sand.

"Why not? This island welcomes anyone, so anyone can walk its trails. And I'm *anyone*." Kristine hopped over the hard-backed creature, then bent down to knock lightly on its shell. "Hello in there. Can anybody hear me?"

"Well, you've been here some two weeks, and I've never seen your hair messy," he said. "You remind me of Ginger, you know, on *Gilligan's Island*."

She looked at the top of the palm tree, its own mane blowing freely. It never bothered to tidy itself. The raccoons of the island don't bother to brush their hair and the spiders, well, their webs are a mess, always under construction. "I didn't realize I came across that way. I don't want to be Ginger! Marianne was always my favorite. Let me be her instead!"

She felt like a foreigner in a strange place and knew that in order for a place to become comfortable, it had to feel so with her. She respected this place and didn't want to be an intruder, overwhelming the salty scent of the air with her strong *Red Door* perfume.

"I bet you spend a ton of money at spas. I hear they've got tons of those spas in the Netherlands."

"I'm not from the Netherlands, Denver. I'm from Holland, Michigan. A Dutch city in the state of Michigan, the *United* States."

Denver used his walking stick to tear down a banana-colored spider spinning a huge web. The spider fell hopelessly, probably already beginning to plan where next to rebuild after the devastation caused by man. No wonder their webs were a mess out here. "Gosh, hope the Ginger comment didn't offend you. That's why I classify people as vessels, less offensive."

"Right. You told me you're a make-shift raft in need of repair. So, what sort of vessel do you think I am?"

"You? You're an underwater ballistic submarine."

That was definitely not the answer she expected. "Oh, how glamorous. One moment you say I'm a Ginger, the next an underwater... what kind of submarine did you say?"

"Ballistic," he stated.

"Ballistic." She paused to look at him questioningly. "That' doesn't sound like a compliment."

"Well, what were you hoping to be?"

"I was hoping I'd at least be a luxury liner or a cruise ship, like the love boat!"

"No, no way. You hide the imperfections of your life. Nothing bad shows on the surface. Your sadness is deep and...hey, I don't for a *single* minute believe your life is perfect. You look like you've got it all together, but you don't," said Denver in his rough, splintery voice that sounded nothing like his singing voice. "That's all I'm going to say about you as a vessel right now."

"Why? I don't know a thing about submarines. I mean, you've got to tell me more, anything."

"Nope. You need to work on yourself. I've got my own repairs to do."

They passed the water tower, the owners' private home, and, after discovering the small size of the island, arrived back at the staff house. The moon replaced all clocks, and the crickets played wildly as the island dressed for the occasion called night, so unlike its daytime attire.

"Hey, let's go for a drink at the bar," said the make-shift raft.

"No thanks. You go without me. I've got plans."

※

She didn't know what Howard had in mind, only that he had promised to turn her boring white canvas into something interesting. Having just been told she was a submarine—and all she knew of subs was that they were ugly and gray—she felt desperate to brush new strokes of color onto her own canvas.

She made her way to the old splintery dock with the shallow, brackish water below. There she joined the man with scruffy auburn hair and together, lying on their backs, with the ripples of water breaking against the moorings beneath them, they watched a lightning show overhead. Distant thundering rolled through the heavens like bowling balls striking their pins. They could see dark, angry clouds mounting the horizon, and the gulf turned murky and mean. For an instant, they spotted fireworks going off near Sanibel Island.

As they talked, they stared up at the gathering madness. Both enjoyed talking about deep things. Howard pointed out how scary the sky was, while Kristine explained what she knew about the enormous gravitational spiral nebula called the Milky Way Galaxy. Howard described gut instinct, while Kristine described intuition. Howard shared his feelings of loss, as Kristine discussed grief. Both talked of loss in their own words but neither discussed what they had lost.

Kristine wondered if the tide affected blood as it does the waves that draw near, then far again. If so, the moon seemed to be bringing everyone on the island close for one moment, distant the next. She appreciated the moon as never before. It was the governor of night. Tonight's yellow moon formed a perfect circle, unlike any she had ever drawn or traced. She had never taken notice of the moon before, at least not like this.

Howard sat up and whipped a flat stone. They heard it hit somewhere out in the water. "So you said you wanted today's canvas to look fun."

"Yes, that's right."

"Then take off your clothes, and let's go swimming."

"Howard! Now that is rude. You brought me down here to skinny dip? Well, goodness, I'd love to see what sort of painting you'd be doing tonight."

"Relax, relax. I'm fooling around," he said, standing up. "You can swim in your jeans if you want. It's your choice. Well, hope ya don't mind if I take something off."

"Maybe I do. Keep your shorts on, please!"

He laughed as he took his straw hat off, tossing it to the side, then proceeded to pull his hair off. Kristine couldn't believe what she was seeing. His beard and sideburns came off too. "Your hair! It's a wig? You're bald?"

"I lost it at an early age. This here wig is great, side burns, beard and all. I wear the hat just to anchor it down a bit."

"Okay. I guess this is what living is all about…taking your clothes off and swimming in the nude and becoming world smart; not just book smart." She stood up and yanked off her jeans, swearing she wouldn't eat so much key lime pie tomorrow.

"That's right, but gosh! Did my baldness inspire you that much?"

Just then, as if flagged down, someone, something jumped out from behind the far bushes, shouting, "Don't you lay a hand on her. She's a sweet, innocent girl, Howard!"

Howard reached for his wig and in one quick step, the long hair, side burns and beard were back in place, but Kristine stood there in her underwear, feeling naked enough.

"Denver, don't do this," called Howard. "I don't have enough fuel in me for this. You know that," he yelled. "Besides, you're just a raft now. Don't go back to being a destroyer again."

"Oh yeah? Well, I'm a destroyer tonight."

Denver, a destroyer, made his way out to the end of the dock and shoved Howard. Howard, by the saving power of adrenaline, picked Denver up and threw him over the dock into the shallow, marshy water below. He struggled in the tangled masses of arching roots for a moment and broke free. It was a collision between a destroyer and a caravel.

"Kristine, get back to the staff house, now!" Denver's voice rang out like a blow horn. "Hurry."

She grabbed her jeans in her hands and half-running, half stopping, enthralled with the plight behind her, Kristine witnessed Denver climb out of the water and up and over the side of the dock. She could hardly see the path without a flashlight, and as she ran through spider webs and branches, she could feel her face getting scraped and cut. Suddenly she hit a small hole and twisted her ankle, falling to the ground. She kneeled behind the trunk of a palm tree and listened to the fight in the distance.

"You're nothing but a selfish spoiled...luxury liner," shouted Denver. "How dare you! How dare you take off for the oceans of the world while I was stuck in the mud! I hate you for it."

"You could have gone the same places. You could have come with me."

"No, I had forces working against me, you know that," yelled Denver.

"I don't believe that."

Denver shoved Howard in the shoulder. "You rich snob."

"I'm richer now than I've ever been, and you know what? It's got nothing to do with green stuff," said Howard, quieting his voice.

"Then why did you follow me out to a remote island? What are you doing peeling potatoes for Christ's sake?"

"I'm here because...because...I love you."

"I don't get it," said Denver. Kristine, still hiding, also didn't get it. Were they in love? No, couldn't be.

Howard continued. "Listen. Listen carefully. A dying man is allowed one wish, is he not?"

"Yeah, okay," said Denver. "Yeah."

"Okay, then take me seriously," said Howard. "I've brought a large sum of money, a fortune too large to even disclose to you now. I've buried it behind the Indian mound, just next to the trunk of that crooked palm tree. You know the one."

"Yeah, yeah, I do," said Denver.

"Now when I'm gone," stated Howard. "I want you to take it and use it. Use it wisely. It's up to you."

"Gone? Oh come on. Don't say that."

"Man, I'm going to be gone and you've got to deal with it…in your own way."

"What should I do with your money?"

"I'm not going to tell you what to do with you. You've got free will and I can't interfere with that. It's the only way I know to help you, to give you a chance. Please don't screw up. It's my one wish."

"Wait. Listen. Did you hear that?" asked Denver.

Kristine took off running for the staff house. More tree branches hit her in the face rudely indicating wrong turns off the path. She kept stumbling, but making her way forward, telling herself she didn't need light, or optical vision to guide her way. She was a submarine, cruising deep in the dark depths of night. But then she heard something loud moving just ahead of her. She knew by its sound that it wasn't a lizard. Its magnitude resembled more of a lurching human. Denver! He jumped in front of her, shining his flashlight into his face and taking hold of her arms.

"Denver, you scared me to death, what are you doing? Where's Howard?" She maneuvered herself back, releasing his grip.

"Kristine, we told you to get back to the staff house," said Denver. "What have you been doing?" His hand felt greasy like machinery.

"Everyone said I'd learn this trail so well that I'd be able to walk it blindfolded, but I've only been here a couple weeks."

"Did you hear the fight between Howard and me?" he asked.

"No. Couldn't hear a thing. Why? What happened?" She couldn't breathe.

"Tell me what you heard, damn it," he said.

"I just told you, I didn't hear a thing. I've been trying to find my way back and all I hear is my body making its way through branches. What happened after he pushed you in the water? Are you okay? You poor thing!" She lied.

"Come on. I'll light the rest of your walk. It's pitch black out here tonight." Denver no longer moved like a destroyer, but now limped onward, smelling of salt and sweat. He walked like a starving, grungy mutt living in the streets of Mexico.

"I'm fine now. You can leave," said Kristine as they walked under the stilts of the staff house.

"What? So Howard can come back and harass you a little more?"

"What are you talking about?" she asked.

"That's why I attacked him. He's got the hots for you, Kristine. Don't trust him. He's no good for you," said the muddy, bloody rabid-looking man.

"This entire fight was about me? Oh Denver, you shouldn't have." she lied again.

Just then, they heard someone running along the path toward the staff house.

"It must be Howard," slurred Denver. "I've had enough. I'm in pain. Help me. I've gotta hide." He pulled himself up the stairs and into the staff house. Kristine followed.

"I don't know where to hide you."

"Your closet. Hide me in your closet," he said.

She allowed him in her closet, but within minutes, Howard had made his way into her room, noticing the muddy tracks leading to Denver's hideout. As he threw the doors open, Kristine couldn't help but notice tears streaming down Denver's face.

Howard shook his head. "Come on now. This has gotten out of hand."

"Howard, I want so badly to hate you, but instead, I hate my own life. I hate what I've made of my own life. I don't hate you. I've never hated you," shouted Denver.

"I know. You don't need to tell me that. I came here to help you. I came here so you could have a second chance. You can do it this time. You've spent enough time whipping yourself on the back. Think. Think real hard about what you want to do with the money this time. Change your life or change your soul. You decide."

There was a long silence, and Howard turned and walked out of the room.

"Get in bed now, Kristine. Don't say a word. Just do it, now!" demanded Denver, then he left her room.

She glanced at the clock at three o'clock and climbed onto her mattress with her clothes still on. Knowing that if she tried counting sheep to fall asleep, they'd turn rabid and kill her. She slipped out of bed to brush her teeth. Squeezing from the bottom up, toothpaste with tiny red speckles oozed out. Ants, millions of active miniature red ants making their way through the sticky white paste. She dropped her toothbrush and screamed.

Denver opened her bedroom door. "Y'all right in here? What's going on? I heard you scream."

"Ants, dirt, my toothbrush! Disgusting. I can never use it again!"

"Well, I kin offer ya my toothbrush, but I drop that thing daily. Now get to bed and remember, when we go to breakfast in the morning, we won't remember a thing about none of this. Ya hear this? Now good-night."

"Wait, Denver. I need to ask you something."

"What now? You need a glass of water? Snack? I am not going to say anything else about the fight, so don't ask."

"No, I just want to know about your song."

The man with torn clothing and a muddy, bloody face walked over, plopping himself down on her mattress. He resembled a Halloween costume. "Oh yeah? What do you wanna know? When my album is being released so you can say ya knew me back when?"

She laughed. "No. I mean...yes, you probably will have an album someday, and maybe you can mix the island sounds into it."

"You mean the clanging pots and pans of the kitchen and the eggs frying on the pan in the morning, things like that?"

"No, of course not. The birds, the rippling water under the dock, the voices at the bar. But hey, tell me about your song and why the words are so sad. What did you lose in life?"

He stood up a moment to pull his cigarettes from his back pocket, then squinted his eyes as if looking for water down a long, empty well. "I smoked the last darn one. Life is tough, and I'm going to tell you something I learned the hard way. I had me a business, fixing air conditioners for people. I worked real hard at it and hated every second of it. Like a raft made of twigs, I just couldn't survive the rough elements and even my hair started falling out. Saved every penny I ever made and carried that money with me for years, nothing to spend it on. I lived simple but had an overabundance saved. Saved for what? I don't know. It just kept growing and growing, sitting around. One day I realized how much I hated my work, my life. Took me a trip to visit a friend in Northern California. From there we went to Reno. Did some gambling. Started on the three-dollar black jack table, nothing major. Each time I lost, I laughed because I was losing the money I earned from a job I hated. Well, those casinos are pretty clever. They don't put windows or clocks in the rooms so you never know when day turns to night and then back to day again. Well I moved on...to a twenty-five dollar table. Started throwing down a hundred here and there. The dealer didn't like me. I got real angry when I lost the five hundred dollars because he got twenty-one and I got thirty. I'm not the best counter. I made frequent trips to the debit machine, my fuel supply to continue, and kept moving on to new tables, all the while telling myself, 'I'm a loser, I'm a loser.' I couldn't stop and didn't realize until later how serious my addiction had become. I dumped my entire load in a matter of days. Yep, that's right. I left Reno with no money."

"What did you do?"

"I didn't know anyone and couldn't find anyone I knew and I walked out of the last casino, a destroyer who wanted nothing more than to sink to the bottom of the ocean."

"How do you and Howard know each other?"

"It's amazing how a lady gives birth to two babies. One grows up to be a destroyer, well, advancing to a make-shift raft, and the other, a caravel, who travels the world accumulating gold and silver. I don't know why we take such different routes. I only know our mothers gave us the basic materials and sent us off into the waters of this world. It's up to us to create the sort of vessels we want to be."

"So what are you going to do now?" She didn't breathe a word about the money she knew Howard had hidden near the Indian mound. She knew it would be best to stay out of that.

"It took me a long time, but I made a choice. I could continue to destroy or I could start to repair. That is why I came here, and just in time, my brother shows up to lend some tools, some very expensive tools. I don't deserve help and it doesn't take much money to repair a raft. I guess I just need to figure out what to do with those tools and in doing so, repair myself. That's all I'm gonna say about that. Good-night."

12

Each day brought a new tub of potatoes. As Howard sat peeling them on a bucket turned upside down in the kitchen, Denver washed dish after dish with the sprayer, and Kristine ran in and out of the kitchen carrying trays with clean dishes, and trays with dirty dishes. They chatted here and there, quickly, only as time allowed. Howard would ask about her canvas. Denver would share a vessel statistic, or tell her about a gorgeous submarine located somewhere out in Asia. Kristine would mutter Spanish and ask them how her accent sounded. No one mentioned the night on the dock, nor the hidden money. They pretended it never happened. She knew better than to ask any questions. She knew this story didn't belong to her.

The nights on the island were so filled with late-night dock conversations and midnight fishing trips that it seemed as if a lifetime had passed when it came time to leave for her first two days off.

She quickly found that days off the island meant a return to the things-to-do world that revolved around a wristwatch as she obediently checked off errand after errand on her to-do list. She got her passport photo taken, registered by mail for classes at the University of Madrid, and bought some clothes for Spain. While opening a pile of mail, she discovered she had been awarded an academic scholarship and decided it would be a great reason to give Ruth when it came time to leave her job at the end of summer.

While browsing through a bookstore, she found a section on *grief*. By now, she had learned she had a choice. She could either be passively grief-stricken and a victim of grief, or she could actively grieve and move toward healing. She read that the grieving process often included four stages: fear, guilt, rage and sadness. She felt stuck in fear.

She moved her way to the self-help section and learned that the occurrences she experienced were commonly referred to as "panic attacks," and that millions of Americans at some moment or other have felt such episodes of sheer fear. For some, the fear goes away. For others, it takes over their entire lives. It becomes debilitating, making their lives impossible. Fear is expressed in many ways. Some can't face crowds; others, heights or bridges or water, some dirt. This is true. They can't stand any speck of dirt in their homes or on their bodies.

As she read that anxiety is the fearful anticipation of impending danger, the source of which is unknown or unrecognized, she felt sharp pains dart through the left side of her chest. She read more, relating to the words on the pages. *The central feature of anxiety is intense mental discomfort, a feeling that one will not be able to master future events.* Yes, in her case, the night. She needed to survive each night so that she could live to see day again. *Physical symptoms include sweaty palms, muscle tension, shortness of breath, feelings of faintness and a pounding heart.*

She hoped that just reading and identifying with symptoms in a book might cure her. Instead, she realized how powerful mind over body can be, when on the way home from the bookstore, she felt dizzy and nervous driving over the long, high bridge that connects Fort Myers to Cape Coral.

Her car collided with a butterfly, killing it, and it bothered her that death comes so suddenly, even to a bug. She noticed the construction vehicles working on the other side of the median, and for a moment, they looked like monstrous creatures with long black antennas and silver claws mechanically moving like predators she had once seen on a horror flick. Engrossed in fearful thoughts, heart palpitations, shortness of breath, and near fainting, she cruised into the far right lane and imagined herself crashing into the stone wall. She watched her car cross lanes and hit other cars, and together, they all went over the bridge. Just the thought of it made her unfasten her seat belt. If the imagined scenario became reality and she did go over the bridge, she couldn't allow herself to be restrained in the sinking car. Like a film inside her head, she could see it all too well, so well that she considered making it happen. She felt the urge to hit the side just to see what might happen. Would it hold? Would she go over?

She couldn't believe she was contemplating such urges. She held both hands on the wheel, not trusting herself. The end of the bridge was in sight, and she slowed her car down to ten miles per hour, but honking horns behind her pressured her to accelerate. She considered crying wolf, pretending her car had died so she could simply stop with her emergency lights on. Instead, she put her emergency lights on but kept going about fifteen miles per hour. She saw the sun setting in Cape Coral about a quarter of a mile away—the light at the end of the tunnel. Behind her, lightning struck in Fort Myers. For a moment, she thought it had hit her car and was causing the pain in her heart. Rubber tires, she reminded herself, and returned her attention to the setting sun. She saw the end of the bridge but feared she would never make it to the end. She would ram her car into the side and go over.

No, that won't happen. None of it will happen. I do have a fear— a fear of dying in my sleep. I am not about to let it become a phobia, an intense and persistent fear of a situation, specific object or activity. I am fully aware that my fear is irrational and way out of proportion, yet I also recognize my free-spirited imagination, which becomes dangerous when out of control.

But despite her psychosomatic diagnosis, still, she secretly believed she too lived with an undetected heart problem. Whatever the cause, her sleepless nights were pushing her to the edge…an edge that was dropping off into a chronic state of sleep deprivation, perhaps leading to insanity.

That night, she called Steve, and they listened to jazz at Peter's LaCuisine in Fort Myers. As she sat across from him, she pictured what their children might look like. One would surely have his blue eyes, while the other her brown ones. Hold on! She put a stop to her thoughts. Come autumn, she'd leave the country, and after that, she'd return to Michigan. Mr. Right wasn't supposed to show up, not yet.

Steve playfully stepped on her shoes under the table as always. "So tell me, what's this island life like? What sort of people go off to live and work on such a small island with nothing to do?" He casually folded his cocktail napkin into an airplane.

"It's intriguing, Steve. I guess they're people who want to step back from this hectic world for a moment. Those who just need to stop a moment, catch their breath. All sorts." She took several gulps of White Zinfandel.

"Then why are *you* out there?" He said, shooting the paper airplane he had folded directly past her.

"It's refreshing. I can breathe out there." She rubbed her eyes, hoping it was just hairspray. No, Steve went out of focus and she felt dizzy. She bent down to pick up his plane once she noticed her shortness of breath. Why at such a calm moment would this occur? She had many hours left until bedtime, until midnight. Not wanting him to see her struggle to breathe, she knocked her purse to the floor and bent down to gather it up. It seemed that bending down helped to clear her airways. Sometimes she'd tie her shoes or fix the cuff on her pants.

"Steve, tell me, what brought you to Florida? I haven't ever asked you that." She needed more air, but didn't want him to see her gasping. How could an attack come at such a calm, relaxing moment, one that provided absolutely nothing to justify a panic attack?

"I haven't told you this yet but I've got bad knees and a bad back. I need hot weather."

"I had no idea. I thought we knew nearly everything about each other." She stole a few more sips of wine, assuring herself that all was safe and nothing life threatening was going to happen. She looked around for escape routes…the bathroom. Then she reminded herself that she was an imaginative person and her imagination loved to tease her. Steve and she were having an outward conversation, but all the while, she inwardly talked to herself, or to the other her. No, the only her. She wouldn't allow these anxiety episodes to turn into schizophrenic voices. *No way*, she told herself.

"I'm determined to stop the pain in my knees from getting worse. That's why I always bike ride and stay active." He took her hands in his and kissed them, then massaged them. "I was in an accident several years ago, a horrible one. I'm sorry I haven't told you, but I don't like thinking about it."

"Tell me more, please." She had never begged anyone on the island to share stories. She would definitely beg Steve, though. She had to know about him, the creative architect from Mississippi.

"I don't feel now is the time. You might just think I'm crazy. Kristine, you've got everything under control in your life and you've lived in a pretty comfortable world. You might not understand."

She wanted to tell him that now, even as she spoke, she was thinking of impending danger, of a heart attack. She wanted to tell him of her psychosomatic illness, her phobia of dying in her sleep, and the panic attacks that crept up on her during most of their dates and most of her nights.

"Steve, I want to tell you something. I need to…"

"What is it?"

"I'm here if ever you feel like talking about your accident."

℘

She arrived at the ugly rental house and climbed into bed by one o'clock in the morning, not ready to sleep. *How could death be so cruel?*

How unfair to take Lauren in her sleep, and Grandma too! Her pillow felt damp as if someone on the beach had stood over it, shaking their wet, salty bodies. She longed to order another café mocha with Lauren or paste together seashell mirrors with her grandmother.

She couldn't help but think about Grandma, who came unglued after her husband had died. Grandma's mourning turned into depression and she started to live most of her days in the past, in the old home in Evergreen Park, Illinois. She had raised her family in that home, in that neighborhood, in that comfort zone. After Grandpa died, she crossed that bridge back to her glory days and never fully returned to the present.

She sat up to stop the stabbing, but didn't have the patience to counsel her breathing. She let it go untamed, and the battle took its course. She hugged her tiger, the stuffed creature that secretly went on and off the island with her. He went everywhere. How could he not? The rugged orange and black fur body had absorbed a good fifteen years of salty tears. As she squeezed his neck, she remembered childhood nights when she lay in bed crying on his shoulder with a recurrent worry. What would she do with Tiger when she grew up and got a husband some day? Could she have both a tiger and a husband? Would Tiger have to be tossed up in a closet? Could her husband be tossed up there instead? No, she'd never let the striped animal get kicked off her bed. He belonged atop her pillow. Well, now at twenty-one years old, he nonchalantly remained hidden *under* her pillow, as king of the bed and most loved of her stuffed animals. Since her freshman year of college, he had held his noble distinction: the only stuffed animal she owned. The others got dumped in Type A cleaning rages, then mourned over in cries of regret later.

Just as she wiped her tears across his scratchy nose, she glanced down and saw an envelope sitting on her floor. There was a *yellow Post-It* note with her Dad's handwriting on it.

Honey, this letter came in the mail for you today. I believe it's from Lauren's mother. Hope you had a nice night with Steve.

Love, Dad.

She trembled. She could hardly open it, so for a moment, she just held it, kissed it, smelled it and held it again.

Dear Kristine:

Doctors say Lauren had a heart condition that we never even knew she had. After talking with some people at the college, we discovered she did many sit-ups on her last night, just before meeting you at the cafe. That activity apparently triggered her final attack. I say final because, according to the autopsy, she had suffered many minor heart attacks in recent months. They all went undetected.

I don't quite know what to write, except I can't continue this mourning. It's killing me. I haven't been eating, or sleeping, or smiling, or going any place fun. Why couldn't it have happened to me? Why my young daughter?

Everything reminds me of my daughter. If I so much as smell someone walking by wearing her favorite Angel perfume, my mind takes me back to the past and I see the two of us shopping for high school prom dresses. Sometimes I go even further back, to the time she dropped her entire plate of hot macaroni and cheese all over the living room carpet. I am so glad now that I hugged her instead of yelling at her.

Every day I've been sitting at her gravesite. I bring flowers but their colors clash with the ugly brown ground. I tell myself this is not the place to sit. My daughter is not there. No, just as Christ is no longer on the cross or behind the rock, my daughter is not in the ground. I can sit at the gravesite forever, but she is not there and knowing that brings me hope.

I'm writing because I had a dream last night. Lauren told me to live in the present and celebrate life, not death. Kristine, I've got to do this or I'll die myself. I'm inviting you to do the same. She talked about you all the time, sometimes saying you tend to worry a lot about things you cannot control, that you tended to see cloudy days as devastating. Now I hope you see that nothing lasts forever, especially the clouds. Let's celebrate life. It's not going to happen immediately. It may take a year or more, but let's try.

Love,
Lauren's Mom.

13

Returning to the island meant stepping into a world without pressed dresses. The color of the sky on a particular day mattered more than the color of clothes she chose to wear. The humidity resting on her skin meant more than the sweat that came from working out in a gym. She enjoyed walking the rugged, sandy path so much more than sweeping and mopping the kitchen floor back home where things like sand and turtles surely didn't belong. Stepping foot on the island meant returning to a world where errands didn't matter. She felt like a college student returning to nursery school but still having the skills and intelligence of someone in their twenties, and that suddenly made everything so simple—not boring, just simple. She felt a sense of elation after returning to the island, her Kingdom of Narnia, as if life off the island tossed her one too many things to do.

Some people never needed to make a list in their lives. They just stored details in their memories, not knowing why they felt agitated and stressed out. Kristine tended to write down every item of every day's agenda, including things that might be considered natural instinct: wake up, eat breakfast (Quaker Oat Life Cereal, something from the fruit family, plain yogurt), shower, bank, post office, etc. This at least gave her brain a break from having to store it all.

On the other hand, she was a perfectionist *and* a list maker, and that combination along with a strong work ethic and Type A personality threatened to drive her to the edge of sanity. Such people needed to make perfectly *beautiful* lists, and if they screwed up one word, or the order of their errands, they felt compelled to crumple them up and start all over again. Making lists coincided with a profile on obsessive behavior, but Kristine's reasons for making lists were entirely practical: a disorganized list meant a disorganized day, and a disorganized day naturally led to a frazzled, unproductive mind.

Island life required no lists. Life just happened there, like the weather. Rain arrived whenever it pleased. Its timing didn't matter. It could hit in the midst of an outdoor party and not care that it was falling on guests' expensive hairdos and drenching their designer gowns. Let them worry about that. And this, they surely did! If rain took into consideration all the events it might ruin on any given day or night, the world might shrivel up into dryness because the rain worried so much.

Tarpon Key was a small mangrove and didn't allow much room for worry. Lists, whether mental or written, would fall through the branches into the murky water. Life there stayed rudimentary. And it forced Kristine to notice smaller things, like a Roseate Spoonbill pacing deliberately in slow motion. Or the smaller Oyster Catcher with its long, curving beak and dainty steps, or Anhingas perched in the mangroves to dry their wings, while the Great and Little Blue Heron stalked crustaceans and small fish in the shallows.

Kristine worked lunch, then walked briskly back to the staff house to change her clothes for dinner. Denver had told her a new vessel had arrived, and Kristine couldn't wait to meet the new waitress.

She looked older than her forty years and was worn down with lines of age and abuse. Together with her sunken cheekbones and pale color, set against thick black mascara, the crevices around her eyes and mouth sculpted a roughness on her face. Only her long, curly brown hair added feminine softness, and it fell around her face like a flag torn by the wind. Her name was Evelyn.

Together, the two cleaned out the piles of old newspapers, empty cigarette boxes and soda cans stashed in the closet of Evelyn's new room.

"Why thank you, sweetie. You're *such* a big help. You look like a college educated girl, am I right?"

"Yes." She wondered about the tough lines on Evelyn's face and what put them there and didn't want to waste time finding out. "So tell me, Evelyn, why are you here on the island?" She tossed the last two beer cans into a Hefty bag.

"I'm in hiding. But I'll tell ya about that some other time. For starters, I need to know your birthday." Evelyn tucked her cleaning rag into the waist of her jeans and opened the window for air.

"My *birthday*? Why?"

"A birthday tells me more than a name. When's your birthday?"

"November 24th."

"Nice to meet you my little shooting arrow centaur."

"What?"

"You're a Sagittarius. We'll talk later."

As Kristine helped train Evelyn in the routine of the restaurant, she wondered why the weatherworn woman was in hiding. Who or what was she hiding from? She certainly didn't require much training. She said she had waited tables her entire life. Well, except for the decade when she danced topless in a bar near the beach. Despite her curiosity, Kristine left the woman alone her first few nights on the island, assuming she might want some initial privacy, the kind she herself had wanted just five weeks ago when she first arrived, before agreeing with John Donne that no man was meant to be an island.

Like a lighthouse flashing in the dark of night, a red glow came from Evelyn's room. Kristine noticed it as she made her way down the dark hallway of the staff house. She planned on sitting outside on the wooden steps for a few minutes, something she often did when insomnia struck. Tonight, as always, she headed towards the front door, but a red light shimmering under Evelyn's partially closed door caught her curiosity. She altered course and peeked into Evelyn's room. Red boat candles, belonging in the restaurant, were glowing everywhere. The woman sat Indian style on the sandy floor with a deck of cards in her hands. In the flickering red light, her facial lines showed up more embittered than they appeared in daylight.

"It's so dark in there. How can you see what you're playing?" whispered Kristine.

"Oh, my little college-educated girl, welcome, welcome," said Evelyn. "Come on in now, come on."

"Let me guess. You're playing a lonely, desolate game of solitaire," said Kristine.

Evelyn laughed, "Oh no, not solitaire, and I'm not *playing*, honey. This is serious stuff. Here, shuffle this deck and draw eight cards. Come on. Don't be a scaredy cat."

A horrible shuffler, Kristine clumsily moved her hands through the cards, while looking at the weird and colorful pictures on their backs. Candle sticks, men with wings, other men with horns, gold wine cups, ladders. She selected eight cards and handed them to Evelyn.

"These are Tarot cards and they're going to tell *me* about *you*. About your past, your present, and if they feel comfortable, your future."

"Okay, but hey, can you skip my past and present? I just want to know my future, my immediate future. Am I going to die any time soon? That's all I need to know." She knew she had asked a serious question, but she put no belief in the cards, or in what Evelyn was saying.

"The cards will tell me what *they* want you to know. I have no control over that, babe." Evelyn laid the eight chosen cards in two rows on the floor and studied them seriously for a moment. "Now this is your past. You were comfortable, surrounded in comfort. I get a strong sense of home, belonging, comfort in people you loved and places all around you and…"

"Wait, stop," interrupted Kristine, rubbing the goose bumps on her arms. "I don't get it. Where are you getting this information? You don't know me, anything about me!"

"It's not coming from *me*, doll. The information is coming from the *cards*, the sprits working through the cards. I told you that. I'm just reading them for you." Evelyn flipped another card from the deck and said, "More recently, you feel guilty you didn't go to her funeral, don't you?"

"*What?* I've never said that out loud to anyone. I've only thought it. What are you talking about?" Her tongue caught a warm, salty tear before it dribbled toward her chin. Suddenly she wished she hadn't stopped at this lighthouse because nothing about it felt safe. She longed to be sitting on the staff house steps instead. Why didn't she stay on course?

"Moving on," said Evelyn without emotion. "Writing. I see writing."

"Sure. Letters. I write letters to my grandmother. My letters keep her going." Kristine crossed her arms, not in defense, but to shield her from the sudden chill.

"Yes. Keep writing those letters. They may turn into something more some day."

"Okay! Stop." She felt as if her immune system suddenly weakened, like a head cold coming on quickly.

"We've gotta finish, baby cakes. Touch as many cards in the deck as possible, then choose four more."

Kristine did as she was told, her hands trembling.

"You asked about death. Well, I can't get any specifics on that, but you are your own worst enemy. Does that make sense?"

"I think I've had enough. This is just too much. It's too much." She left the lighthouse, making her way to her room, feeling confused about what Evelyn and the cards had said. In a way, she liked the attention and what they said, and the fact that they spoke to her and about her. Her God didn't usually get this specific in speaking to her, whereas these cards seemed to know her, perhaps better than her own God? Like an alcoholic taking a sip of vodka, she wanted more. She couldn't wait to know more about her future.

The next day during lunch, a man carrying a dozen red roses arrived on the island by charter. Without coming into the restaurant, he yelled to Kristine through the screen.

"Hey, do me a big favor, will you? Ask Evelyn to step outside. Tell her there's a surprise out here." Everyone, including customers having lunch heard him ask his favor and watched curiously as Kristine ran into the kitchen.

"Evelyn, hurry! There's a surprise for you outside. Quick!"

"For *me*? Oh gosh, oh shit! I mean, a *surprise*?" She walked out the front door and looked around.

Like a jack-in-the-box, the man was whistling from behind a palm tree, and as Evelyn walked out, he popped out. "Evelyn, marry me!" he shouted.

She jumped into his arms crying as he spun her round and round, sending chills through Kristine. Customers clapped. One lady wiped her eyes with her napkin. No one even knew Evelyn had a boyfriend. She only talked about her future and that of everyone else. Kristine wondered if Evelyn had ever forseen this surprise during one of her own Tarot card readings.

Several nights later, Kristine didn't feel like finding her way back to the staff house in nature's total darkness so she grabbed a red candle from the restaurant for just a little added help. Her status had advanced to that of island veteran, and island veterans never carry flashlights.

Those who knew the island didn't need battery-operated light to guide their way. If they bumped into a tree or took a wrong turn, so what? That was part of the adventure that made island life spontaneous and the darkness so emancipating.

As she entered the dark staff house, she anticipated a quiet evening alone since Lawrence had taken Ruth, Howard, Denver and the others by boat to a bar on Captiva Island to go dancing. Instead, the moment she walked down the hall, she could hear Evelyn ranting and raving, her voice ringing out like a lighthouse alarm gone mad.

"Kristine, is that you? Child, help me!"

She ran into Evelyn's room to find her in a rampage, frantically pulling her clothes out of her dresser drawers.

"Oh honey, we're all in danger. You, me, everyone living here." Evelyn's mascara streaked her face like a rabid zebra. "Oh, damn, where's it at? I know I've got more of that blankety-blank fix."

"What are you looking for? And can't you just ask your Tarot cards where it is? I'm sure they'll know."

"Well honey, I sure ain't looking for *this*, although this could come in handy!" She pulled a huge knife out from under the bed. It resembled more of a sword from medieval days, a souvenir from a Renascence Fair.

"Evelyn! What are you *doing* with that thing?"

"I'm giving it a better hiding space, babe," she said, sliding the weapon back under her bed. "But that's not what I'm looking for. Help me! It's a bag of pot, and it's gotta be in here somewhere, unless someone stole it. Whoever stole it better not say anything to Ruth because I know she'd make me walk the plank if she found it."

Together, they emptied out the rest of her drawers, then the closet, where Evelyn found her prized pot in an old sneaker and lit up.

"Honey, you seem uptight. I think you need a reading," said Evelyn, removing her deck of cards from a small box under her bed.

"I don't know, Evelyn. Why can't I just face uncertainty in life like a confident vessel in dark waters moving forward?" It took her all day to come to that conclusion.

"Because you'll get hit with storms, babe. The cards will tell you those storms are coming and how big they are."

"Well, if a storm approaches without warning, I can turn around, or take another route or anchor and wait for it to pass." She fidgeted with the tiny gold cross hanging around her neck, and for a moment, felt ashamed that it shared the chain with a shark tooth.

"As you shuffle, I want you to concentrate on *one* thing, one thing you'd like to know," said Evelyn.

She gave in. She wanted to know her future and she wanted to know it now, but couldn't think of just *one* thing she wanted to know. Instead, she thought of God and prayed part of the 'Our Father.' *Thy Kingdom come, thy will be done, on earth as it is in Heaven.* Then, in an attempt to form a bridge with the pictorial cards, she missed and they collapsed all over.

"Now baby, shuffling ain't your talent, so don't try overachieving." Evelyn laughed raucously.

Starting over, Kristine shuffled conservatively, no bridges this time. Evelyn took the fifty six-cards with the twenty-two additional pictorial cards and arranged them on the floor.

"These pictures represent the forces of nature and virtues and vices of humanity," she explained. "Okay, according to this first card... hmmm...That's odd. This here card tells me there's a strong power or force at work in you right now."

"What kind of force?" Kristine continued to pray silently.

"A *spiritual* force of some sort, honey. Whoa, weird. Never seen *that* before. And this second card here, this second card is telling me your reading is *over*, not to continue."

"Does that mean I'm about to die or something? I have no future?"

"No, just that we shouldn't be doing your reading right now, and I'm not going to argue with this force, whatever it might be."

"Evelyn, do you believe in the Holy Spirit?"

"Honey, I wouldn't play around with such powerful cards if I didn't. I only give these card readings because I think some people are in need of a message, and the cards bring that message. Don't you want a message about your future?"

"Yes, I do. Then again, no I don't. There's a bright lighthouse out there, one I know I can trust, one you can trust too, if you want to. I want so badly to trust in this light, even as tidal waves come my way. I admit, my faith has been weak lately, and I've been looking around for life vests to cling to, but knowing the future surely won't make my life better in any way. And if I get hit in the face with a sudden cold one, oh well, that is life. Evelyn, have these cards ever really helped your life in any way?"

"My life. Ha. Let me tell you bout my life, my endless cycle of Hell. Just name it and I've experienced it—rape, abuse, near starvation from no money, no food, and divorce. Did I mention spouse abuse? Got so bad I had to have surgery."

"Evelyn, would you like to know about the lighthouse I rely on?"

"No! Not now, please! I don't want to hear about anything right now."

Kristine stared at Evelyn, a ship fallen victim to piracy, a life controlled and possessed by someone else. The women cried together on Evelyn's bed. They cried because the pirate that did this to Evelyn classified not just as an enemy to her, but to all of womankind.

How can such a wounded life ever be repaired? Kristine wondered before saying anything. "What about your fiancé and your engagement?"

"I can't marry that wretched man. He's the one who beat me up to the point of needing surgery."

"But Evelyn, the proposal, the tears…"

"Yeah, yeah, yeah. Tears of fear! It was all a damn act to save my life, babe. You're such a naive romanticist. I didn't want to disappoint you. You were so happy for me. How could I tell you the good old truth?"

"That's ridiculous, Evelyn. I can handle *your* truth. Why'd you say yes to his proposal?"

"Call it acting, my dear, acting. I'm good, aren't I? Yeah, that was all a big act. I came to the island to hide from him. He said he was going to kill me because I tried breaking up. Believe me, he *will* kill me! I escaped to this island without telling a soul, not even my daughter. I hoped to stay out here long enough—I don't know how long, just long enough for him to get on with his life. But, he found me. I don't know how. The whole proposal scene, it was done publicly because he knew it would be the only way to get close to me. As he swung me around, he whispered in my ear that he'd kill me if I didn't return. I told him I had to finish my week at work in order to get any pay at all." Evelyn pulled out a different box of Tarot cards she had tucked behind one of her pillows and started shuffling the deck.

"Do you think he might show up here again?" asked Kristine.

"Hell yes, with his gun! I've seen his gun close up. Believe me, I've almost felt its bullets. It would be just like him to charter a boat out here and show up at night when we're all sleeping. There's no way I'm gonna sleep tonight and neither should you—for your life's sake!"

With no locks on the front door of the staff house, or on her own bedroom door, Kristine wanted to stay awake and alert. She finally understood Evelyn's anger, her attitude, the toughness of her voice, and the lines on her face. She remembered all the tales of domestic violence her father dealt with as a police officer, a job he worked during college and now again while in Florida. There could be violent and potentially life-threatening situations for anyone present.

Hours passed, and Kristine tried returning to her room, but Evelyn begged her to stay. "I'm scared to death to go to bed, honey. He might kill me, while I'm sleeping. Oh honey, this is probably all so strange to you. Your life is so good."

"I understand your fear of not wanting to sleep, Evelyn. In my own personal way, I do."

"I'm gonna do some reading now, some card reading that is."
"Sure. I'm going to write a letter to my grandma."

※

Dear Grandma:

Everyone has fears in life. Some fear the future. Some fear physical threat. Some fear addictions. Some fear love. Some fear financial starvation or homelessness. At first, I was afraid of these strangers I had to live with on this island. Now, I depend on them. I like them. We are meant to be here, living and breathing together at this time and place. There's nothing more exciting in life than converting strangers into friends. It's worth staying up late for.

Instead of relying on Tarot cards, I need to patiently live out God's timeline in my life. Why would I let a deck of cards, or the unknown spirits at work in them, dictate my future? What if they told me one thing, when in reality, another thing was supposed to happen? As a result, their advice could make me stray from my real destiny. The cards, or the person reading the cards, might predict some pretty strong things, and it might change the whole course of my life. The joke would be on me then because I let them steer me. As Denver would say, "I thought you were a darn stronger vessel than that."

14

The women sat on Evelyn's bed, one smoking pot while shuffling Tarot cards, and the other writing to her grandmother, until morning. Kristine could still feel the puffiness around her eyes that night when her parents came to the island for dinner. Lawrence had chartered them out for their wedding anniversary, and she couldn't wait to serve them in the rustic candlelit restaurant.

She had thought a lot about them lately and wondered how the move to Florida had been working out for them. She wasn't the only one who had left behind a comfort zone. Back in Michigan, they had had a thriving business, even a passionate business. But the more it grew, the more it had taken all of their time, morning, noon and night. This inched them towards wondering what life might be like, not having the pressures of owning their own business. In addition, they caught a group of employees stealing thousands of dollars from the cash register. This pushed them another inch, as they lost some of their entrepreneurial energy, and with it, their penchant to trust people, especially employees. It led them to working longer and harder hours. Meanwhile, Grandma endured lonely but therapeutically warm winters in Florida. Their empathy and desire to bring the family closer to her pushed them the rest of the way, and they sold it all and moved to the South.

Kristine's father immediately landed a job on the local police force, declaring it would only be temporary, until he and his wife found the right sort of business in Florida.

"I miss you two. I miss a lot of things." She sat down just as her father took his first bite of prime rib. "So how are you both handling your southerly migration so far?"

"Your father's mind still smells the waffle cone batter heating up on the griddle every morning," teased her mother as she peeled a hot shrimp.

"I miss pride of ownership," said her father. "I'm glad to be a police officer again, but hey, I haven't done this kind of work since college. The demands have changed somewhat. Maybe I've changed. I'm only twenty years older." Her father fed her mother a bite of his mashed garlic potatoes.

Kristine stole a sip of her mother's iced tea. "What do you miss most, Mom?"

"Oh, I'd say preparing the bakery goods each morning as the bed & breakfast guests came down to chat in the strawberry room." She squeezed lemon on her shrimp. "Even more than that, I miss working side by side with my husband and my girls."

"And Grandma, poor Grandma. She hated her lonely winters in Florida," added Kristine. "I still can't get over the fact she died just after you got here."

"Well now, let's look ahead. Tell us, Kristine, how are you preparing for Spain?" asked her mother.

"For starters, I need to start turning all these after midnight fishing offers down and start reading the assigned books for my Spain semester. The first book I have to read is, *A World History of Our Own Times*—a five hundred and seventy one-page history book."

"Do you have time out here?" Her father loaded a ball of butter onto his baked potato.

"I'll make time. I've got five more books just like it lying on my dirty floor, coated in dust. My foreign language academic counselor said that as an American representative in Spain, I should be able to answer intelligently any political or historical questions people may ask me concerning the U.S."

"That could be scary for our country!" he teased.

"Hey, I could tell them what sorts of fish we have in our waters. Now isn't that a lot more interesting?" she asked.

"Yes, but can you tell them in Spanish? That is the real question," her father joked.

Toward the end of their dinner, she felt tempted to leave the island with them, especially after last night's scare. They were her lifeboats, and she felt so safe with them. But, no, she couldn't go back. She had to stay. This place allowed her to stay up all night if she wanted. She needed this world right now.

She walked alone to the staff house. It stood on its stilts, silently, the second night in a row, blending in with the still palms all around it. The familiar mixtures of voices, like birds in the trees, were nowhere to be heard. Some had gone fishing, others sat atop the water tower, and Howard was hanging out down by the docks. As she entered the door that welcomed everyone, no matter how rich, poor, smart or stupid, she stepped into an atmosphere at least twenty degrees warmer than the eighty-degree night outside.

A lizard with half a tail ran down the hall in bliss. She herself staggered, a human tossed into a snake cage. It didn't take a heating and cooling expert to diagnose a broken air conditioner. She felt like screaming for Denver, but he wouldn't be back until morning. He always liked to repair things and people, and he seemed to gain momentum from helping others who were stuck.

Unlike the dry Midwest summer nights, and Florida's typical humidity, this heat was overbearing. Kristine began dripping sweat so profusely, she felt as if her head were hanging over a pot of boiling water on the stove. The more her salts and fluids ran off, the more she wondered if this is what it felt like to be trapped inside a dryer, or worse yet, to be stuffed into a plastic bag inside a microwave—dripped dry. She considered telling Ruth, but it was too late at night for her to call a technician. Besides, he had to come by boat, and it would be morning before he could get here. "Hey, Mr. Kool Aid," she cried, "where are you when a gal needs some refreshment?" But he only appeared to children.

To keep her mind off the deadly heat, she started writing a letter to her grandmother. She considered shoving it into a bottle and sending it that way. Better yet, maybe she'd squeeze herself into the bottle. But she didn't see any bottle, just the infamous coffeepot, and who ever heard of sending a letter in a coffeepot? She started a letter but couldn't find the words to describe her summer on Tarpon Key, an island named after a big fish with a silver belly.

Her room provided no air and she felt locked in a sauna, unable to breathe. The very thought of not being able to breathe triggered an attack. Her breathing became more labored. She had dumped her paper bag weeks ago, determined to combat the ridiculous problem without it. Now she needed it as a claustrophobic needs to break free from a seat belt as it tightens against her or him during a sudden stop in traffic. Frantic feelings tumbled about inside her. She wanted a window, a refrigerator she could climb into, a Popsicle, anything for relief. She tried to stay calm and slowly inhaled one breath at a time.

"Girl, pack a bag cuz you and me are going to have a slumber party," whistled Evelyn from down the hall, an unsteady branch that separated one type of bird from another.

"What are you doing here? I thought you went island hopping and dancing with everyone else. Is this heat making you sick, too?"

"Sweetie, this heat's going to dehydrate us like lizards and kill us in our sleep. But don't fret, babe. I've got a solution." She tossed her cigarette butt into the toilet and reached into her back pocket for another.

It seemed Evelyn routinely shared a fear of sleeping. Her boyfriend never came to kill her that night, but she always feared something getting her in her sleep. "But Evelyn, where can we go? Should I get dressed?"

"No, there's no time for wardrobe and makeup. We need to get our bodies outside where the temperature will be at least be one hundred degrees, a breathable, survivable temperature. This environment is for the lizards, not humans. I feel like I'm in a tank at the aquarium."

"Great. Hadn't obsessed on that one yet," said Kristine, suddenly feeling like a reptile.

The women set out in pajamas, carrying pillows, blankets, and melted candy bars. Holding Kristine's hand firmly, Evelyn led the way, skipping and singing, "Lizards and spiders and snakes, Oh My! Lizards and spiders and snakes, Oh My!" She sang her rendition of *Wizard of Oz* lyrics for a good five minutes before Kristine caught on and joined in.

They skipped all the way to the restaurant and went inside. "Will we get in trouble for being in here at night, Evelyn?"

"Hell no. We need fluid in our bodies. It's a matter of life or death, and no one can argue with us about that. Come on. Let's get some ice-cubes and tea."

Outside again, a mouse ran over Kristine's toe and she screamed, running into Evelyn.

"Oh babe, you're okay. Come on. Let's go catch some *zzzzz*'s on the dock."

The dock might have worked, but once they got there, they met up with a determined gang of No-See-Em bugs. Scratching and squirming, Kristine suddenly saw how hilarious their situation was. "This is crazy! This is not normal. Look at us, lying out here on a dock on a tiny little island at this time of night."

She looked at Evelyn, her new friend, and started to laugh. She couldn't stop. Tired, irritated from bugs, she couldn't stop laughing. She laughed until her armpits itched, realizing she had forgotten what that felt like. Tears rolled down her cheeks and her stomach hurt. Evelyn just stared at her with a smile, then lit her cigarette.

"Oh child, you're still in the sweet stage."

"What?" Kristine wiped the tears from her eyes.

"The sweet stage. Tell me something, how do you like your coffee?"

"My coffee?" asked Kristine.

"Yeah, your coffee, and be specific. Order it like you'd order it in one of those coffee shops brewing up on every corner in this country."

"Okay. Ahh, let's see. I'll have a tall mocha with whipped cream, chocolate shavings and a few chocolate covered espresso beans on top, please. Oh, and a chocolate covered almond biscotti to go with it. No lid. I like to eat the whipped cream off right away."

"What else, dearie? Any added sugar?" mocked Evelyn.

"Yes, one blue packet. I'll add it myself." She landed from her flight of laughter as she answered.

"I knew it. I knew it. Let me tell you something, babe. I drink Folgers and I drink it black. I brew, pour and drink. Nothing more. You see, life, like coffee, progresses. And as you grow older and move on through life, you'll eventually skip the sugar, the chocolate, the whipped cream, all in stages. You'll go to that one or two percent milk. But hey, like wine, it's all part of growing old. You start off in life needing the sweetest wine there is, like that strawberry junk, the Lambrusco, or the sangria, whatever. But soon, you tolerate it drier and drier and come to my age…on second thought, you'll be much older than me, you'll drink dry wine and black coffee."

"Sure. It's like ice cream. The little kids used to come in our shop screaming for blue moon, or bubble gum, or any of those obnoxiously colored flavors. They had no idea that blue moon was really almond flavor. They appreciate ice cream for the color and craziness of it. As they get older, they'll start liking nuts or chocolate, and you know what's odd? The old ladies always ordered black walnut. I don't know why, but I never served that flavor to anyone under sixty it seemed."

"Yeah, well, I hate ice-cream. Always did, even as a kid. I guess I skipped the sweet stage altogether."

"Evelyn, let's figure out some way to make your life better. I mean, you don't have to be treated so…"

"Make my life better? Oh, shut up! What are you going to do, plop some whipped cream in my coffee? No, I don't deserve better. When I was a little girl I dreamt of Prince Charming picking me up on his pony and taking me off to Fort Myers Beach and all. I wanted to live in a mansion some day with hanging glass chandeliers."

"Sometimes our dreams just don't happen the way we once wanted them to."

"Yeah, well, I've never had much to offer. No brains, no money, no education. No, I don't deserve any better in life."

"Evelyn, you deserve peace of mind, happiness. You deserve to be treated well, nothing less. It's your right to be treated like a person."

"Ahh, get a grip, my little romanticist. You still believe in those rosy little tales, don't you? *Ha ha ha ha ha ha.* Oh, come on, I'm teasing."

"No, it's okay. I just don't think it's that funny."

"Girl, you've never been treated bad by a man in your life. You've probably never even had a man. But if you did, and he treated you bad, what would you say to him?"

True, she hadn't ever truly been in love and therefore, had never truly been hurt, nor abused, nor abandoned. She had to think fast before Evelyn might reach out and bite her for being naive. "Ahh, well, getting back to your situation, you will survive!" It was all she could think of and now she knew that dancing and singing to Gloria Graynor music with Lauren did serve a higher purpose. "That's right. You will survive. I'm assuming that, that at first you were afraid, you were petrified, I mean…how he did you wrong…and how to get along."

Kristine paused to imagine her and Lauren back in the dorm room and to remember more of the words. Evelyn stared with interest, so she continued. "And now he's back…from outer space."

"He sure is, babe. And it's not even Mars," added Evelyn. "There's gotta be a planet way far out there that some of these men come from, and it's not Mars. It's much worse."

"Well, you should have changed that stupid lock," recited Kristine. "If you had known for just one second he'd be back to bother you."

"True," added Evelyn. "But I thought I'd fall apart mentally, you know, at him trying to get to me."

"Of course, you thought you'd crumble, you thought you'd lie down and die."

"Exactly. That's exactly how I felt."

"Oh no not you, Evelyn! You're not that chained up little person."

"I don't want to be," she said.

"You're not! And ya know, why? You're saving all your loving for someone who will love you!"

Evelyn wiped her nose and sniffled. "Well, not to change your subject or anything, but I've got us an idea! Let's go to that old vacant cottage, the one that used to belong to some German doctor years ago. We'll sleep there. Never seen it, but I heard he lived in that attic above the cottage," said Evelyn as she flipped Kristine's hair into a sloppy bun atop her head.

"That place is eerie, don't you think? It reminds me of some A-frame cottage in a Stephen King novel."

"Getting there, that's the spookiest thing about it. We gotta cross that fragile little bridge over the murky water in the dark. Hope you can handle it."

With the bridge behind them, both agreed the obscurity of the attic might be spookier. Holding a candle, they climbed up the steep stairs of the A-frame cottage overlooking the gulf. The walls consisted of old, brown panels and the ceiling slung low, forcing both women to duck as they stumbled up the stairs like Halloween guests scurrying through a haunted house. Evelyn pulled the top mattress off the bed and let Kristine sleep on the bottom mattress. Reaching into her big well-stuffed cloth draw bag, she pulled out her stash of mini Reese's Peanut Butter Cups.

"Care for some caffeine and protein disguised as fattening yet comforting little treats?" Evelyn looked like the old lady in Hansel and Grettel, but Kristine took the candy anyway.

15

"Wake up, child! We gotta get ready for work." Evelyn stood like a hunchback in the low-ceiling attic.

"Whoa. What's happening? Are we late?" asked Kristine, looking around to reorient herself.

"No, not yet. But no time for dilly-dallying. Better run back to the staff house quickly so no one catches us in our evening gowns." Evelyn's eyes frantically peered out the triangular-shaped window like a suspicious, hallucinating drug addict.

"Evelyn, how did you wake up without an alarm clock?"

"Never slept," she announced matter-of-factly, pacing back and forth.

"Why not?"

"Okay, if you wanna know. There was this enormous lizard sitting on your back. The thing was huge."

"An iguana? Bright green?"

"No, no iguana. Look! He's sitting on the windowsill now. I took it upon myself to keep an eye on it for you. Who knows what it could have done to you, while you slept."

"You do think of anything to stay awake, don't you," mused Kristine. But again, she understood the strangeness. It seemed everyone on the island possessed an oddity of her own, and Kristine proved no exception.

The island, like a daytime talk show, represented a microcosm of the world. Everyone had an interesting personal issue to share.

Kristine showered and showed up for work. Evelyn took a bit longer. She showered and never showed up for work. Instead, she quietly left the island on the morning staff boat, never saying good-bye to anyone. As Kristine ran into the kitchen for a basket of rolls, she wondered how Evelyn would survive. She didn't have money, nor food, nor a job and the cards surely wouldn't provide her with these basics.

The woman with the huge sword only half-hidden in her partially open suitcase stepped off the staff boat at the marina, as the man with a sketchbook under his arm stepped on the staff boat. Their paths crossed momentarily as he offered her help with her suitcase. "My, my, my, aren't you someone's fine catch?" she muttered to him. "Why would you want to help an old wretch like me?"

"You deserve as much help as anyone else and hey, people like to help people. So accept it." He took her belongings and set them on the dock, then stepped back onto the boat. He had an agenda for going out to the island. He had finally decided to share his story and it would be the very first time telling it since it all had happened.

"Steve!" Kristine dropped her dirty rag, ran over to the screen doors and hugged the good-looking man standing in the doorway. "Steve! How did you get out here? I'm so glad you're here."

He answered shyly, "Lawrence, the man who drives the boat, did me a huge favor. He says he'll take me back to the marina in an hour. He's a great person. You can see it in his eyes."

"You've only got an hour? Is everything okay? Did anything happen?" she asked.

"Kristine, I've gotta know. Are you all right out here? I mean, here you are living on a small remote mangrove in the middle of nowhere."

"Steve, I love it out here. It's busy, hard work, but I *have* to stay."

"You don't have to. I'll take you back on the boat with me today, if you want."

"No, of course not." She wiped sweat from her forehead and started to wipe down a dirty table.

"I miss you and it seems like I'm losing you. After this, you're off to Spain." He took the rag out of her hand and tossed it on the table, forcing her attention.

"I know. And after Spain, I'll be back in Florida for Christmas. And after that, back to Holland for a semester of school. Then, who knows where I'll go. There are so many places to see yet. But then, after all of that, I'll be back here in Florida again. We've gone over it again and again. Oh, and look at me, planning every semester of my life. Who knows, maybe I won't do any of these things. Maybe I'll die in my sleep, or something."

"*What?*" he asked. "What are you *talking* about?"

"I don't know. I just hate saying good-bye. If I get too close to you, we'll have a horrible good-bye ahead of us," she said.

"I know, I understand, I really do." He took both of her hands and held them tightly, not minding her bitten nails and dryness from cleaning.

"What is the worst good-bye you've ever had to say, Steve?" she asked.

"Come with me a minute. I'll tell you. I need to tell you something."

"I can't come with you. I've got a million tables to clear." She looked around and saw Ruth joining in on the mess left by the lunch crowd.

"Kristine, you've served everyone, people are leaving, and now you've got dirty tables. Big deal. The lunch crowd is over."

"Okay, okay." She took him by the hand, leading him out the front door and down the path to the shore. They sat down on the hot sand, and he started to take his shoes off. She did the same, not knowing where this would lead.

"Put your toes in the water. It's warm."

She laughed, then glanced back at the restaurant, worried that Ruth might be calling for her. "You are an interesting one. I'll say that much."

"I want to tell you about the worst good-bye I've ever had to say, Kristine. I'm going to tell you some things about myself, and I hope this won't scare you away from me."

"Nothing will scare me away, don't worry about that." She had heard it all. After getting to know her island friends, she truly felt nothing could scare her away.

"As I've mentioned, my father was high ranking in the military, and we lived all over the world, including Spain."

"Spain? You lived in Spain? How could you not tell me?"

"Well, we were only there a few months. We moved to Madrid some years back, and after just getting there, I was hit by a car. I was nineteen years old, and I don't remember a thing about the accident itself. I do remember everything that happened in the hospital, however. Everything!"

"Oh my goodness." She covered her mouth with both hands. "Your knees, your back…"

"Yes, that's why I have pain at times," he said. "I watched from above as the doctors worked on me, Kristine."

"From above?"

"Yes. I know it all sounds crazy, but I saw my mother crouched down on the floor in the corner of the waiting room. She cried, out of control, and was screaming out to me that she loved me and didn't want me to leave her. I saw my father kneeling down next to her, also praying that I would live because he couldn't stand to see his wife in so much pain. Back in the emergency room, the doctors covered me and declared me dead. I saw and heard this all from above, as if I were floating near the ceiling of the room. I saw my life all around me, as if I were watching one of those panoramic movies at Disney World, you know the ones."

"You watched your life like a movie?"

"Yes, from start to the time of the accident. I felt absolutely awful for all the times I ignored people in need, and I felt incredible satisfaction for every time I quietly helped a stranger. I realized those were the moments that brought quality to my life. I watched and judged my entire life, and then I went down the tunnel we all hear about and I can't describe the place I saw at the end of the tunnel."

"That is the place you always talk about? The place that doesn't compare?" She took the sketchbook from under his arm and flipped through it. Some pictures were in black and white, some in color. Others were coated with black paint, as if the artist got frustrated and later tried destroying them.

"Yes. God cannot be reduced to human words, or my attempted artwork. He cannot. I did not want to come back to life, but I was told it wasn't my time. I kept hearing my mother crying out to me. I entered my body and felt miserable because it was so heavy and painful. I didn't want to be back. I didn't want to say good-bye to the place I just visited, and the God I just saw. I was so comfortable there."

She had both hands covering her mouth, but now she rubbed her arms to tame the geese running up and down her arms. She closed her eyes, opened them again, and put both hands around Steve, hugging him and rubbing his back. She did not know that sort of good-bye. She couldn't imagine a good-bye like that. "No, no place I go in this life will ever compare to where you've been, Steve."

"But it's not a competition. I have to savor this life for what it is and not compare."

"What is this life?"

"This life is about people, doing small things for other people. It's about doing things that others don't see, things that don't bring rewards and recognition, just things. Treating others as you yourself would want to be treated. That famous phrase is the truth!"

"Steve, you are so right for me."

He laughed. "Thanks, but my timing is off. I still want you to go out and see the world and do what you're meant to do. Promise to be careful in those streets of Madrid and remember that this life is good but the next is better."

"Are you sure you couldn't come along to Spain with me this fall? Oh, but I'm so sorry for saying that. How could I say that with the accident? Oh, you probably don't ever want to return there again."

He reached over and splashed some water onto his legs. "No, it's okay. I'm just into different things now. Back then I wanted to travel the waters of the world. At this point in my life, I just want to stay put in my comfortable little world where I've already established some close friends and all. I've left enough friends in my life, moving from one place to the next for many years." His answer came long-winded, without a breath.

℘

The Mississippi steamboat left. Every time it picked up a load of passengers in life and got to know them, it would just have to drop them off again. She felt tempted to leave with it, to remain the longest passenger it has ever had, but she knew she couldn't. Soon she'd be leaving for Spain, and the steamboat couldn't make it to the Mediterranean Sea. Sure, steam-powered vessels do indeed cross the ocean, but the operating costs are high. It wasn't willing to pay those costs. Only the underwater ballistic submarine could go this time, and it would go solo. It needed to go much further than just the rivers, at this stage in its life.

16

Kristine knew that Marie, the new bold, blunt, borderline obnoxious Italian waitress from the East Coast, didn't need any privacy or time to adapt. The slightly overweight woman seemed to have every male customer falling in love with her the moment she laughed. She had the resonant sort of laugh that echoes across a room, making everyone wish they were over chatting with her. Her laughs exploded as uninhibited outbursts from the gut, and they were contagious. A single laugh ranged from high to low tones and came out so friendly, it made Kristine re-evaluate her own laughing style. *Goodness, if only I could laugh that boldly, that boisterously,* she thought. She wondered if every bit of stress and disease got shot right out Marie's body every time she laughed. She always used her forefinger to delicately wipe tears from her eyes, tears of laughter. Men laughed with her even if they were sitting across the room from the laughing area.

"Well, you've survived your first night waiting tables on this mangrove out in no-man's land," said Kristine.

"I think I like no-man's land," laughed Marie.

"If you're up to it, I'll be out in front on the chairs. It's a great way to unwind." Kristine poured herself a mug of hot chocolate as a defense in the unusually breezy evening air.

"Yeah, that sounds good. I'll pour myself what you're drinking and add a dose of Bacardi," answered Marie.

"Great. Meet me outside." Kristine waved to the few stragglers hanging out at the bar, as the aroma of prime rib from the kitchen followed her outside. The white wooden chairs felt cold against her bare legs, and the night wind kept stubbornly blowing her hair wildly across her face, interrupting her view of the navy blue water with its bobbing boats. She closed her eyes and could breath, something she never took for granted.

"Kristine, that prime rib smell is like an aroma therapy treatment. My pores are just eating it up." The wooden screen door slammed behind Marie. A second later, it slammed again.

Two male guests left the bar, in trail behind her. They were history professors and owned a forty-foot sailboat anchored about fifty yards from Tarpon Key. They had taken a small inflatable dinghy from their boat to the island for dinner and were anchoring here for the night.

"Have you women heard of Spook Island?" asked the one leathery-skinned historian.

"Oh yes, actually my customers talk about it all the time," Kristine sipped her hot chocolate. "From what I hear, everyone who has ever tried getting there has run into some sort of difficulty."

"Well, we think we know where it is, not too far from here. What do you say, would you two like to venture out and give it a try?"

"We'd love to." Marie stated loudly with no fear. "How are we going to get there?"

"We'll take our inflatable dinghy. It should be durable enough. Come on. Let's not waste any time."

"It's pretty late. Shouldn't we find it during daylight?"

"Kristine, it's called *Spook Island*. Any place with a name like that requires a night search," laughed her newfound friend from the East Coast. Again, her laughter got completely out of control and all four adults were totally engrossed in hysterics for about five minutes. The chorus of laughter allowed Kristine a moment to study and imitate its style, and no one noticed as her laugh started blending with that of her new friend.

Cramped in the errant rubber life raft made for two, the four set out for Spook Island. Their extra bright flashlight seemed to lighten only a small circle of the black rippling water ahead. They had paddled about one hundred yards from Tarpon Key when the wind picked up and became stronger. Cold waves splashed their faces.

"My toes are cold," whined Kristine.

"I think we had better re-route to our sailboat," stated the forty-five-year-old professor of ancient civilization. "Not because her toes are cold, but these waves are starting to hit us."

"Can't we just go back to Tarpon Key?" Kristine massaged her toes that stuck out of her sandals.

"Not with this wind. We're closer to the boat, and it would be safer to get out of this dingy as soon as possible."

"Well, that'll be all right. We want to be safe," said Marie, still holding her mug of hot chocolate with Bacardi. "We'll sit in your boat until the wind dies down, then you can bring us back."

"I'm getting nervous. This isn't good. Look at these waves. Where'd they come from?" exclaimed the long-winded professor.

"Marie, throw your mug overboard. We don't need the extra weight!" teased Kristine.

"You got it. I refuse to be the one who drowns us all!" She tossed it into the blackness and laughed. They all laughed.

They made it to the boat, but according to the radio, the winds gave no indication of dying down. They talked for about an hour, as the waves swayed the sailboat and it tugged and strained on the lines to its anchor below. No sign of calming wind.

"Let's have some fun now," one of the men said as he reached over and kissed Marie's neck. "There's not a whole lot of privacy here, but you women don't mind."

"I'd like to go back to the island now," said Kristine. "We both have to work early, and it's already after midnight."

"Well ladies, we'll take you back in the morning, but we're not going out in the dingy in this weather. Besides, we didn't take you out here just to catch some *zzzzz's*."

"Kristine wants to go back, and so do I!"

"We told you once, we're not taking you back. There's too much wind."

"But this is a *sail* boat. I thought these boats relied on wind. Why can't we go back?" asked Kristine.

"This isn't *wind*, this is a *storm*, and we're *not* going to take you back. Not tonight."

Kristine whispered to Marie rudely in front of them. "I want to go back to Tarpon Key now!"

"You heard what she said, she wants to go back to Tarpon Key now, so either you'll take us or we'll dingy ourselves back!" Marie blurted out.

"Be our guests. Take the dingy and your lives."

The two women jumped overboard into the dingy and were off.

"I know we're crazy, Marie. What do you think?"

"I don't know what to think. I want to get back too. And there's never anything wrong with a little adventure in life."

"Yeah, that's what my adrenaline is saying right now." Paddling like crazy, they tried to steer for Tarpon Key.

"I hope you know how to steer because I don't."

"Oh sure, like I drive dinghies every day in New York. What a great way to get through traffic. Is that what this thing is called anyway? A dinghy?"

"Dinghy, raft, inner tube with a bottom. I have no idea."

"Whatever, no problem. The dinghy should follow the same course as the wind is blowing, and good God, it's blowing toward the island." Kristine coughed on a wave that hit her in the face. Covering her mouth, she dropped one of the plastic oars. "Oh no, quick! Help! Use your hands, Marie!"

"No, don't lean over. This thing is filling with water. We'll just have to let it go."

"I'm drenched. Are you?"

"Kristine, look what we're sitting in! Five inches of water!"

"What if a shark goes by? Are we safe, Marie?"

"No, but steer zig-zag and we should be fine. They can't chase us if we steer zig-zag." Marie paddled with her hand, trying not to lean too far over.

"You're talking about alligators. Alligators have eyes that can't move in the zig-zag manner. Sharks have better eyes."

"Well, what do you expect? I'm a New Yorker. This is new to me! Look back, I can hardly see the sail boat," said Marie, gulping a wave. "No gentlemen awards for them tonight."

"I need to know. Were they being bullheaded, or wise?" But before Marie could answer, Kristine changed the subject. "I'm going to get sick, Marie."

"It's just a little seasickness. You can make it."

The direction of the waves worked to their advantage, and they noticed the current miraculously carrying them straight toward their island. Both were hugging each other under the slanting rain—in part for comfort, but also so that neither would fall out of the deflating dingy.

"We're in the only inflatable dingy out tonight," said Kristine, partially laughing and partially screaming. The waves had become so high that she lay down in the dingy for shelter. Though terrified, she forced herself to laugh some more. Soon, it came out naturally. She laughed so hard, her gut hurt. She wondered if her laughing had reached a higher plateau than Marie's at one point. Finally, she was laughing so much she felt drunk from laughing. She swore that from this moment on, she'd force herself to laugh loudly, just like Marie, whether alone in her room or whenever something silly was said. She looked around, hoping to see Lawrence somewhere out shark fishing or Captain Edwards tarpon fishing. No, they weren't foolish enough to venture out in this storm.

"We're the only daredevil women desperate enough to try such a thing, Kristine." At this point, the dinghy had reduced its services to that of a kick board, no longer something they could sit in. Instead, with both arms holding onto it, they used leg power to kick their way back to Tarpon Key. Kristine's foot cramped into a charley horse, but they did reach shore.

With the hair on their arms standing straight up from the cold, they ran back to the staff house, not realizing they did so without flashlight, candle, nor moon in sight. Marie clung onto Kristine's arm all the way.

"Good night, Marie. It was nice meeting you," said Kristine, tiptoeing into the staff house, her skin stinging from salt water and her finger joints stiff from the cold.

"Yeah, nice meeting you too. See you in the morning."

"Hey, Marie, has anyone ever told you you're absolutely crazy?"

"Every day of my life."

"Well, I'd call that an understatement."

℘

At around four o'clock in the morning, Kristine heard jazz music coming softly from down the hall. She got out of bed, poked her head out the door and noticed the glowing yellow crack under Marie's door. Why wasn't Marie sleeping? Everyone else was sleeping, everyone but Kristine, and now, Marie. And if Evelyn still lived here, she'd be awake dealing with some sort of anxiety. Denver—he wasn't even singing his depressing old lyrics at this hour. But now Marie, a new night owl lived here, awake for whatever reason, and Kristine wondered why. A little voice from within checked her: she needed her own rest though, so she decided to reach out to Marie another time. Returning to bed, she softly sang the lyrics to a B.J. Thomas song. *He's the light in the darkness, shining through brighter days. He's the light in the darkness, guiding me each step of the way.* The words helped her drift off to sleep.

17

Kristine left early on the morning boat for her two days off. As the boat took off at high speed, she looked back, wondering about Marie's story and why she stayed up all night. The next chapter of that novel would have to wait. Looking ahead, she could see Steve sitting on the edge of the dock waiting for her as always. She lived a dual life and felt like two completely different persons living in two distinct worlds.

She liked this part of her world, the one with Steve in it. They spent the morning together at the mall, walking and talking and spending money.

She wondered if love had a sense of humor because every time she first saw him, she would drop something. At the marina, she always dropped her purse or suitcase as soon as she heard his voice. Once, when they met at a café, she dropped her hot mocha, spilling it down the front of her shirt, and watched in embarrassment as it flooded the table. Another night, she dropped and shattered a light bulb the moment he arrived at the rental house to pick her up. Yes, love played hilarious jokes on her every time she saw him.

"Why are you always dropping things?" he had asked her when she dropped the bottle of opened wine into the sand the night they saw the sunset.

"I have no idea, but I can't help it."

Later she said good-bye to Steve and walked into a tiny café in Cape Coral to meet her father for coffee. Her mother and sister had missed their family in Michigan and returned to visit. Her father had gone as well but had come back early for work. She spotted him instantly. He looked handsome in his navy blue police uniform, and she felt proud to walk over to his table, kiss him on the cheek, and sit down. He held the daily paper in one hand and a cup of coffee in the other.

"How was Michigan, Dad?"

"The new owners are now selling hot dogs in the shop. I don't know that it goes that great with ice cream," he said.

"Oh no. Yuck."

"And they painted the front door a much darker pink."

"I liked the old pale pink. It was always a pale pink," she said.

"Yeah, I know. Couldn't believe it."

"What else did they change?" she asked.

"They're redecorating Mom's guest rooms upstairs."

"No. You're kidding. They can't! We wallpapered those together, all of us."

"Yeah. Wait till they find all the letters you girls scribbled in marker on the walls under the paper."

"Oh, that's right. Hey, they're still carrying the same flavors, aren't they?"

"Yep, but they added some sorbet down on the end," he said.

"That's no good. No, they can't start getting so complex like that."

"Tell me about it, and you know how you girls used to draw the daily special in chalk on the chalkboard?"

"Yeah, what happened to it?"

"They asked me if I wanted to take it or they were going to dump it."

"How could they? Customers loved those chalk drawings."

"I know. I've got the board in the car now. It still has your parfait picture on it. Some of the whipped cream smeared off, but we'll preserve the rest of it." He sipped his creamy coffee.

"Good."

Toward the end of lunch, her father got a domestic violence call and had to run.

"Oh Dad, one more thing. Quick, what types of fish live in Lake Michigan?"

"Well I'll be darned. My daughter is asking about fish?" He laughed.

"Yeah, I'm really curious."

"Okay, well, there's perch, bass, catfish, tuna, smelt, sturgeon…Do you want me to go on?"

"Thanks, Dad. I love you."

She hugged him, though his bulletproof vest was in the way, then watched as he waved to the café owner and walked out the door. Through the window, she could see him get into his squad car. The kaleidoscope he lived in now looked so blue. She squinted, hoping to see the magnitude of colors that once danced around him. A simple shake in life and everything changed so quickly, and so significantly.

Afterward, she picked up her round trip plane tickets to Madrid. They cost twelve hundred dollars, and she paid with her own cash—*her summer goal met!*

18

Kristine felt drawn to the rustic bar and, when not outside on the dock talking with co-workers after work, she sat in the dark, candle-lit bar for hours, surrounded by dollar bills that hung on the walls and strangers that sat on the stools. She watched the men talking together at the bar. Some were millionaires of the mannequin sort—their complexions were as clear and pampered-looking as their wives—and others, plain old rugged-looking anglers. A dollar bill may have meant nothing to one man, yet a lot to another, but still, they all scribbled their names in magic marker and taped their money to the walls. Then, they ordered their drinks and hung out together as if class and social barriers didn't exist. They had all arrived from different walks of life and had different stories. She couldn't help but hear their voices, like the tides, drift in and out of her hearing range.

"I killed a five-foot long alligator here on the island once," said one man. "Yeah, that's right. Cooked it for dinner, tasted great."

After a few sips of Chianti, she heard that same voice add, "I also caught this shark." He held up a tooth he wore on a gold chain around his neck.

"*You* caught a shark?" asked a lady sitting at the end, also overhearing his story. " On purpose or by accident?"

"Oh, I set out shark fishing for the night. Caught it on purpose," he answered across the bar.

Just then, Lawrence took a seat next to Kristine and began talking to a man next to him. "Yes, that's right. I love these magnificent mangroves and this entire area. It's in my blood, my history," said Lawrence. "The Calusa Indians, Spanish Conquistadors, they all loved this magnificent area."

"Kristine, would you like to try a rum and pineapple juice? It seems to be the drink of the night," said the bartender.

"Sure. I'm getting kind of tired of red wine and that whole French paradox thing," she replied.

"So what do you think of our waters out here?" he asked as he stabbed a pineapple with a plastic sword and set it in her drink.

"I'm from the Midwest. There we have hunters and fishermen, but it's different." She sipped her new drink and wiped her lips with a napkin. "Well, Midwesterners fish too, for trout, bass, things like that. But here, you're talking *alligators* and *sharks*. It's *different*."

Lawrence spun his barstool around. "Kristine, this gentleman and I were just discussing life's journeys. Tell us, what's one of *your* greatest journeys in life, dear?"

"I don't have one."

"Дear, life isn't worth living if it's a life without a journey. You've got to have one."

"No, I don't."

At that point, Howard and his three-piece wig, which nested an inch too far to the left, walked into the bar and signaled Kristine to meet him at the dart board. "Oh, I'm quite horrible at darts," she said.

"Listen to me," said Howard, aiming the dart at the board. "Remember that Spanish contact I told you about?" He shot the arrow, making bull's eye. "Well, here's his name and number. He lives in Madrid. His name is Ignacio. Call him Nacho for short. He's about your age. Look him up when you get there."

"But, will he…"

"No questions. Just look him up," said Howard as he handed Kristine the darts and started walking out of the bar in a hurry. "Oh, one more thing. Promise me you'll ask him to play the piano for you."

"The piano?"

"Yes, remember the piano." Howard left the bar, and Kristine stood there with nothing to do but toss the dart. She missed the board altogether and almost hit Marie who just walked in.

"Hey Marie, you look tired. What's up? Not sleeping at nights?" she asked.

"Kristine, I don't know if I'm going to make it out here."

"It's the feeling stranded on a remote island phase. Believe me, when I first got here, I felt it too."

"No, it's much more than feeling stranded. I really need to talk to someone."

"First, tell me why you came out here. Then, maybe I can help."

"I saw this place mentioned in a tiny blurb in *The New York Times* travel section. It said something about a person wanting to do a little dance when they first stepped foot on this remote island get-a-way."

"So you wanted to get away. From what?"

As Marie downed her rum and pineapple juice, she started laughing. She laughed until tears rolled down her cheeks. The laugh differed from her usual one. It was a pathetic sound, as if she knew she should be crying instead of laughing, or as if her emotions were taking control and playing nasty tricks on her. Tears poured out. Kristine stared. That's how it always is for the second party. It's not the type of laugh or cry that needs to be shared. It's a lonely, emotional breakdown moment. Kristine couldn't have joined in if she tried.

"Marie, you've come to the right place. Don't leave, whatever you do. Stay here. I don't have any answers for you. My only advice is this. Do not leave this island until the answers come to you. You were meant to stop here for a reason."

"I'm thinking of leaving tomorrow, of returning to New York because I'm in love with someone there, a good man but a dangerous situation."

"If you leave this island, you are pushing yourself against the wind. You will only wind up back where you started from—confused and in need of another escape. Give it time."

Just then, the band returned from their water break and started singing more great hits from the *Doors*. Denver walked in and took the hands of both women, kissing them tenderly. Ruth also showed up and, for a moment, the voices of everyone living on the island and everyone visiting the island blended like a symphony. The colors and stories added so many notes, and the candlelight was so dim that the bodies could hardly be seen. It was a room of voices, of stories, of lives anchoring for a moment, long enough for a drink and maybe more. Someone offered Kristine a drink and when she turned around, Marie had left.

Lawrence made an announcement, asking if anyone in the bar felt like going shark fishing with him. He was leaving now, but everyone was tired and all declined—everyone but Kristine.

Midnight stood as the border between two worlds, night and day. Night no longer meant time to fall asleep, no more futile attempts to drift off or struggles *not* to drift off. She celebrated the fact that she no longer had just until midnight. The sound of the boat making its way through the water sounded like a little kid splashing in the tub. She felt refreshed and wanted to swim but knew the difference between the safety of bath water and the ocean here. This water housed all creatures great and small, toothless and not toothless, full and hungry, all down under.

Lawrence showed her Cayo Costa State Park, part of the chain of barrier islands with the Charlotte Harbor on one side and the Gulf of Mexico on the other, only accessible by boat. The ten-mile limestone-based island stood completely undeveloped with a thick forest of pines and oak and palm hammocks in its interior, and mangrove swamps on the bay side. He claimed it was one of Florida's most primitive state parks and promised they'd step foot on it another time, during daylight.

They anchored about two miles north of Tarpon Key, where there were no other boats within sight. Except for a multitude of hawks overhead, nothing else could be seen. There were no stars, no clouds, and the moon was barely visible. Just black outer space and serene surroundings. No wonder Lawrence walked so freely in life.

He turned a bright flashlight onto the dark waters and pointed it toward glowing eels. Kristine wondered if the long, slithery snake-like creatures glowed naturally or only because the flashlight shone on them.

"Tell me, Lawrence, did you ever get nervous out here? I mean, what if your spotlight burns out?"

"It has burnt out and it will again, dear." He shifted some bait boxes over to one side of his tiny steel boat.

"What did you do? It's so dark."

"Dear, every one of us will lose our light or compass at some point in life. What do we do then?"

"We take out a flashlight or battery-operated radio?"

He smiled. "Long ago, ships didn't have compasses, or lights. They navigated by stars."

"But that was a long time ago. People are different today. We need modern guidance." She laughed.

"Let me tell you of one particular journey, dear, that happened long ago, when bad weather made sailing horrible. Although it was the worst season for sailing, the pilot set out because he didn't want to stay where he was. He had nice weather at first, but that changed quickly. He did anything to survive, even passing ropes under the ship to hold it together."

"Did this happen around here?" She looked around and could hardly see a line separating the black water from the horizon.

"No, somewhere near the coast of Africa. The men did all kinds of ingenious stuff out there. They tossed a weighted, marked line in the water, and this let them measure the depth. Every time they tossed the line, the water got less and less deep, indicating some kind of land."

"Well that must have been good news."

"No, they feared they might crash into rocks, dear. This fear made them drop the anchor, and they prayed for daylight."

"Sounds like something I can relate to in my own way."

"Of course you can. We've all had our dark days of life, dear, and even darker nights."

"So what did they do?"

"The sailors wanted to escape the ship so they dropped the lifeboat down into the sea. A man named Paul told them that unless they stayed with the ship, they wouldn't be saved. They listened."

"They must have been scared to death."

"Paul assured them not a single strand of hair would be lost from their heads. Then he urged them to eat. He broke bread and gave thanks to God. In the morning they saw a sandy beach."

"I've made journeys like that, Lawrence. I've never sailed the seas and I've never been shipwrecked, but I've spent endless nights wondering if I'd ever see the light of day."

"Then you've been through adventures in life, Kristine. Don't underestimate the journeys you've gone on. They don't have to be geographical or physical journeys. Everyone has their dark days of life when the storms seem never-ending."

"Lawrence, where did you hear of that story?"

"In the Bible, the book of Acts, chapters twenty seven and twenty eight," he said.

Several dolphins playfully escorted their boat back to Tarpon Key, and Lawrence explained that they have a high order of intelligence and a complex language of their own.

℘

Kristine loved being outdoors, but she had never enjoyed it the way she did here, under the stars on the ocean off the coast of Florida. She couldn't remember ever closing her eyes while standing outside in Michigan, in the yard or anywhere. Why didn't she ever do this before? *What does Michigan's air smell like? What does it feel like? Do its stars differ from these stars? Does the moon look different from Michigan than it does here in Florida?* She regretted never taking the time to savor her own state's environment.

She longed to stand outside in her yard in Michigan, to close her eyes, to smell, to feel, and to tear a leaf off a tree and hold it in her hand. She would do that when she returned. She promised herself to notice all of nature more, to feel it and enjoy it. Even if it meant doing an angel in the snow, she would do it. She tasted the salty tang of the air as she took in a breath and felt the warmth of the night's temperature on her arms. She looked up, saw no stars, then closed her eyes and inhaled deeply. She could *breathe*.

℘

Much happens between the hours of sunset and sunrise. Sometimes, issues become clear in late-night conversations or spells of insomnia. Other times, they work themselves out in our dreams, as if our brains surrender to some other existence and in the morning, our subconscious minds have it all figured out for us.

The restaurant sounded boring without Marie's laughter in the morning, and Kristine knew she had left for New York City. It was by no means a coincidence that this New Yorker had spotted the tiny blurb in *The New York Times*—a blurb so powerful personally to her that it motivated her to journey from the Atlantic Ocean to the Gulf of Mexico to find the tiny island she had read about. After all that, how dare she turn and head against the wind without giving the island a chance? In a matter of time she would hear it echoing, calling her back, whispering for her to escape for a moment, perhaps a lifetime, to go somewhere that allowed her to look at her life through a telescope from far away, to change that life if need be.

Howard no longer sat on the upside down bucket in the kitchen. After the game of darts, he had caught his own private charter off the island, never saying a word to anyone as to where he was going or why he was leaving. Denver acted shocked, although Kristine wondered if he might know more.

19

Like reading entries in her journal, the days flipped by quickly. Some days hardly got the descriptive entries they deserved, but recording life was becoming a preoccupation for Kristine. Sometimes, while observing life from a safe ten feet away, she would rather have dropped her pen and paper, and played the part of a character, to have become emotionally and physically involved without any thought or purpose. Just how obsessive could a diary or an on-going letter to her grandmother truly become? She wondered. Well, for the detail-oriented perfectionist that she was—creating daily lists of things to do that had to be so artistically and grammatically correct—any correspondence, no matter how short and insignificant, was becoming a novel in the making.

So much of life never gets put down in ink, and as a result, will be forgotten as soon as one's memory fades or the person who experienced it dies. Kristine wrote about the things that mattered most to her, of the personalities and issues facing the strangers on the island. In doing so, she could feel her circle of comfort growing wider, as did her worldview. This was reflected in her collection of shoes.

Some shoes fit. They weren't necessarily her style, or from stores she'd ever shop at, but they did fit. She made them fit. If it meant putting on eight pairs of socks, this she would do. But some styles felt so out of proportion to her own feet, she couldn't get them on even when she tried, socks or no socks. These were the times she wore wooden shoes, not minding that others wore flip-flops.

Why write of shoes? *Grandma would surely relate to such a metaphor,* Kristine wrote. *Her tile sandals, allowing her toes to get wet, walked her down the beaches of Sanibel Island each spring when Kristine and her sister came for a visit. Her red satin slippers escorted her to plays and dinners, easily sliding off when the lights were dim and her toes requested freedom. The Indian Moccasins slowly and silently walked her to the coffee shop each morning in Saugatuck, then quickly walked her home, fueled by caffeine. Those thick rubber white gym shoes that matched perfectly with her bulky gray jogging suit, trekked her comfortably to the family reunion in Michigan one cold Christmas. The grandchildren had wanted so badly to rescue Grandma's tiny body from that oversized gym suit. Finally, her furry pink slippers—they went to pizza parlors and danced to Elvis in her apartment. Perhaps they took her the farthest.*

Nights passed swiftly, as fast as it takes to tie a shoestring. Kristine wore cream-colored high-heel strapped sandals for her date with Steve. He picked her up at her parents' rental home, and they spent the night snacking from a picnic basket and lying on a blanket on Fort Myers Beach, down near the nearly deserted tip that overlooked Sanibel Island.

"Hmmm, treating every date like it's our last, I like that, Steve." She rubbed the silky petals of the roses he gave her.

"And treat each day like it's your last. My philosophy is that you should do at least one thing a day that you'll remember. I don't mean errands or tasks, but just one unique thing. For instance, years to come, I might not remember anything about today, but I will remember the roses because they're something I did for you, not me." As he spoke, he carefully stacked seashells into the shape of a building in the sand.

She opened a package of wheat crackers and started spreading one with crab dip. "Your job as an architect is going to have lasting impacts. You're designing some of the most modern-looking condominiums in

Bonita Springs. Look what you're contributing. You're like an artist whose work will exist long after your life does."

"Unless a hurricane comes along." He popped a green grape in his mouth. "Nothing physical is permanent."

"Okay, okay. A tornado, a sinkhole, a hurricane might take down a building or two, but that's out of your control. Without acts of nature, your buildings will stand tall and proud for years to come."

"I'm not sure that buildings are the legacy I want to leave behind. I've got to leave a legacy, but I'm not sure what. What kind of legacy do you want to leave?"

"I can't think of anything concrete that I could leave."

"Your diary, or those letters to your Grandma. Maybe some day the letters will become a novel. If not, leave them for your own grandchildren. That's a legacy in its own way."

"I don't know that I could ever be content with anything I write, especially not something as lengthy as a novel. What if I put so much time, as I know I would, into making it my absolute best, and then find out, thanks to reviewers willing to remind me, that it really is a horrible book?"

"Christine, that is why we enjoy the process leading up to our goals. That is why we must enjoy the journey toward our goals as much, and perhaps more, than the moment we reach those goals."

He collapsed his shell building and kissed her quickly on the lips.

꽃

She awoke on her second day off the island with a strong craving, and because Solomon says there is a time for everything—a time to be silent and a time to speak—the time had come for her to be silent and alone. After weeks of company and listening to the stories of others, she wanted now to listen to herself. She longed for this time as much as one might for a day at the spa, a mud mask and pedicure, the works. She needed silence as badly as a woman balancing on a trapeze, as if a single noise might shove her into midair, tumbling to the ground. Solitude sounded as comforting as lying in a bed with feather pillows and cotton sheets and covered with a big cozy blanket. She neither knew nor cared what she might say to herself, nor what she might hear. Perhaps she would mentally pamper herself for existing in a constantly changing world. There was no harm in pampering one's soul from time to time, acknowledging its journey.

She drove over the causeway to Sanibel Island, then drove further to Captiva Island. Her mind told her hands exactly where to steer the car. She needed to go there. She needed to go someplace related to her comfortable past, yet one that would invite her to walk toward the future, stopping first to enjoy the present, of course. Grandma had spent her winters in a condominium on the beach. Every spring break of every year in high school, Kristine and her sister went there to visit. Every morning they walked the beach of Captiva. Before each trip, they'd count down days. When the annual trip to Florida rolled around, they savored those days, and when it passed, they remembered them.

Much older and alone now, she grabbed a handful of the sizzling hot white sand and let it sift through her fingers. She tossed the broken shell chips into the water and started walking along the crunchy seashore, a forced emporium. At first, she noticed the shells in a detached sort of way. *Florida Fighting Conch*—three-inch-long shells, rich in orange and brown to deep mahogany shades—seemed to be the majority. They shared the sand with scallops that looked like stone fans, and whelks, which were orange, white and brown, like little pounding tools. She felt guilty stepping on the external skeletons, so she kneeled down, not minding the summer's warm waves washing up to her. She dug her hands in the wet sand and discovered coquinas, shy and buried just under the surface of the sand. Each time a wave came in, the miniature pastel-colored shells would be revealed for a second, before the live creatures inside managed to pull their shells under again. A few shorebirds down the beach looked to be feasting on the coquinas, and Kristine got up and ran toward them, interrupting their breakfast and forcing them into the air.

She walked for miles, someone at the low end of conchology, appreciating shells for their looks, nothing more. She knew nothing about them, only their beauty. She wondered if architects ever modeled winding staircases or the interior of homes after the intricate mollusk homes. She'd have to ask Steve. Her beach combing lasted for hours and her appreciation turned almost obsessive. Her neck ached from looking down, but if she looked up, she might miss the most spectacular beach worn specimen of all. Fragmented seashells that once were whole and gorgeous somewhere out in the Gulf of Mexico were now getting smaller and smaller with every foot that walked the beach. She stayed selective. The shells of dead mollusks went in her purse, next to her lipstick and car keys. Seashells with living, slimy creatures inside were pitched into the waves. As for the starfish and sand dollars, it was hard to tell if they were alive or dead, so she tossed them back into the water. Her eyes followed the flying fuzzy starfish until it hit the water and sank. She squinted as she looked across the channel, past Northern Captiva Island. Somewhere out there, too far away to see, Tarpon Key grew like a mangrove out of control, a world invisible from here. But soon the summer would be over, and she'd leave on the staff boat for good. As she thought about leaving her comfort zone, she felt the newly hatched caterpillars in her stomach nibbling on their eggshells. The stages kept on coming and going—thanks to a couple of eggs that complete their development and later reproduce.

She remembered walking one day on the beach with Grandma, asking her the difference between butterfly and moth. "Butterflies are the angels of emotions and they come out at daytime," Grandma had answered. "Moths come out at night, like that which is dark, honey."

"Wouldn't your clothes smell better if you used butterfly balls?"

"Yes, but moth balls are meaner, tougher, better fighters."

She had walked the beaches of Saugatuck many times with Grandma and Jane. She and her sister would take the old wooden ferry across the river and bike to the beach, then make it back in time for their five o'clock shift in the ice-cream shop. Michigan's beaches were different from the beach she now walked in Florida. Lake Michigan turned her toes numb; the Gulf of Mexico felt like bath water. She wondered why Michigan's sand was yellow and Florida's, white. She used to grow tired making her way through the deeper, dune-covered Midwestern sand as compared to this hard flat Southwestern sand. She wished Michigan had fuller seashells like Florida but felt safer swimming with creatures of the lake as compared to saltwater creatures. She jumped over a jellyfish and watched a stingray glide along like a creature from *Star Wars*. In Michigan, she swam comfortably after the minnows with nothing to fear. Here, the Gulf of Mexico was too big and unpredictable for her to risk casual swims like that.

20

"Ruth, where is Denver this morning?" She asked when she returned to the island.

"He left. He left for good, Kristine. He said he had inherited some money. Seventy-five thousand dollars, so he claimed. Like I really believe that! Oh well, you know Denver." Ruth took a white filter off the shelf and started measuring five tablespoons of coffee grinds.

"I wonder what he's going to do with that kind of money?"

"Well I don't think he was telling the truth. It's a nice fantasy, and I'm glad to see he's got a good imagination. I couldn't help but laugh when he told me. I thought it was kind of funny."

"I hope he anchored here long enough to repair himself. I hope he spends it wisely."

"What?"

"Nothing. I'd better get ready for work."

℘

Like an old schoolhouse, that year after year seated different students in its same old wooden chairs and scribbled its perennial lessons on the same old chalkboard under the same old roof, nothing ever changed on Tarpon Key—except its visitors. They were always coming and going like ships, anchoring for a moment. Ruth, Lawrence and some of the island cooks were an exception to the rule. The cooks had stayed there many years, artists at their craft, broiling halibut and baking key lime pie day after day, to the utmost perfection. They liked the kitchen, their domain.

Having worked lunch, Kristine ran back to the staff house and changed into an evening dress. With time to spare before the dinner guests arrived, she plopped herself down on the mattress, wiping her eyes with the corner of the pillowcase. She missed the strangers she had grown to love in such a short time. She thought of Denver, the makeshift raft, and wondered if he had gathered enough twigs to fix his weak spots. She hoped he had taken enough time to repair himself, so much so, that he might arrive at his next destination stronger than a tanker.

She prayed that Evelyn wasn't victim to any more abuse. Some day she might realize she deserved a good life, and that she was as much of a person as anyone else. But first, she needed to get to know and trust God—not the strange spirits speaking through a deck of cards. What had they offered her thus far? They wouldn't even reveal who they were.

Howard remained the mystery of all mysteries. After his disappearance that morning, no one spoke of him again. Kristine couldn't wait to look up his Spanish contact. Maybe he could offer some clues concerning this caravel.

Marie sent a postcard from New York City, stating that some day she might make her way to the island again, but the timing of her last voyage hadn't felt right. She wrote that she lived in a crazy and dangerous comfort zone but that leaving would feel too uncomfortable. She lived like a buoy, bobbing up and down for breath, hanging in there. Kristine still wondered what sort of rough waters she was treading.

The world itself lost much value as people came and went so suddenly. High school students in Colorado were shot down in class. John F. Kennedy, Jr., his wife and sister-in-law crashed into the waters off Martha's Vineyard. They had been on their way to a wedding, of all things. Office workers were shot down in Atlanta, Georgia. A train wreck in India took hundreds of lives. Midwesterners died of summer heat stroke. Over 12,000 people died in an earthquake that shook Turkey during the night. They had gone to sleep not knowing the hour of their death. The quake itself lasted 45 seconds. Mourning and grief for all these victims would last for years. Death had come in a cruel manner, manifesting itself creatively in many costumes. These people, many young in age, had come and gone so quickly, too quickly.

Back in Michigan, students were buying their books and returning to campus where classes would be starting soon. Kristine tried imagining herself walking the campus in Holland…its perfect comforts of life and its pristine charm…and the bright young faces. She instead felt thankful for her living, breathing lessons on the island. Although she couldn't picture herself a part of university life just now, her mind rushed her through its seasons, and she longed to rake the lawn and smell the burning piles of orange crunchy leaves on the side of the road leading to her dormitory. She craved a mug of hot chocolate with marshmallows, and feeling her toes warm in front of the residence fireplace. She wanted to feel the first snowflakes of the season land on her eyelashes. Suddenly everything went gray, like a landslide burying her thoughts of both the future and the past.

She tried hard but in no way could she imagine herself in Madrid. She couldn't picture anything about Madrid, a place so far away, a place she had never seen. She blocked out all anticipation and allowed herself no expectations. She reminded herself to live only in the present and opened her letter to Grandma.

℘

> Dear Grandma:
> I've met a lot of interesting "ships" (short for friendships) this summer. It is good to anchor, every so often, in life. Eventually, anchorage spots become comfort zones,

where we fill up on wisdom, stories and interesting relationships. We need to rest in one place every so often too, before we can fuel ourselves to move onward again.

Yes, we're all just ships coming and going, and we're all propelled through life by different things, some by oar and sails and others by paddles and poles. Some have steam engines and boilers and some have internal-combustion engines or outboard motors. Some go through life in a purely recreational manner, while others stay practical. If a vessel is determined enough to stay on course, it will be strong enough to resist the waves banging against it. Some of us take on water and sink from time to time, while others constantly work to stay afloat. I've met all of these vessels.

I haven't begun to prepare for my journey to Spain. Why should I? I'd rather just live the moment and the moment is still anchored at Tarpon Key. I'll think about Spain when the time comes to set sail.

॰

That night during dinner, Ruth called her into the office. "Kristine, I'm so sorry. This letter came for you today and I forgot to give it to you. Please forgive me. It's been so busy around here."

"Thank you."

Kristine delivered a basket of warm muffins to a couple, then took a seat at a candlelit table in the empty front room. She tore open the letter and held it close to the flame of the candle.

Dearest Kristine:

I wanted this letter to arrive romantically, as a letter in a bottle, but the post office wouldn't deliver it that way and I can't control the currents of nature. Who knows where the bottle would have ended up if I just tossed it in the water and wished it toward Tarpon Key? Anyway, right now I'm sitting at the marina writing this to you. I know you're just a few miles out there, but without my owning a boat, it feels so much further. This fact has frustrated me many nights. Once I woke up in a sweat. In my dream I held on to a log and tried making my way out to see you, but the log broke and I woke up choking for air.

Anyway, I just got a call from my father telling me my mother is not feeling too well and it would be wise if I came home to see her. I think it might be serious, so I'm taking off right away. She brought me into this world, and when I died, her cries brought me back again. I owe this visit to her. My flight leaves in two hours.

This is not a letter of good-bye. I know I won't see you again before your trip to Spain, but still, I am not writing to say good-bye. Instead, I'm writing to remind you that you're entering a unique time in your life and to make the most of every minute and every person you meet. Don't declare someone your Mr. Right until you've met lots of different people.

Please remember, as you go through life, some things might be challenging and other things downright stressful and scary. Just remember too that this life is good and the next is better. I know that for sure.

I love you and always will. You know where to find me if the currents in your future lead you back here. I still remember the white roses I gave you. I think they might have given me more pleasure then they gave you. But that is my philosophy. Doing things for others makes life better. Those are the moments I like to remember.

If ever I decide to travel again, I will certainly let you know. Perhaps some day we can cruise the seas together.
Love,
Steve

She wiped her eyes with the letter, smearing the ink on a few words. She ran outside staring up at the sky, spinning around for a moment, searching for the moon. Sure enough, the moon and its fullness stood above, controlling the night. She looked out across the water and tried imagining Steve sitting on the dock miles away at the marina, but the night was black and she could see only the flickering white of a few sail boats anchored just past the island. She glanced at her watch and knew he had already landed in Mississippi. She looked back at the restaurant windows, warmly glowing from candlelight and remembered she had customers waiting for their dinner. She reminded herself his letter did not mean good-bye, yet he was older and would surely move on, as would she. She stepped into the ice-cream freezer in her mind. She had to. She had customers who were hungry and paying a lot of money for a once-in-a-lifetime dinner on a remote island in the middle of nowhere.

The caterpillar in her stomach had completed its feeding and wandered to a sheltered area where it could rest and cocoon.

21

Kristine awoke extra early to the sound of rain beating down on the staff house roof. It had never rained in the morning before, so this downpour she intended to enjoy. Ignoring the sudden rush of blood to her head as she bolted upright and bounded out of bed, she felt dizzy and almost fell to the ground. All summer she had wanted to shower in the rain. Now was her chance. She forced herself up and squeezed into her bathing suit, then grabbed her bottle of shampoo, conditioner and a bar of soap.

Outside, despite the cloudbursts, a miraculous slice of sunshine streamed through the green fronds of the palm trees, producing a tiny rainbow. She knew exactly where she wanted to shower, but had to close her eyes because the rain was coming down so hard. After she made her way to the top of the Indian mound, she raised her arms in triumph and, laughing with joy, began doing an imitation of a rain dance in honor of the Indians who had once inhabited this land. No one could see her. She had made sure to look around. Besides, who woke up this early in the morning? And if they did, they were probably eating breakfast in the restaurant, not frolicking out in the rain. She lathered her hair and rinsed it. The rain provided ample rinsing. She looked down, and her imprints in the mound started to flood. She looked up, but the force of the rain pounding on her tender eyelids hurt. Rain in Michigan would have to pound for forty days and forty nights just to equal one day's rainfall in this tropical area of Florida.

She opened her mouth and gulped the torrents of water streaming down her body. The rain was hitting so hard that she couldn't tell she was actually crying as she suddenly thought about the young woman who would never graduate from college, nor bake another batch of chocolate chip cookies, nor kiss another guy, nor walk down the aisle arm-in-arm with her father. More thoughts of her friend flooded her mind. Lauren would never be a grandmother rocking in her chair, reminiscing about things of the past. She would never be a Mommy either. Her tears joined the rain drenching her.

Lauren used to describe a future nursery as if she were with child. Instead of nursery rhyme characters and commercialized patterns, she had planned on painting clouds toward the ceiling and soft blue waves on the wall near the floor. She said she'd get pictures of boats, a tugboat would be one of them, and she'd frame them in white wood on each of the four walls of the nursery. It hadn't mattered that Lauren didn't even have a boyfriend at the time of these aspirations. She was a romantic and knew it would all happen some day. That was the kind of woman Lauren was. She and her husband would have a baby boy, and his name would be Noah. After Noah, they would have a baby girl and name her Grace. She would raise her son to respect women, to wash dishes for his wife some day, to tell his mother 'I love you, Mom,' to care for creatures abandoned on the side of the road, and to adore Jesus. Kristine once teased her that Noah would end up a monk with all those traits, but Lauren continued talking of Noah as if her entire life would suddenly make sense and become important once she was a mother.

Now the idea of Noah's ark was dead. It hadn't survived long enough to bring Noah to life. The pain of thinking about what might have been washed down Kristine's face along with the rain as she stared at the mud massing about her feet.

Suddenly, she wondered if she made the most of her summer at Tarpon Key. Did she appreciate the songbirds that proudly sang every morning? Did she truly listen to the strangers around her? Did she convert them into friends? Did she touch their lives as much as they did hers? Did she learn from them? She felt as if the doctor had just granted her one more day to live and she wanted to savor everything—the saltwater air that so often blew her hair into her eyes, the afternoon wind, the squirrels running down the sandy trail in front of her, the view from the top of the water tower—all these things and more. Time ticked by too quickly, and she felt frantic—frantic because she would never be twenty one years old again. That time had come and gone, nothing would be the same and nothing could match it, ever. She already envied her younger self just starting her adventure on the island three months ago.

It was then that she had left behind the comforts of her hometown, her family business and her best friend. She left on an adventurous journey through dark, wavy, unfamiliar waters. But worse than the mystery of the waters, she didn't know herself, or what class of vessel she was. It took Denver to tell her that. As she rinsed the conditioner from her hair, she remembered those dark days of not knowing how to grieve, or handle death, or deal with loss or change or new things to come, whatever they might be. She also realized she had moved on.

Summer had slipped into Fall, and later that day she would be leaving on the three o'clock staff boat. She looked around as the downpour switched to dribbles and wondered what part of life ever remained constant. Shadows fluttering about caught her attention. She looked up to find five white doves flying overhead. Their feathers were as smooth as petals of white tulips as they nestled on higher ground, away from the mud. She had never seen doves around the island and felt her spirits soar as she listened to them cooing, one to the other. They reminded her of Lauren's angels, and she thanked God for lending her Lauren's angels for the summer. She now offered them to someone else in need.

The doves lifted their wings and, in the twinkling of an eye, disappeared behind a palm tree.

※

Before the lunch crowds arrived, she had piled her suitcases in a closet in the restaurant. Now, in the bar, she took a dollar from her purse, grabbed a black magic marker and wrote on the bill: *Ships come and go, anchoring for a moment—Kristine Longheart*. She handed it to the new bartender and ordered a diet coke. He laughed as he taped it to the ceiling of the bar. Next, she signed the guest book at the hostess stand: *Tarpon Key, a magnificent place definitely worth a second visit*.

Once her last table of customers was gone, she gathered her suitcases and said farewell to the bartender, the cooks, then Ruth, standing at the hostess stand by the front door. "Go, don't even think about getting a hug from me. Get out of here, Kristine."

"This is not easy, Ruth. I don't want to go."

But she could sense Ruth was not comfortable with good-byes, so she walked out, letting the screen door gently slam shut behind her.

She walked down the sandy trail to the staff boat. Without looking behind her, she kissed two of her fingers, then extended her arm behind and waved just as Grandma always did at the airport in the fall. It was the authentic good-bye wave. The only thing missing was Grandma's tinted black sunglasses that she always put on first thing in the morning on the day of her departures.

Lawrence started the staff boat, and for a minute, Kristine could feel the eyes of the dock master on her. Ignoring his compassionate regard, she sat tearfully savoring the smell of the salty air. One of the nation's bald eagles swept above her in search of a channel marker to land on. For a moment, she felt sure she saw the national bird, endangered or threatened, she didn't know which, flying in sync with its cousin, the osprey. Donning her sunglasses, she watched Tarpon Key grow smaller and smaller as the boat sped away at top speed. She didn't think for very long about the pelicans and laughing gulls following the boat. Instead, she found herself already mourning the tropical mangrove located at a channel marker in the Intracoastal Waterway, just eight miles south of Charlotte Harbor. She didn't know which she loved more, the people or the place.

She noticed the boat slowing down sooner than usual and realized Lawrence wanted to talk. "Dear, you must read some of Hemingway's works. Please, I can't stress enough how magnificent you will find them. Especially now that you've lived in the tropics, and now that you're off to Spain. You will appreciate his magnificent writing. *Death in the Afternoon* might better prepare you for a bullfight. Do be open-minded when you go."

"I will, I promise I'll read Hemingway, and I'll try to be open-minded at a bullfight."

"Dear, it's been magnificent having you on Tarpon Key and I know you'll move on with your life." He had a sparkle in his eye. "But I also know this place will remain in your heart forever. Do come back and visit. You owe that to yourself."

"Thank you for that first boat ride to the island. I didn't know if I should take the job or not, but you convinced me. Thank you."

"Kristine, you have such a bittersweet look on your face right now."

"I feel bittersweet. Bitter because I don't want to leave the island and sweet because I'll have such good memories of it."

"Well, you've got quite a magnificent adventure ahead of you."

"Yes, Spain. It's time to think of Spain now."

22

"Is the bittersweet look gone? It better be because the time has come," she told herself in the mirror. "You've got to think *Spain* now."

She fought back tears, hugging her father good-bye after he turned the volume down on his police radio. Almost late for work, he didn't offer his many fatherly cautions so typical of him. "What can I say? You're going to another country today. At this point, I can only tell you to use your common sense, and I know you will," he said. "Oh, and perhaps most importantly, do not carry luggage or anything on the plane for anyone else."

"I know, Dad, stranger danger. Besides, I've got way too much of my own luggage." An indecisive, always-be-prepared person, she only wished she was the type to go to Europe with a pair of Levis and a white T-shirt, but no. First she made a list, then she packed. Wardrobes meant complexity. There might be an early morning chill, late afternoon heat, rain, or wind. Clothes served several purposes…weather barriers, fashion statements, camouflage, or notice-me standouts.

"I love you, honey."

"I know you do. I love you too, Dad."

Later that day, her mother and little sister took her to the Fort Myers airport. It had been raining off and on since she woke that morning, but now the rain came down as hard as if the angels above were tossing water balloons. Suddenly, like an adult terrified of cold water hitting their hot skin, she didn't feel ready to leave the country. She wanted another day at home with her family and after that, another day on Tarpon Key. She wanted time with her mother, to shop, enjoy lunch, drink coffee, make cookies.

Her mother was thinking the same. "I wish we had had time for coffee," she said, just as a bolt of lightening lit up the window and an explosion of thunder blasted from a Heavenly microphone.

"I wish I had decided on the later flight. I wish we had just ten more minutes. I love you, Mom."

"I love you, too."

Neither could say another word. The time had come to leave. She walked the plank alone, the last to board the plane. A backward goodbye wave didn't satisfy her. She turned to see her mother in tears, arm-in-arm with her little sister, who didn't understand where or what Spain meant or why her big sister had to go there.

"I love you, Kristine," whined Katie.

"I know you do. I love you too. And hey, call me Kristini."

"Mommy, why does Kristini gotta go bye-bye?"

"Because it's her time to leave the nest and we love her, so we have to let her go, honey."

A fleeting picture of Katie, the pink little body newly arriving in the world a few years ago, crossed Kristine's mind. She was glad her mother had invited her into the delivery room on that special day and wiped her eyes. Welling tears blurred her vision as she boarded the plane. She could sense the already seated passengers, strangers, wondering about her story and why she cried. She wondered herself. She knew. She hated good-byes. When she thought of it, she was mourning because she wouldn't be saying 'hello' to Lauren at La Guardia Airport in New York, where they had planned to meet. They were supposed to be going to Spain together today. Lauren had promised to be her walking, talking dictionary, her interpreter, and best friend. She didn't know if she should be mad at Lauren for dying, or at herself for continuing onward to Spain without her.

She cried about anything she could think of. She cried for her tiger on that awful first day of pre-school when she carpooled with the bully-to-be. He punched Tiger's beautiful orange and black head until it almost bled. He twisted Tiger's gorgeous thick neck until it almost broke. He pulled Tiger's belly button until it fell onto the floor of the car. If only her mother had been driving that day. Her mother never would have let that happen to Tiger. She was glad she had a Mom who cared, who understood her love for Tiger, and who sewed his tummy button back on, and who made him a cake that night, and who bought him a new pair of pajamas. Yes, her Mom loved Tiger too, and this made her cry more—this time for the lightning bugs that the bully used to smear against the sidewalk, their God-given glow smeared out of them. Okay, okay, she told herself. Get off the bully memories. As Grandma would say, "Life is a bowl of maraschino cherries, and the red dye is poisonous."

She fidgeted with the seat belt that first felt too tight, then too loose. She found herself next to the emergency exit and considered changing seats, but then decided she liked the idea of having an easy escape if needed. She looked at the orange and maroon patterned seat cushion and imagined herself holding onto it as she flew through mid-air, landing in the Atlantic Ocean. But no, she'd never make it that far, and the very thought of an instant explosion that could end her life made her bend down and touch her toes. She could control her breathing, but not the plane. No, the pilot would control the plane. She considered walking up front to meet him, but the flight attendant started talking on the microphone so she stayed put. She again bent down, this time pretending to fuss with her purse under the seat. She caught a little air that way, not enough. She reached up to redirect the air control, aiming it in her face, and asked the people on both sides of her if she could turn their air controls towards her too. For the first time, she carefully watched the flight attendant describe the oxygen mask procedure.

Suddenly she felt the urge to jump up in front of everyone and go crazy. How would she go crazy? She didn't know. She could scream and jump about and pound on her chest. Maybe they'd let her off the plane. The oxygen mask instructions confused her and she wanted to test the procedure, but knew that people would stare. The last thing she wanted when she couldn't catch her breath was people watching. It only made it worse. A drink, she would order a drink immediately, a kahlua on the rocks. That would do.

"Pray; don't panic. Pray; don't panic," she chanted under her breath, then closed her eyes. *Oh dear God, please employ all my guardian angels to leave me, and instead put all their efforts into guiding this big plane. Please help the pilot steer and whatever else a pilot needs to do. May the Holy Spirit guide this man-made vehicle through the mysterious skies and repair any possible mechanical mishap.*

The darn creatures in her gut decided to rehearse again, but the plane's take-off disturbed their choreography and they scattered about inside her. She felt dizzy, as if she could feel the earth circling the sun. It seemed to be going faster than normal, but it couldn't be. That would cheat our calendar days. No fair. The earth must take its full three hundred and sixty five point two days to rotate fully. No speeding allowed.

She put the headphones on and for a minute she couldn't believe what she heard. She took them off. No, it can't be. She put them on again and closed her eyes, singing along with the music in the headphones. *I've spent oh so many nights feeling sorry for myself...*

She felt a nudge from the man next to her and realized that her singing was too loud, but couldn't resist. *I've got all my life to live, I've got all my love to give...*

As she sang, she observed the faces of everyone around her. The man who had nudged her had deep lines on his forehead. He must be stressed. He must be planning something big, something on this flight.

A baby cried two rows back. The baby must sense something about to happen. Sometimes young ones were more in tune with such things. She saw a woman rubbing her eyes. *Oh dear old me, she too notices this plane going too fast.* The teenager next to her looked completely zoned out. Perhaps the plane had reached too high an altitude. She studied the teenager for quite a while, her guinea pig, an indicator of the plane's oxygen level. For a good hour he zoned in and out, in and out, his eyes rolling to the back of his head.

As she sipped her second kahlua, she felt somewhat better, so she ordered another. Then she felt great and made a phone call home.

"Mom, hi, it's me."

"Honey? Honey, where are you? I can hardly hear you."

"I'm about ten thousand feet over the state of Virginia, Mom. I was just thinking how much I already miss you and I wanted to let you know that…you know, just in case something happens to this plane."

The man next to her cleared his voice and folded his newspaper. She knew he was eavesdropping but didn't mind.

Her mother's voice cracked. "Oh, we miss you too. I felt much better knowing you were out on that island than I do having you in some other country. Are you okay up there?"

"I'm okay, but there's not much oxygen, I'm noticing. It's just not normal at all."

"What? I still can't hear you too well."

"I said there's not a lot of oxygen up here. I think they're having problems. I think we've gone too high." She yelled much louder and the man cleared his voice again and looked around. The women seated one row ahead also turned and gave her weirdo glances.

"Did you bring a paper bag, honey?" asked her Mom, safely grounded in the kitchen of the rental home.

"No, but the plane has oxygen masks, and let me tell you, every person on this plane is going to be using them in a minute. It's getting worse, Mom."

Just then, the man seated next to her got up and disappeared behind the first class curtain.

"The guy next to me looks like an espionage spy, Mom. You should see him. He's got really deep worry lines on his forehead, and he's compulsively biting his lips. He's up to something. I know he is."

A woman in front of her also got up and disappeared behind the first class curtain.

"Now don't worry yourself. Don't do this to yourself. You're going to be just fine. Say a prayer."

"I did, but I still can't breath. It's driving me crazy."

"Honey, I don't like to ask this, but you're not drunk, are you?"

"Of course I'm not drunk, Mom! I just called to say I…I'm sorry, I just can't stop laughing…I…I love…it's so funny…no, I'm not drunk…of course not…I love you, Mom. That's all I've got to say."

Two flight attendants, the man who was seated next to her and the woman in front of her all returned at the same time. "Are you okay? Are you afraid of flying?" One of the attendants reached over and whispered quietly.

"Hey, Mom, I've got to go. I'm getting some special attention now from the flight officials. They're giving me a pair of wings to wear. I Love you, Mom."

"Wait, honey, you are on the flight aren't you? I mean, you're not lying are you?" She blew her nose. "Did you somehow get off the plane, and you're afraid to let us know you just aren't ready for Spain?"

"Everyone, say hello to my Mom, please."

"Okay, you *are* on the flight. You be careful now and call us when you get to Madrid. Are you going to make it?"

"I will survive. I will survive. I've spent oh so many nights feeling sorry for myself. Don't worry. I will survive. Oh, and Mom…thank you for making that cake for Tiger." Kristine hung up the phone and followed the attendant up to the first class area.

"I'm not doing good. I feel like I'm going crazy on this flight. It's as if I'm having a claustrophobia attack or something. I'm also leaving another comfort zone and I've never been good at that."

"Why don't you sit up here in this empty row? It'll give you more space. You know everything is under control, and the pilot is excellent." She waved her manicured red fingernails as she spoke. "His landings are always very smooth. We'll be going down very shortly now."

"Can you just knock me out? You know, hit me right here. I swear I won't press charges when I wake. I just think it would be better if I'm out cold for the rest of this flight."

"No, of course I won't hit you, but I'm sure some of the passengers back where you were sitting would love to. No, I shouldn't say that. They were a bit concerned about your conversation with your mother though. Now are you going to be all right? I've got to prepare the cabin for landing. It's time already."

"Sure, just one more drink please."

℘

> *Dear Grandma:*
>
> *Here I sit at La Guardia Airport in New York. Lauren hasn't arrived yet, and of course I know she won't come. Lauren was never late. She warned me not to be late for this flight and her last words were that she wouldn't board without me. But here I am, selfishly about to aboard the plane, alone. I still feel guilty, as if I don't deserve to go. I missed her funeral, and now I'm on my way to Spain without her. I have to respect what her mother wrote me in that letter. I have to celebrate her life, not mourn her death. It all takes time. Sometimes I slip back into grief.*
>
> *I just traded in some American money for pesetas, but I still don't understand how the two relate to one another. I*

gave one hundred dollars and got nine thousand pesetas. What a deal, I think?! Oh well, if I didn't have a ton to learn, this wouldn't be a learning experience. It'll also get easier once this kahlua leaves my system.

♫

At *Barajas* Airport, just nine miles outside Madrid, Kristine showed the taxi driver the address she had carefully tucked away in her purse. She silently applauded herself for having written it down in advance and now rewarded herself by sitting peacefully and passively in the back seat of the taxi, no verbal efforts needed. She had also decided to keep a pad of paper and a red crayon in her purse at all times, hoping she could simply scribble pictures of whatever she might need. She had chosen a red crayon on purpose. Lauren used the same color to scribble her goals on the white paper tablecloth that night. Now, in the back seat of the taxi, Kristine used the red crayon to draw a toilet; then a stick figure sipping a glass of water. Well done. Her most urgent, yet basic needs jotted down on flash cards, stored in her purse, just in case her Dutch accent dominated and perhaps completely trampled over her classroom-learned Spanish accent.

The taxi turned off a busy metropolitan street and pulled up to the curb of a narrow street, lined with meat markets, bread shops and tall apartment buildings decorated with black cast iron balconies. A woman in her late sixties stood on the curb holding a long thin loaf of white bread. As this woman watched Kristine carelessly toss the taxi driver some money, she wiped her hands on her food-stained apron, aggressively pushed some fallen strands of dark gray hair back into the clip of her bun, before holding her hands out to welcome the young woman from America.

The taxi driver deposited the luggage on the curb and drove away. Kristine held her hand out to the *señora*, but instead the Spanish woman walked up face to face and kissed her, once on each cheek. Kristine could smell the juice of freshly minced garlic on the woman's skin. Rosario placed the bread under her arm and grabbed two of the heaviest suitcases. Kristine felt embarrassed, as if the woman might be judging her a materialistic American unable to leave home without just about everything she owned shoved into that baggage. She placed her hands over those that smelled of garlic, but after a tug of war, surrendered, allowing the woman to drag her load up four flights of stairs.

The climb up the stairs felt long, like walking up the Eiffel Tower. All the way up, the out-of-breath woman offered her new guest a fast flow of shouting words, as if the climb itself had bonded them forever, more so than together reaching the top of Mount Everest might. The words came loud and fast and there seemed to be no space between them. The words, sentences and perhaps even paragraphs went unrecognized and sounded like static in her mind, or worse, like the sports station blaring as she sat captive in some athlete's back seat. The words hit hard and fast, and with her hands full and her dictionary tucked away in her pocket, she felt caught in the midst of a rainstorm with her umbrella at home.

"*Baño*," Kristine said once inside the apartment. It trigged no response. "*Baño, necesito baño, por favor.*" She felt her bladder ready to burst, like a water balloon hooked to the faucet, as big as it's going to get. Okay, if her words didn't sound familiar to Rosario, pictures surely would, unless Spanish toilets were designed differently from American ones. As she flashed the crayon drawing of what looked like a stick figure sitting on a donut, Rosario took grab of her hand and pulled her down the long, dark hallway with wooden floors.

After the water balloon popped, Kristine tried communicating again. "*Agua, por favor.*" No one could convince her that 'agua' didn't mean water, yet Rosario again stared in misunderstanding.

"*¿Qué?*" asked the woman.

"¿*Agua? Agua, por favor.*" She had heard the word on Sesame Street her entire life and the puppets pronounced 'agua' no differently than she was saying it now. But then, they were American puppets. Would Spanish puppets say 'agua' differently? How many ways could one possibly say it? After attempting some more unique pronunciations of the word, aware her Spanish professor might expel her from being a Spanish major if he heard, she took out the picture of the stick figure sipping a glass of water. Proving the worth of pictures, Rosario hurried down the long hallway once more, this time to the room at the end, the kitchen.

"No hurry, it's not that urgent," Kristine mumbled to herself as the woman slid around the corner, returning with a glass of *agua*, which still means today, and has always meant in the past, water in Spanish. "*Agua, agua, agua*," practiced Kristine out loud.

The tour of the apartment differed from the tour of the staff house. Kristine knew that Rosario spent most of her time cleaning to make the antique wooden table shine, the silver teacups in the hutch sparkle, and the bed linen smell like a breeze of fresh autumn air. For a moment she feared she might feel claustrophobic in her new room, which was not much larger than a walk-in closet, but the ceiling was high. The colors of the apartment, mahogany, rust and shades of brown sang out calmness and peace, like the colors of crisp leaves. Anything bright or pink would clash like a budding tulip in October.

Rosario pulled a chair out from under the dining room table and, with dramatic hand movements, motioned for her to sit down. Then she shouted over and over in Spanish something about soap and twins and *Christina, Christina, Christina*. It sounded as if she were saying there was a bar of soap that had a twin named Christina. Then the woman dramatically turned on the television and waved toward the screen.

Oh my goodness gracious! I can't believe what I'm seeing! Kristine covered her mouth with her hand. *It's a Spanish soap opera, and I look exactly like the woman on the screen only she's Spanish and not a true blonde.*

Rosario shook her head in disbelief as well, staring at the television, then at Kristine. "*Christina, Christina, ¿si? ¿si?*" She walked up to Kristine and again kissed her once on each cheek, then joined her hands together as if saying a prayer. Kristine felt so welcome, as if this woman had been counting down the days of her arrival. For their first hour together, the Spanish *señora* and the American student sat at the dining room table eating marinated black olives and watching a soap opera called 'Christina.'

At supper, they broke bread and ate. Rosario's chair remained empty as she ran back and forth into the kitchen for more courses to the meal. She had a keen eye for when the family wanted the next course and only then would she introduce it to the table. It started with red table wine, white bread and more olives. As she brought out a platter of anchovies stuffed with garlic and strips of pimento, she explained that life is meant to be savored, just like a meal. "Never rush any part of it," she said in Spanish, and Kristine proudly translated to English. "The appetizers are as important as the dessert. *Si*, the beginning is as good as the end."

Her husband sat on the end of the table, but didn't have the end-of-the table personality that one might expect. He closed his eyes as he chewed, opening them only to glance and smirk at his grown daughter across from him, his two grown sons, and Kristine.

Next Rosario brought out bowls of stuffed squid boiled in its ink, fried shrimp with cloves of garlic and seafood soup.

"Oh my goodness! My soup is alive! *Esta viviendo*, look!" Kristine screamed. "They're still moving!"

The tiny black snails must have been freshly dumped into the soup and hadn't boiled enough to be dead yet. They squiggled around frantically, taking cover under the hard-boiled eggs.

Kristine suddenly felt like a baby. She couldn't possibly eat this sort of food, no! No one had prepared her for this. Perhaps instead of all the grammar and history textbooks, perhaps her college curriculum should have included a Spanish cookbook. All eyes stared at her as she watched the creatures move about in her bowl. She brainstormed her escape quickly and knew all she had to do to break the silence was to start up a conversation.

"Um...um...*estoy embarazada*." There, she said it, or at least something like it. She told them she is full, or maybe she said embarrassed. She didn't know which came out.

Silverware dropped, as did a half-chewed anchovy from the father's mouth. Rosario covered her mouth like she did many times during the soap opera, and the grown children started talking rapidly all at once. Now she had a bowl of living creatures and an entire Spanish family in an uproar, all because she said she was full. It must have offended them.

"No, no. *Estoy lleno por que comi en el plano*." She gestured her hands to demonstrate that she ate while up in the sky in the airplane.

Rosario shouted something loudly, grabbed a maroon-colored velvet pillow off the sofa and shoved it down her shirt and into her stomach. The father pointed to his wife's stuffed stomach, then to Kristine's and questioned her.

"Oh dear, what did I say? No, I'm not pregnant. Oh no, misunderstanding. Wait, wait." Kristine slapped her stomach then flipped through the pages of her dictionary and sure enough, the word *embarazada* meant pregnant.

The family forgave the misuse of language but laughed and joked about it for quite some time. The grown sons and daughters laughed and spoke too, but Kristine didn't know what they said and didn't try to understand. The trip to Spain had been accomplishment enough. Perhaps she'd try interpreting another time. Now, she needed a rest.

Soon, the anchovies were eaten, and Rosario brought out a pan with various cold sausages, patés and small pieces of goat's milk and other cheeses. No one spoke a single word of English, and they all took turns speaking with their new arrival. After each of their questions, Kristine realized she only offered them little more than silly *goo goos* and *ga gas*.

Rosario served a colorful meal. Kristine could taste garlic, onion and tomatoes in the yellow rice topped with green peas and strips of red pepper. Rosario's husband took on the responsibility of educating Kristine on his wife's *comida*, slowly explaining that rice is a popular ingredient in Spanish cooking and any firm, white fish can be used with this dish. He patted his wife's plump behind as she filled his plate and everyone laughed some more. Then he picked up a mussel and a clam, and bragged that his wife spent much of her day cleaning the ingredients for this dinner. He shouted something at her and she ran into the kitchen and returned with a bowl of shells, as if to show Kristine where the seafood originally came from.

"*Mas, mas,*" said the husband as he broke off more white bread and dipped it in his rice.

Mas meant more, so Kristine got a second helping and a third after that.

After the ever-so-lively meal, Rosario brought out a bowl full of pears and apples, and they all continued to feast, proving the end was just as significant as the beginning.

23

As the sun started rising over the city of Madrid, so did the aroma of baking bread from the shops below. Both reached the cast iron balcony of the apartment ten floors up. The noise of the waking metropolitan city worked like an alarm clock each morning, drawing Kristine to the balcony. But Rosario scolded her for standing out there with bare feet, so this morning she put on a pair of socks and shoes and headed down the long hallway to the kitchen for their morning ritual of cookies and milk.

As she headed to the noise of Rosario clanging pots and pans, there was no evidence that the Spanish brothers, Diego and Michaelangelo, had been sleeping on the floor. Rosario always picked up their pillows and blankets as soon as her sons stood up each morning, and there seemed to be no resentment toward Kristine for having stolen their closet of a bedroom. The *hermanos* were fully grown men in their mid twenties and still living at home, now sleeping on the floor, and they held full-time jobs and had social lives in the city streets below. Some nights Kristine heard the brothers sneak in at around three o'clock in the morning, but it never upset the parents. And by the time she awoke, even Margarita, the daughter, had left for the day. She too stayed out until very late and Kristine wondered how they spent their nights on the streets of Madrid.

Was it anything like the nights on Tarpon Key? She missed staying out late, but interpreting a foreign language took so much of her energy, she collapsed into bed each night. This didn't mean she fell asleep right away. Often she lay on her back, staring at the high ceiling above her. It didn't matter that the brown paint looked dull and old. Sometimes she saw scenes of Hemingway novels acting themselves out, or ships coming and going, or tulips blooming then dying, or a clean white paper tablecloth or a pure white canvas—she didn't know which. At times the nights felt so never-ending and agonizing that she wondered if Michaelangelo both loved and hated the ceiling of the Sistine Chapel.

As she took her seat in the kitchen, Kristine wondered so many things, but didn't feel linguistically confident enough to ask. *I wonder why Rosario's husband, Lorenzo, has such a gigantic stomach! I wonder why everyone leaves the house, but Rosario. She cooks and cleans all day. I wonder why that dead animal is hanging on a rope upside down in the kitchen with its head cut off, and blood dripping from its neck into a pan.*

Suddenly, as if she had just finished listening to a motivational tape by Anthony Robbins, she felt a power within herself and knew she had to turn those pictures on her ceiling into words that could be used in the kitchen with Rosario, in the city streets below, and in the classroom. She closed her eyes and made the decision to advance her language quickly and return to adulthood, wondering no more. She would have to act quickly since she only had one semester, so she started by making it her goal to learn from Rosario in the kitchen each morning.

The *señora* poured warm milk into a mug and placed a roll of flat cookies on a plate next to a jar of marmalade. She never sat down with Kristine, but instead wiped counters, scrubbed the floors and poured more milk each time it got low. As the American woman nibbled on *galletas* and complimented the marmalade every other bite, the Spanish woman poured out her life, and boldly shared her opinions about everything.

Though barely understanding one another's native words, the women communicated. Kristine grew empathetic as Rosario's eyes saddened. She felt homesickness as Rosario's voice lowered. She felt anger as Rosario's hand wildly flailed in dramatic gestures around in the kitchen, and she felt frustrated as Rosario wiped her dirty hands on her apron and closed her eyes in silence.

Rosario told her how she missed her aunts, uncles, cousins, sisters, and brothers living in Pamplona. She shared how her husband loved food so much that his stomach had grown bigger and bigger by the day, and how she worried about his ever-growing *estomago*. She mentioned how her life consisted of nothing but cooking and cleaning, and how the collapse of the Franco Regime had accelerated a social/sexual revolution in her country and how, along with the downfall of Franco, came a downfall of morals. The *señora* liked the fact that birth control, abortion, divorce, homosexuality and adultery were all illegal under Franco. Now, *la gente* do all of these things and litter in the streets, pick public flowers, skip church and sunbathe nude along the coastal beaches. She shook her head in a tempered disbelief as she spoke.

Was Rosario saying she missed *Francisco Franco*? A man who ruled the country with an iron fist for forty years? Kristine spread some pear-flavored marmalade on another cookie and sipped her warm milk.

The mornings came and went, as quickly as the marmalade in the jar disappeared, and the two women continued communicating in a way that demanded more than simply traditional talking and listening. It required a keen observation of tones, hand gestures, facial expressions and body language. Kristine well understood her *señora* over morning breakfasts.

During the christening of a new jar of plum marmalade one morning, she slowly asked Rosario what she feared most in life.

"*Nada. No tengo ningun miedo,*" replied the woman as she hit the jar against the counter to loosen the lid. Fear no, anger yes, *si, si*. If fears won't go away, get angry at them. Drive them away because fears are the enemies! A Roman Catholic, a believer in Christ, Rosario explained that Christians shouldn't fear much, especially death! *El muerto* should hold no terrors because it is only the beginning of eternal life with God. If you're not ready to die, you're not ready to live, she shouted to Kristine in Spanish. She gave the sign of the cross and blew a kiss up to the ceiling.

℘

Kristine missed the mornings with Rosario, but her next two weeks were spent sight seeing throughout Spain with a group of other American students from various Midwest liberal arts colleges. The foreign studies program grouped them together initially to minimize culture shock and develop English-speaking contacts, should they be needed throughout the *semestre*.

Together they toured *El Museo Del Prado* and *El Palacio Real*. They drank pitchers of *sangria* and ate *tapas* in *masones*. They climbed to the top of the Roman aqueducts in *Segovia* and walked the Alcazon castle where Queen Isabella and King Ferdinand gave Christopher Columbus permission to go to the United States. It also claimed to be the castle that Walt Disney modeled his castle after. Their last few *dias* together were spent in and around *Cantabria*, a town lying along the Bay of Biscay, better known as *El Mar Cantabrio*. There they hiked the *Picos de Europas*—mountains in Northern Spain that rose to almost nine thousand feet—ate in exquisite restaurants, slept in bed and breakfasts and savored life.

℘

> *Dear Grandma:*
> *A mural of heaven! Some day, my dream is to own property in Los Picos de Europa and on that property I'd like a Spanish-style inn. I can't take such magnificent nature for granted. As our bus trudged up the winding*

mountains, wild bulls crossed the dirt road in front of us. Let me tell you, bulls do have the right of way in Spain, and they can take as long as they like.

I also spotted a tiny, solitary fisherman standing on a stretch of sand at the foot of the immense weather-beaten cliff. I wonder what his catch options are in water like that. Tarpon? Shark? Wales? I'd love to go fishing with him. I hear those waters host some of the finest seafood in the world. Then again, I heard it from a boastful little old Spaniard who was chopping wood. These people are so proud of what they have, of their magnificent country.

Hiking through the mountains was so treacherous, we got dizzy, but I felt like it was the highest and closest I've ever stood to Heaven. It began down pouring, and I fell quite a distance, cutting my knee, but I still felt such an exhilarating high. I felt in tune with God and his beauty, his art.

I don't think I want to return to Madrid. It's such a busy city! It's too much of a culture shock from the island. Maybe I'm just in that purgatory stage, lingering between two comfort zones. Will I ever love Spain as much as I loved the island?

Anyway, I took photos of my seafood soup at night. In it were foreign looking shells far different than the shells of Sanibel Island.

૭

After spending the night in a quaint valley inn, situated in the mountains of Spain, Kristine dreaded leaving the next morning. She longed for more time to walk with the roosters of the country and to talk to the old toothless, parched-faced farmers chopping wood in their backyards.

The natives of the valley had an ignorance that seemed pleasantly pure. She wanted to sit in the geranium and laundry-filled porches of the little inn and write letters to Grandma. She liked the cold, wet valley air that cleansed her pores. It reminded her for a moment of Michigan's chill. About this time of year the crispy leaves would start to fall, delicately covering the ground of Lauren's gravesite.

The tour bus left, and the group spent the next three nights at a luxurious three-star hotel in a city called *Llanes.* There they drank *Sangria* and *Cedra* and ate fried squid and *tapas* under the moon overlooking the sea. They swam the icy waves of the *Mar Cantabrio.* Kristine and some other Americans lay down on their backs in the sand near the shore so the waves rushed over their bodies, stealing a breath or two. They danced way past midnight at flashy *discotecas.* They lived a lot and slept little.

Kristine liked her new friends, but knew they'd have to separate back in Madrid. She was here to live the life of the Spanish, and hanging out with fellow Americans would spoil that. The entire group of American students made plans to sightsee in France, and they were already purchasing their train tickets. They tried persuading Kristine to go along, but she refused. No, she needed to experience Spain, to live the life of the Spaniards. Playing American tourist would ruin that. She only had a few short months in Spain, so why leave for France? She needed to make the most of her time, getting to know the Spaniards. France could be another trip, another semester, or an after-graduation reward. She didn't know and she couldn't think about France or any other country now. No, she could only think of the present and the present was Spain. The others went without her and she was glad.

24

Back in Madrid, the city felt cold, crowded and dirty compared to the Spanish countryside, but Kristine knew it would only be a matter of time before she found that one special place—the water tower, the dock, the rustic bar. It might be a challenge finding it in a metropolitan city, but she felt determined. She would eventually discover a place to think, to dwell, to escape. Such secret places made time go by more slowly and new places a little more comfortable. Rosario had two such places in life, the apartment and the church on the corner. She made daily stops at the meat market and bread shop but spent most of her time in the apartment or at mass.

The day before classes began, Kristine had mailed a letter to Ignacio Guillermo. She kept it brief, simply stating that she had met a friend of his family's while on a little island in Florida. His name was Howard. She included her Spanish family's phone number and suggested he call to arrange a time and place to meet.

§∂

Dear Grandma:
I especially feel drawn to the Prado Museum and the Centro de Arte Reina Sofia National Museum. I plan to

return often. I realize now just how many stories a museum has to tell. Every painting, every piece of art represents a story. When I first stood outside the glass showcase of Picasso's final "La Guernica" at the museum, I could almost hear the voices of crying mothers with dead babies, screaming soldiers in pain, and dying horses. The twelve foot high, twenty-six foot long canvas shared a gruesome, destructive story of the Spanish Civil War.

Then the Spanish tour guide explained the symbolism behind it. The open mouths signal the person is alive, while the closed mouths mean the person is dead. The toro represents the country of Spain and hope for overcoming Fascism, while the arm holding the light points out the hope for Spain. The picture itself depicts the saturation bombing of a Basque village by German planes. I feel guilty now, but at the time, I couldn't help it. I took a photograph of La Guernica, and I don't think I was supposed to do that. As the guard came running, I hid my camera under my shirt and took off.

And Palacio Real! What a great place to hold a wedding. But since the Eighteenth Century, its sole purpose has been to hold receptions for the royal families and ambassadors. A few Spaniards asked me why there isn't royalty in the United States. I told them there are. We call them "celebrities," and they live in Hollywood.

As for culture shock? Well, I've grown up near Midwest cornfields and streets lined with tulips and I've never taken a subway before. Now, I have to take a subway that announces the stops in Spanish. I guess I also tend to smile at everyone who walks past me in the city. Our tour guide noticed and told me not to be so friendly, it could be 'peligroso.' It seems a bitterly cold thing to do, but I guess I'll smile less.

℘

With a less than typical smile, she proceeded to walk about a mile to Madrid's *Complutense* University for her first day of classes. Dressed in black velvet pants, a red and black Spanish-looking button-down sweater bought in Florida, and new black, pointy European shoes, she felt fashionably dressed with the rest of the Spanish culture around her. Her blonde hair, with no dark roots, and her fair complexion were sure American give-a-ways as she walked the downtown streets, stopping along the way for an *espresso* topped with milk and a thin triangular tuna fish sandwich on white bread. As she walked, male voices called out several *'rubias'* to her. This meant blonde, and she knew they were only complimenting her. She looked just like a Spanish soap opera star. In America, she'd glare back, but in Spain, she knew men were only throwing out compliments as they shouted things out to women walking by, a cultural thing. As long as they didn't bark or meow like a cat, she didn't mind so she smiled a 'thank you' and continued walking, no eye contact. Women hate men gawking, yet if they don't gawk, they secretly wonder why.

Like the hour hand of a clock, she felt in sync with the hours of Madrid. Street life awoke at around eight in the morning, shut down for *siesta* from around two to four o'clock, then picked up again all afternoon and ticked well into night. Restaurants overflowed with people between the dinner hours of nine-thirty and midnight, bars were packed by eleven-thirty, and traffic continued until three.

Her time for education had come. As she walked under a huge stone arch in the northwestern part of the city, she could see her destination, the campus, just a couple of blocks ahead, west of Madrid. Under the fresh colors of the morning sky, the campus appeared as a scribbled-down item on her life's list of goals. In a few minutes she'd be sitting in a classroom, officially a foreign student studying abroad. If she had a question, oh well. If she didn't understand something, oh well. She was told her professors would not understand English. And if they did know just a bit, they wouldn't let her know. While in *their* country, she would speak *their* language. Those were the rules. She felt scholarly, so she dipped into her book bag and took out the fake eye spectacles she bought at K-Mart for five dollars.

"*Perdoname, Señorita, perdoname.*"

She heard his voice louder than the other voices on the street and her woman's intuition told her he was talking to her. *Don't look and definitely don't smile,* she reminded herself. *You're not in Holland, Michigan. You can't be nice to everyone.*

She tried hard to act in a PMS sort of way, both glaring and ignoring the voice from behind her. She put her spectacles on, stared straight ahead, and pushed her hair behind her ears in a bold, confident manner.

"*¿Puedes ayudarme, por favor?*" The male voice was asking her for help.

She stopped to look in a bakery shop window but wasn't looking at croissants. In the reflection of the window, she could see a man in a car pulled up to the curb. Rolling down his front window, he beckoned to her. *Okay, in times of potential crisis, a glance can't hurt.* She turned and smiled.

"*¿A donde esta el calle norte?*" He only needed directions to North Street.

She took full notice of the Mercedes and the man leaning out the front window. She hadn't seen a lot of nice cars since she got to Madrid. No, actually, for some reason, she did feel a bit safer knowing he drove an expensive car. In a stereotypical way, it meant he might be educated, professional. Maybe he enjoyed the prestige of owning classy transportation or maybe he drove long distances to work from a home in the country, a hidden getaway, and needed a well-engineered car—her imagination took over. *Okay, he could have stolen it, or could have smuggled drugs or something. Okay, you're analyzing things way too much,* she told herself. *You've already smiled so the damage is done.*

"*Yo no hablo espanol.*" She just told him—in Spanish that is—that she didn't speak Spanish. *Smart,* she sarcastically told herself.

"*¿Porque estas aqui, en Madrid?*"

If she understood him correctly, he had just asked her why she was in Madrid if she didn't speak Spanish. "*Porque, estoy estudiando a la universidad de Madrid.*"

She pointed at the university campus straight ahead, feeling quite confident that she had constructed a solid sentence. Words came to mind and one by one, they formed a complete sentence, probably not in the right conjugation, but they made a sentence.

In a slow, educated Spanish dialect, he said, "*Un estudiante. Si, si. Pues, poly vu Frances?*"

Did she speak French? *¡Oh, por favor!* She just spoke the most perfect *espanol* of her *vida* and now he wanted to know if she spoke French as well. Well, they weren't wasted moments after all, she told herself, those times washing her hair in the shower. She did know some French because she spent every morning reciting and memorizing the French descriptions and "to use" instructions on the back of her hair conditioner bottles. Yes, she could speak a little French, as long as the conversation centered on shampoos and hair rinses.

Removing her fake spectacles after they fell down her nose, she replied, "*Si, la solucion demelante. Mode d'emploi. Appliquer sur les cheveux propes.*"

The man laughed. "*Tu eres Americana.*"

She nodded and smiled. He guessed that right. She looked and sounded American—whether speaking Spanish or French. She studied his eyes behind real eyeglasses, amused eyes, and felt curious about his story. Like so many men, fine age lines only added to his appeal. Why was it that aging men grew more handsome, while women just got more wrinkled? She wondered why she understood his Spanish better than any other Spaniard she'd ever heard. His words came clearly and easily, and listening to him, she felt as comfortable as she might if standing in her favorite section of the bookstore. She understood his words as quickly as it took her to read the titles on the spine of a book. She didn't have to read the fine print; the title said it all. Maybe he just spoke slower than the other Spaniards, out of courtesy.

She asked him if he spoke English, to double check that their conversation didn't just take place in English.

No. He spoke Spanish, Italian and French, and explained that the people in his country tend to speak fast so she shouldn't get discouraged. He told her that soon she'd be dreaming in Spanish.

He put his car in park and opened the door. She suspected she had gone too far, that she should never have smiled or stopped in the first place. Her tour guide had warned her, but she lived in Spain now and wanted to learn the culture. How could she do that without chatting with its people? The distinguished man getting out the car wore a gray turtleneck with black dressy pleated pants. He came up to her and stood too close, invading her comfort zone. She took a couple of steps backward, but he drew closer again. She reminded herself to buy some gum later because Spaniards like standing face to face when they talked. They conversed with no fear of spitting or coffee breath. And up close, they still talked just as loud as Americans who are standing several safe feet away from each other. She understood this about him, so he didn't offend her.

In Spanish, the stranger told her she spoke proper Spanish and started to chuckle. His laugh grew louder, more effervescent, and didn't stop.

She stared at him in disbelief. Feeling offended, she asked him why he was laughing. What had she said?

After a few minutes, he wiped his tears and confessed that her Spanish sounded quite antiquated, at least a few centuries old. He told her to imagine a Spaniard in the modern-day United States, but speaking Shakespeare.

"Great. Thou art a complete weirdo," she mumbled to herself. She had no idea that her choice of words included ancient verses only used in *libros*, though books were where she learned most of her Spanish. She defended herself by telling him about the Ancient Spanish literature class she took at college last semester. No wonder her words sounded a bit outdated. But, that's why she came to study in Spain, to transform words learned from a book into living breathing conversation.

From her language style to her clothes, the observant outspoken stranger sounded as if he were writing a commentary. She felt alienated and abducted, and wouldn't have been surprised if he had drawn out a silver needle to probe her next.

Instead, he asked about her red and black sweater. Where had she bought it?

Simple question and simple to answer, she thought. She told him JC Penny's in Florida.

He laughed again, for quite some time, and once more, she didn't understand why. Then he asked her how she liked wearing the pointy shoes of *Europa*.

She desperately needed to complain to someone about the narrow eighty-dollar pair of shoes she had bought, and felt like a native as she yelled at the black torture devices on her feet. She told him she couldn't wait until the end of the day so she could change into her comfortable American loafers. He bent down and touched her shoes, and that she found very odd.

All this time, his car engine was still running, so finally he excused himself, *un momento*, and returned with the keys. "*¿Perdoname, como se llames? ¿He sido hablando, pero no he preguntado su nombre?*"

She caused a moment of silence, understanding his question, but debating whether she would actually give her name to a strange older man in Spain, a stranger with a fascination in her clothes, her shoes and the ancient style of her language.

"Kristine." She replied.

"*¿Christina?*"

"Kristine."

"*Christina, que hermosa! Como el fatima del opera!*" He kissed her once on each cheek, then asked for her last name, too.

"*Christina. Christina de los Estados de Unidos.*" She smiled. He'd have to settle for that—Christina from the United States. "*¿Quien esta?*" She asked his name out of politeness.

He played along with her game. "*Yo soy Rafael. Rafael de Espana.*"

She asked Rafael from Spain where in Spain he lived.

He explained that he came to Madrid frequently on business, but lived on a yacht in northern Spain. He worked as a fashion designer in Spain, Italy, and France.

Sure, she thought, suspiciously, feeling ahead of the game. *I've read Danielle Steele. He probably wishes he worked as one. What an innovative way to capture my attention! Me, a young, naive Americana falling for a pretend European fashion designer. Please, Rafael, just be yourself. You're a nice hombre. Besides, I'm not attracted to you because you drive a Mercedes, nor because you dress well. These things don't make a person. Better yet, I'm not attracted to you at all. You're too old for me. I just understand your Spanish better than anyone else in this country. Normally, I go for personality, but for some reason, I can't seem to translate personality yet. All Spaniards have the same personality to me at this elementary stage in my language interpretation.*

"*¿Que?*" She came out of her English-language daydream, realizing he had just asked her something. Her mind took a moment to translate it. *Oh yes, what time does my class start?* She glanced at her watch, but like a cruel joke, it looked as if it spoke another language as well. She was too nervous to figure out which dot meant which hour. That required more translating. She knew she shouldn't have bought a watch with dots. Her mother, grandmother and her sister all had watches with numbers you could read. Problems with telling time ran in her family—well, for the women anyway.

Again, Rafael asked her what time her first *clase* started and when she told him nine-thirty, he glanced at his black leather wristwatch and laughed, telling her it was now almost ten-thirty. They had been standing on the curb under the arch for an hour, speaking in Spanish.

"Oh no, no! My first class in Spain, oh, and my second too! *¡Tengo que ir!*"

He continued laughing, as if her missed class meant nothing. "*Mañana,*" he stated.

"*¿Mañana?* Tomorrow? What do you mean?" She asked with disgust.

"*No te preocupes, hay mas clases mañana,*" he said.

"Of course there's more classes tomorrow, but today was my first day of classes. I am worried!" She knew her words had switched to English, but that happened under pressure.

"*Mañana, mañana, mañana, Christina.*" He kept laughing, then pressed a button on his key chain and the trunk of his Mercedes popped open. Inside lay piles of white blouses with transparent, opaque floral sleeves neatly placed over silky skirts. With his nod of approval, Kristine took a closer peek and touched the soft fabric of a pale pink blouse.

"*Te gustan las ropas, Christina? Tu puedes tenerlos, si quieres!*"

Had he just offered to give her some clothes? She felt almost sure he said they would probably fit her, and that she could pick one or two for keeps. No, that would be an embarrassment if she didn't hear him correctly, so instead she shook her head and walked back to the sidewalk.

"*¿Te gustan? ¿Te gustan?*" he asked in the same tone Rosario used when she asked if Kristine liked dinner. He grabbed a blouse and held it up to her.

"*¡Si, me gusta mucho!*" How could she *not* like such incredible looking European fashions?

"¿¡*Christina, por favor, me gustaria tomarte a un restarante, si quieres?!*"

She accepted. They agreed to meet for dinner. First, he'd be out of the country on business and said he wouldn't be back until early October. So they agreed to meet on October fourth at six-thirty.

He asked where he should pick her up, and she remembered that her Spanish family never had anyone up to the apartment. She didn't want to expose her Spanish family's apartment to some *stranger danger*. She was the one to stop, turn, smile and talk in the first place, so she'd pay the consequences if this guy turned out to be a foreign creep. She told him she'd meet him on the main corner of *El Corte Ingles*, the seven-story department store that stood a block from the family's apartment.

Rafael flipped throughout the pages of a black leather day planner and scribbled the date, time and place, then drew a big heart and wrote 'Christina.' He wrote the exact same thing on another page, ripped it out, and handed it to Kristine as a reminder. *Wow, that's confirmed*, she thought.

As he drove away, he waved his hand out the window until he could no longer see the young woman with schoolbooks in hand, turned in the opposite direction from the college and headed for the *Prado Museum* at the other end of Madrid.

Visiting the museum clicked. It immediately became her place—a comfort zone in a big city in a big country in a mammoth world. *The world is large and easily overwhelming and that is why it must be broken down. That is why people of all ages need to find their hangouts, their escapes, and little hiding places in life*, she wrote to her grandmother later.

While staring at the works of sixteenth to eighteenth-century Spanish artists on the main floor of the *Prado* Museum, Kristine felt guilty for skipping her first two classes in Madrid. She blamed Rafael partially for her first skipped class, but she had had plenty of time to make the rest of her classes. Instead, she chose one of the world's most famous art museums and convinced herself that she must live with such decisions. A museum could teach more than a classroom. Eventually, instead of feeling guilty, she felt risky, dangerous and terribly adventurous. She told herself not to make eye contact next time, just to keep walking, even if someone needed directions. Besides, who would dare ask a blonde with not a single dark root for directions in Madrid? *What a yahoo*, she decided. She couldn't wait to write Grandma all about this character who seemed to have popped straight out of a romance novel. Yes, Grandma would love the details about Rafael.

She heard the tour guide say in Spanish that the broad spectrum of paintings reflected the personal taste, religious beliefs and political power of the Spanish Crown dating back to the reign of Ferdinand and Isabella. She listened, she learned, she thought. The *Prado* Museum became her place to stare and think, stare and think.

She decided not to tell anyone of her encounter with Rafael. She had plenty of time to decide if she would dare meet up with this *hombre* on October fourth. He himself probably wouldn't remember her in two weeks, let alone their scheduled date. Besides, she didn't want him for a date. She considered him too old, much older than Steve. Would she actually stand on a corner waiting for such a man three weeks from now? Probably not, she decided later, while looking at Goya's works downstairs.

℘

For the rest of the school week and the following week, she arrived early to reserve a front row seat and left each class with a severe headache. Listening and trying to recognize the Spanish words of her professors proved straining. In one class she was taught something about Spain consisting of two great kingdoms for two whole centuries of its history, Moors and Jews, if she heard right. Both had diverse dialects. The Spanish civilization during Moorish supremacy thrived. There were more schools built, and many were free so poor people could attend. She caught fragments of facts, nothing more.

As the days passed, her mind worked overtime to listen, interpret and take notes that flipped back and forth from Spanish to English. She felt confused, not knowing in which language she should take her notes. Her brain heard Spanish, and tried to convert the Spanish into English. Should she take notes in Spanish or English? She worried that straining so much might create an indented fault line on her forehead. Late at night, she looked up the meanings of unknown words in her Spanish-English dictionary, then studied her notes from class thoroughly.

After closing her dictionary, she would sit in bed late at night and noticed an old familiar problem returning. A terrible knife-like pain darted through her heart, accompanied by shortness of breath. Drained as she felt from interpreting classes, she fought off sleep and stubbornly stayed awake for hours. She didn't mind not sleeping at night—she only wished she knew of something productive to make of the night, like tarpon fishing or water tower talking. Soon, she promised herself, she would get to know Madrid at night.

℘

> Dear Grandma:
> When I can't fall asleep at night, I just look forward to the next day's siesta. This entire country naps a couple of hours a day. I always thought napping was a sport for babies. Maybe some Spaniards throw tantrums, but probably not. Owners close up shop, business people keep sofas in the back of their offices for resting, and insomniacs refresh themselves.
> I love the concept and wonder if I might be influential enough to take the siesta back to America with me. But where would everyone go to nap? At least in Madrid, they can walk home to their apartments, or lie on a bench in one of the many parks. I guess Americans in the corporate

world could bring mats and nap in the hallways or conference rooms. The lights could go off, and there'd be blankets handed out, and a stardust lady to tap naughty nap takers on the shoulder.

But no, only babies and cats nap, and for good reason. There'd probably be too many sexual harassment claims centered on naptime in America. People would have to lock their doors and sleep safely in their offices behind closed doors.

Could the United States handle closing down business for an hour every day? Naptime would have to be mutually declared and perhaps made into a law. The siesta only works if everyone goes down for a nap at the same time. Winston Churchill napped daily and claimed that when the war started, it was the only way he could cope with his responsibilities. If I were president, I would declare a war on stress and mandate every U.S. citizen to take a one-hour nap every day. I wished my country would wake up to the benefits of the siesta, especially because everyone might then have more energy for fiestas and for appreciating the night.

As she napped during the next day's siesta, she awoke to Señor Lorenzo calling her to the phone. It was Ignacio, Howard's mysterious contact.

25

He received her letter and wanted to meet but had some questions. At first, he spoke *rapidamente* like everyone else in Spain, but then he picked up on Kristine's low level of Spanish comprehension and slowed down, reassuring her that she spoke Spanish quite fine. Talking on *el telefono* was always more *dificil* than talking in person.

She agreed. The phone made the language barrier more difficult.

He said that neither he nor his mother had any recollection of a man, let alone a friend named Howard, living in Florida. In fact, they didn't have any American friends at all. After much hesitation, he decided to meet her anyway, just in case the name Howard might eventually ring a bell.

Kristine apologized, telling him she felt foolish and wanted to forget the entire thing. If he didn't know a Howard, there must be a mistake. There must be another Ignacio living in Spain, and somehow, she probably messed up part of his telephone number or one letter in the correct spelling of his name. She could accept all this and move on. Surely her life didn't depend on meeting Howard's contact.

The man on the phone insisted they meet, telling her to call him 'Nacho' for short. He said Friday night worked best.

She asked if she could bring some friends along. She hadn't made any friends yet, but just talking of them might lend the impression she was protected—the higher the number the greater the protection.

"No!" He insisted she go alone.

What-ifs crowded her mind as they had done on that first boat ride to Tarpon Key. She imagined a strange plot, a kidnapping, a mugging, a mysterious plan set forth by both Howard and his stranger European contact. She told the man at the other end of the phone that it was nice talking with him but to please forget the entire thing.

And then he tempted her with the one thing she had been craving to do for weeks. He asked her if she had seen Madrid at night.

"No," she told him. She'd been staying in the apartment with her señora, studying at night.

"So you know *nothing* of Madrid," he declared in Spanish.

"But I do know some things. I'm taking several very intense classes, all taught in Spanish and by Spanish professors," she replied defensively, also in Spanish.

"*Si*, but you are missing out on the one most precious aspect of Spanish life. *El noche!* If you don't know the night, you don't know the people *de Espana.*"

She thought of tarpon fishing and late-night dock conversations. It was true. Night is valuable. She agreed to meet and suggested six o'clock.

"No," he told her, "night doesn't begin that early. Nine o'clock."

She told him to pick her up on the curb below her Spanish family's apartment.

"No," he said again, and told her to meet him inside Madrid's Opera House Friday night at nine o'clock, Row ten, Seat B.

"What? *¿Que?*" she asked, still uncertain if her translations were 100% accurate or if her mind had turned reality into some surreal semblance of things she thought she heard and thought she said.

"*Yo tengo dos* tickets to a visiting orchestra performance. I will have *uno de* those tickets waiting *para ti* at the ticket box when you arrive. You only need to give your *nombre* to the *persona* inside the box."

"No!" She was adamant. She told him she preferred meeting him outside before the performance.

"No!" He said that he wasn't going to stand outside, risk her tardiness and miss a single moment. He told her the Opera House is located opposite the *Palacio del Oriente* and asked her if she knew where that was.

"*Si, si*," she answered. Of course she knew of The Royal Palace, the second most stunning tourist attraction in Spain. How could she *not* know where Philip the something-in-seventeen-something built a home suitable enough for a Bourbon monarch? It did catch her eye every so often as she walked by, and she had gone for a tour with an English-speaking guide. Alfonso the something was the last person to live in the palace, yet Franco's body was still there today. Yes, she could certainly find Madrid's Opera House just across from the palace, and she could probably find Row ten, Seat B.

"*Adios.*"

"*Adios.*"

They hung up.

℘

Dear Grandma:

There's something I will never again take for granted back in the United States and I can only daydream wishfully about plugging it in, turning it on, filling it with water, and feeling the steam rise forth. Yes, ironing. It took me an hour to persuade Rosario that I needed to iron, let alone wash my clothes. After a fun game of charades, she took out the ironing board, but explained that I'd have to pay her first, and that I could use the washing machine only once a month.

I know I shouldn't complain. Life could be tougher than this, but it happened the same day that I was in the midst of shaving my legs in the shower when Margherta, my Spanish sister, shut the water off. She explained to me that shaving my legs was costing her family money and that I shouldn't do it daily, rather, like washing my clothes, I should shave monthly.

Well, I suppose if I am to live the Spanish life, I need to adhere to this Spanish family's rules. Attitude adjustment needed. May the hair on my legs grow free and wild!

℘

She thanked God that the hair on her legs didn't grow too long by Friday night as she walked a couple miles to Madrid's Neoclassic Opera House. She noticed nothing spectacular along the way. She could only wonder about the mysterious man who would be sitting next to her in Row ten, Seat A. She thought it odd to arrange a first encounter under such circumstances. Why was he so adamant about meeting inside? Was he really that uptight about missing a single moment of the performance? It was only a visiting orchestra, and he was a *Madrileno*. They're the ones late for everything.

She followed his orders, telling the man inside the box office her name, and he handed her a ticket for Row ten, Seat B. She went inside and found her seat, the second from the aisle. There was no Nacho. A woman sat on her right, but the seat to her left was still empty. *Look who is early and look who is late*, she thought. The lights dimmed, and she could hardly see a thing. Now she wouldn't be able to see what Ignacio looked like, at least not until the performance ended. That is, if he showed up.

He did. A man took the seat next to her nearly a quarter of the way through the first performance and made no apologies for his tardiness as he whispered into her ear. "I have been a fan of movies, of musicals and of the night for more than four years now," he said in his native language. "I always make a point of arriving late."

"*¿Por que?*" She asked him why.

"*Porque.*" He told her that when the sun sets, the movies start and the curtains open. Only then does he arrive.

"*¡Que mysterioso!*" she said, finding him to be more interesting than the performance on the stage.

Suddenly he took her hand and slowly lifted it in his, placing it on one side of his face. "*Aqui. Por favor*, feel my emotions. Feel," he whispered.

She felt embarrassed touching his face. A handshake of introduction, or a kiss on each cheek would have been fine, but feeling his face? She didn't want to offend such a deeply intense individual, so she kept her hand on his face. Since she couldn't see a thing in the darkness, she closed her eyes and felt his face, as might a person without sight. For a moment, she felt peace and calmness. But then, as she started to move her hand over to the other side of his face, he stopped her abruptly. She sensed something shocking, something *bad* as the man next to her seemed to be responding in tune with the music, as if it were controlling him.

At the end of the first song, he clapped loudly. So loudly she couldn't help but notice, and she told him his clapping almost sounded better than the performance.

He laughed. A new song started and he asked her what she found beautiful.

"*Agua.*" She told him Lake Michigan, the Gulf of Mexico, and the Mediterranean Sea.

"*¿Por que?*" He asked her why she liked the sea.

"It has depth," she said. "What do you find beautiful?"

"*El noche.*" After saying he found the night most beautiful, he excused himself to go to the bathroom in the middle of the performance.

A good twenty minutes passed. Row ten, Seat A remained vacant. She walked home alone.

A few days went by and she began feeling uneasy about Nacho. Perhaps he got sick and had to take off. Perhaps he got mugged on the way to the bathroom, or he lost his ticket and they wouldn't let him back in. She didn't get mad. She became curious, and it drove her crazy not knowing why he liked the night so much and why he had disappeared so suddenly. After all, it was very rude to leave a young woman alone and not to escort her home. She called him up.

"*Hola.* You never told me why you liked the night," she said slowly in Spanish, ignoring mention of his bad manners.

"*Si, si.* It brings out my best features," he answered in his native tongue.

"*¿Que?* What features? Your mysterious side?"

"You might not like me in the light."

It had gone far enough, and she told him it was all too strange. "Let's just forget we ever met," she told him. "This was all a big mistake. *Adios.*"

"*¡No!* I will pick you up at eight o'clock on the curb below your family's *apartmento.*"

She gave him the address and they hung up.

ʂ

Dear Grandma:

The other night I was attempting to make my way through the dark hallway to the bathroom when I heard an awful noise. It grew louder and more ferocious with each step I took. Suddenly, the noise was right below me, and horrified, I realized it was Señor Lorenzo. I had mistakenly routed myself into their bedroom and was standing over their bed. I've never heard such a snore in my entire life. It had a Spanish accent to it. I started to shake with laughter as I stood there, frozen and blinded, with my hands gagging my mouth.

℘

With her Spanish family gawking out the window above, Kristine stood on the street below, waiting for Ignacio. Rosario never offered to invite him upstairs because in Madrid, the street served as the meeting place, the center for all excitement and socializing. As her family shouted from the window above, she grew nervous that perhaps Ignacio had forgotten about her. Lorenzo laughed, telling her not to get so upset over time, that a half hour late meant nothing on a first date. She felt uptight because she didn't know what Ignacio had to hide, and she hadn't told her Spanish family a thing about their first meeting at the Opera House. All they knew was that she was meeting a friend of a friend from the United States, and they assumed it was for the first time.

At around eight forty-five, he pulled up to the curb in an old-fashioned bright yellow car. As he got out, she saw he was a good looking, short and stocky Spaniard with dark features inherited from Moorish invaders of long ago. He walked right up to her and kissed her *dos veces*—once on her left cheek, once on her right cheek.

Then she noticed a horrible scar on the left side of his face. He wore a patch over his left eye and his skin appeared burnt, wrinkled, and pink. Was this his secret? Was this why he loved the night, and showing up late, and leaving before the lights went on? As she stared at it, he showed no signs of insecurity, so she closed her eyes and slowly moved her hand over the left side of his face. He let her do this. Then she opened her eyes and kissed him once on each cheek. She didn't say anything about the scar, nor the other night. And neither did he.

They strolled to a nearby café in the heart of Madrid and drank *chato*, a small glass of red wine, and ate some *tapas*, or appetizers of fried fish, slices of sausage and prawns in butter. The café was crammed full of shouting Spaniards and Nacho's voice blended in perfectly. His opinionated personality made him a sort of genius, except when it came to remembering whether or not his family knew a Howard from the United States. Kristine described Howard's physical appearance, his personality, the island, but still, nothing came to mind. Nacho declared the entire thing suspicious but said he didn't mind. He enjoyed meeting her anyway.

He lectured passionately about the Constitutional Monarchy, shouting out his own views, then wanted to know her views on political figures, domestic and international issues, literary authors and more. He picked her brain and frighteningly, at times, he seemed to have a better understanding of her own country than she did. As he spoke and as he listened, his thick, bushy black eyebrows nervously twitched and arched in sync with the words. *Tranquilo, tranquilo*, Kristine thought.

Espresso-intoxicated Spaniards still swarmed the café at one o'clock in the morning. A nearby table of students sat flipping through textbooks and highlighted notes. A woman across the room stood in a corner wiping her mascara-drenched face with a napkin as her friend shouted words of comfort at her. Young kids crowded a small table, trading CD's. For Kristine, keeping cafés open in Madrid long after midnight was an insomniac's utopia. They were therapeutic refuges from the world, philosophical havens and retreats for modern-day mourning. She thrived in this city of night owls and looked forward to the next day's siesta to refresh.

All at once, as if just the thought of insomnia triggered her problem, she felt short of breath, as if there wasn't enough oxygen for everyone in the cramped café to share. *I'm so sick of this*, she thought, and ordered *tequila* at the bar.

"Tequila should calm me down a bit," she announced in English, before downing the shot.

"*¿Que?*" asked Nacho.

"Oh, never mind. Tell me, what's the name of this café? Oh, wait, did I just say that in English? I think I did." The shot of *tequila* was doing her no good. "*¿El nombre de este cafe?*" she asked again, this time in Spanish.

"*Yo no lo se.*" Nacho said he did not know it.

Kristine asked the woman sitting on a stool next to her the same question.

"*Yo no lo se,*" replied the woman.

"You don't know the name of this café either?" Kristine felt frustrated. She liked this place, despite its close air, but she wanted to know its name. She then asked the bartender.

"*Yo no lo se,*" he replied confidently.

"*¿Que? ¿Que?* How can you *not* know the name of the place where you're working? That's absolutely nuts! *Mas tequila, por favor.*"

As she waited frantically for her next drink, Nacho told her there were more bars in Madrid than in any other city of the world. He said there was something like eight thousand bars.

"Oh, as if that's any excuse for not knowing the name of the bar you're in right now. Well, I don't even know if this is a bar or a cafe. It serves both liquor and coffee."

She downed another shot of *tequila,* disgusted that everyone she asked, including the bartender, did not know the name of the bar, café, whatever it was that they were in. She waited for a thank you from her lungs and within minutes they were so busy breathing normally, they didn't have time to thank her and she was pleased. She wanted another, but also knew she didn't want to mask one problem with another. Yes, masking problems could lead to self-destruction. "Let's go, *vamanos.*"

On their way toward the door of the crowded café, she stopped to ask one more intelligent looking man the name of the place.

"*Yo no lo se,*" he said.

"You do not know it either? *Estupido,*" she mumbled. The *tequila* was triggering her temper. She ran outside and looked at the sign on the door. It read, '*Yo no lo se.*' That's right. The name of the place was, 'I don't know.'

※

The next morning Kristine stared at the cookies and milk, and Rosario realized something was wrong, so she asked her guest what Americans eat for breakfast. Kristine liked the morning snack but could still taste the *tequila* from last night, so she answered honestly, "*huevos.*" In case the woman didn't understand, Kristine pantomined breaking an egg against the counter and pouring it into a pan.

"*¡Si, si, si! ¡Tortilla Espanola!*" responded Rosario, and she went right over to the refrigerator and took out three brown eggs. "The most widely eaten dishes in my country, *Christina*," she said in her native language. "I teach you how to make the *tortilla*, or Spanish omelet."

As she chopped two medium-sized potatoes into fine matchsticks, Señora Rosario bragged that the French stole the idea of the tortilla from Spanish chefs at the court of Louis the something after he married the daughter of Philip the something in 16-something. Kristine understood most of what she said and wondered if the *señora* now spoke more slowly or if she herself understood more than before.

Often, the women in the kitchen watched each other more than they listened. And now, Rosario wanted to know all about her encounter with Nacho, her *hombre mysterioso*. As she shared the events of last night, Kristine sensed understanding as the woman carefully watched her face, as if watching her soap opera. Kristine made sure to accentuate her hand gestures because that too helped Rosario to better understand. The woman watched her gestures as if watching someone conducting a symphony. Both only listened to ten percent of each other's words, but *las mujeres* communicated.

"*Pues,*" said Rosario as she chopped the small onion, "*Un amigo bueno.*" Kristine nodded, "*Si, si.*" Nacho might be a nice friend to have.

Rosario fried the potatoes and onion together slowly in oil, without browning. Then she beat the eggs well, added them to the pan, and let them fry for a moment as well. She asked Kristine if she saw the morning paper.

"*No, no he leido a nada. ¿Porque?*" Kristine had not seen it.

Rosario placed a plate on top of the omelet and turned the frying pan upside down, then slipped the *tortilla* back into the pan on the other side. She handed Kristine the *El Pais* newspaper and pointed to a small article on the second page.

Kristine sat down at the table, but for the moment ignored the article. Instead, she wanted to watch Rosario in the kitchen so she could recreate the Spanish *tortilla* back home some day. She watched how Rosario inspected the eggs.

She liked breakfast, and as she ate, tried reading the newspaper Rosario gave her. The article that she had pointed out reported Spaniards, and especially *Madrilenos*, sleep less than any of their European neighbors. She certainly agreed with that report. *Maybe it's all the espresso they drink,* mused Kristine.

Rosario left the kitchen, and when she returned, she had a suitcase in hand.

"*Rosario, ¿adonde vas?* Kristine asked where she was going.

For the first time Rosario sat down, setting her chores aside as she spoke and cried. She was homesick. It didn't matter that she was in her sixties and had a family of her own, grown children and all. She missed her extended family in Pamplona, and that family meant cousins and aunts and uncles and second cousins and great aunts and uncles and more. But her husband had a good job at the post office downtown and they would never move back there, not now that the kids were grown and living in Madrid. Her children liked this modern world, their home, and moving back to Pamplona would mean leaving them behind.

Her husband and kids made the trip to Pamplona only twice a year. Rosario and the kids took one extra trip each fall and would be leaving today. She would be meeting her sons and daughter at a specific train stop since they were leaving work early. She bragged about Pamplona as if she herself had designed it. She described it as a prosperous city with high-rise apartment blocks, nice lawns and factories, if Kristine understood correctly. She said Pamplona was so old that, from the 10th to the 16th Century, it was the capital of the kingdom of Navarre. After the Civil War, she said her people had changed it into a flourishing city. She boasted that her people were hardworking, religious and conservative.

As she wiped her eyes with her dishcloth, she said she loved that city but her husband was from Madrid. She said she often regretted having fallen in love with a man from another city because it forced her to choose between her man and her family, and her man would never leave Madrid. She chose Lorenzo and ever since they had lived together happily in Madrid.

26

Rosario was queen of the house and wore the crown of the kitchen. Her absence and the power she held triggered a sort of celebration of gluttony for her husband Lorenzo, and incidentally, for Kristine.

The rebellious fiesta began immediately that night at supper with a pitcher of fruit-filled *sangria*. Lorenzo insisted that Kristine write down the ingredients of his infamous *sangria* made of *vino tinto*, liquor, brandy, sugar, pears and apples. He added the ingredients with pride, as if turning water into wine. Then he urged Kristine to make the second pitcher of sangria, as he watched with the impish grin of a little boy, claiming that his wife had put this recipe to rest long ago.

As Kristine chopped the fruit, Lorenzo drank glass after glass, telling her he had fallen in love with his wife because she was from Pamplona and Pamplona had better *fiestas* than any other city in Spain. He said he had been disappointed to learn that his wife never liked the annual *fiesta* in Pamplona. She thought it overwhelming, but he hoped he would one day convert her into a party animal. He said years ago, he and his father would have *fiesta* after *fiesta* almost every day.

"Do you have a lot of *fiestas* today?" she asked in Spanish.

"*No, no mas,*" he answered honestly.

"*¡Que triste!* I bet you really miss those *fiestas.*"

"I miss them but it is not sad, *Christina*. Never say the old days are better than these. The church tells us this."

Lorenzo admitted he felt guilty and knew his wife would not like the *fiesta* he was hosting, but he added *la comida and bebida* (food and drink) were his only rebellions in life. He knew he acted in disobedience toward his wife, the domestic queen, but couldn't resist his passion and respect for food. As Evelyn would have said, Lorenzo had never outgrown the sweet wine stage of life. He diluted his coffee with sugar cubes and *leche* and the normally mellow, loving father couldn't harm a fly. He'd even caught bugs in a glass, then let them free outside. He served as an all-around obedient husband who appreciated his wife's home-cooked meals of lentil soup, garbanzo beans with carrots and olive oil, octopus and *paella*. He just needed his sweets and sangria once in awhile and knew that meant sneaking. Rosario long ago prohibited such indulgences out of worry over his mammoth stomach.

After the sangria, he opened a white paper bag full of an assortment of *galletas* and *dulces*—his favorite being nothing more than gourmet chips of some sort dipped in a candied glaze of chopped peanuts.

Between chomps he lazily sang, "*Da da da de da de da.*" To Kristine, it sounded like the tune from *If I Were a Rich Man*.

She tried asking if he saw *Fiddler on the Roof*, but the word fiddler wasn't in her *dictionario*. Still, she felt sure she heard this Spaniard mumbling this Jewish song.

"*Da de da dee da de da,*" he sang as he controlled the outpouring of the *sangria*. This *fiesta* wasn't about to end, not until the last drop was drank.

"*Mas, mas, Christina,*" he announced as if he were a ruler. But he was no ruler, just a harmless, hard-working man who liked to party. But he made it very clear that once he slurred his first word, he always stopped drinking.

"Are you sure of that?" asked Kristine in a slight Spanish slur. "Are you saying you do not drink to get drunk?"

"*Nunca, nunca! Yo no bebo demasiado porque los espanoles tienen la dignidad.*" He said, never! Spaniards only drink to enhance their perspective and wit, but once they get drunk, they've lost their dignity.

"*Tengo una pregunta*," said Kristine. "How does Madrid flourish despite the fact that the people shut everything down to nap every afternoon?"

"Divine intervention," he said in slightly slurred Spanish. "Divine intervention."

℘

Lorenzo took advantage of his wife's absence for the rest of the week. One *fiesta* after the next, every night he'd open the little white bakery bag of goodies as if he were Santa Claus dipping into his sack of toys.

Despite these late night indulgences, something significant clicked for Kristine during the day. As she sat in the front row of her History of Spanish Civilization class, she took notes in Spanish without thinking about translations, conjugations or meanings. She no longer strained to interpret the professor. Without any delay in her mind, she now understood her classes, and her headaches disappeared.

She felt on top of the world. The pages of her Spanish grammar books were now alive. She felt emerged in Spain and its culture. At last, she could understand her professors, Lorenzo, and the people on the streets of Madrid, and that meant she had become fluent in Spanish. As if the joy of it all fueled her, she regularly left class and walked the streets of Madrid for hours, alone, yes, but as a loner, no. Doing things alone didn't make her a loner. She needed time alone, time to think about herself in relation to the world around her. She wanted to enjoy her own company. Why shouldn't she? She'd have to be with it the rest of her life. And still, after death, she'd again have to live with her mind, her soul, spirit, herself. She walked under the luminous blue sky that Velazquez once painted and felt the warm air blanketing her skin.

Though she considered herself happy, biologically and emotionally, her moods fluctuated like Picasso's erratic eras in painting. So, in the next minute, she felt outraged, in a dark blue mood. Deep down inside lurked despair. Grandma and Lauren were no longer just a phone call away. Her parent's home in the country had been reduced to a memory. She could never scoop another ice-cream cone in her family business again. She felt far away from her sisters. She felt furious, fed up with her breathing problem. Breathing was the source of life! She walked faster.

Others were walking, too. Punks with rebel hair, mothers with grocery bags and toddlers, and business people with briefcases followed the rhythm pulsing through the streets of Madrid. They strutted rather than walked, with an egocentricity about them, arrogant almost. Into the darkness, people walked. The nights belonged to everyone.

She thanked God that she liked herself. She could walk alone and still enjoy herself. She walked through Gran Via, a major thoroughfare in Madrid, past cinemas, shops, and fast-food restaurants. After several miles of thinking her own thoughts, and making her own observations, she knew her walking had become obsessive but she could neither stop nor slow her pace. She had too much to see and think.

Some people go through life with burnt taste buds, numb to details. She wanted to notice everything. She walked past a crowd and could smell someone wearing *Eternity*. For every birthday, Grandma got *Eternity* something—perfume, lotion, foam bath. Yes, Grandma always got fragrance and pajamas, usually purple. As she walked, sometimes Kristine wore her headphones and listened to a Mecano tape over and over again. They were a popular Spanish group. Other times she listened to the streets that sounded just like she always imagined city streets to sound—the Lego utopia city of her childhood imagination.

Everyone contributed a vivid unique sound to Sesame Street. The electrician climbing the pole, the garbage men running parallel to the truck then hopping aboard, the window washers ascending the rope, and the woman in the second-story window yelling '*Adios*' to her husband leaving with a briefcase. It looked like the Lego city she created on her bedroom floor. Everyone participated in the city.

But then she walked past a bucket and a gray bundle crunched up on the sidewalk outside the *El Corte Ingles* department store, and for a moment, felt guilty about her nightly *fiestas* with Señor Loenzo. She had no *pesetas* to donate to the bucket so she sat down on the cold pavement and smiled at the ancient, black eyes sunk inside the hooded flannel shawl. Still out of breath from her walk, she couldn't talk, and if she could, she didn't know what to say. She didn't know why she sat down next to the stranger. For a moment, a long moment, she heard silence, and she thought the homeless bundle, nobody's grandmother, might want to share her story.

Unlike story sharing on Tarpon Key, there was no wine, nor rippling currents, just an empty bottle of *tequila* and the sound of honking horns. But the woman, like every other homeless, and every other living creature, had a story to share and Kristine felt like listening.

Out from the black flannel, a scaly, wrinkled hand wiped a cold tear from her eye, but said nothing. Kristine didn't recognize this woman as any character in her childhood make-believe cities, and she had owned all sorts of plastic people for her lego city.

She knew that wearing this woman's shoes would be horrible because typically in Spain, children, grandchildren and extended families don't allow their aging mothers to sit in rags begging for money. Then again, she wasn't wearing any shoes. In such cases it's okay to live for tomorrow, thought Kristine. How could a frozen, hungry woman sitting next to the gutter actually live for the moment? After about five minutes, Kristine got up and walked away.

Like descending into Hell, the subway's escalating stairs took her deep into the earth at least ten floors down. She learned slowly, but she learned. No eye contact. Look straight ahead. Which line to take? Sometimes she got confused. Attention Deficit Disorder, maybe. So she'd just ride. Any line, any color.

Once she hopped on and a little old man grabbed her, pulling her off just before the doors shut and the subway took off. Whispering in Kristine's ear, he warned her about some "*peligroso*" stop. That meant dangerous. His eyes speckled with blue, green brown and yellow, an artist's palate as he held her hand tightly, walking her to another stop. He nudged her to board. As he stood outside on the subway platform, he waved through the closing glass doors. His angelic-like eyes looked familiar. He then pulled out a straw hat with a hole in the top and put it on his head, laughing. It couldn't be Howard without the sideburns, without the beard. No, Howard wasn't that old. But he did have Howard's same bluish-gray eyes. They waved until the subway car pulled away, and she could no longer see the stranger.

She always power walked past the Iranian travel agency, and slowed as she passed the two fountains in the park, taking a favorite bench outside the *Prado* Museum. Here she tried to memorize the photographic grandeur of the fourteen mammoth white arches, sculpted with various statues, leading to the museum doors. She appreciated the art of the tall, slender black lanterns, and the stone-carved figures surrounding her in the park.

She knew it might be easier returning to visit Tarpon Key someday than it would be returning to this country in southeastern Europe, so she wanted to remember everything. That way she could at least return in daydreams. As a submarine that had traveled from Lake Michigan to the Gulf of Mexico and now the Mediterranean Sea, she never wanted to forget the route she had traveled.

She decided to surface and allow herself some reminiscing in life. Without it, she knew the things that were once a part of her would suddenly die. A cool autumn Madrid breeze tickled the hair on her arms. If only she were a speck of dust that could sweep her up and carry her away. *Take me with you. Are you blowing to the West? Toward the United States? Where does wind die out? How far does it travel?*

Her daydreaming relaxed her like a catnap. One blink woke her. Her eyes settled on the white pillar of the museum, and she remembered that life was but a passing midst. Dust to dust, ashes to ashes. No, she wouldn't want to be dust. She wanted to be a person.

A homeless man filled with much character woke her from her daze, then assured her he had no intention of begging for *dinero*, though he felt entitled to it.

She told him she had no cash and asked him why he thought himself entitled to money.

In a blend of Portuguese and Spanish, he boastfully claimed to have some sort of noble title in life, that his nobility dated back to the Middle Ages, to the time the Christians started reclaiming land from the Arab invaders.

She asked him how someone so noble could end up homeless.

He admitted, with a grunt, that everyone grabbed on to some noble title back then, so a noble title wasn't too significant in today's Spain. It was hard to compete when the whole country was noble. That's why he was left homeless, he said.

She asked him if the claim to nobility explained why Spaniards don't seem to stress themselves with work and school. She told him she noticed a noble attitude in many of the Spaniards.

He asked her how so.

She explained it was the way they drank and ate, as if they pampered themselves by feasting and eating *mas, mas, mas*. Then she realized she had said this to a bum who probably never feasted. She apologized.

The bum confessed he was homeless because he didn't think he should work. He was too noble to work.

Having never met a more arrogant, but charming bum, she got up and walked inside the museum for her fifth time that semester. Each time left her more entranced, more invigorated with confidence, determination and inspiration to accomplish something significant in life, but at this stage, she didn't know what. She refused to worry about her future now. She was in the moment, and the moment meant Spain. She believed that, when it came time to do something significant in life, she would know. Ideas would come to her, doors would open, and people with a purpose would pop into her life. She would be ready, but for now, for today, she could only think about the moment and the moment wasn't college in Michigan, nor Tarpon Key. Her moment was Spain—where her greatest present accomplishment might be doing laundry.

After hours in the museum she walked the several miles back to her evening economics class. Afterward, she knew she had options. She could return to the apartment, or she could walk back to *Calle Preciados* and drop by the corner of *El Corte Ingles* at around six-thirty and see if a black Mercedes showed up. After all, it was October fourth.

27

She casually stood outside the doors of the crowded department store that sold Levis for about ninety-three dollars a pair. Feeling indecisive, like a woman impulsively ready to spend money but also fearful of wasting that money, she started to walk away, then turned back once more, as if giving the black Mercedes one last chance. She remembered its driver saying that if the corner looked busy, he wouldn't park the car, but would instead pull up along the curb so she could hop in. As cars came and went she considered the investment. Did she really want to step into the car of a unknown foreign man? What would it cost her? Was there a return policy? Would he return her to the curb if things didn't work out?

Suddenly, she didn't want to invest anything of herself with this stranger and she started to walk away. She felt proud and without regret, a woman choosing to leave the expensive clothes behind, a woman walking away, having spent nothing. She just started to realize how much she had when she noticed the same gray fabric from earlier, still sitting on the piece of sidewalk square, now, hours later. She asked the homeless gray bundle if she had seen a black Mercedes pull up to the curb. But no, she hadn't.

She sat down again on the cold pavement next to the woman. They didn't talk. Instead they listened to the sound of coins dropping into the bucket every couple of seconds. Some coins landed with a splash. Others sounded like a single droplet of light rain. The bucket never went dry. The people of Spain wouldn't allow it to and the old woman, probably noble, surely seemed to be surviving off her country that cared.

Kristine looked up, as if giving Rafael one last chance. *He's just some stranger in a big country far from home. How can I possibly get in the car and drive away with a man who doesn't speak English?*

She suddenly felt horribly foolish for making plans with him in the first place, so she quickly squeezed the cold hand next to her, stood up, and started crossing the street in the direction of the apartment. Why of course he had forgotten about her, their encounter, their plans to meet on a crowded corner of all places. And she too would make it a forgotten moment, and him, a forgotten stranger.

As she reached the other side of the street, she felt someone yanking her sweater from behind. Her heart made a record breaking leap over the high jump as she arched around, ready to protect herself with a fist, but she couldn't hit the little old woman under the gray shawl, frantically flinging her cane in the air and pointing it toward the department store.

A black Mercedes had parked along the curb, and Rafael stood with a bouquet of purple, yellow and red tulips on the corner. He held the flowers as if he actually understood where the American woman came from, as if he knew somehow that tulips made her want to dance and scrub streets with buckets of cold water and old-fashioned brooms, as if he knew that tulips marked every corner of her hometown, and that now they might make her homesick. He formally held the flowers, yet casually looked around, as if his fifty-five minutes of tardiness meant nothing at all.

The two women re-crossed the street together. The older took her seat on the corner. The younger accepted the bouquet of tulips and got in the car.

They drove about ten minutes to what Rafael kept calling *el museo de cera*. Kristine had no idea what the words meant, nor where they were going. She didn't care as she softly caressed each of the silky petals.

"*Me gustan*," she told him she liked the flowers. "How did you know that tulips are my favorite flower?" she asked in Spanish.

"*Son preciosas como ti.*" He told her they were as precious as she was. Then, he asked slowly in Spanish. "Of all the flowers in *el mundo*, why are they your favorite?"

She carefully laid out the correct Spanish words in her mind before speaking. "I'm from Holland, Michigan. It's a *ciudad en los Estados Unidos* that holds an entire festival for tulips."

"A festival of tulips? I've never heard of such a thing," said the Spanish stranger next to her.

She paused a moment to translate his words, then responded slowly. "People have been celebrating the flowers for hundreds of years, since 1632, when the interest in tulip growing exploded over in Holland, the country." She tried hard to remember the words of her high school teacher when he lectured about the flowers. "Tulip growing developed into a craze, and there was wild activity in tulip stock, and people asked outrageous prices for a single bulb." She noticed him staring more at her than at the road he was driving down, so she stopped talking.

He waved her on to continue. "*Mas, mas. Quiero escuchar mas.*" He said he wanted to hear more.

She continued in fluent, yet slow Spanish. "The tulip situation got out of control, and finally, after so many of the Dutch went bankrupt, the government stepped in to regulate the tulip trade."

He smiled and said in his native language, "And *Christina*, after all of that, the tulips survived and still stand proud every spring."

"*Si, Si*," she answered.

Following their drive, Rafael parked and they walked into a building where they were greeted by the king and queen of Spain. Kristine peeked into an ante room and noticed Michael Jackson standing as he might on the cover of his *Thriller* album. A short distance away she noticed John Wayne, then Hitler! For a moment she wondered if she had died and well, was she in Heaven? Purgatory? Hell? She couldn't make a judgment like that as she thankfully realized *el museo de cera* meant wax museum.

They began their tour in the political room, and Rafael stopped in front of Franco. Kristine remembered all that Rosario had said about the ruler. How his collapse triggered a social and sexual revolution in her country and a downfall of morals. How divorce, birth control, abortion, homosexuality and adultery were all illegal under this stern man. How she actually seemed to miss Franco's control.

Kristine wanted to know Rafael's opinions as he stared eye-to-eye with Franco, the wax figure. "*Rafael,¿que piensas de Franco?*"

He spoke clearly and slowly, and it only took her mind a second to translate his Spanish words into her English words. In fact, she heard his Spanish words as English in her mind. He was better than any history book she has ever read and more interesting than any class she has ever taken.

"With the collapse of Franco, my country jumped from dictatorship to democracy overnight, *Christina*." As he spoke, he looked back and forth between Franco and his American guest. "It marked the last Fascist regime in Europe." He looked angry and shook his head, as if scolding the wax figure in front of him.

"*Mas, mas. Quiero eschuchar*," she said. "I told you about tulips. Now you tell me about Franco."

"Forty *anos* of dictatorship and order at the expense of freedom," he continued. "Anyone who protested against the restrictions on speech and press and assembly were disciplined."

"It must have made many people mad," she commented.

"*Si, la gente de mi pais* were afraid. You would be too, *Christina*. But Franco had power, too much power. He was empowered by the army, church and the Falange Party."

The Franco question proved better than asking why people on Tarpon Key had given up civilization to live and work on the tiny mangrove. Both were personal questions it seemed and both made her want to know more. She wanted to know how Rafael's life personally changed after the collapse of Franco. She knew now that he and Rosario had different perspectives. Rosario seemed to miss the stern order Franco insisted upon Spain. Rafael despised the man.

"*¿Su vida esta muy diferente sin Franco, no?*" She wanted to know if and how his life changed when Franco no longer had power.

"Ahhh, si, si," he replied. "Franco limited the cultural and intellectual aspirations of my people. With Franco gone, the fashion industry spawned. Women used to wear mostly black. Without Franco, they immediately started wearing some of the most daring colors." He laughed. "I remember the modern statement the models made as they walked down the European runways in wild colors for the first time. *Las mujeres* mostly dress daring in the city. Country women are still conservative."

"*¿Por que?*" She wanted to know why they dressed in black in the country.

"*La muerte,*" he said. "Death is all over, *Christina*. In the country, they mourn for several years after the death of family. Because they have such large *familias*, they're always mourning someone, and always wearing black."

She wondered if wearing black might actually help someone overcome grief. Maybe she should have worn her black dress instead of that pastel bikini right after Lauren died. Then again neither Lauren, nor Grandma would have wanted her to go around wearing black for months. Lauren once said that black darkened her eyes, and Grandma, well, she only wore purple.

"*Estamos de moda, Christina,*" Rafael declared proudly, as he turned and walked toward the next room.

She couldn't argue. They did look like a country in style now!

They entered the dark monster movie room, where the damp coldness reminded Kristine of a cellar. They were the only ones touring, and she wished the museum had more customers. As Rafael took hold of her hand tightly, she felt sudden fear. Not from the mummies and monsters, but from the older man wearing glasses, walking by her side and now holding her hand.

Who was he? Why did she get in the car with him in the first place? How did it all start? What if he's married? Well, if he is, this luxurious older man is a Titanic heading for disaster. Suddenly a sharp pain struck her chest. She couldn't breath and her legs shook. Her vision blurred and she knew she was losing *the-mind-over-matter* battle once more. She tried to listen to Rafael's slow, clear Spanish narration of the tour, but instead she wondered if he knew CPR. She dropped her purse so she could bend down and catch her breath, but don Rafael insisted that he be the one to pick it up. She didn't want to die, not here in the wax museum, not here in Spain. The figures around her looked real—real and dead, as if they should be resting in coffins instead of standing around in a basement, staring into space.

As they entered the political room, Rafael's voice grew louder, filled with excitement. "*El es un amigo muy especial, Christina. Y el tambien.*" He pointed to a wax person. "Once, we were friends and look there! We too were friends! Now, they are dead. Now, they are wax sculptures in a museum."

She knew Rafael had important friends. Anyone made into wax after death is important. She knew Rafael was important. Anyone who is merely friends with wax sculptors must be important himself. She now wondered about Rafael and his friends. She wanted to know who they were, but at this point, she was only half concerned with the stories of the wax figures. Most of her attention went to talking herself out of a panic attack in the cold, dark, creepy museum. Not only was she standing in a spooky looking room with a mysterious man, but she was with a man who had friends turned into wax!

She felt relieved when the tour ended and they drove away. After awhile they parked the car and walked for quite some time to Café Gijon, located near the *Plaza de Cibeles* at the edge of the prestigious Barrio de Salamanca, a wealthier side of town. It was a chilly night, so once inside the warm café designed cozily with polished paneling and gilt mirrors, Kristine didn't want to leave. It didn't matter that they both had already drunk two coffees. Neither felt ready to venture out into the windy night, and something about the century old café stirred a desire for fine conversation.

They stayed in the café almost four hours, discussing a novel Kristine was reading for her Spanish literature class. *Pascual Duarte*, a novel she could hardly understand, turned out to be Rafael's favorite, and he offered her a lengthy analysis of it. Rafael waved his hands as he spoke, as if his hand gestures were part of Spain's language and as important as words.

"The 1942 novel, by Camilo Jose Cela, was written in a type of realism known as *tremendismo*," he said. "Do you know what *tremendismo* means, *Christina*?"

"No, *¿que significa?*" she asked.

"It features the antihero and an insistence on the ugly, harsh aspect of life. The author won the Nobel Prize for literature in 1989. It is my favorite book and I've read it several times."

"Why do you love such a depressing novel?" she asked in Spanish.

"*Porque.*" He looked down. "I have had several depressing moments in life."

"*Digame.*" She told him she wanted to know more.

"*Mañana, mañana.*" He told her he'd tell her another time.

She thought about the sentence in her mind, translated it to Spanish, then said it. "Would you like to meet me another time? I really enjoyed our discussion and I am already craving another."

"*Si, si.* But we must carefully choose our cafés," he whispered.

"*¿Por que?* Don't they all have good coffee?"

He laughed and shook his head. "*Christina*, choosing a café in Spain is like favoring one political party over the other. Cafés have reputations. There are right-wing and left-wing cafés, cafés for artists and cafés for writers. There is a café for everything."

"Just like there is a time for everything. But tell me, what is this café known for?"

"What did we just discuss?" He asked in Spanish, but Kristine understood it like English.

"Literature."

He smiled, giving her a nod of approval then responded slowly, "You have your answer. Hemingway loved this café the most."

℘

Rafael wanted to drop her off in front of the apartment, but she insisted he drop her off on the same corner where they had met earlier. She liked him and their evening together but didn't dare expose her living quarters to him, just in case, she wanted her privacy. Besides, in Madrid, a night without the moon meant nothing. On the island, the moon's absence was surely noticed and it meant closing her eyes and walking the trail in her mind. But here, the city lights lit her way. She saw some clouds glowing yellow and knew the moon hid behind them and as she walked a couple blocks back to the apartment she thought of their plans, of meeting the following week, same time, same place.

Her fingers went numb as she climbed under the covers and lit a gardenia-scented candle beside her bed. The tiny apartment felt cold this late at night, but she couldn't resist. She had to write about her conversations with Rafael.

℘

Dear Grandma:

I'll call him Rafael de Espana. He transforms Spanish into more than just grammar off the pages of a book. He brings it to life for me. He takes the language barrier away. As he speaks to me slowly and without shouting, I feel way beyond the culture shock and, I think, homesickness. I think it's time to stop crossing off days in big black marker on my calendar. As I lie in bed and hear his views of Spain and fashion and his people in my mind, I no longer quietly hum the National Anthem. I love this country now. I started loving it the moment I started breaking the language barrier. I love it a little better now that I have Rafael as a friend. This may sound dramatic Grandma, but I know you love reading romance. And I don't mind living it.

28

On July 18, 1936, many painful letters were written. The rightist revolt had been launched. The National Socialist parties of Italy and Germany fully supported the army and had decided to seize power and destroy the Second Republic. This decision began the Spanish Civil War. The Republicans set up camp in the urban areas of Madrid. The rebels, who called themselves the Nationalists, moved in from Morocco. They were led by General Francisco Franco as they entered Barcelona, establishing themselves in the provinces of Catalonia, Murcia and Valencia...

Like armies of rebels, ants moved their way through the veins inside Kristine's left arm, heading toward her shoulder. Then the professor explained that the death toll, an omen of sorrow for the Republicans, sounded early in 1939, when Franco's forces, after weeks of bitter siege, entered Barcelona.

A bow-and-arrow, no, it was a sword. No, the date was 1939—a *bullet* struck Kristine in the heart and she bent over at her desk to catch her breath. She declared herself crazy. How could a lecture alone cause a panic attack? And though a lecture on war and death, she herself didn't have to fight. In fact, with the war long since over, it no longer posed any sort of threat to her, an American studying in Spain sixty something years later. Still, she felt in danger, fearful of something.

The professor continued. The Nationalists had control. They had disciplined and well-armed troops. They were led by experienced generals and had plenty of materials from abroad. They were described as if they were on sort some of a Holy Crusade to crush the infidels as they chanted, "Long Live Death!"

Kristine's attempts to catch her breath became loud sighs of frustration and forced yawns. A lost battle, she ran out of the classroom door. Alone on the sidewalk outside, perhaps where the Republicans once established their base of support, she felt ridiculous that such symptoms could be coming from her mind. She had developed a bad habit of having panic attacks.

A soldier wounded while simply listening to the history of the Spanish Civil War, she started running toward the big hospital she had seen just a few blocks away. She allowed no time to talk herself out of this one. She was dying. Her mind convinced itself of that. As she ran, she thought of Steve, and wondered if she was running to the same hospital he went to the day of his horrible accident here in Madrid. She ran faster for herself, and for Steve. Kristine didn't have to run for Steve because he was fine now, safely back in Florida. Her mind forced her to run faster just thinking about the seriousness of Steve's accident.

She knew the word *corazon* meant heart, but her Spanish under pressure came out broken, as she explained her pain to the nurses. After sitting in a crowded waiting room a good hour, the nurse led her into a bigger room with tons of other sick people lying on beds, then told her to take her shirt off. Looking around at the crowded room and the dark-haired men drooling over her light hair, she didn't want to take her shirt off, so she asked for a curtain, or something.

"Americans are a bit more modest than Europeans," she explained in Spanish.

The doctor with messed up hair appeared completely over-burdened with ill people seeking free medical care. Kristine felt like a pathetic character in the musical "Jesus Christ Superstar"—just one more body demanding the doc's attention. "Heal me I'm hurting. Heal me I'm bleeding. Heal me, I'm dying."

Unfortunately, none of the doctors spoke her native language, and in a time of crisis, English would have been comforting.

It became all too familiar to her last hospital encounter back in Cape Coral, Florida. The doctor's assistants hooked the ECG up to her chest. As they rapidly talked medical terminology, she lost all capability for translating. Abducted by outer space aliens, she lay on the cold table looking up at the bright fluorescent light. Speaking their own language, they poked her and stuck her with things, then debated amongst themselves.

After the ECG, they led her in a wheel chair into a waiting room. A few moments later an unfamiliar-looking man in a white coat asked her questions. He wanted to know her symptoms. She had a perfectly fluent Spanish conversation with Rafael, so why couldn't she have one now? Why hadn't she ever read the Spanish version of those family medical encyclopedias? She had no idea how to say heart attack in Spanish. Then again, she did just leave the Spanish Civil War lecture, in which the professor used the words *golpe* for military attacks and the word *guerra* for war. Close enough. She'd give it a try.

"*Tengo un dalor en mi corazon, como un golpe o una guerra. Si, tengo un guerra en mi corazon.*"

She judged the doctor's silence as poor bedside manners. Then he stared to laugh. He laughed from his gut so hard, tears came streaming from his eyes. Meanwhile, she lay on the hospital bed with stabbing sensations piercing her heart. She thought it over, rehashed her words. She knew what she had said. She had just told the young Spanish doctor that she had a war or some sort of militaristic attack on her heart. The more the doctor laughed, the younger he looked.

"Well good, I'm glad I'm a stress relief for you. So can you treat wars of the heart, doc?" She said it in English but didn't care. She cried, while the doctor laughed. "I'm feeling better, doc. You must think I'm a hypochondriac wanting attention, and the hospital is the only place for me to get it."

Finally, he managed to pat her on the knee and ask her some slow, simple questions requiring no more than a yes or no answer. She must have answered one too many no's because he then wheeled her into the same ECG room that she got wheeled into before with the nurses, and began hooking her up, again.

She felt like a child on a merry-go-round, lying that she had not yet been on the ride, and she felt guilty, but didn't know what to say to stop the ride from starting. It was too late to admit she already went through the ECG with the other little men in white suits.

"Worry no. I explore you," the doctor said in his attempt at speaking English.

"Explore me? Goodness doc, that's worse than me having a war of the heart."

Just then the nurse that hooked her up last time to the ECG, returned.

"*Hola!* I should have died in battle!" said Kristine.

The nurse began waving arms and shouting loudly at the doctor. Both stared down at their abductee, so confused! She just answered no to the ECG question five minutes ago. Unhooking her, they took blood instead.

An hour later, the doctor explained something about stress and wished her well. She left the hospital alone, alive, and feeling like a soldier sent home from war. She just didn't feel like being sent home to her Spanish family's home. Instead, she walked to the corner of the *El Corte Ingles* department store. She arrived too early for Rafael, a Spaniard who never let time get the best of him. He'd show up in an hour, well, probably an hour and a half. He never seemed to care about time. No one in Spain seemed to care about time.

She had never had a homeless person as a friend before. They didn't exist in Holland, Michigan. Well, there was a shelter and it may have been full, but they never sat around on the streets, and they never begged for money. She took a seat on the sidewalk next to the gray bundle, and she thought of the children back home dressing up like bums about this time of year. Greedy trick-or-treat children, and she was always one of them.

Again, they sat side-by-side in silence for a few moments. Then, in slow, clear terms, Kristine started talking about her grandmother and Lauren. It felt so good to talk about it, as if the seeds of a pumpkin were being scraped out of her, and someone was carving a smile on her face. She spoke some words in English, but mostly in Spanish. She told how they had both died of heart attacks in their sleep just a few months apart. She couldn't stop. She shared how Lauren was supposed to be in Spain now too, but her destiny hadn't allowed it. She told how, for many nights, she had mourned in her sleep, how she had missed the funeral. She noticed the woman listening, interested, so she said more. She said she had feared that she too might die in her sleep, and that the fear had turned into a phobia of falling asleep, and that it had progressed into full-blown panic attacks, during the day.

The dry, cracking hands of the old woman reached inside her deep gray, dirty woolen blanket that she wore as a shawl, and pulled out an embroidered handkerchief, yellow from age. She looked Kristine in the eyes for a moment then patted away her tears with the cloth.

"*Gracias.*" Kristine didn't know what else to say. A submarine reaching the surface, she just exposed everything. The silence felt naked. She had undressed too much. She changed the subject, asking the old woman where she got the pretty handkerchief that looked like a precious antique. She didn't know the woman's name and she had just shared everything with her.

"*¿Come te llamas?*" asked Kristine. "What is your name?"

"*Triste,*" answered the woman. And Kristine interpreted it to mean sad, but if the woman wanted to be called Triste, she would call her that.

Triste's hand squeezed Kristine's hand, as she shared her own story. "*Tengo muchos anos,* I am very old," she said in broken, choppy Spanish sentences, and sometimes, paused a moment before stating the next. "The churches, they tried taking me in. I am *muy* proud of *Espana*. I never have hunger. *La gente de espana*, they fill my bucket *cada dia*." As she spoke, she never smiled nor looked Kristine in the eyes. "I am a woman, very stubborn. I don't want strangers to take me in. If I had *familia, si,* I'd go in. *Pero* I have no *familia*. As a young woman I watched my country go mad."

Kristine had heard about the destruction and wastage of the Spanish Civil War in class, but now she saw the ruins in the dark eyes of this woman.

"Franco and his war killed my parents, my brothers, my newlywed husband. It killed my grandfather and uncles and everyone I ever loved. I have been mourning ever since, *muchos anos.*" She stared at the people walking by and continued. "I have come far. I went from wearing a black shawl to wearing a gray shawl. People called me *loco*. They told me to stop mourning. I told them 'no!' The tragedy of my country has wounded my soul for life. I made a decision. I chose to mourn one year for each of my loved ones lost in that war. Then, I decided to mourn for every Spaniard who died in the battle. I sentenced myself to mourning for life. Now, an old woman on the sidewalk, I am proud of the years I have put into full-time mourning. I sit on the sidewalk, watch strangers go by, and pray for them. I pray that *Espana* will never divide in such an animalistic manner again. *Si,* I will pray and mourn until the day I die. It is my purpose in life."

"Well, blessed are those who mourn," said Kristine, reciting what she had learned in school of Jesus' words and the Sermon on the Mountain. "Blessed are those who mourn, for they will be comforted."

The woman held up the handkerchief, saying it one time belonged to her mother. It was the only thing she grabbed the day she died, and now, it had years and years of tears soaked into it. "Go, get on with your life, my dear. Live life," said Triste.

A paper bill floated down, landing into the bucket like an autumn leaf falling from a brittle branch, and Rafael reached his arm out to Kristine, helping her up from the sidewalk. She wondered if he minded her sitting on the ground with the homeless, but if he did, he wouldn't have dropped money in the bucket himself, she decided. She kissed Triste once on each cheek and squeezed her hand tightly. She didn't realize until she stood up how long she had been sitting there. Her buttocks felt sore and cold from the cement.

The older Spanish man and the younger American woman walked a couple blocks and stopped outside a high-rise hotel.

"No." She said in Spanish outside the hotel. "I will not go to a hotel *contigo*, Rafael. We are *amigos, no mas!*"

He looked accused of wrongful action as he urged her inside the lobby. "*Una sorpresa* for you on the top floor, *nada mas*," he explained in Spanish. "Nothing more."

They took the elevator to the twenty-sixth floor and stepped out onto a balcony glowing from candlelit tables and stars overhead. She felt like a voyager arriving in another world, another life. As one waiter led them to an intimate corner table and another poured red wine into their glasses, Rafael pointed to the three men with instruments. "They're playing the tambourine, some sort of bagpipe, and castanets," he commented.

The live instrumental music became intoxicating. Under its influence, everything possessed extra vitality, and she couldn't help but notice the details all around her. She swished the velvety wine around her glass and nibbled on some assorted cheeses, cubes of yellow, orange and white. Looking down at Madrid gave her the same sort of feeling she had experienced sitting atop the water tower, looking down on the island. But instead of palm treetops, these were rooftops. The lights from the city below looked like white Christmas tree bulbs.

Her toes tingled as she felt tipsy from just a few sips of wine on an empty stomach. "Do you know, Rafael, where light comes from?"

"*Digame*," he said, aware of the trick question.

"Those lights you see below us, the city lights, they're really just lightning bugs reincarnated."

"*¿Que?*" He didn't understand.

She switched to English and continued. "The fortunate little things once smeared against the cement by bullies and now shining so brightly again. I toured the Edison home back in Fort Myers, but I know the truth. It was really just a reincarnated lightning bug factory."

"*Tu eres una mujer muy interesante.*" He said she was a very interesting woman, although he didn't understand a thing she just said.

"*Gracias.*" She felt dramatic, a woman in a black and white movie, as she tried to decipher where the man-made window lights of the city ended, and the large celestial bodies composed of gravitationally contained hot gases emitting electromagnetic radiation started. Music and another sip of strong wine influenced her imagination, so she decided not to take another sip until she had some real food in her stomach. She no longer had to promise herself to live for the moment, she was living the moment and she appreciated it, every detail.

"*Te quiero, voy a ir a America y casarme con tu,*" Rafael broke the silence by telling her he loved her, he was going to America with her, and he wanted to marry her.

She ignored his comments, at least for a moment. She first needed another cube of cheese. As always, she understood his Spanish quite well, so she didn't have to double guess what he had just said, all in a single sentence, completely out of the blue. Had Rafael, her friend and tour guide turned himself into the stereotypical romantic male Spaniard? They hadn't yet kissed and now he wanted to marry her? First, she had no intention of kissing him, ever. Second, she didn't want him in that sort of way. She wanted him as a friend, a conversationalist, a companion, a shoulder to lean on in times of foreign distress, a man who could teach her about this country, its people, their passions and fears. She wanted him for all of these things, but not for Mr. Right.

She let his words linger in mid-air as the wine spoke to her mind. As she stared at the miles of city lights, she pretended she was a queen, looking down upon her kingdom. The wine spoke in a deep, romantic tone, telling her to consider his proposal. She had a difficult time standing up to its overpowering and seductive voice. She needed to hear Lauren's voice at this moment. Together they'd laugh at Rafael's proposal, but hadn't Lauren said she wanted to fall in love with a distinguished Spanish gentleman? She needed a pen and paper to write Grandma a letter, leaving out not a single detail. Grandma would surely say, "Now, now, now, forget it young lady! Stick to your senses! Your father would kill you, but keep writing me letters, and don't leave out a single detail!"

The waiter set down a platter of *bacalao a la vizcaina*, which she recognized as cod, tomato, thyme, red pepper, bayleaf, onion, garlic and fried croutons.

Rafael, the king, took her hand and in his native romance language, continued with his poetic proposals. "I will design you a wardrobe. I will brand name it 'Christina.' I have already begun to create the skirt, pants and blouse with you, my *preciosa*, in mind. Now, I only need to measure your waist, and I thought I could do that after dinner."

"No," she said in English. "No," she said in Spanish. "No," she said in French. No, being universal in almost any language, he understood. He was not going to put a tape measure around her waist.

Why can't he make you the wardrobe without measurements? asked the wine.

She peered deeply into his brown eyes, the same color as hers, and said once more, "no!"

"*¿Porque?*" He dared to ask why.

"*Por que.*" She answered because. She swigged some more of the seductive speaking wine, then bent down, not to catch her breath, but to reach into her purse on the floor and pull out a red crayon. Rafael closed his eyes, as if savoring his bite of food, and Kristine started to write on the white linen tablecloth. In English, she scribbled down, 'Home.' Writing it on the tablecloth now turned it into a visualized goal. She felt more focused now, ready to handle his proposals. Nothing could possibly distract her from returning home. Then again, is home Michigan or Florida? She did not know. She would figure that out later. Home definitely meant the United States of America, and that was good enough for now.

Rafael opened his eyes and for a moment stared at her scribbles, then grabbed the crayon from her. As the waiter approached the table, he quickly covered the red markings with his bread plate. Then, when the waiter walked away, he asked, "*¿Escribe?* You wrote on the table? What did you write? *¿Porque?*"

"I like to sometimes write out my goals. Americans do this all the time. Seeing them makes them more active and achievable. Besides, life is so hectic that we tend to live our lives by a list of errands. Without the list, we hang out on the sofa eating chips and pop. We go to pieces without a list of things to accomplish."

"*Ahh, si, si, Americana,*" he said. "But why on the tablecloth? *¿Por que* not on paper, *Christina*?"

"It's an American custom," the red wine lied. "*Lo siento.* I didn't realize the Spaniards do it differently."

He lifted his bread plate and scribbled down, '*Ser feliz.*' He moved the plate over the words, hiding them from the waiter.

Kristine translated it as, 'To be happy.'

She slid the candle centerpiece over and wrote, 'To return home, alone.'

He took the crayon and wrote, '*Ser feliz con Christina,*' to be happy with Kristine.

She took the crayon and broke it in half. Tablecloth scribbles made her nervous now. Perhaps they might scribble out loud and death might hear and come knocking.

Next, they feasted on *cochinillo a la segoviana*, suckling pig roasted over a wood fire and basted with lard and seasoning. Once the food overpowered the wine, she turned the conversation over to more intelligent things, like the religion of Spain.

"Does everyone in Spain practice Catholicism, Rafael?"

"Franco had forced it upon us all. But today, we worship in whichever denomination we choose."

"What have you chosen?"

"Because it was once forced upon me, I am still confused. I know many who struggle with this, still today."

℘

As he pulled up to the corner of *El Corte Ingles*, he took out his black planner and flipped to the end of the week.

"I like you. I like our conversations. But Rafael, your proposals at dinner made me nervous, you understand that, right?"

"*Si, si.* I understand. I will continue to wine and dine you, *Christina*. You will fall in love with me soon, ¡*mañana!*"

"No Rafael, that is *not* the goal of our meeting. I will *not* let that happen. As I said, I enjoy talking with you. I enjoy you as a friend."

"And you do not enjoy romance? How sad, *que triste*."

"Yes, I do, but not now. I have to leave Spain in a few months and I cannot allow myself to fall in love with a man from another country."

"Is it my age? I thought American women appreciated older men like they appreciate older wine."

"I appreciate many things in life and have much to look forward to. I need to graduate from college and move close to my family again. Spain is only temporary for me." She grabbed his day planner and flipped it forward three more weeks. She'd meet him then, no sooner.

"Then I am only temporary."

"*Si, si*, you are. So am I. Everything is temporary, Rafael." She got out of his car and started to walk down the sidewalk.

"Then what do you want from me that is permanent?" He called out the window.

She walked beside his car as he slowly drove. "Your friendship for now and your memories for later."

"And what do you want from me that is temporary?" he asked.

"Tell me your last name. For now, all I want is your last name."

"*Rafael de Espana*," he said.

"Oh. Well, don't you want to know my last name?" she asked.

"I know it. *Christina* precious angel, *Christina de los estados unidos*."

He drove away, leaving her to stand on the street corner, a tulip standing tall and proud, waiting for the photographer to snap its photo, but then, the man with the camera drives away. Now with him gone, she wanted his attention, she wanted him to pick her, to take her home and place her in a beautiful vase and give her water and care for her, admire her. She stood alone now, without his interesting facts, his sophisticated Spanish, the smell of his foreign cologne, his romantic little sayings, his coming on to her. She wilted and walked away, realizing she was just one flower in a world so full of beautiful petals. Three weeks seemed a long time and surely so many others would bloom before him in that time and she might be forgotten. Yes, she might never see him again.

She climbed in bed and lit a candle. She didn't want to wake her family by putting a light on that could be seen under the curtain of a door. She picked up a book she had been meaning to read for quite some time, *A Death in the Afternoon*, a documentary study of bullfighting by Ernest Hemingway. The more she read, the more she admired this American man who had become so close to the Spaniards. He knew them from the inside, which was her goal, although she knew three months would never be enough. She wanted more time. She read Hemingway, and his work provided her with some short cuts, some things she didn't know about the Spaniards, things she didn't have time to find out on her own. She read for hours and appreciated him for passing on such important information.

29

Dear Grandma:

It was a field day for me. My entire Spanish family left me alone. They had something to go to in some nearby town and kissed and hugged me good-bye a million times before leaving.

As soon as they left, I shaved my legs and ironed all my clothes. I felt both naughty and panicked the entire time. I feel guilty for all the water and electricity I must have used. At least I didn't wash my clothes. Washing clothes means I would then have to hang my underwear outside on the rope overlooking metropolitan Madrid. Rosario does the entire family's underwear once a month, all in one huge, collective load. Then it hangs outside for a good two days after that. Lorenzo had a colorful pair so big I thought it was the Spanish flag. I guess I wouldn't mind my undergarments hanging in the country, but in the city? No way! Not mine!

Spain and Tarpon Key certainly have something in common: Night life. For the islanders it's tarpon fishing or dock chatting. For the Spaniards it's walking the city streets *or hanging out in cafes all night. I'm not saying all insomniac's need to relocate to a remote island or Spain, but they should certainly keep in mind that not everyone in this world goes to sleep at nine o'clock. Maybe as they sit in their recliners or pace down their hallways, they can think of such places in their mind, knowing they're not the only people awake at such odd hours.*

※

Mañanas came and went, and as she crossed the corner of *El Corte Ingles* department store on her way home from school, she thought of Rafael, hoping he might drive by. She regretted the three weeks delay, but had no phone number for him, and didn't know his last name. Why hadn't she at least got his number? Why hadn't she insisted on getting his last name? Why hadn't she given him hers? Where exactly did he work? She kicked herself about Rafael from Spain, her secret source. That's all she knew. She kept him her secret, never telling anyone about him, not even Rosario.

As her Spanish improved, she discovered exciting things she never knew about her Spanish family. For instance, Diego and Michaelangelo, her brothers, were singers in a popular band. One afternoon, when Rosario and Lorenzo went to mass, they invited two band members up to the apartment and asked Kristine for help. They had been singing a song for quite some time now and needed the words translated. They wanted to know what they had been singing about.

"Sure," laughed Kristine. "I can easily interpret this song for you. Winter, Spring, Summer and Fall. *Invierno, primavera, verano, y otoño.*"

The men with guitars laughed, admitting they thought winter, spring, summer and fall were names of American women. As they continued singing songs from Crosby Stills and Nash, then the Beetles, in English, but with strong Spanish accents, Kristine laughed until she cried. She no longer felt embarrassed about her weak Spanish skills upon arrival to their country. At least she could differentiate seasons from names.

As if a wonderfully exciting storm had arrived, the brothers quickly decked themselves out in pale blue silk suits and rushed out the door, grabbing her along. They passed Rosario and Lorenzo returning from mass and kissed them affectionately.

"*Hasta Mañana*," the parents said.

"See you tomorrow? Where are we going? *¿Adonde vamos?*" Kristine asked Margherta, who joined the storm chasers.

"*Mis hermanos* are *muy* popular and tonight, they have a concert. We want to take you."

Kristine suddenly felt sheltered, as if she had been hiding away in some basement for the last few months, having no clue as to the excitement all around her. How could she not have known her Spanish brothers were in a band and that they actually played at concerts and were popular? Had they discussed it over dinner? Had she zoned out due to interpretation problems? She had heard them sing now and then, but just casually, in the shower or before bed at night. Surely, these were the signs she missed. How could she live with people, yet not know the weather patterns of their daily lives? Then again, this happened all the time. People lived under the same roof where one person took cover from a storm, the other chased after the same storm. One declared it a sunny day; the other saw the rain. One liked walking with an umbrella; the other liked getting wet. Neither knew how the other felt because neither truly listened nor asked. Well, that wasn't going to happen anymore. Her new and improved Spanish competency would no longer allow it. She could now run the trail blindfolded. She could understand words, sentences and paragraphs without straining.

They took the metro, then the *autobus* to the *pueblo*. With about three hours until the concert, they drank wine and ate bits of skewered meats, omelets, olives and ham in a nearby noisy bar. Waiters were clinking glasses, everyone was heavily engaged in laughing and shouting, and the television in the corner served no purpose, but it stayed on, adding to the noise. Two friends joined them, and when they first walked in the door, Kristine couldn't help but stare. They were imitations of Ricky Ricardo. One had shiny black hair slicked back and he wore a black sports jacket with Spanish embroidery. The other had brown curly hair, huge brown eyes and wore a yellow-flowered tie. They all wore the narrow, torture-inflicting black shoes and looked like they just stepped out of *GQ* magazine, European edition. They talked slowly for Kristine, bought her drinks, and persuaded her to order what they called the *sardinas*, a popular Spanish appetizer. Basically, it was a sardine on a platter.

Outside, the stage stood decorated in festive, brightly colored paper ornaments. Sausage and *tortilla bocadillas* were being prepared on an open grill and three one hundred-year-old looking women were dancing hand-in-hand next to a group of young rowdy teens. Two little boys were throwing a dried chicken foot at a screaming girl, who picked it up and whipped it back. Everyone was singing, dancing and clapping.

The brothers pulled her up on stage and publicly taught her how to Flamenco dance to their modern Spanish rock. Once she understood the apple concept, she caught on just fine. She discovered it as simple as reaching her right hand up to pick an apple from a tree, then with a special added twist of her reach, bringing it down toward her mouth and taking a bite, then another twist, and tossing it down to the ground. *Pick, twist, bite, twist, toss.* It was that simple. Together, everyone picked, twisted, bit, twisted and tossed over and over again.

As if the hours of pigging out and dancing weren't enough, after the concert they caught a taxi to some downtown dance clubs where they met up with more friends. As they stood in a long line for one club, Kristine noticed Margherta standing on the street, calling for a taxi.

"Wait, Margherta, why are you leaving?" Kristine called out in Spanish.

"*Porque. Porque.*" The women stared eye-to-eye for a moment, then Margherta hopped in a taxi and drove away.

The interior of the *discoteca* looked foreign, like something from the twilight zone with green glowing fluorescent lights, several floors and balconies to dance on, and a huge rectangular swimming pool in the center. After much dancing, Kristine pulled Diego aside and asked him where Margherta had gone.

"*No te preocupes,*" he told her not to worry but didn't answer her question. "*¿Estas cansadas, Christina?*" He asked her if she felt tired. After all, it was around three o'clock in the morning.

"*No, estoy bien. Me gusta la noche.*" True. She did appreciate the night. Several months ago she had dreaded it; now she lived it passionately, savoring its every hour.

Diego pulled her over to a quieter corner so he could better be heard. "Spaniards call the hours from midnight to morning *la madrugada*. Often, when *la madrugada* passes unnoticed into *la mañana*, there's no point going to bed."

They proved it. After the disco, they all walked to the Chocolateria de San Gines and ate strips of fried dough called *churros* dipped in melted chocolate.

At six-thirty in the morning, they took a taxi back to their parent's apartment. No one worried about curfews because Spaniards view night differently, not as a time to stay safely inside; but as a time to satisfy their lust for fine food, drink, conversation and dance. Margherta pulled up in a taxi at the exact same moment. Her eyes were red, and Kristine wondered why she had been crying. No one said anything as they quietly tiptoed up the wooden stairs to their parents' apartment. The exciting night had ended, and they were tired.

℘

Siesta time came every day at the same time, keeping people inside like Florida's summer rain and lightning. No one dared to control, nor alter the details of this national tradition, but instead respected it and closed down shop and halted business until it ended each day. Kristine respected the *siesta* in Spain and always dozed off as peacefully and simply as a person put to sleep by falling rain.

She needed this hour of sleep. It became the momentum necessary to stay awake through the nights in Madrid. A night out with the Spaniards felt like getting sucked up in a tornado and blown through the city streets in a sensational pattern. Madrid's younger generation called it *la movida*, the late-night scene. They took their nights of eating, drinking, talking until sunrise, dancing and riding the streets in taxis seriously, probably more so than their next day at work. But they never got drunk, nor did anything illegal or stupid. They just lived the nights like storm chasers, lustfully and passionately making the most of such fast passing moments.

As sure as a tornado warning, she knew *la movida* would suck her up again, and it did. Nacho picked her up at seven o'clock, and they spent time sipping coffee and talking at a small table outside in *La Puerta del Sol*, an oval plaza surrounded on all sides by cream-colored eighteenth century buildings. She couldn't help but imagine Steve sitting with his parents at perhaps the same table years ago, trying his first cup of strong coffee. She missed him now and wondered if some day they might find themselves standing under the same clouds and in the same rain again.

Later, they hit the *tapa* circuit, walking while chomping on blood-red *chorizos*, mushrooms in oil, potatoes with garlic mayonnaise and manchego cheese all the way from *La Puerta del Sol* to the Prado Museum, and down the streets *Carrera de San Jeronimo* and *Atocha*.

Afterward, they drove to Old Madrid and walked along the narrowed cobble streets lined with wrought iron balconies until they came to a cave-like neon-lit bar. Inside the bar, the whites of everyone's eyes, as well as the drinks, glowed a shamrock green.

Nacho started a game of pool with a stranger, and Kristine leaned against the brick wall, studying his face and his constantly twitching black eyebrows. There was still so much she didn't know about him. Weeks had gone by without his calling and she imagined his life must be very busy. Doing what, she couldn't be sure. He often kept their conversations to politics or his opinions of historical events. They just skimmed the surface with one another, and she liked that he never tried kissing, holding hands, or proposing marriage.

As she watched him hit three solid balls into some holes, she wasn't ill nor tipsy, but felt dizzy and confused to the point of frustration just thinking about how Howard must have known Nacho's family. Had Nacho lied to her? Probably. There was no reason for Nacho not to remember an American friend of the family. As much as she tried telling herself it didn't matter anymore, it still drove her crazy, and her frustration clashed with the black and white checkered floor beneath her pointy black buckled Spanish shoes. The beat of the music made her mind jump back and forth, rehashing every word Howard had ever said to her, trying to pin down some sort of clue.

Nacho studied the table seriously, but glanced at Kristine each time before shooting, raising an eyebrow without a smile. She started fidgeting with the gaudy silver ring she bought in Toledo when suddenly it hit her like the blue ball just hit the red ball. The piano! Howard said she must ask Nacho to play the piano for him! It was around three o'clock in the morning when she yelled out, "*El piano,*" and Nacho hit the red ball so hard it flew across the room and cracked down onto the floor.

No one picked it up. Instead, he signaled her to follow, and they headed for the door. Outside she asked Nacho if he was any good at the piano. His demeanor signaled the mysterious rush of a category three hurricane making a dangerous turn at the last moment. "Yes, I am good," he answered brusquely. "Why does it matter you?"

"Wait a minute, Nacho! Did you just say that in English? No? Yes, yes you did!"

"*Si, si*. I speak very little *Ingles*."

"Little? No. I don't think so. You speak fluent English, don't you? I mean, that sounded pretty good to me."

"No, please, don't compliment."

"Nacho! How *could* you not tell me something so important? How could you? You said you don't speak any English. Why would you lie to me about that?"

"In my country, we speak my language. If you don't learn the language, you don't learn the people," he shouted behind to Kristine who was almost running down the cobblestone street to catch up.

She felt as impressed as the time on the island when Howard of all people suddenly switched from jabberwocky to perfectly fluent Spanish. "I want to know the people of Spain. I want to know you, but you are very mysterious, Nacho. I don't know that you want me to know you. Can you understand me right now?"

"No." He laughed, stopped and turned around. "*Si, si*, good."

"Nacho," she called out to him, nearly out of breath. "Just think of all the good conversations we could have had by now if you only told me sooner you speak English."

He stopped again in the middle of the narrow street, raising his arms toward the black sky above. "What, what do you want to talk about?" He looked at his watch. "We talk now."

She stepped up to him, eye-to-eye. "The piano. Play the piano for me. Let's find a piano."

"*No se*. It has been a long time."

"So it's true. You do play the piano, or you used to?"

"*Si*. I used to play every day, every *minuto*, but today, no. Today I don't play anymore."

"Nacho, *por favor*. I am leaving your country very soon. I beg you to play for me."

He rolled his eyes as he opened the car door for her. "Okay. I take you to my piano."

As he sped down the cramped and curvy roads in his bright yellow car, Kristine sat in silence, shocked at the discovery that her mysterious friend spoke English and proud of herself for remembering the key that might unlock his secret.

"*Vamos.* We go to the apartment of my mama. She is not home tonight, and I respect her. If she were home, we would not go there now."

Asking people why they had come to Tarpon Key had always proved fascinating. She now tried a new question with Nacho, hoping to achieve similar results. "Nacho, why do you play the piano?"

"Stupid question," he replied with his lips and with his hand gestures that always danced in tune with his emotions and that meant they hardly ever stayed put on the steering wheel.

"No. Don't say that. It's not stupid," said Kristine. "I don't come from a musical background. Music isn't my domain. Do you understand me? I am envious of people with a talent for music. I just wonder why you hit the ball across the room when I said the word 'piano.'"

"*Tranquilo, tranquilo.* You wait." His eyes frantically traveled from her eyes to the rear view window to the radio, but never to the road ahead it seemed. She decided not to talk any further until they had arrived safely and she could step out of this carnival ride.

If there were a ticket booth outside his mother's apartment, people would surely purchase tickets to get in. Art sculptors, statues, and white rugs stood upright and still, making Kristine self-conscious of her own posture upon entering. As in a painting, the dark object caught her attention immediately, the only dark item in the elegant living room. Nacho walked over to the black piano bench and picked up a gold and ash colored vase that rested on the bench like a bouquet of flowers on a gravesite. He carefully placed it atop the piano before taking a seat.

"I am angry at you, Kristine," he said as he cracked his fingers.

As she stood in the center of the white room, she felt a sudden chill, similar to that which entered the dorm room just before Lauren had died. "Why are you angry at me?"

"Wait. Just wait. *Un momento.*" He stood up and walked over to a white candle. After lighting it, he dimmed the lights and returned to the piano bench to sit down again. He pushed the sleeves of his white oxford up, as if performing steps of a ritual. "This is serious," he said.

"Playing the piano for me is serious?"

"No," he scolded. " I don't play for you." He compulsively moved the vase to the left about an inch. Then he moved it to the right about two inches, and back to the left again a quarter of an inch.

"Then whom do you play for?"

He didn't answer. As if he had forgotten he had a one-person informal audience standing before him, his fingers hit the keys, and his nervous facial glitches and eyebrow twitches danced in tune with the notes. At times, she noticed his scar, like an etching carved into petrified stone. It neither responded to the music nor to the movement of his facial muscles. She wondered what had caused it. But then, as if the piano contained some mysterious electricity, it jolted him. The lines on his forehead deepened, and his eyes closed.

As she stood alone in the large room, Kristine suddenly felt fear. The death of her friend frightened her. She too would die some day. Her other loved ones might also die. She had no control over its timing. It would arrive when it liked, a thief in the night.

His music switched keys, and now she felt guilty. She should have stayed in Michigan long enough to attend the funeral, to comfort the family, to wear black. She should have met Lauren twice a week for coffee instead of once a week. Sure they studied together nightly, but she should have insisted they have more fun together. She should have told Lauren how much she loved her as a friend. She should have this and that. She should have... she should have...

The music exploded into storms of octaves echoing each other as Nacho's hands pounded the keys almost violently now. She felt anger bursting from the keys or going into the keys—she didn't know which. Lauren had left her at a very bad time, just before their semester in

Spain. She had never said good-bye. How rude! Kristine felt angry at the thought of life ending without warning, mad that God had made it all part of some plan. Nacho also looked angry, as he too looked afraid, then guilty. They both seemed to be taking the same journey.

His music slowed and she felt sad. She wanted to block out the music, but it demanded sensitive listening. If she let herself cry, she could have donated enough tears to form a man-made lake.

Sweat dripped from Nacho's face and she felt exhausted watching him, tired from going through the stages of grief. When his fingers stopped, the room filled with a lonely quiet. The silence ached, so she had to say something, but she self-consciously knew that her voice sounded ugly after such gorgeous notes. She stood still, alone, in the center of the room, her arms hanging awkwardly beside her.

"Nacho, who did you lose?"

He stared at the vase. "My father," he said, then slammed his hands down on the keys.

She jumped. "Why don't you play the piano anymore?"

"I do not know what notes might come out. *Mi padre*, he died of cancer one year ago. He was my, how you say it, *mi maestro, mentor de la musica*. I am prodigy, but he was mentor."

"I'm so sorry."

"No, I am. He died when I was in law school. I had no piano with me. A man tries to cry in the shower so the two waters blend. I couldn't cry in the shower and I stayed at school. I wish now I had gone home, but nobody is taught how to feel, how to be."

"I'm glad you played for me."

"No! I no play for you!" he pounded the keys again. "I play for *mi papa*, for his spirit."

"*Lo siento.*"

"I played violin in Madrid's symphony before *mi padre se muerio*."

"I'm embarrassed to admit that I've never gone to a symphony," she said.

"You, go to symphony! It is the greatest form of team, I tell you. Not flesh, but team of spirits. You, go!" Nacho closed his eyes and struck the keys some more.

Her questions about Nacho, his intensity were answered. He was a child prodigy, mentored by his beloved father who had recently died. He hadn't played the piano since. He had been numb until tonight. Now she wanted to know how Howard fit into all of this.

"Howard! Who's Howard?"

Nacho stopped playing. "Howard was the American man traveling Europe with the backpack. He shared a room of the hospital with *mi padre*. Howard suffered cancer too and I played *el piano* to help them both sleep. But Howard said he could not die in hospital and he left."

"Yes, he left for an island in Florida," added Kristine.

"I don't know. He said he went to help a brother. He got a funny wig, a funny hat, and a mask of hair for his face, too. Doctors said he had some time."

"Nacho, I'm so glad you decided to speak English tonight."

30

She could hear catwalk music blaring from Rafael's Mercedes as he pulled up to the well-lit commercialized corner of *El Corte Ingles*. European shoppers with bags full of expensive clothes, perfumes and cosmetics scurried about the corner, and at times, it seemed that the mutter of their voices rang louder than the blaring traffic noises.

Kristine looked at her wristwatch. It was nine forty-five. This time Rafael was only ten minutes late, but she no longer minded his typical tardiness, the entire country's lateness for that matter. A culture that runs behind schedule allowed her to do things she might not normally make time to do. But since Rafael had showed up only a few minutes late, it left her no time to chat with her homeless friend, who again sat on the same sidewalk square between the same two sidewalk cracks.

A wave will do for tonight, thought Kristine, as she glanced over at Triste. Instead of a return wave, however, the old lady frantically flagged something small and purple in the air. She knew Rafael sat waiting in his car, but she ran over to the woman anyway.

"*Aqui. Para ti, mi amiga preciosa,*" the old woman said, handing Kristine a tiny purple cloth bag.

"For me? This is for me?" Kristine took the gift and started opening it but Triste grabbed her hands.

"No. *Ahora, no. En los estados unidos, si.*" Triste begged her not to open it until she returned to the United States.

"*Bueno, bueno.* I'll wait. *Gracias.*" Kristine stuffed the sack in the bottom of her purse.

Triste pointed to Rafael and flagged her to go now. "*No te preocupes. ¡Vive!*" She told her not to worry; but live. Go live life!

Rafael wore a black turtleneck and gray dress slacks. His shoes always shone and his cologne always smelled like a brand new car. Kristine didn't recognize it as *Polo*, or *Obsession for Men*, or *Calvin*, but she knew the scent meant a night full of conversation, rich food, red wine and culture.

They left the skyscrapers and city traffic behind and drove about fifteen miles into country hills filled with ancient tall pines. Kristine wondered what might be in the purple sack in her purse, but she promised not to open it until she left Spain. She couldn't wait to know and felt tempted to peek early. She wondered if Rafael minded her befriending the woman. He and Triste shared one major opinion. Both disliked Franco. The woman mourned the damage he had done to her country and people during his autocratic rule. Rafael celebrated the fashion and freedom that came to his country following his death.

"Rafael, *no te gusta Franco, ¿no?*" She wanted to make sure she understood well that he didn't like Franco.

"Some give credit to Franco," Rafael answered in Spanish. "After all, he never opened Spain to Hitler and that is very positive. But I give him very little credit. I made one mistake in life many years ago, one mistake very horrible. Because of Franco, I've had to live with that mistake, and my life has not been good."

Kristine unrolled her window so she could feel the cool air hit her in the face as they drove. "What sort of mistake?"

As they pulled up to a ranch-style restaurant, Rafael put his fingers to his lips and shushed the topic, giving Kristine a subtle indication not to ask again. "This restaurant, where I am taking you, received five forks, *cinco!*"

"Five forks? *¿Que significa?*" She asked what that means.

"It means I only take you to the best." He answered in Spanish. "*En Espana*, we rate restaurants on a scale of one to five forks, based on the quality and price."

A hostess greeted Rafael by name and led them to a candlelit table on a glassed-in porch on the side of a cliff overlooking some nearby chestnut trees and evergreen oaks in the distance.

A wandering flamenco dancer dressed in orange, purple and yellow stopped in front of their table to perform, and Rafael leaned over to Kristine to whisper loudly his opinion of the dancer. "This dancer is emotionally uninhibited. She is more concerned with experiencing the very moment than with anything else in life."

Kristine didn't understand. She only saw a dancer. "Do you know her?"

"No. Watch the Flamenco. Watch her moves. She is completely carefree and has an attitude toward *la vida. La musica* and dance are her ways to express it." Rafael sat silent for a moment and the song and dance seemed never-ending to Kristine.

"*¿Que piensas? Digame, Christina. Digame in ingles.*" He asked her what she saw in the dancer, but asked her to describe it in English, not Spanish.

"That's odd. You want me to describe what I see in the dancer…in English?"

"*Si, si, en ingles, Christina. Ingles.*"

"Okay, sure. I can do that but you won't be able to understand what I'm saying," she replied. "Oh well, I'll describe what I see. I see a dancer. A dancer in a colorful costume who's getting a great aerobic work…"

Rafael interrupted by gently pushing her chin toward the dancer. "*Mira.* Look at the dancer, not me," he urged in Spanish.

"*Si, si,* I see a dancer, one who has a story to tell. It's a long story because she's been dancing a long time now. She wants to share her story. She wants to express it. This woman is expressing a story about…death. She has some things to say about life and death and things worth doing."

Kristine forgot about the man sitting beside her, and instead, only noticed the lines on the gypsy's forehead deepen as her voice turned rough, like sandpaper. "Oh dear, this song is tormenting. She is looking, her eyes shut now. It's regret… it must be."

As her neck jolted and her eyes rolled around, the woman didn't seem to notice the couple at the table. "She's looking back on her life, the hardships, the frustrations, and how she handled them, or how she let them handle her. What else can it be? She's dancing through the dark moments of her life," announced Kristine, who could feel her own face responding to the scene before her.

Then the gypsy's teeth showed and her forehead crevices disappeared. "Peace," declared Kristine. "She has found peace in the present. She is going to focus on things worth doing, things she can control, her attitude toward hardships."

"I thought Flamenco was always happy-go-lucky," continued Kristine. "I thought Flamenco was simply a reach, pick, twist and toss. I was wrong. This woman is releasing every stress she's ever had, I'm sure of it. This is an emotional outburst, and she's not afraid to express herself. We shouldn't be either, should we? The fact that I allow my own body to panic is crazy. I want to Flamenco, not panic. She expressed her story so passionately. Rafael, I'm glad you made me truly watch this. *Gracias*."

The woman moved on to another table. In Spanish, Kristine told Rafael she felt like dancing the Flamenco, too, because it looked so therapeutic. He held her hand tightly and smiled, staring in her eyes.

"*Algun dia*, some day," he told her. "I'd like you to do your Tulip dance for me."

Kristine laughed. "Oh, my Dutch dance? Okay, some day. I need my wooden shoes to do it."

Three waiters catered to their table. One opened a bottle of red wine, another laid cloth napkins on their laps, and the third opened their menus. As Rafael raised his glass of dry sherry to his mouth, she caught glimpse of his gold wristwatch that whispered five minutes until midnight.

Suddenly, she wanted to know why Rafael never told her his last name. Who was this older man sitting next to her? To be fair, she reminded herself, she had never disclosed her last name, or the whereabouts of her Spanish family's apartment.

They picked at the plate of cold *serano* ham, sausage and shellfish. Rafael ordered a bottle of sparkling *cava*, Spanish Champagne. She demanded his last name.

"Rafael. *Yo soy Rafael de Espana*," he replied.

"Okay, Rafael from Spain, say something more, please. *Mas, mas.*"

"*¿Quien eres, Christina?*"

"Who am I? *Yo soy Christina de los Estados Unidos.*" Two could play this game.

He poked his long, tiny fork in the plate of octopus salad, asking her if she ever considered staying in Spain *mas de solamente un semestre.*

She told him she missed her family back home, so "No."

He said if she ever did consider it, he could provide her a job in the fashion industry. He held a fork of baby eels dripping garlic butter sauce up to her mouth, urging her to taste. She tasted and he urged her to taste more.

"*Mas, mas,*" he insisted.

She tasted more. He said if ever she considered staying in Madrid a little longer, he'd find her an *apartmento* and pay the rent. He sampled the grilled crayfish off her plate, then asked if she ever considered traveling around all of Europe and the world.

"No. *Yo no puedo, Rafael,*" she stated boldly. "I can't travel the world, as much as I would love to. I have college waiting for me in Michigan."

"*Si, Si, entiendo,*" he said he understood. "But you would have a far superior education with me. The world has so much more to offer than a textbook, *un libro*. You see the world with me."

"No. Traveling costs money. I have to put all my *dinero* toward school right now. Please stop with all your offers."

"*No te preocupes, Christina.* I will finance your travels. And then, I will finance the cost of attending the *universidad*. Marry me, then travel with me."

"No! I've read all about Don Juan men like you, so stop trying to convince me. Besides, I would miss *mi familia* horribly."

"*No te preocupes, mi preciosa.* I will fly your *familia* here for several months out of the year. I will buy them a house in the mountains and they can rent out rooms."

"No," she said. "No."

"I can come to *los Estados Unidos*. You teach me English. During our engagement, I could grow close to your *familia*."

She laughed. That wouldn't work. He wasn't that much younger than her own father. Oh no, that would never work. "No," she stated again.

"I build a home in America, but I still have to travel much to *Europa* on business. As long as I have your precious face, I can design clothing anywhere in the world."

"Wait, wait, wait! *Un momento, Rafael!*" She had no problem being firm with her words. She knew the persistently romantic reputation of the stereotypical Spanish man. She told him there would be no wedding, nor consideration of a wedding. They shared a friendship, and a special one for that matter, but nothing more! If he couldn't accept that, this would be their last night together. She stood up and walked to the bathroom.

As she passed a table where the Flamenco dancer now performed, she noticed a young woman wiping her eyes while watching the dancer. The woman's hair shone black and straight, and her skin light, but the man who held her in his arms had much darker skin. As the woman dropped the napkin from her eyes, Kristine stopped dead in her tracks. It was Margherta. The women spotted each other at the exact moment, and Margherta looked like a deer caught in the headlights of an oncoming car.

As Kristine walked over to her Spanish sister's table, the young man generously pulled up a chair, offering her a seat. "Hello. How are you?" he said.

"Hello. *Hola* Margherta. You speak English," she said to the young man, as she glanced back and forth at both young people.

"Yes. My name is Ron and obviously, I'm American, as you can see, my skin is much darker than Margherta's. Margherta refuses to learn English, but one of these days, I'll teach her. In some odd way, beyond my understanding, she feels it might be disloyal to her mama." He laughed, then kissed Margherta on the cheek, wiping a falling tear from her cheek.

"Is Margherta all right?" asked Kristine.

"She's fine. She gets absorbed in watching the Flamenco dancers. Did you know those songs and dances are made up of Arabic, Sephardic Jewish, and African music?"

"No, I had no idea, but I found the dance quite moving myself. She was at our table earlier."

"Everyone proudly says the Flamenco reflects the region's multicultural heritage. I know that's what Margherta loves most about it anyway, the multicultural heritage."

"Margherta, *estas bien?*" Asked Kristine, worried they were ignoring her.

"*Si, si.*" She smiled then waved her hands for the two to go on talking without her.

"Margherta and I are very much in love. But, from one American to another, can I ask you to keep our secret?"

"Of course, but what secret?"

"Well, you can't tell her mother about us, don't tell anyone. Some day, very soon, we'll tell everyone. But she's not ready now."

"I don't understand."

He took a sip of his wine and continued. "Okay. I'm a lawyer from New York. I'm fluent in Spanish and French and pretty much German as well. I love languages. Anyway, two years ago I came to Spain on business and met Margherta. I found her adorable from the start. We met while in line to buy a tuna sandwich at a café. Man, was she ever fascinated with the United States, you know, like it was some other planet. I found her curiosity so cute that we talked all night, in fact, until morning. We talked like this night after night and, well, you probably found that the Spaniards love their nights. They don't stop talking. Five nights felt like five years with Margherta."

They laughed and Margherta joined in.

"So why the secret?"

"Well, you know Rosario. She's, well how do I put it? She's from the older school. It's like she almost misses Franco's control. She adores her children, her country, and might I say the old Spain? That's the problem. I'm not from Spain, and my skin is black. This mattered to her. She has no idea we're still seeing each other. She has no idea we're so in love and those feelings are not going to die."

"Well, she herself fell for someone from the city. She's from the country. I find her homesick all the time, and she's lived in Madrid for far longer than she ever lived in Pamplona," said Kristine. "Do you think she's worried Margherta will marry you and move to the states?"

"Yes, but we haven't really made that decision yet." He finished his wine and nodded to the waiter to pour another. "Maybe we can live in both places. I'm pretty close to my family back there, and you know how close their family is here. I just don't know yet."

"Oh, Margherta." Kristine squeezed her Spanish sister's hand tightly, and Margherta reached over to kiss her on the cheek. "Where are you staying?" she asked Ron.

"I'm renting an apartment downtown, both here and in New York. I get here every chance I can."

"And no one knows of your relationship?"

"Her brothers do. They take her out with them all the time, then she catches a taxi to meet me. They all feel so guilty for it, yet they all respect their parents so much. Telling them might only hurt them."

Just then, Rafael, in all his tallness, came walking around the corner, looking at his watch and looking worried, as if he feared that his date for the night and for the past several months had left him and his proposals forever behind.

"*Rafael, aqui, estoy aqui,*" Kristine called him over to their table.

"*Ahh, Christina, Christina.*"

"*¿Quien eres?*" Margherta asked the well-dressed Spaniard now standing at their table.

"*Es Rafael. Um…Rafael…de Espana,*" answered Kristine, noticing how European his gray black hair looked slicked back, almost long enough for a pony tail should he choose.

Rafael introduced himself to both Margherta and Ron, kissing them each, once on each cheek. He and Ron spoke in Spanish for several minutes as Kristine whispered into her Spanish sister's ear something about Rafael helping her with homework and showing her Madrid's hot spots and being her friend and picking her up on the corner and treating her wonderfully. Margherta laughed and told her to have him come to the apartment instead of the corner.

A few moments later the waiter walked over, indicating to Rafael that more food was waiting, hot, at their table.

"Ron, my Spanish is pretty good now, but please, just in case, let Margherta know I've kept Rafael my secret until now. He's so much older than me and hasn't yet told me his last name, or where exactly he lives, or a phone number, yet I like him more each time he picks me up on that stupid corner. Yet I make him meet me there in case he is some crazy man."

"Kristine, this is no crazy man. Ask him some more questions, you'll see. He is very well known."

She stood up and put her arms around Rafael. "Did he tell you that?"

"No, he didn't have to. I know who Rafael is."

"Who?"

"Someone who really thinks highly of you, Christina of the United States. I like that one," he laughed. "Get to know him on your own, just as you're doing. And soon, give him your last name."

"I'll keep getting to know him, but I'll ask Margherta when I get home tonight exactly who he is and what he's trying to hide. Simplify things a bit."

"I don't think so. Margherta and I have our own secret, and we respect the secrets of others. You won't get a single clue from either of us." He smiled. "Now go, have fun. It was great meeting you."

"You too and tell Margherta I will never mention your secret."

"I'll tell her. I love her so much that nothing but death could ever come between us."

As much as she loved food, especially authentic Spanish cuisine, she neither tasted nor smelled anything the rest of the evening, as if all her senses drifted directly into her conversation with Rafael. They touched on the subjects that convert strangers to friends and then topics that turn friends into couples. He talked about growing up an only child since his mother couldn't have any other children. She talked about growing up with sisters, one being so many years younger. He told her he had reached a crossroads in life, for he had come to understand the difference between spirituality and religion. She told him she grew up Catholic, yet attended an all-Dutch school. Later her parents left Catholicism for a charismatic congregation. Now, she knew she loved God and that the Bible was his word. But that was about all she knew.

He whispered that he loved his work yet loved life more. She admitted she tended to turn life into one big productivity checklist but over the last several months her perspective had been changing. He told her he wants to treat a wife like a queen, he had it in him to offer a wonderful life to someone willing to accept it. She told him she had so many things to do yet in life and finding Mr. Right wouldn't happen for years yet. They discussed all of this and much more, without mentioning their last names.

He dropped her off on the corner, telling her to consider his proposals. It was mid November and he had to leave for Italy on business. He wouldn't be returning to *Espana* until mid December, but that should allow her plenty of time to make a decision, he said.

§◌

Thanksgiving, truly an American holiday, arrived and went without turkey, sweet potatoes and family.

Thank you, Lord, for creating such magnificently unique people, and for letting me get to know them. Thank you for all of our differences and similarities. There's a million different jobs, checkbooks, cars, houses, and lifestyles out there, yet there's only so many emotions. This means, no matter how different we all are, we all share the same emotions. And death, well, it's prejudiced against no one. No matter how much wealth we acquire, no matter how strong a fortress we build around ourselves, death will find each one of us, break down our walls and penetrate our protective armor.

She spent her next few weekends on bus trips to nearby Toledo and Salamanca, and a ten-hour train ride to Barcelona. There she found a cathedral with unlocked doors so she went in and knelt in the very last pew. She recognized the song, *Ave Marie*, Grandma's favorite. It had been played at her funeral. Kristine tried to pray, but her thoughts quickly jogged up the aisle to the front row, just as Grandma always used to lead the entire red-faced, furious family directly to the first pew when they arrived late. Dressed in satin oriental slippers, the petite woman used to say that running into church was her only form of exercise, so she might as well make the distance all the way up to the front.

Kristine, still sitting in the back of the church, watched up front as Grandma dug through her purse for butterscotch candy. Kristine listened and waited for the loud whisper. "I do not have a temper so don't think that I do but I just can't get this damn candy wrapper off." Grandma always said that, and sometimes, she said it so loudly that Kristine feared the priest overheard the word damn. "Then I'll go to confession after mass and take care of it," Grandma would say. Damn and Hell were the only swear words Grandma ever used, so she confessed.

The smell of sandalwood drifted throughout the church and like the waves hitting the beach, each time Kristine breathed deeply, another whiff of sandalwood assailed her.

She smiled, knowing that the woman she loved so dearly had returned to her Maker, like the seashells she found while walking the beach, the ones too gorgeous and loved to be kept, the ones tossed back into the water where they came from. She lit a candle for Grandma and left the church.

As she walked and walked, she found herself replaying Rafael's proposals over and over in her mind, like shifting from one canvas to another, painting one, then the other. *A worldly education...learning from people and lands rather than from pages of a textbook...a bed and breakfast for her parents in the mountain's of Spain...a job in the European fashion industry...doing what? Who knows? Does it matter?*

The canvases she painted in her mind would surely make Howard proud. But suddenly she felt disturbed. She didn't love Rafael in the husband sort of sense, nor in the boyfriend sense. She loved him as a friend and absolutely nothing more. On the other hand, she had always wanted a friend for a husband and they had never kissed so perhaps a kiss would add some red or at least pink paint to the painting in her mind. She told herself not to think about this man, or his proposals, any longer, but she couldn't help it. He stayed on her mind. As she saw new things in Spain, she could hear his slow, sophisticated Spanish explaining the significance to her in a passionate way. Yes, Rafael walked passionately through life, all the while carrying some sad secret. She would welcome any story, any secret that might come whispering through his lips, the lips she now craved to kiss for the first time.

On December 18th, she turned twenty-two years old and each person in her Spanish family kissed her *dos veces*, once on each cheek. Rosario made *paella* and a chocolate glaze torte, and everyone drank *Rioja* wine. A few times Kristine caught Margherta deeply involved in a daydream stare, but other than that, they never spoke a word about either Ron or Rafael. Perhaps she felt that sharing it with others might further betray what her own parents didn't know. Kristine respected this.

After eating a piece of torte, Margherta handed her a box of dark chocolate and together the women indulged in the moment, perhaps to satisfy the cravings they each had, one for Ron, the other for Rafael. Why did chocolate do this? It terrified Kristine that chocolate brought Rafael to mind. Didn't that mean something serious? Love?

The women closed their eyes and savored each bite. They did this until the last round truffle disappeared. Overdosed and fatigued, they lay on the hard wood floor of the apartment holding their stomachs and laughing at first, then crying from feelings of gluttony and abuse to their stomachs. Kristine realized the limits to indulging in the moment and dreaded how she might feel tomorrow. She thought of Rafael always telling her, "*Mañana, mañana, mañana*," then she decided that eating like there's no tomorrow could literally lead to no *mañana*. But they did it in honor of their men, one a lawyer in New York City and the other a fashion designer off somewhere in Europe. Yes, men had this effect on women. It was the men's fault.

Despite the chocolate overdose, *mañana* came anyway, and Nacho, layered in T-shirts and a thick oatmeal sweater, took her for ice cream and a walk through a nearby park. He didn't care if he drew attention to himself as he sang, "God rest ye merry gentleman, I dunno the rest of the words."

Kristine nudged him, hoping he'd quiet just a bit, then realized it was his country and he could do as he pleased. His voice echoed through the chilly park, while a group of little boys tossed a couple of pennies at him.

"I'm just a man who loves to sing and play life key by key," he sang his own words to the holiday tune that reminded Kristine of a list, not exactly a things-to-do list, but a Christmas shopping list. She already bought her mother some blue and silver earrings from a day trip to Toledo, and her little sister a purse shaped in the fashion of a dollhouse at *El Corte Ingles* department store. Her father would get a leather day planner from the Sunday market in the street, and her older sister a Madrid T-shirt and some European brand of blush and lipstick.

As they walked and as he sang, her mind journeyed further from the materialistic list, to a place she had never visited before, a place that might put the North Pole out of business. Instead of costly objects, her mother needed to know how much she loved her as a friend, not just a mom. Her little sister needed to know how much she would always be there for her as she grew up, when she might need someone to talk to about boys and dating and anything else. Her father needed to know how much she loved him. Her older sister needed to know that no matter how far apart they might be living, she would always love her as a friend and a sister and no distance could fade that love.

Nacho's Christmas carol ended. "Let's get you some ice-cream, no? That always makes you feel better. Come on," he said.

She longed for peppermint stick ice cream, but the counter they stopped at didn't carry it. In its place, she ordered some chocolate nutty flavor in honor of her mother who loved nutty flavors. She took a bite of her sugar cone and promptly missed her father, who always took over her cones once she demolished the ice cream. She looked down at the fresh chocolate stain on her white blouse and missed her little sister, the child that stained every shirt she ever wore while eating ice cream. She pinched an inch on her stomach and thought of her older sister, who always worried about getting fat, yet always had a cone in her hand. She spotted a wreath on the door of a shop and reminded herself it was December, so the shop back home would be closed. Instead of eating ice cream, her parents were probably sitting on the dock of the rental home drinking drambuie right now. They always drank drambuie in December, and gin and tonic the rest of the year.

She looked around at the park benches filled with Spaniards deep in discussion. She noticed the birds of the air and wondered if they had Spanish-sounding chirps. She smelled the aroma of bread from a nearby shop and wondered how she'd survive in America without bread at each dinner. She looked at her friend walking beside her and wondered what she'd do without seeing his beautiful face full of expression, emotion and drama as he talked. She wondered if she might be better off staying in Spain a little longer. It would spare her from having to say good-bye.

"There. Do you feel better after your ice-cream, Kristine?" Nacho asked as they reached the street in front of her apartment.

She didn't tell him that ice cream also brought on horrendous homesickness. "*Si, si.* I am better, Nacho. Except now, I don't know how to say good-bye to you." She looked up at the balcony lined with stockings to see if Rosario were watching. She wasn't.

"Friends don't say that, Kristine. No good-byes between friends." Nacho spoke like an expert on the subject of saying good-bye, and his confidence made him so believable.

"But I'm leaving you're country, you know that. I'm not going to see you any more."

"You see me more. You see me when you hear the piano, when you go to orchestra. You see me when you close your eyes and remember me."

"I don't want to go. I don't want to just remember you. I want to listen to you, to hear you, to see you with my eyes. I like what I see with my eyes. You know that, don't you, Nacho?"

"*Si, si. Claro*, of course. But I want you to see things without eyes, too. Go and see the world without eyes. You'll see new things. Now go, leave. *Hasta luego.*"

"Okay, okay. See you. See ya later. *Hasta luego*, Nacho."

31

Screaming, clapping people nudged her from all directions and she couldn't hear a single word Rafael kept shouting into her ear. As they sat in the stands on a Sunny Sunday afternoon, waiting for the initial pageantry to start, she felt disgusted that so many people were waving flags and cheering for the onslaught of a bull, as if cheering a touchdown. She thought that reading Hemingway would prepare her, and it had, until she sat in the bleachers herself and now had to see things with her own eyes. She knew it was her first time and her emotions were taking over. She knew she wasn't allowing the facts of bullfighting to penetrate her mind, and that she had allowed herself to revert back to ignorance.

Here sat the only still body in the bleachers and her face stuck out in the crowd, her nose red from fighting back tears, Rudolph the Red-nosed Reindeer amidst a group who cheered and probably called her names, had they known the thoughts now rushing through her mind. She didn't want to ruin Rafael's time, but then again, she didn't want to hide her feelings either. She always smiled and laughed and acted so polite on the outside. This time, she refused.

Rafael fanned her face with a folded brochure and explained that the *corrida de toros* wasn't a sport but a spectacle. He told her that his country respected it as art, and asked her how many paintings, sculptures, music, dance and literature revolve around football?

"*No mucho*," she answered. Nonetheless, the poor bull. She told him in ancient Egypt, Mesopotamia and Crete, that bulls were the objects of worship. Her ancient civilization professor once told her so. "Now look at them."

The black creatures stood in their little pens in the arena below. "They look so naive and adorable," said Kristine.

"No! Fierce and untamed," shouted Rafael.

She asked him how they trained bulls to "charge."

He said they aren't *trained* to charge. He said *toros* are born with the instinct to attack anything that threatens their predominance.

She laughed when the Spaniard next to her said bulls don't know the cloth is red. They're colorblind.

As the bulls grumpily stood in their suffocating pens, she blew her nose, aware that such creatures, only five years old, would soon experience what Rafael called the ultimate test of their existence: their performance with the bullfighter. He said that bulls live a spoiled, noble, enviable life, spared from slaughterhouses.

She disagreed, and like a rebel in an animal research lab, she sat in Madrid's *Plaza de Toros*, feeling compelled to run down the bleachers and let the five-year-old creatures loose. She felt foreign, and Rafael was a stranger with different values. For the first time in her life, she longed to be at an American football game.

Like the energy of a bull, rising and rising as it sits in the tiny pen waiting to defend itself, her own questions…about Rafael…who he was…why he never told her his last name, were also rising. She had to know. She felt sick from not knowing who he was. Yes, she loved his company. Yes, she learned a lot of culture from him, and yes, she once craved to kiss him, but the chocolate took care of that and now, she demanded to know more! She too prepared to fight.

"*Rafael, tu estas un hombre muy mysterioso. ¿Quien estas?*" She tried to sound both serious and mad, but knew her tone in Spanish always came out the same. That of an American with a Dutch accent, carefully choosing words with the right meaning, and hoping she made the right choice as she said them.

"Christina…"

A loud trumpet sounded, interrupting him. She couldn't compete with the crowds as they sprung from their benches, jumping up and down. It was an opening parade of some sort. Men fashioned in Sixteenth Century clothes entered the arena on horses. The three bullfighters, killers, *matadores*, celebrities, or whatever they're called, walked into the arena wearing colorful costumes and black hats.

Their objective obvious: to kill a bull, she told Rafael.

"No!" he shouted, offended. He said the objective is to artistically and intricately maneuver the cape and *muleta!* And while doing so, to elegantly dance with the bull in all its animalistic *brutalidad.*

She had never thought of it that way before.

Individual teams accompanied the three bullfighters, and Rafael explained to her that the team members handled all sorts of things, including using the cape and placing sticks in *los toros*. He said the team members once dreamed of becoming *matadores*, bullfighters, and it may have been their only ambition in life for quite some time. But they never made it past the novice stage, so they're just part of the teams now. Only *matadores* have the right and permission to kill fully-*grown toros*, he added.

Some workers entered the scene and smoothed out the sand in the arena, and Kristine's mind paved over Rafael's proposals. She knew his offer to stay in Spain sounded good and she found herself considering it, but first, she demanded once more that he tell her everything. She asked for his last name again and didn't know why she felt so obsessed with the question, when she herself never told him her own last name. She felt bothered, perhaps because he kept his secrets stuffed so far down, like toys stuck in the toes of a stocking. She couldn't wait any longer. Everyone else shared their stories, their fears, and their feelings.

Why wouldn't he? She asked him why he wouldn't tell her. Then she said it.

"I will never see you again, Rafael," she told him in Spanish.

"No!" He yelled louder, as if she triggered his temper. He warned her never to say such a thing again.

Everyone in the arena below stood in designated spots. The president of the *corrida* took out a white handkerchief and waved it, and a bull charged out of the tiny pen after a morning of rest.

"Rafael!" Kristine yelled.

His eyes followed the action in the arena below, but he answered. "I do have secrets."

Those words alone struck her. Fear, like the charging bull. But then she glanced in the arena below and decided that no one feared anything. She saw no fear in the bull, or the matador, as if dying meant nothing in the arena below. How could a young man stand face-to-face with a ready-to-charge bull yet show no fear? She herself, sitting safely on the bleachers next to a stranger in some ways and a friend in others, felt more fear than a matador ready to be charged at. Crazy. But her fear wasn't crazy. It felt real. Rafael knew she would soon leave his country, and he'd never see her again. So maybe he planned to kill her out of passion, like the scene in the arena. It must be passion in the arena below. Why else would these young men make this their life's ambition? Passion. It had to be. A passion planted so long ago and shared by an entire country.

The initial stages continued, and the *torero* was experimenting with his cape and the bull. "His objective, Christina, is to find out if the *toro* favors one of its horns over the other. Yes, the *torero* needs to get in touch with the animal's natural tendency. He needs to test the bull's eyesight and try to understand and learn whether it charged in a long, smooth manner or short and choppy," said Rafael in Spanish.

She glanced back and forth from the bullfight to the man next to her, as if watching his face for reassuring clues. Some sort of clue that would reassure her that the blood below meant nothing serious. She also watched the man about to battle a bull. His good posture and perfect walk proved that he felt no fear. She glanced around at the Spanish faces in the bleachers around her. They looked as if they loved life too much to fear death. She envied them.

The matador led the big black animal into the center of the ring. The *picadores* stabbed the bull. "In order for the bull to follow the cape smoothly, it needs to be slowed a bit. Its head must be lowered," explained Rafael. The picador pierced the animal with a few knives, correcting any defects in its charge. "Now, the bull won't hook to the right anymore, and it won't swing up its horns as often. *Tal cosas* could have killed the matador if not adjusted."

A trumpet sounded to signal the final act of the drama. The matador, with sword in hand, asked the president if he could kill the bull. The president gave permission, and the matador dedicated the animal's death to his mother!

The creature, now angrier than ever, jumped around, arching its shiny black back and neck and kicking up its hind legs. Rafael watched below as he confessed. "*Soy triste.* I have been unhappy for many years, Christina. My wife only wants my money. She does not want to talk to me. She does not care what I say or what I feel. We are not friends. We are strangers and we always have been. Our marriage has confidentially been declared a mistake. She loves my possessions, not me. She doesn't laugh when I laugh, and she doesn't cry when I cry. Her face looks like stone."

After positioning the bull exactly where he wanted it, the matador lifted his sword to shoulder level and waved the *muleta* slowly, to guide the dangerous horns past his right hip. His target: a three-inch wide opening *entre* the shoulder blades.

"If he misses the target zone, he'll hit bone, and the fans will be outraged at him," said Rafael. The steel thing hit the target, but it wasn't well placed, and it didn't kill the bull.

"The matador must be scared to death."

"Death is not the enemy, Christina. Fear of death is," stated Rafael.

She wanted to scream at him for having a wife. She couldn't believe it. She knew he had a secret and she continued to meet with him. He was also an older man, and of course he should be married. This, she should have expected. She couldn't get mad at him and his situation, nor could she get mad at this country for its custom. In fact, she couldn't take her eyes off the scene below and the more she saw, the more she wanted to know…about the Spaniards, the country, and Rafael's sadness. "*Digame mas, mas.*" She told him to tell her more.

"When I pulled up to the curb to ask you for *direcciones*, I noticed *tres cosas*," said Rafael. "*Primer*, I noticed your expressive eyes as you listened when I talked." He pointed to her features as he spoke, staring at her. "*Segundo*, I noticed the several differing tones of your voice. *Tercer*, your smile. Our friendship developed genuinely. My money is not important to you, no?"

The matador used a shorter sword fitted with a cross-bar close to the tip. As he pierced it into the base of the toro's skull, Kristine looked around at the fans to see if they, too, were crying. No, they were clapping. Only Rafael had tears rolling down his cheeks. She wanted to tend to Rafael, but had a hard time taking her eyes off the arena below. It said so much about Spain, and the people as a whole. It revealed so much about the people, perhaps more than any conversation could ever reveal. She knew she needed to go, again and again, to buy a season's pass.

She felt ignorant for judging the bullfight, and so guilty, that she once again considered staying in Spain a little longer. She and Rafael could go to more bullfights next year, and she could watch, listen, and learn a little more each time.

The bull hit the ground and people shouted louder as a team of mules dragged the dead animal out of the arena. Everyone waved handkerchiefs.

Rafael pinched her ear. "They are requesting that an ear be given to the matador," he said in Spanish.

"Well, not mine," she shouted back in Spanish.

Rafael laughed. "No, not a human ear, the bull's ear. The matador gives the ear to the butchers in exchange for the bulls body." The matador ran around the arena once, as if the waving handkerchiefs meant more than applause. Another trumpet sounded, which meant time for the *segundo* bull to enter the sunny arena. The crowds cheered for *mas, mas*.

"*Christina, estoy sufriendo,*" whispered Rafael as he stood up and tugged on her sweater so she'd follow him. The fight wasn't over, but he led her down the bleachers and out to his car.

They drove into the country with the clear sky overhead. "Bullfighting *hoy* isn't all that it once used to be, Christina," said Rafael. "Now it shares the fame with soccer matches. *Tambien*, there have been changes in Spain's economy. Many ranches were sold. On the ranches in the past, owners could selectively breed *los toros*. Breeding the right sort of bull for a fight almost classified as an art, or a science, I don't know which. No, bulls of today don't always have the space for exercise and natural grazing and ranches. They aren't as wild as they once were."

As they drove over soft rolling hills, Kristine stared out the window, catching a glimpse of a white patch of slow moving animals. They were sheep and for a moment, they reminded her of a Bible verse she had memorized and recited back in school, one that had never made any sense to her. "The Lord is my shepherd, I shall not be in want. He makes me lie down in green pastures, He leads me beside quiet waters, He restores my soul."

Sheep always brought this verse to mind, and now she closed her eyes and said a silent prayer as Rafael continued talking about bullfights. *Oh dear Lord, I want to be more like the sheep, that are so dependent on their shepherd for protection and guidance. I no longer want to be frightened and passive. I want to be wise, wise enough to follow You as you guide me through life.*

The smell of a dead skunk on the road interrupted her prayer, drifting her thoughts to death instead. She continued to recite more of the Psalm in her mind. "Even though I walk through the valley of the shadow of death, I will fear no evil, for you are with me, your rod and your staff, they comfort me."

Dear Lord, I am afraid of death because I am so helpless and cannot save myself from it, nor those I love. I can become stronger and wiser in my life, but none of these traits will save me from death. I know that my only comfort regarding death is the fact that you will walk me through it just as you walked with Lauren and Grandma. I thank you for your presence and the comfort that knowing this brings me. Amen.

They pulled up to a brown acorn style cottage, and Kristine pleasantly noticed horses, not bulls, nor sheep, grazing behind a white picket fence. Several smaller cottages were lined up and down the hill.

Rafael got out of the car, telling her to stay put. As she watched him disappear into the office, she quickly rummaged through his glove compartment, in search of anything that might have his last name on it. But, like her own glove compartment, Rafael kept a tidy car with not a crumb of evidence.

He returned to the car and told her he had rented some horses for a few *horas*, but she refused to take part in the adventure. She credited herself as too smart for that, and perhaps borderline paranoid. She refused to be murdered somewhere in the country in Spain on her semester abroad. She also noticed her mind getting a bit dramatic, but she blamed it on television and movies. A simple horseback ride in the country on a gorgeous, calm day almost always led to murder in the movies.

"No. I don't want to ride horses at a time like this. You're married, and you should be riding horses with your wife." She knew she said it in English, and she felt a nervous feeling in the pit of her stomach, moths killing butterflies and taking over.

They sat together on the trunk of his Mercedes, which was parked inconspicuously under the shade of towering trees.

"Ay, Christina," Rafael reached above him and pulled an oak leaf off a low-hanging branch. "I married so young and I discovered many years ago that my wife had cheated on me, over and over again. I should have known I loved her more than she loved me. I should have read her face. She looked like stone." He made an awful stone face, freezing all his expressions for a moment. "No laughter, no tears, no yelling. Numb to life. I've never seen any emotions come from her. Many times I've wondered if she is made only of make-up and designer clothes, my designer clothes, and nothing more."

"Well, you did choose her to be your wife and now, you probably have a family with her—kids you are responsible for."

"No, Christina. She refused to have children, telling me only after we were married that children demand too much attention. The truth is, she demands too much attention, and children would take that away from her."

"You wanted children?"

"*Si, si, claro que si.*" He extended his arms up and outward in similar fashion as the trees around them. "But she went and had surgery without telling me. In Spain, do you realize how abnormal this entire thing is?"

"Rafael, this is abnormal for anywhere in the world. Have you considered divorce?"

"*Si, si.* No, no. My country, under Franco didn't allow divorce."

"But Franco is dead, Rafael."

"And Catholicism lives, Christina."

"So, because a religion lives, you must die. That doesn't make a lot of sense to me," said Kristine.

"I will not die!"

"No, but you are living a dead life."

"I am alive now that I know *Christina de los Estados Unidos. Si*, I am alive again."

"*¿Quien estas, Rafael?*"

"No. My name is not important. I want you to know me, Rafael." He pounded on his heart.

"I can't know you if I don't know your past. I do not know you," said Kristine.

She got up and walked away and he followed. "I practiced law, as many college students in *Espana* do. Then, I inherited millions from my father. He once owned many banks throughout Spain, so I do not have to work, ever again. But designing clothes is my passion in *vida*, my only passion, next to my new friendship with you, *mi preciosa*."

She felt a smile for the first time since they had arrived at the ranch. She tried to contain it, but couldn't. She didn't want to be a stone, numb to emotions, especially to a man so appreciative of details she had never even thought of before. Emotions happen like reflexes, yet Rafael cherished them after years of living without them.

"Follow me," he said. "I have a surprise for you."

He popped the trunk of his car and took out a pile of black dresses and white cotton tops with sheer floral sleeves. "Try them on for me, *por favor*."

"Where should I try them on?" she asked.

"*Aqui.* Here."

She laughed with the excitement of new clothes yet felt horribly shy, embarrassed to model in front of a man who worked with top European models on a daily basis. Her emotions ran in circles. She felt so honored that he wanted to give her this wardrobe. She also felt insecure that perhaps it was a hint that her clothes were ugly. Anxiety took over. What if they didn't fit past her thighs? Then again, he must have known what he was doing when he picked them. He said designing clothes was his passion—maybe he had designed them. She felt like hugging him, yet at the same time hitting him for being married. She felt in love, yet she was frightened. Were these the emotions he saw and liked on her face? Well, Rafael deserved some credit himself. He was a man who provoked many emotions, and he stirred hers all at once.

"I designed them over the past few months, with you, Christina, in my mind."

She walked behind a tree trunk, wishing it were a thick baryon tree instead of an oak tree. He could see part of her, she was sure, but hoped he saw her stomach, not her thighs. She didn't mind him seeing her stomach. She minded her thighs. She slid her top over her head and unsnapped her pants. As she struggled to pull them off, she knew the tree trunk no longer hid her butt. She tossed the pants on the ground and grabbed the black dress, hanging on Rafael's finger. She pulled it up, wondering if it might get stuck at the waist. No, of course not. Designed by a successful European fashion designer, of course it would fit. Well, now she'd find out if he really designed it for her, with her in mind. Yes, it pulled up over her waist and up to her neck perfectly, as if painted onto her body. If there was such a thing, she would declare it her soul dress, a dress made just for her, a dress so in tune with her body, her style, her emotions. If the dress had cost four hundred dollars in America, she'd get a job and find a way to buy it. She'd grow old wearing this dress that he designed just for her, sexy yet conservative.

"I help you. I help you." He piled her long blonde hair in a bun on her head and zipped the dress up to her neck. "*Si, si.* I made this for you, *Christina,* for you."

She believed him now as she walked with a sway of her shoulders, once around his Mercedes, spinning a couple times, then returning to where he sat on the car.

"*¿Te gusta?*"

"*¡Me encanta!*" She loved the dress, but knew she'd never have a place to wear it. She didn't live a soap opera life, nor did she attend the type of American parties that called for this sort of dress. She longed to be a part of a social world that wore these dresses. However, no matter how dressed up she might become, she wanted to remain full of emotions, full of life.

He grabbed her around the waist and pulled her close, kissing her for the first time on the lips. "*Te quiero,*" he whispered in her ear.

"No, no." She wiped her lips and backed away, not sure where this dress and its maker might take her.

"*Si, si. Te quiero,*" he said again, smiling.

She knew his words meant both love and want and this, she had to stop. Despite the fact that he married a stone, he was still married to that stone. She wanted to kiss him, to hold his hand, to walk to places she had never seen with him, but she refused to do this with a married man. She felt pity for him, yet he had choices to make concerning his marriage, his situation.

"*Te quiero,*" he said, pulling her close again. Then he whispered something else in her ear and she had to pause to interpret what she thought it meant. Yes, if she heard it correctly, he wanted to sleep with her.

"No!" shouted the woman from Holland, a woman raised in a town declared more conservative than the country of Holland, the town where people didn't dare bike ride on Sundays, or dance in public, or say the words, 'Holy cow.'

"*Si, si.*" He kissed her neck slowly this time, whispering, "*Mas, mas.*"

"No. I have to tell you something, Rafael." She pushed him away.

"*Si, si, digame,*" said the man from Spain, a country with a rich history of passion and drama, a country drunk on romance. "*Te quiero.*"

"You cannot have me, Rafael. You cannot love me."

"*¿Por que? ¿Por que?*"

"First, you are married, and I am not about to destroy something that might potentially be sacred. You and your wife must make a decision. I'm certainly not going to influence something so significant. I don't want to live with that burden. Be a man and do something about it. Don't think you can go on living in a miserable marriage while wining and dining me on the side. Forget it." She had said it all in Spanish and for a moment, she wondered what Dr. Laura might say. If only she could make a quick call to the radio show.

"*Ahora, ahora, te quiero.*" He stood closer again and continued with his lines. He still wanted her.

She allowed him to kiss the back of her neck, and it sent chills down her spine. In the romance novels, the woman would be swept away into mad passionate love. Grandma would be skipping ahead a few pages just to get to the steamy part of this letter. But this wasn't a romance novel. This was life, her life. She couldn't help that she grew up in a conservative Midwest town, a town that called marriage sacred and sex as something made for marriage. She closed her eyes and let Rafael slowly unzip the dress and kiss further down her back. But then she thought of her high school Bible teacher, of all people, and his phrase of the year: *The body is the temple of God.* These darn psychotic voices in her head again! She thought of Rafael's wife, wherever she might be and whatever she might be doing right now. She drove herself crazy with thoughts and wondered why her mind worked so darn hard as Rafael slowly pulled the dress down off her waist. Then she thought about life. This was her life, no one else's life. It was her life and why would she want to screw it up? Why would she let a few romantic moments in Spain screw up her entire life to come? She opened her eyes and put an end to it all.

On the corner of *El Corte Ingles,* he offered one more time to buy her and her *familia* plane tickets to *Espana.* He said he'd set them up in a little ranch in the country. He also promised he would leave his wife. He said there was nothing sacred about their arrangement and had he known back then that his wife would take such a malicious turn in life, if he had seen through her insincerity, he never would have married her. He had tried every attempt imaginable at making the marriage work. He would never break such a commitment without first trying everything to save it.

"No, *Rafael de Espana,* no," she told him and got out of his car.

She didn't know what else to say and didn't want him to see her cry so she put her sunglasses on, although the sun had gone down. She turned her back to him, kissed her two fingers, extended her arm back and started to wave, without turning to peek. She could see him in the reflection of the department store window, just as she did the first time they met. He didn't know she could see him as he wiped his eyes on his sleeve and made the sign of the cross. She started to walk away, but kept waving. She walked with a purpose. What purpose? She didn't know, just the sort of purpose that says this good-bye is forever. She heard his car drive away, and as badly as she wanted to turn to look one last time, she didn't. The backward wave would have to do and she felt like a hummingbird that flies backward to back away from flowers whose nectar they've been sipping. Just like these small birds, her legs and feet felt too weak to walk, but she had to. She couldn't fly.

32

Mañana came all too soon and with it, sad thoughts of leaving behind her Spanish life and all the comfort it had recently started to bring her. Sure, there'd be another tomorrow, but it would be a tomorrow in Michigan, not Spain. She wanted to stay anchored there just a little longer, in the country that lusted life and stayed up all night. She wasn't ready to pull up anchor, yet her life and college degree were calling her back.

Maybe someday she would return to Spain to operate a bed and breakfast in the mountains, live on a yacht in Barcelona, or rent a tiny studio apartment near her Spanish family and write letters to Grandma, morning, noon and night. By now, her emotional roots were so tightly interwoven with her family back in the States that relocating to Europe would only generate heart-wrenching good-byes and years of bitter homesickness.

On her hands and knees and in a temper, Rosario scrubbed the wooden floors for hours, moving Kristine's heavy suitcases over every few minutes so she could clean the floor under them. It took no words to understand her loss. She had allowed a stranger into her apartment, her kitchen, the most private and intimate aspect of her life, and now that stranger was leaving.

Kristine felt an adult butterfly emerging in her stomach, pumping body fluid through its soft veins and expanding its wing. At quarter to nine, she kneeled down next to her *señora* to rest before her flight, and placed her hand on the woman's hands, blistered from cleaning. Rosario stopped, and for a moment, the two sat in silence on the floor, listening to traffic and voices from the street below. They didn't need nor attempt to talk. Both heard the same sounds outside and both felt similar pain inside. The woman handed Kristine a sheet of stationery. There was a quote scribbled in English, and Kristine knew Rosario had gone to great lengths to get this translated. It read:

What do you have to fear? Nothing.
Whom do you have to fear? No one.
Because whoever has joined forces with God obtains
three great privileges: omnipotence without power,
intoxication without wine, and life without death.
                              —*St. Francis of Assisi*

The others left the apartment earlier in the evening because they had weekend social plans brewing in the streets below. Lorenzo walked next store to mass, hugging Kristine tightly before he left. Rosario said he used mass as an excuse so he wouldn't have to say a formal goodbye. He, too, felt the loss of a daughter, but at least he had his job at the post office to keep him busy. He could socialize with others. In a day or two, he would be fine. Rosario, however, didn't have a social life or a job outside the apartment. She would always miss her American student and had already begun the paperwork to get her second student the following year.

The woman pulled herself up from the floor and opened a drawer in the antique hutch, withdrawing a notepad and broken red crayon.

"I've been looking for that for weeks," laughed Kristine, curious.

Rosario giggled like a bashful girl and handed her a crayon drawing of a house. Inside the house was a huge globe of the world, and inside the globe of the world, was the body of a stick person. Kristine stared at it for a moment, but it didn't take her long to realize that Rosario was thanking her for bringing a new and unknown part of the world into her apartment, her world. Kristine tucked the hand-made picture in her pocket, along with half of the crayon. She told Rosario to keep the other half. Perhaps she could start this tradition with her future students as well. They might all leave Spain with a similar crayon drawing, something worth so much more than expensive souvenirs.

Together the women dragged the luggage down the many flights of stairs to the street below, and Rosario flagged down a taxi. She kissed Kristine on both cheeks, closed her eyes and made the sign of the cross, then blew a kiss as her American daughter climbed into the taxi and drove away.

The taxi headed down the narrow street, and Kristine didn't trust herself to turn around to see the *señora* standing alone on the curb with her dirty apron and strands of hair falling from her bun for fear she would burst into tears. She did however catch a glimpse of Lorenzo, standing in a bakery window eating a huge cream puff. She laughed for five minutes at the man who claimed to be at mass.

Next, the taxi stopped in traffic at the *El Corte Ingles* corner. Cars were honking, and one man got out of his car to yell at someone in another car. She ignored the scene and instead watched a homeless woman, sitting on the pavement outside the department store. People were dropping coins into her bucket here and there, but the old woman never smiled. Then a man dressed in black velvet pants and a black turtle neck walked over to the woman and handed her what looked like a cup of something warm to drink, still steaming. He sat down next to her and opened the woman's hands, placing the mug between her palms, and held them for a moment.

Kristine tried unrolling the window of the cab, but it may have been on safety lock. She tried opening the door, but the cab started to move. She pounded on the windows. One more smile, one more wave. She had to tell them both—the millionaire and the homeless woman—how much she loved them. She wanted now to tell Rafael how much she appreciated him, and that of all the Spaniards she grew to know, she loved him the most. She wanted to thank this mystery man for taking such good care of her, teaching her about the Spaniards from the inside out. She wanted to remove the excess sweaters that had crowded her suitcases and wrap them around Triste. She loved this country and she loved its people. She loved Rafael. If she could stay just a little bit longer.

"Wait. Let me out. Stop!" She cried either out loud or to herself, she didn't know which.

The taxi driver just stared in his rearview mirror and kept driving. She felt like an animal in a cage being taken away, somewhere. She was leaving the country she now loved, the country that taught her to live life and not fear death. She frantically opened the little purple sack her grief-stricken friend had given her and wiped her eyes with the white embroidered handkerchief that Triste had used for mourning. It probably had some sixty years of serious tears soaked into it.

She held it tightly as she watched out the back window of the cab. The gray bundle and black velvet next to it grew smaller and smaller, as did the nation's capital, located in central Spain at the foot of the Guadarrama Mountains. She noticed herself already mourning the Spanish city situated two thousand feet above sea level, the highest capital in Europe. And she didn't want to leave the country bordered by the Atlantic Ocean and the Mediterranean Sea. She didn't know which she loved more: the people or the place. The tears in her eyes clouded her vision, turning the scene behind her into a Salvador Dali surrealist painting.

At the airport, she had a good hour before her flight. She took out her red and gold-lined journal and continued the letter to her grandmother.

℘

Dear Grandma:

TIME, WEATHER AND DEATH—*these three words transcend any culture and any language. These three things are completely out of our control, yet everything is planned around them. Even if a fiesta is planned for mañana, TIME moves on at its own pace, turning that fiesta into nothing more than a memory. WEATHER behaves rudely, when it likes, pouring on the guests of the fiesta. DEATH, should it be told, shows up just before the fiesta. And for that person, who may have been living in a count down of anticipation, the fiesta never comes. This is why people fear death. They cannot control it.*

33

Her breathing and chest pains still teased her every so often, even though she anchored herself securely in an old familiar place—an apartment with some mutual friends on the campus in Holland, Michigan. It was the apartment she and Lauren had picked out together and planned on sharing after they returned from Spain.

Kristine had a lot of homework to do and a class to attend, but none of that mattered at the moment. *Mañana,* she told herself. She could always go to class and study tomorrow.

Today, she decided to place the important things at the top of her list. And this meant she had choices, several stages, just as a woman at the beach could choose to take her shoes off and safely walk along the shore with nothing more than her toes getting wet. She could further choose whether or not to take her clothes off and tread the chilly water waist-high. After that, she might shuffle her feet fearfully, paranoid of jellyfish or stingrays biting her. Or, she could choose to dive under, getting her hair wet, forgetting about her make-up. Yes, a woman could choose to go only as far as the white shallow waves washed gently against her, or she could ride the waves and risk being dashed on the mammoth spikes barricading the great ocean beyond.

Aware now of her choices, the degrees to which she could participate in daily life, Kristine refused to bury herself in the sand and all her daily lists of things to do. Granted, she would not ignore responsibility, or productivity, but she would transform a tedious list of errands into a life-changing map simply by adding one magnificent thing a day, something that might bring significance to her day. She promised herself she would start the New Year facing the wind like a windmill, with sturdy arms embracing the winds and generating beautiful and unlimited energy. And as the wind died down she would rest, knowing with fresh faith it would soon start up again.

Spain, Tarpon Key, and *Till Midnight* with Lauren were moments she might never forget. And she knew she might never cross paths with vessels as magnificent. In fact, her life might never be that exciting again, but it didn't matter. She no longer feared death. Sure, her anxiety attacks every so often returned, but not concerning death. She knew at once that it had turned into a bad habit, started by her mind, and anything at all might trigger it. She only needed to break the mental habit now and she would.

She remembered what Nacho once said, "Go to the symphony." Well, she couldn't. She had no cash, nor time, nor information about any symphony. So she bought Ludwig Van Beethoven's Symphony No. 9 in D minor, Opus 125, and played the cassette in her car as she drove around campus. Her mind traveled farther than campus, farther than Tarpon Key, farther than Spain. How could it not? She was appreciating one of the highest artistic achievements of the human mind. As she listened to the sweeping majesty of Beethoven's greatest work, the campus changed before her eyes. It became more cultural, more beautiful. Just because she didn't have a lot of money, nor time, nor resources, didn't mean she couldn't add a few sparks to her now-ordinary life and now, even in winter, she could find creative ways to feed on the nectar of flowers. Suddenly, just as she turned right onto College Avenue, Beethoven's stately music erupted. Startled by the unexpected sounds filling her car, she accidentally switched lanes, cutting someone off behind her. Horns honked and she laughed, because it actually fit well with Beethoven's piece, a rebel bassoon player, a naughty spirit.

When the music came to its magnificent finale, she realized what it was she needed to do, something very important. Kristine walked alone to *Till Midnight* and took a seat at the tiny round table on the sidewalk. The tulips she and Lauren had seen together last spring had disappeared, their season of stardom past. As sure as the seasons would come and go, new tulips would return to take their place in the same soil come early May. As she looked around, the day seemed to stand still. No candles were lit and a closed sign hung on the restaurant door. Despite the chilly air and the light snow, the tables were already covered with paper tablecloths, sheltered by an awning and heat lamp above. The staff scurried about inside, preparing to open in an hour.

Aware of the hours of studying to do, but even more aware of the special things in life that come first and should always fit into any hectic schedule, she sat at the same table where she and Lauren had last planned their future together. She noticed silver-frosted clouds draping the horizon as she pulled out half a red crayon from her purse and wrote on the white paper tablecloth.

She started with Lauren's main goal and wrote, *Live the present*. She remembered the passionate battle with the tarpon and she heard Captain Edwards voice, then wrote, *Find a domain and bring passion to your life*. Yes, she would turn her letters to Grandma into a first novel of some sort, and writing would become her domain. She remembered Denver classifying her as a submarine and telling her it's okay to feel down. She wrote, *Surface your feelings*. She could see the letter from Lauren's mother in her mind. She scribbled, *Celebrate life*. She watched a waiter inside scrubbing a table and thought of Ruth, and wrote, *Find an island where you can stop and think. Think things you've never had time to think about and notice things you've never noticed before*. She could hear Howard's voice directing her to write, *Start fresh daily, adding beautiful colors to your plain white canvas*. When she thought of

Evelyn, she wrote, *Face uncertainty in life like a confident vessel in dark waters heading toward the lighthouse.* She heard Marie's loud, boisterous laugh and scribbled, *Add laughter to your life.* She could hear the motor of Lawrence's boat, as loud as his voice and wrote, *Don't ever underestimate the journeys you've been on, and look for the magnificent, not the bad, in things.* She thought of Steve and jotted down, *Hop, skip and jump toward goals, enjoying the process as much as the destination.*

Voices travel far, perhaps farther than any voyager in history. She could hear Rosario's voice all the way from Spain saying, "Life should be savored, just like a meal and the appetizers are as important as the dessert." She wrote, *Don't rush any part of life. The end is as good as the beginning.* She could almost taste *sangria* as she thought of Lorenzo and wrote, *Indulge in fiestas but never lose your dignity.* She felt the chilliness of the seat she now sat on, and it reminded her of Triste. She wrote, *Get on with your life. Live life!* She remembered the Flamenco dancer and with a smile wrote, *Dance away anxiety.* She noticed a tray with red cloth napkins near the door and thought of the matador and wrote, *When death comes around, stare it in the eyes.* She closed her eyes and could hear Nacho's music. She had already gone to a symphony as he had suggested, a symphony in her car, so she opened her eyes and wrote, *View the world without eyes for a change.* It was as if she had forgotten Rafael's voice. She couldn't write anything as she thought of him. Their time together had been incomplete. She longed to know what she might have learned had she spent more time with him.

She put her crayon down and stared at the frozen flowerbed where last year's tulips stood in a perfect line, waiting for the infamous tulip festival to begin. The cup-shaped solitary flowers died each year, but every winter their bulbs divided under the snow-packed earth and more new ones bloomed in the spring.

She spoke as if someone sat across from her. "No, a believer in God and all that is spiritual, I will not fear death! Death will be the start of eternal life with God. For now, while I'm alive, death will serve as a reminder."

At the end of her new list, she added, *Remember the tulips. Just as their season of stardom comes and goes, you too will one day pass.* As death was added to that list, it seemed to put everything into perspective. She now valued her time and the moment and neatly folded the tablecloth with her new scribbles. This one she would bury at Lauren's gravesite in the spring. She would place it in a special chest, dig a hole and plant the most gorgeous tulip bulbs she could find around it. And every spring after that, her tulips would grow and bloom and spread new life in Lauren's memory.

She rose from the table and did what she had wished she had done before. She made an angel in the snow. A few passing cars honked. She took a handful of snow and tasted it. Still in angel position, she closed her eyes and felt the refreshing coldness of Michigan's wintry mantle. When she opened her eyes again, the robust clouds overhead seemed to shimmer in shades of white she had never seen before, matching the snow beneath, and in the far distance, the horizon between sky and earth blurred where the grayish whites met. Thin tree branches wrapped in snow looked so perfect that she could almost swear someone had taken a bottle of Liquid Paper and carefully painted each twig in opaque white.

She lay in the snow a good five minutes. Things she had never pondered before drifted through her mind. One could determine the life span of butterflies by capturing them and marking their wings with a square-tipped marking pen, then watching for them later. She didn't want to be captured. She didn't want to know the number of her days.

ℓ

Dear Grandma:
Everybody will lose someone or something they love at some point in this life, as we know it. A loss can be a family business sold, a move from a hometown, distance from a

big or little sister. It could mean the end of lifelong friendships. Losses great and small come in various ways.

Some people will grieve; others will be grief-stricken. I recommend actively grieving, I mean going on a grief journey. Grieving is a long process. You have to rediscover the world about you.

Some will turn their grievances into fears and phobias. Others will turn their grievances into an appreciation for life, for the living moment itself, the present.

34

Dictated by time zones, the New Year would arrive first in Spain. With just 45 minutes left before the millennium, Rafael knew his Spanish custom of tardiness might postpone a meeting or delay a luncheon, or make Christina stand desperately by herself on the corner. Alas, he knew that his tardiness would not, could not, prevent the New Year from coming. He wanted so badly to take hold of the skinny little hands of the clock, to twist and pull them until they fell off, to put the worldwide celebration on hold until someone with tools could repair them and set the clock in motion once again. No, though he could not control time, or the coming of the New Year, he could control his own decisions, and this—this he would do. He had to!

Sitting in the leather seat next to him, his wife shouted and cursed at him. "Drive faster!" she demanded.

They were late for the event of the century—wining, dining and gossiping with Spain's best, Spain's royalty, and most gorgeous and impressive people. As he drove slowly in the direction of the *Palacio Real*, he dreaded entering a New Year with no love, no children to call his own, nor a friend to share his emotions with. He couldn't stand thinking about spending another year with his wife and her materialism, rudeness and hedonistic selfishness.

They had driven to *Palacio Real* hundreds of times before, so he had no excuse to give his screaming wife as he made a wrong turn and drove an extra couple of blocks before stopping his car on the corner outside *El Corte Ingles* department store. For years, words like '*loco*' and '*estupido*' left her mouth like balls at a batting cage, hitting him head on. Now, they only rolled past him. He refused to look at her, but through the corner of his eyes, he saw her throw her hands up in a tantrum as she belittled him with crude names. The combination of her perfume and hair spray smelled like a gin cocktail and made his head ache and his eyes water. He watched out the window as a woman walked by with two babies in a double stroller, and again he felt desperate to become a father. He mourned the thought of his wife never wanting to have babies. She had a right not to want them, but she had never told him this. In fact, she had once lied saying she wanted children. She had said it simply to get him to marry her. Her self-centeredness burned his stomach. As the young mother turned the corner, he started the car, ignoring his wife's cursing, and drove to the palace. He knew he had changes to make in the New Year. He would make these changes. He would do so…*mañana! Mañana, mañana, mañana!*

℘

The gray bundle stood in the long line at the corner shop that often served the homeless free soup. The city celebrated, getting ready to welcome the New Year. She reached into her pocket and felt the wrinkled paper the American woman had handed her. She smiled, thinking of the romantic young woman from another world faraway. The woman had reminded her of herself years ago, before she had allowed death to take over her life. She didn't know what she would do with the piece of paper that had Kristine's full name and phone number scribbled on it. She laughed at the naive girl's crazy offer. If she had understood her sophisticated textbook Spanish properly, this girl had invited her to go to America. *Si, si,* she had invited her to stay with her family there. How *loco*! She would never leave *Espana*. Impossible dreams, but the romance of it all made Triste smile as she carefully folded the paper and tucked it in her pocket, then sipped her warm soup twenty minutes before midnight.

ஐ

Dressed in a red and black-checkered flannel nightgown, Evelyn peeked out the window of her trailer home near Fort Myers Beach.

"Goodie. The moon is just about in its midnight position," she said out loud to the brown stale plants sitting around in their pots. They had suffered and died in captivity, and were now the framework of a spider's mansion. "I think I'll touch the cards now and see what they have to offer me for the New Year. Maybe they can get me out of this Hell hole," she said, looking around at the fist holes that provided rude peepholes into her bathroom. Cheerios added design to the coffee-stained fabric table booths.

Just outside, the man who beat her so many times walked up the pathway and pounded on the door. "Open up. I know you're in there. I brought you some good stuff. Let's party like it's 1999," he shouted.

She opened the door, hoping he wouldn't break it down again, but this time, he knocked her down, laughing as she crashed into the table, bruising her knee.

"Don't lay another hand on me," she screamed.

"Oh yeah? You know you deserve it."

"I do not deserve it. No one deserves this kind of treatment," she told him.

"Oh? Whoever told you that?"

"Some smart, educated girl I meant once."

Evelyn picked herself off the floor and stood up. "Yeah, she told me I deserve a better life and you know what? I've been thinking about what she said. As simple as it sounds, no one has ever said anything like that to me before. I've been giving it a lot of thought, and ya know what? I agree with her."

"A few stupid words have inspired you?"

She picked up her deck of cards, tossed them at him and ran out. She knew exactly where she was going. She had read about the woman's shelter just a few weeks ago, and all she had to do was get to a pay phone and make the call. Yes, she deserved better than this. The cards had told her nothing about leaving this crazy man, so she had made this decision on her own. She would enter a New Year and a new life, both at the same time. She would run and not look back, and this time she would make it on her own.

※

"There's room for two more," Denver shouted, as he waved people onto his houseboat. "Okay. I'll come back for the rest of you in about a half hour."

"Happy New Year," shouted the voices in line. "Happy New Year, and thank you for helping us."

"But O the ship, the immortal ship! O ship aboard the ship!" Denver shouted out a famous quotation from Walt Whitman. "Ship of the body, ship of the soul, voyaging, voyaging, voyaging."

He left with his group of about 15 people down the Sacramento River. Television crews swarmed over the area, but he refused interviews. He didn't want publicity. He simply wanted to carry out his plan. He simply wanted to make the most of his second chance, to spend every penny his brother had given him, in the most productive manner. Each time he took a group of 15 homeless people down the Sacramento River, he offered them hot apple cider, cheese and bread, fruit, and a pep talk.

"You're all vessels," he told them. "You're all vessels in need of repair, and believe me, you can repair yourself." He had been doing this for months now, and cameras had been following him ever since. "I'm going to sing you all a song that I think you can relate to. It's called, 'Life is so sad, life is so sad.' Then, I'm gonna lend ya 'all some twigs, some twigs to start repairing yourselves again."

The homeless appeared to be interested in his message, and often times, Denver had them join hands and close their eyes. "Give us this day, our daily bread," he would often say, reciting the 'Our Father.'

℘

"And forgive us our trespasses as we forgive those who trespass against us," whispered Howard. A nurse entered his room and handed him a party favor, but he felt too weak to blow. He glanced at the clock on the white wall and counted down, as he did all night, not for the New Year, but for when his brother would be finished with the boat rides and would stop in to visit him. He knew he wouldn't see another year and perhaps another night. It didn't matter now. All that mattered to him was that his money had gone to a good cause and that Denver had repaired himself. He could rest in peace now.

℘

"I guess this is Happy New Year," Marie said as she lounged on the black leather couch in their luxury studio apartment in New York City. "You won't let me turn on the television, and I still can't believe you didn't want to go see the ball drop in person. We could have been there, you know."

"Too risky." The man she loved peered through the blinds, holding his hand on the gun hidden inside his black coat. "When this is all over, babe, I'll take you out to wherever you want to go. I promise you that."

Just then, the phone rang and as she went to answer it, he yelled, "No! Honey, no! We can't let anyone know we're here. It's just not safe, and keeping you safe is my first priority. You know that."

Again, the person calling hung up for the fiftieth time that night. It had been as if the ringing of the phone became the countdown to midnight, and she feared what might happen after twelve. A bomb? She didn't have a clue because the man she loved had told her nothing about his business.

"Honey, why don't you get a new job in the New Year," she said.

"Don't be crazy. I can't leave the family. You know that."

She closed her eyes and for a moment, dreamt of a place far away. It called her. Some day, she might leave the not-so-comfortable city behind and go there to think, to reevaluate her life and how she might walk away from it all. Why did she have to be in love with someone so dangerous? Some day she would sail away by herself and stay. She just didn't know when the currents would work in her favor.

℘

At twenty minutes before midnight, Captain Edwards watched the moon overhead and the stars that dropped more magnificently than the ball in Times Square. He had recently made the local news for catching a one hundred and thirty-pound tarpon near Sarasota, Florida and in the New Year he would catch an even bigger one. Apparently, the man he had taken fishing that night had published a novel, had become a state senator and the father of quadruplets shortly thereafter. It must have been a very motivating battle.

℘

Kristine wrapped the scarf around her face to shield her skin from the winter wind as she hurried across the airport parking lot at ten minutes until midnight. What a place to celebrate the New Year, she thought, as she ran up the elevators and to the terminal, rubbing her fingers together to warm away the numbness. She could hardly wait to see him. It didn't matter that their New Year kiss would happen in the luggage area and that her teeth would be chattering from the cold. She had it all planned. She would toss her arms tightly around him and tell him how much she missed him, while she was in Spain, and that he was her Mr. Right. He only had to wait until she could graduate. Then, she would move to Florida, to escape the cold that kept her inside, that kept her cuddled up every night, that prevented her from spending the nights on a dock or taking a walk or swimming in the nude at midnight, fun things like that. Yes, she would find a job in Fort Myers, living close to her parents and close to him.

As the plane landed at five minutes till midnight, crazy passengers passed around paper party hats and noise-makers. Steve didn't feel much like celebrating. He felt confused over his decision. He knew that by taking the assignment overseas, in Japan, he would not be able to see Kristine this summer, or perhaps, ever again. He didn't know if Japan was the sort of place Kristine would like. She did mention she wanted to travel and had seemed disappointed when he had once said he was done with traveling. Maybe it would be a surprise for her. She could finish college, and then move to Japan. He wanted her for a wife and hoped she might consider his proposal. He would find out after the long weekend. He would break the news tomorrow, not tonight.

35

The sun rose and set some 365 times. Fridays arrived, but Mondays crept quickly around the corner every time. She reached the end of her journal, her letters to Grandma, and saw time flipping by like the pages of a book. She wanted to read life slowly, paying attention to the details and, sometimes, reading the same sentence twice. She couldn't ask summer to take its time. Winter arrived when it liked. Fall had so much to do in such little time. She would never be able to control the timing of the leaves turning orange, nor turning crisp, nor falling, nor the time it took people to rake them into piles and burn them before the snow. She could only control her own pace, and she wanted to walk through life, slowly.

Once in awhile her breathing troubles still haunted her, and she continued writing about her episodes, allowing her out-of-control thoughts to be expressed through writing. Often she prayed. Sometimes she would close her eyes and visualize herself on the dock of Tarpon Key or in the park outside the *Prado* Museum in Madrid. She no longer feared death. That fear and its ridiculous obsession belonged to her dark days, or, in Picasso's language, her "blue period" of madness. She painted with a rose palette now.

As her days grew busy from the demands of graduate school, she handled things well and simply remembered there was a time for everything.

She cried at the thought of the cold, dead ground where the tulips once stood. She smiled when she thought of spring and the ducks arriving from the south. She closed her eyes and laughed at summer and the people lining up to buy ice cream. She went through the motions of the backward good-bye wave just thinking about fall and the ducks heading south again. Yes, there was a season for everything and this, God knew.

On February 14th, at four o'clock in the morning, her friend in residence ran into her room. "Wake up, wake up, quick! There's a crazy man on the phone speaking Spanish. I hung up, but he keeps calling back, and he's shouting, '*Christina, Christina!*"

As if riding the wings of a butterfly, Kristine flew to the phone so quickly she could hardly catch her breath. "*Hola?*" she said as she held the receiver tightly to her face.

The man on the other line said he couldn't refuse the wrinkled piece of paper that Triste had one day waved before him. He had tucked it away for quite some time, then, with the help of an interpreter, he called the college and tracked down the graduate school she now attended.

They both had so much to say, and several times, they both talked at once, and then laughed. His voice came like an echo across an ocean, and she tried hard to picture his face but the waves were too high. She had no photographs of him, only those in her mind. Still, they had faded with time. As he spoke of his life in recent years, she stared at the tulips standing proudly in the vase on her desk. The voice on the phone said he had spotted her standing so tall on her first day of classes, and that he picked her, of all people, to ask directions.

"You spoke funny Spanish," he said in a strange English accent, "but you stood so tall and proud, like a flower."

"Rafael," she said, smiling. "You've been learning English. I'm so proud of you."

They talked long enough to generate a phone bill that could have paid for an expensive four-course dinner. Neither knew how to say good-bye, so Rafael finally took charge.

"*Te quiero Christina de los Estados Unidos. Te quiero.*" He hung up before she could get his phone number, and, once again, she had forgotten to get his last name.

Awake, she didn't care about time. She'd always have the next day's *siesta* to catch up.

℘

>Dear Grandma:
>
>*You'll never guess what time it is. It's four o'clock in the morning, and being awake at this hour reminds me of the sleepless nights I went through after Lauren died. I don't know that I'll ever hear from Rafael again, and I don't know that I'll ever make it back to the island.*
>
>*Last night I had a nightmare. I was holding on for dear life on a raft I made myself out of a few logs and ropes. Of course it was dark out and the waves stood high. With my hands in the Gulf of Mexico, I paddled my way toward a little island but never made it there. My raft fell apart, and a big boat rescued me. Unfortunately, they were heading for the mainland and refused to take me to the island.*
>
>*I don't know why I crave to return. My life is comfortable now, like a warm breeze blanketing my skin. I once lived inside pink walls that smelled of waffle cones. When the cone broke, I felt so cold. I wondered why anyone would ever want to leave a comfort zone. Now I find myself loosening the bedding at night so my toes can stick out. Yes, I feel confined when my toes can't breathe. Anyway, now I value the voyages we take from one comfort zone to the next.*

36

Kristine had been rocking for hours, sitting by the window and hearing the chimes every time the breeze made its way over the foreign water just a block outside her window. Her empty tissue box sat on the hardwood floor next to her rocking chair. Her hair, now gray and somewhat purple, lent her a look of wisdom, of a seasoned woman who sailed through life, through choppy water, through calm water, through storms and through sunsets. There were no more tears left when she closed the letters to her grandmother and closed her eyes. She liked to close her eyes and listen. Often she saw things she couldn't see when her eyes were open.

Outside she heard the distant motors of boats and footsteps of people walking down the streets. She remembered when the noises outside her window had once sounded so unfamiliar, foreign to her ears, as if the people here had worn different shoes with different heels than the people back home. It had all felt so uncomfortable back then. She opened her eyes to see the familiar pictures of her children, now fully grown, hanging on the wall in front of her. Noah, her first born, was now in his late forties and living in Ann Arbor, Michigan, of all places. This, she was glad of. He lived so far from her, yet so close to the world she grew up in, her old Midwest comfort zone. It had provided her with a wonderful place to visit several times a year, ever since he had started and graduated from the University of Michigan. She was proud of him, a Spanish professor.

They always visited Noah in early May. Afterwards, they would drive to Holland for the Tulip Time Festival, in which she proudly wore a Dutch costume and scrubbed the streets in the parade. Something about wearing wooden shoes always reminded her of who she was and where she came from. It still didn't matter after all these years that her blood wasn't Dutch. She had decided years ago to participate, to become a part of this comfortable town, regardless of ethnic background. This she had done and continued to do every year, scrubbing those streets with pride and passion, always dumping a cold pail of water on her husband's head when he least expected it.

With disposable cameras full of tulips and windmills and yellow sand dunes, she and her husband would then head south. To her delight, their daughter, Emma, had met a man from Florida and together made the South their home. At first it had sounded so terribly faraway, but with the right financial resources, a love for adventure and travel, and a good book to read on the flight, the oceans of the world felt so much smaller than they once had.

As she rocked back and forth, so too did her thoughts, rocking from the past to the future, and now, she couldn't help but count down the hours until Emma would arrive. She stood up and walked over to the pantry. Good, she had plenty of espresso beans. Then she ran her hands over the white paper tablecloth and fidgeted with the bouquet of country flowers standing tall in the vase. She set two white candles in holders next to the flowers, then opened the drawer of a hutch and pulled out a box of crayons. She scattered the crayons across the center of the table and sat down. She did this every time she had guests. They seemed to like the activity and often said it changed the course of their future simply by altering their daily activities. It put things into perspective. Yes, the tablecloth scribbles did this for people.

The chimes of the clock down the street struck twice, reminding her she had just an hour before her daughter would show up and the two could begin to sip coffee and catch up on life's daily details as they did several times a year.

She could smell the aroma of olive bread in the oven and felt the tightness of her skirt around her waist. She glanced at her wedding photo hanging on the wall, and her wedding dress to this day still amazed her. She knew she had bragged about that dress for years, but how could she not? Never had a gown been made so perfectly designed to fit her body. Well, it wouldn't fit now with all the olive bread she had enjoyed through the years, but it certainly fit back then. The fabric had felt so personal, so comfortable, as if painted on with a silk brush. It made her smile knowing she had made the right decisions concerning her Mr. Right. Now, hindsight offered nothing more than pleasant memories of her life gone by.

She walked over to the crucifix hanging on a nearby wall and thanked God for the years she had lived, long past her naive fears of death. She knew that without the spirit of God in her life she would never have had the energy or courage to leave old comforts behind and enter new waters. "For thine is the kingdom and the power and the glory forever," she whispered.

Just then, she could hear the cane of her husband as he made his way into the room. He walked slowly now, slower than ever. The arthritis in his knees and elbows only allowed him short journeys from the bedroom to his favorite chair on the porch or to the kitchen for some home-cooked *paella*. Kristine loved taking care of him because he had always taken care of her, always. Their age difference only mattered physically and only started to show in the last few years because he had always stayed active, passionately becoming involved in life and its activities. His mind was still as sharp as when they first met, and this is what she loved most about him. Besides, she had known he was older when they met. She knew it when they fell in love, and she knew it when she chose him for her husband. Back then, she knew so much about him, yet so very little.

"Dear, there's something I haven't told you in a long time," he said.

"Yes, what is it?"

He took her hand in his and kissed it. "Just that... *Te quiero Christina de los estados unidos, te quiero.*"

She laughed. "I love you too, Rafael de Espana, and you just told me that an hour ago."

The End

Kristine's Final Scribbles On The White Paper Tablecloth

1. Live the present.
2. Find a domain and bring passion to your life.
3. Surface your feelings.
4. Celebrate life.
5. Find an island where you can stop and think. Think things you have never had time to think about and notice things you have never noticed before.
6. Start fresh daily, adding beautiful colors to your plain white canvas.
7. Face uncertainty in life like a confident vessel in dark waters heading toward the lighthouse.
8. Add laughter to your life.
9. Don't ever underestimate the journeys you've been on, and look for the magnificent, not the bad, in things.
10. Hop, skip and jump toward goals, enjoying the process as much as the destination.
11. Don't rush any part of life. The end is as good as the beginning.
12. Indulge in fiestas but never lose your dignity.
13. Get on with your life. Live life!
14. Dance away anxiety.
15. When death comes around, stare it in the eyes.

16. *View the world without eyes for a change.*
17. *Remember the tulips. Just as their season of stardom comes and goes, you too will one day pass.*

About the Author

Christine Lemmon's portfolio includes a variety of jobs: radio news producer and on-air host in Fort Myers, Florida; newspaper reporter in Grand Rapids, Michigan; managing editor of a business magazine in Atlanta, Georgia; and publicist for a non-fiction publishing house in Sacramento, California. While growing up, she worked in her family's businesses: a bed & breakfast; horse ranch; home converted into a restaurant; and an ice-cream shop in Saugatuck, Michigan. For one semester of college, she also studied in Madrid, Spain.

Presently, Christine is most content in her role as wife and mother, while writing her second novel. She invites you to visit her website: http://www.tableclothscribbles.com.